Very Best Wishes

M.G. Beatty

THE KING OF KINGS

M. G. Beatty

MINERVA PRESS
LONDON
MONTREUX LOS ANGELES SYDNEY

THE KING OF KINGS

ISBN 1 86106 893 X

First Published 1997 by
MINERVA PRESS
195 Knightsbridge
London SW7 1RE

Printed in Great Britain for Minerva Press

THE KING OF KINGS

Contents

Acknowledgements

Thanks mostly to my lovely Luke who is my inspiration in all things.

Thanks to the quiet country lanes; the gently rolling fields; and the meandering river of my local village wherein I could see the ideas for this story developing.

Thanks to the rich and varied life I have led and to the people I have met – some good, some bad; some happy, some sad; some kind and some not so kind; and to one who was downright evil.

Thanks also to my kitchen table for keeping me company throughout the days and nights spent in the writing of this book.

And finally, thanks to all the frogs and toads and all the creatures of the river banks and forests who hop, jump, dive and swoop giving us all so much pleasure and enjoyment.

THE
REGION OF SEAXE
(and beyond).

Chapter One

Moha's Decision

Moha moved slowly along the island's river bank to where Mars was sitting. The evening was just turning to dusk and the river reflected the colours of the night sky with ever changing combinations of reds, blues, yellows and greys, all of which appeared to dance upon the gently rippling water.

Moha's mood had taken on the mellow autumn day. Indeed he could have been the very day itself. His kind, warm and friendly disposition mirrored the benign weather of the late and welcome Indian summer that was being greatly enjoyed by the river-side community.

The sound of a soft rustling nearby caused Mars to turn around. He had already recognised the movement as that of Moha and he greeted him with a friendship born out of great love and respect.

Moha was the current king of the local frog community of Seaxe. This was a vast area which extended all along the river bank from the Boathouse in the south-east to Kingfisher's Bridge in the north-west. His community were happy and content with their lives knowing that they had such a warm-hearted king who cared so much for their well-being.

In the eyes of the frogs of Seaxe Moha was a giant in every way. His boundless enthusiasm; energy and devotion; and the great care and attention he gave to their needs and safety was met with unswerving loyalty coupled with great respect for their king. He was, without doubt, much loved by his community.

Moha towered above Mars and the young frog felt secure in his presence. Mars looked admiringly at the giant bullfrog noticing once again how the distinctive olive green markings below his eyes and across his mouth ran handsomely down to the top of the shoulders of his muscular forearms. Moha's upper body was a deep golden brown with darker brown patches competing with lighter corn coloured patches for space across his broad back. His hindlimbs were firm and powerful and were attractively marked with darker brown bands. When he sat up the kindly king revealed an underbody of light tan akin to the colour of autumn leaves freshly fallen from the horse chestnut trees that grew in the nearby wood.

Moha sat himself down next to Mars and for a short while they both gazed westward out across the river to the far bank. They could see a great number of frogs, both young and old, either playing or busily chattering amongst themselves making the most of the evening's warmth before the cool of the night took over from the slowly setting sun.

"Mars my friend," began the king. "I am growing old. My body aches more with each passing day and my mind is tired. I have decided that this coming winter will be my last as king of Seaxe. A new king must therefore be found for our community."

The richness of Moha's voice rolled softly yet with great clarity across to his young companion. They were the words that Mars had for some while expected yet hoped he would not hear.

Moha continued. "The time is right for me to stand down and make way for a more youthful king. A king who is more abreast of all these new ideas and practices being suggested by the Anurian Council. A frog who can maybe see the benefits of the proposed changes in a way that I cannot."

"Come now," replied Mars. "You have many winters left before you as our king. These new ideas are as yet without substance and to entertain them without much prior thought and consideration would be foolhardy. We really do need your wisdom and experience to ensure that any change is implemented with every frog's understanding of what it means and what are its benefits. Otherwise change will be made just for the sake of change. We must prevent the fragile whims and fancies of frogs who have little depth from entering our culture without proper thought and consideration being given to their consequence."

Mars could see from the sad expression on Moha's face how difficult this moment was for the old bullfrog. In his young heart he knew, however, that the old king's mind was already firmly made up and that he would not have reached such a momentous decision

'Mars my friend,' began the king. 'I am growing old. My body aches more with each passing day and my mind is tired. I have decided that this coming winter will be my last as King of Seaxe. A new king therefore must be found for our community.'

without Moha's great love both of his community and for all the frogs that lived therein would have been his prime concern whilst coming to such a resolution.

This winter would, for certain, be Moha's last as king of Seaxe.

*

Moha, as is usual practice in the frog community of Seaxe, had been appointed king by the Anurian Council. This council is an august gathering of some of the wisest and most learned members of the community who have been fairly and democratically elected, on an area by area basis, to represent their fellow frogs. They numbered sixty in total and met regularly in order to discuss all issues concerned with, and directly related to, the community.

Furthermore, and something which again is the normal practice of the Anurian Council, the king is chosen from candidates who come from outside the local community. This is actually a tradition of all frog communities and is considered to be a sensible thing to do. It is thought that by bringing in a fresh face it will both encourage new ideas whilst at the same time avoiding the possibility of king's being selected who may already have developed close allies or indeed enemies that exist within the community.

Thus Moha had travelled a great distance from his home community of Somset, which lay far to the south-west of Seaxe, to become king of the Seaxe frogs.

When the Anurian Council first considered his appointment they liaised with their counterparts in the friendly and happy ponds of Somset in order to find out as much as they could about what they already considered to be a very fine frog indeed. They were, not surprisingly, greatly encouraged by what they heard from the wise council of Somset who confirmed their already unanimous opinion of Moha's eminent suitability. The giant bullfrog was therefore appointed with much enthusiasm by the Anurian Council of Seaxe.

Moha's great size, strength and powerfully handsome physique, coupled with the caring attitude he maintained towards his fellow frogs, made the latter feel instantly welcomed and respected when in his presence. In addition his rich mellow voice, surprisingly soft yet able to carry across vast gatherings of frogs, served to give his community a sense of belief and deep trust in what he said. Such attributes gave Moha great charisma and he was much adored by his community.

Moha was quite clearly a very fine appointment by the Anurian Council. This being so it was a matter that was often mentioned, to any frog who may wish to hear (or not as the case may be), by those older frogs who had served on the council at the time. Indeed such frogs were considered very wise for their great foresight and they may, therefore, be excused if they are heard to recount with relish and delight, even for the umpteenth time, how it was that it was they who had determined the appointment of Moha as king of Seaxe.

To the outsider that kind of story-telling may sound a little like boasting or bragging, but to the frogs of Seaxe it was a tale worth hearing time and again especially if it became even more interesting and worthy of praise in the retelling. It's wonderful what a little elaboration around the edges can do to enhance the flavour of a well known piece of history, and, as you will soon find out, when it comes to the masters of adding spice to a story then you need look no further than a frog.

*

It was now in fact only the most elderly of frogs who really had knowledge of what life had been like in the days before Moha had been declared king of Seaxe. In most other frog communities those inhabitants of advancing years, when describing their lot, would probably have been heard to say, "...the old days were the best..." or "...when we were young food was plentiful and we always had full and satisfied tummies..." or even "...things aren't like what they used to be... more's the pity..."

However in Seaxe it was quite different. The elders, as they sat upon a lily pad passing the time of day with their younger friends and relations, would (with a few exceptions of course as there will always be a cantankerous old frog or two) be more likely to be heard to say, "...the young should make the most of the present as these are without doubt the golden days..." or "...you young frogs have never had it so good..." or even "...you know I can't remember summers being so long and warm nor food so sumptuous and plentiful when I was a young frog..."

Of course, young frogs being young frogs, they had never known any different. It was quite understandable therefore that they took their high quality of life under Moha somewhat for granted. After all is said and done what did they have to compare against these "golden frog days"?

It was also understandable, again young frogs being what they are (which is, and they won't like to hear me saying this, a little immature and extra specially green about the glands), that they might also be tempted to think they could provide for the frog community at least as well as Moha. You may even hear one or two of the more cocksure youngsters say, "...somewhat better actually given half a chance...!"

We'll look at some such frogs a little later on in this story but for the moment we will return to Moha and Mars as the king had some exciting, but at the same time quite startling, news for his young friend.

*

After informing Mars that he would be relinquishing his position as king, Moha had suggested that they walk together along the island's bank whilst there still remained some warmth in the sun. As they did so the large muscular body of the king looked even bigger in contrast against the much smaller frame of Mars. Notwithstanding their marked difference in size, Mars was regarded by his friends and acquaintances as being a very handsome and athletic young frog of medium build but with a fine physique.

Mars was a brown frog with beautiful markings over his slim body. He had very smooth skin that was predominantly of a bronze hue but which contained darker brown and deep red shades that were particularly striking in the late sunlight of this autumn evening.

As with the other brown frogs in the community (as distinct from the green frogs) Mars had a prominent black patch that started from the rear of his eyes and tapered to a point a little way behind his mouth and eardrum. His underside was a mixture of marble and ivory colouring which offset his upper body most splendidly. He was indeed an altogether most handsome young frog.

Moha had carefully selected Mars for one of the senior roles in the Seaxe community and the position he held was entitled 'Frog With Responsibility for Health, Food, Safety and the Environment'. This meant he was charged with the task of ensuring that the community was at all times a safe and healthy place in which to live and that the acquisition and provision of an ample supply of fresh food was regularly maintained. For frogs, as you will see as you read on, such matters are paramount and so the importance of Mars' role, after that of Moha's of course, was considered second to none.

It's as well to say at this point, especially if you are wondering at the length of Mars' title, that frogs should be forgiven for attributing rather long names to important community positions, as such protraction is inevitable when one has many hours to occupy sat lazing amongst the reeds or lounging upon a comfortable lily pad considering how best to describe roles of such significance.

Frogs holding such highly valued and well regarded senior positions were chosen by the king and these appointments were therefore his personal responsibility. The Anurian Council, on the other hand, considered that their responsibility for making appointments to prominent positions started and ended with the selection of the king.

The Anurian Council were mainly concerned with overall frog policy and they vested in their King considerable authority for determining strategy and taking day to day decisions. However, if the king were to prove unworthy, then the Anurian Council of frogs would be honour bound to admit their failing to have made a good appointment and withdraw the king's powers as soon as was considered appropriate. In such disastrous circumstances, all members of the council would be expected to stand down from their prestigious positions as an expression and admission of their mistake in appointing a poor king. They would subsequently, and as soon as possible, be replaced by a completely new body of elected frogs.

In the case of the current Anurian Council of frogs, as has already been mentioned, they had proudly boasted for many a long year (in a most acceptable way of course) of their wise decision to appoint Moha as their king – the king of the Seaxe frogs.

Mars was in fact one of seven frogs who had been appointed as seniors in the Seaxe community. These other senior frogs, about whom you will no doubt hear a good deal more later on in this story, are known by name and title as follows. (The reader should be aware that although the order is of no real significance, as all the senior positions are of equal standing, it must be said that it is Mars who is generally considered by the community at large to be the unofficial deputy leader to Moha):

Firstly there is Kejon whose role it is to administer to the elderly frogs. His title is that of 'Frog with Responsibility for those Older, Wiser and More Knowledgeable of Frogs'. It should be pointed out that age, in the frog community, is held in high esteem. This is largely due to the fact that the elderly are considered to have worked hard for their fellow frogs in the past, and, if the current young and adult frogs are now benefiting from their earlier labours, then they should accordingly be respected for such distinguished service.

Secondly there is Geelan. His role is to preside over the younger frogs and his title is accordingly that of 'Frog with Responsibility for the Young, Adolescent and those Frogs Approaching Adulthood'.

Thirdly there is Brylil. His duty is to oversee the adult frogs. These frogs are those who have grown out of adolescence but are not yet old enough to be regarded as either more wise or more knowledgeable than their compatriots. They are more regularly classified by the frog community as 'worker' frogs or 'warrior' frogs although it should be stressed that since Moha took over as king the need for the Seaxe frogs to be 'warrior' frogs has long since been redundant. Moha's reign was particularly notable for the peace he had brought to the community and for his ability for diplomacy with other frog communities, whether located near or far. Brylil's full title was therefore 'Frog with Responsibility for Industrious Frogs and for the Maintenance of Union and Harmony'. His title was especially long because Moha wanted to instil a peaceful attitude in the adult frogs. In the days before Moha became king, Brylil's predecessor was simply entitled 'Chief Warrior Frog'. During Moha's reign, however, that title, and what it clearly suggested to the frog community, would of course never do.

Fourthly there is Chrich whose remit is to care for those frogs who for some reason or another have fallen on hard times (as can happen in even the most well run of communities); or who are physically handicapped in some way; or who have committed some wrong against their fellow frogs and are therefore clearly in need of help and assistance. The title Chrich has been given is 'Frog with Responsibility for those Frogs More Unfortunate than Others'.

Fifthly there is Lebish whose purpose it is to organise learning for the frog community and to ensure that the 'worker' (or adult) frogs carry out their many individual tasks in the best and most appropriate way possible. Lebish is additionally responsible for information, which basically means he has the job of advising the whole community of important events in the frog calendar and of any other matters of relevance to the local frog population. Thus Lebish operates under the rather grand (some frogs, if they were to be overheard as they sat upon a lily pad, would say rather "too grand") title of 'Frog with Responsibility for Educating the Young; Commissioning Further Training for Adults; Ensuring Quality in all Matters; and Providing Valuable and Accurate Information'. Actually it is well understood, by frogs who know about such things, that it was Lebish himself who created this title, advising Moha that his previous title (now long since forgotten) was a little on the light side and really did not capture the importance of his role – "not by a long stretch of water!"

Finally, and making up the other six senior colleagues of Mars, comes Josmi. Now it must be said, especially for you, the reader, to better understand the role of Josmi, that frogs like nothing better than to muse upon a lily pad or by the river bank, particularly on a warm summer's evening, in order to consider the possibilities of '...this and that...' and wonder '...what if...' or '...pose a whole range of scenarios that if they were actually applied would give rise to all sorts of eventualities...'

The likelihood of course of many such eventualities ever occurring in reality was rather remote, as frogs, although having the most wonderful imaginations, do not quite have the wherewithal to make such extraordinary things happen in practice. It is, as many other creatures of the river bank would say, a rather endearing feature of the frog that they have been accorded such fertile minds yet not quite the practical application to develop the many marvellous ideas they had in order to bring them to fruition.

Bearing in mind what has just been said Josmi's title was quite appropriately described as 'Frog with Responsibility for Encouraging Ideas and Concepts for Discussion and Consideration'.

So there you have the leadership structure of Seaxe – Moha as the king together with his seven senior frogs, with each of the latter having their own particular responsibilities for different aspects of the community's business.

As the leading management group the king and his seniors all met together on a regular basis in Moha's chamber in his residence on the island in order to discuss all manner of things. However, how this gathering of frogs actually performed as a group may come as a surprise to you if you expected them to have full and frank discussions culminating in corporately agreed decisions. Those frogs in the community who know about such things would tell you, if you asked the question of course, that very often Moha and Mars' six senior colleagues would say one thing when they were all alone together but when they met with Moha and Mars they would more likely than not say something quite different. They would almost certainly agree with the wise counsel of their king when they sat with him at one of these regular meetings even though they would probably vehemently disagree with such points as soon as they were away from the king's chamber.

This was a constant source of frustration to Moha as he well appreciated his senior colleagues had ideas of their own but that they ultimately lacked the confidence to make decisions. This was primarily because they were worried that they may personally have to stand up and be counted if things subsequently went wrong.

Although Moha did all he could to encourage free-ranging debates on all matters under discussion, there were occasions when it was necessary for him to personally make a speedy decision when certain issues demanded swift action to be taken. Moha knew only too well that when a particularly tricky situation arose, then, with the exception of Mars, the other six senior frogs would take a month of blue Sundays in February to reach anything remotely like a resolution. Even then their proposed course of action would normally contain so many 'ifs' and 'buts' as to make it quite incomprehensible and unworkable.

*

Moha and Mars continued their walk along the water's edge occasionally hopping onto a lily pad every now and then but soon returning once again through the reeds to the island's bank.

"Mars, my loyal and trusted friend, are you aware of the long standing tradition of the Anurian Council which is that only frogs of our community can be considered for the kingship of Seaxe?" Moha had gradually slowed down to a very gentle pace before stopping. He now turned towards his friend and looked deep into Mars' eyes as he asked this question.

"Yes I am," replied Mars. "It is because the council regard outsiders as being free from all the influences that may have been developed whilst living within the community. Influences that may encourage favouritism towards close friends and relations and that may even lead to unfair practice or corruption."

Moha thought for a moment before speaking again and then he said, "I must say, young Mars, that if I were able to change any of our ways then I would wish to change this tradition. Although our community is happy and content I know that we are far from being perfect. It is also a concern of mine that with regard to our leading and most senior frogs some of them, at this moment in time, are either too young, or, like me, are nearing the end of their days as 'responsible' frogs. I would ideally prefer to spend several more winters helping to develop the minds and abilities of the younger seniors before leaving them open to whoever may come from the outside.

"I am very worried that the younger seniors like Geelan, Brylil and Josmi have not yet determined in their own minds clear pictures of our community and what it takes to make it successful. They need to develop that understanding in order to maintain our prosperity and make further improvements. Without such mental pictures they may fail our frogs or be swept away by a new king's opinions before they have formed firm views of their own.

"Chrich is of course past his prime and should now be gently winding down. He is a good frog but his keenness is ebbing with age and, although he still performs his role well, he has neither ambition left nor the stomach for change.

"As far as Lebish is concerned it is him who I fear may fare worst of all. He is so easily led, and, although he can expound on almost any subject with apparent great intellect, his thoughts are nevertheless jumbled and unstructured. Do you know I recently listened to him speak to a large gathering of young frogs on the value and uses of good information. He spoke without pause for twenty-five minutes and, during this time, he exuded great intelligence and learning throughout the talk and accordingly received a substantial ovation from his listeners.

"After he had left the meeting I sat amongst the bulrushes and discussed his presentation with some of our young friends. Of Lebish's poise and performance they spoke in great admiration but, when I asked them to explain to me what they understood of the content of his speech and what it might have meant to them, none gave me the same account. You see Lebish had confused them so much for he had spoken without direction and with a great many contradictions. The young audience had, however, been quite carried away by his uniquely entertaining style of presentation. So much so in fact that they had been encouraged to watch him rather than listen to what he had to say.

"I truly fear that Lebish may be vulnerable to any of his peers if they recognise his weaknesses and wish to see him used for some unfair or corrupt practice.

"Oh Mars. Listen to me going on. Let's hope and trust that the new king will be kindly and wish to build on our strengths and not make change for change's sake. And yet..." the old king gazed into the far north. "...and yet I have a feeling in my glands that there are troubled times ahead."

Mars felt uneasy at his wise king's words. He had never before seen Moha look so worried and he intuitively knew that this foreboding must be taken seriously. His reply, therefore, came softly and with a sense of resignation as the issue was not in his control.

"We must have faith in the wisdom of the Anurian Council. What else can we frogs do? After all the decision on the appointment of the king is theirs by virtue of our tradition."

The king moved closely to Mars' side and lowered his large head to be level with the young frog's ear. "It is in the greatest of confidence that I shall say to you that when I informed the Anurian Council of my wish to stand down as their king they asked what were my thoughts on the selection of my successor. I advised them that if it were possible to change our traditional method of selection then I would suggest that you be chosen to lead our community."

Mars was physically moved. His mind spun for a few moments and the colouring on his underbody visibly flushed a deep golden and pink hue.

"My King... Moha, I am greatly honoured by your words and support, but surely it cannot be possible for our council to change the custom and practice of our forefathers as these are the ways that have been handed down to us since time immemorial?"

Mars knew the answer so it wasn't really a question. Of course such time-honoured and established frog traditions would not change. After all is said and done why should they? The council will feel confident that they can find a frog of at least the same calibre as Moha, maybe even more capable. They too, like the celebrated frogs who sat on the council that chose Moha as king of Seaxe, will similarly want to say, to whomsoever may wish to hear, that they were responsible for appointing the new frog king who was every bit the ideal successor to old Moha.

*

The sun had dipped far below the distant horizon and the sky was now a mixture of deep reds, purples, pinks and greys. A chill wind had also suddenly blown up from out of the north. The two friends shivered, and, feeling strangely uncomfortable but not quite knowing why, turned around and headed for home.

Chapter Two

The News Breaks

The Anurian Council had work to do. Through each of their members they had agreed to simultaneously inform their respective areas of the community that Moha had decided to retire as king. This method of spreading news had become good practice in the dissemination of information and was an approach strongly encouraged by Moha on the recommendation of Mars.

Such a development had been greatly opposed by Lebish. He had never been backward in hopping forward to volubly give advice to the king that information should, in his opinion, be carefully channelled on a very 'selective' and 'need to know' basis. He would always add that information is the province of the senior frogs, and too much of it in the hands of the adults; the elderly; and in particular the young, could be a very dangerous thing.

Lebish had not forgiven Mars for such an intrusion (as he called it) into his area of responsibility. What irked him most of all, and caused him to have a deep-seated hatred borne out of his jealousy of Mars, was that the current practice of making information available to all frogs was considered by the community at large to be a most welcome and gratefully received commodity. They appreciated the fact that they were kept in the picture as important events occurred rather than being kept in the dark as Lebish would have preferred to have treated them. They indeed felt valued by Moha and Mars' thoughtful attempt to keep them fully abreast of what was happening in the community.

Lebish inwardly seethed as he watched the whole community debate the intended resignation of their king. Why should they get to hear of this decision so soon after he and the other seniors had only just themselves heard? He felt that he and his other senior frog colleagues should have been privy to such information long before the "brown and green masses" (as he would often disrespectfully describe the frog community at large) had been informed. If he had been allowed to determine the way in which the community should be told of Moha's resignation then he could most certainly have designed a far more sophisticated and complex information system that advised the community through seniority or perhaps by age or alternatively on the basis of area by area.

As was normally the case Lebish's muddled mind pondered this way and that without reaching any conclusion. He satisfied himself nonetheless that anything he could have thought up would have been infinitely better than the method now being used by the Anurian Council. It was indeed, therefore, a very disgruntled Lebish who huffed and puffed and scratched his fat belly as he wondered what on earth, water and all the lily pads in Seaxe were the "brown and green masses" going to do with such important information. After all, if he had personally found it difficult enough to deal with the news of Moha's intention to stand down at the end of this coming winter, surely, therefore, lesser frogs would have found it quite impossible to cope with such a statement.

As usual, of course, Lebish considerably overestimated his own ability and greatly underestimated that of his fellow local frogs.

*

It was also necessary for the Anurian Council to spread the message of Moha's resignation to other frog communities, both near and far, beyond the boundaries of Seaxe.

Issues of such great importance were not to be merely passed on by frog to frog and community to community as it was quite probable, given the extravagant imaginations peculiar to these creatures, that such news would very likely be expanded upon most generously and become, with the regular telling, something quite different to the original fact. It was therefore common frog practice in Seaxe to send groups of frogs, headed up by seniors, to visit other communities in order to formally explain important news, thus ensuring that the same message reached every frog community in a consistent manner and at the same time.

The reader may, at this stage, spot another of Mars' methods of how to more appropriately issue information as it was once again as a result of one of his proposals to Moha that they accordingly decided to utilise the senior frogs in such an important exercise. Lebish, as you can imagine, this really being his responsibility, had most aggressively and vehemently opposed this "silly idea" (as he referred to it) as being wasteful of the seniors' time and quite unnecessary. His view was that frogs would find out in time that Moha was resigning - that is if they were even interested in such an event - and anyway what business was it of theirs to know about such matters? When Moha heard of this attitude he winced for he knew that Lebish really did have potential but that he also needed to be carefully nurtured to help him develop into a useful senior member of the frog community. The pity was of course that Moha would not now be able to personally guide this senior frog and it worried him for he knew that Lebish could just as well be swayed by bad as well as by good influences. In this respect Moha's major concern was that Lebish had not yet learnt the difference between the two and that he was probably more inclined to be lured by the dubious glamour that more often than not accompanies wrongdoing and corrupt practice.

So it was, and notwithstanding Lebish's groans of protest, that the parties of newscarriers were assembled. Each party consisted of one senior frog and nine other members of the community. These latter frogs having been selected on the basis that they had shown great promise in community work which indicated bright futures possibly even as candidates some day for senior status.

It was decided that Geelan would spread the news westwards; Brylil would make for the south; Chrich would be venturing east; and Lebish, to his obvious disgust, would be heading for the region known as the Near North. Kejon and Josmi were to remain in Seaxe in order to deal with any enquiries that may come direct from distant parts.

You may well be wondering why our newscarriers were being sent west, east and south, but, in the case of the north, only to the Near North. The reason, and this is something that you will be unlikely to hear another frog tell, is that the Far North is considered by all frogs to be a bad and desolate place where wickedness and evil are regularly practised.

Young frogs will hear only once the story of the Far North and, once heard, are forbidden to speak of it again in general conversation. Such talk by any frog is regarded as sinful and, if overheard by a frog who should know better, the offending frog will be sent to Chrich who will treat the individual in order to make him or her a more acceptable member of the community. Such a frog would be considered to be a very 'unfortunate' frog indeed if they were unable to contain such information and felt a need to discuss or speak out in public on this forbidden topic.

Chapter Three

The Story of the Far North

For the benefit of the reader, and whilst no frog of the Seaxe community is within earshot, it will be safe to tell you the forbidden tale of how the Far North came to be regarded as such a wicked and evil place.

In days gone by, in fact a generation before Moha's reign, it is said that one sunny summer's morning from out of the north, as far north as any frog could imagine, there came the blackest and thickest clouds that had ever been seen. Stories are told how on this day, which had started warm and hazy and quite typical of any other summer's day, the air unexpectedly turned very cold and the happy chattering and croaking of the birds in the trees and frogs on the river bank strangely stopped.

Some will say that a chill breeze from out of the north was how it began and that this had caused any frog going about his or her everyday business to suddenly shiver and remark to friends how unusually cold it had become for the time of year.

The breeze rapidly became a strong wind that brought clouds rushing across the sky. Clouds that rolled and raced and were so low that they appeared to whip and buffet the very tops of the trees in the forest.

Then there came the darkness as the sun was extinguished by coal black clouds that had seemingly all merged to form one huge and all-enveloping blanket over the land.

These clouds then brought a deluge of rain and hail that pummelled the ground, lashed the trees and tormented the river. The vicious wind that raged through the woods tore great oaks from the earth – oaks that had proudly stood for a hundred or more winters. Younger trees and bushes were simply ripped up by their roots and sent flying high into the air.

Then, from out of the pitch darkness, came flashes of brilliant light as forked lightning ferociously attacked the tallest trees driving blazing streaks of fire deep into their trunks sending cascades of burning embers hurtling to the ground.

The now turbulent river ran wildly along its course breaking long established curves in the river's bank and smashing reeds and rushes in its wake. The banks were no match for the crazy torrents of water and the river irresistibly forced its way through to flow out and over the surrounding countryside.

The storm raged on for a day and a night, although in truth no frog could tell when the day had ended or the night had begun for the blackness was unrelenting throughout save for the white slashes of lightning that tore into the trees.

It is said that the noise of the storm, with the thunder roaring; the trees crashing; and the river pulverising all that lay before it, was so great that no frog could hear a croak or a cry for help.

Frogs, birds and all the other creatures of the forest and river bank communities were scared beyond their wildest imaginations. Those frogs that could not find shelter in time were thrown up into the air or rolled across the ground like dry autumn leaves. A great number of frogs who had clung in fear to bulrushes and reeds were merely swept away by the raging river. Many, even though they thought they had found safe havens such as in rotted tree trunks or sheltered river inlets, were nevertheless mercilessly wrenched out of their sanctuaries and tossed pitilessly to perish in the elements, such was the ferocity of the storm.

When the tempestuous winds had finally subsided, and light returned once more to the forest and river banks, the scene was one of great devastation. Just how many frogs had perished or disappeared could never be counted. What trees and vegetation remained standing looked ragged, wretched and torn. River banks that had once nobly boasted smooth curves through which the river gently meandered had become crumbled ruins of broken earth and were now merely sad reminders of the savagery of the storm-driven river.

Although a great number of the Seaxe frog community had been taken forever by the storm a very strange thing had happened in that many new frogs had appeared. What was even more strange was that these frogs were all from the north and some even from the Far North. The explanation for this phenomenon, and you would probably have to hear it said by a very close friend if you were to believe it, is that these newly arrived frogs were actually brought into Seaxe riding high above the trees upon the wind. Not that this was voluntary of course as no frog in his right mind would choose to venture so far above the ground – unless of course you were of the tree climbing fraternity, although there were no such frogs within many hops of Seaxe and its neighbouring communities.

Those northern frogs who had lived to tell the tale said that the wind in the Far North had begun with a squall; the squall soon became a whirl; the whirl then turned into a gale; and, before any creature had time to take cover, it finally formed itself into a savage and twisting tornado which pulled into its centre everything that lay in its path which was not firmly tied down or rooted.

Hundreds and thousands of frogs and small creatures were sucked up in this way and were spun round and round and round until they were so dizzy with spinning and so very frightened that they no longer knew where they were or where they were going. In this way many creatures had been taken from their homes only to be thrown across the land and deposited in strange ponds, fields, rivers and forests. Light-heartedly, as frogs of today have long since forgotten the terrifying derivation of this phrase, present day frogs will casually describe a heavy storm as "It's raining tadpoles and frogs".

Thus there was a rich variety of frogs in the community of Seaxe that ranged from the native green and brown frogs, who were the local indigenous population; to the descendants of the rather larger brown frogs, whose parents and grandparents had originally landed with a considerable bump from the Far North on the night of the Great Storm. Since that time all of the frogs in Seaxe, regardless of their origins, had lived together happily and harmoniously.

Interestingly, the brown frogs who had arrived in Seaxe in these rather unusual circumstances actually mixed extremely well with the local frogs and the whole community thrived in a peaceful and calm atmosphere. As you read on you may find this happy environment rather surprising for reasons that will become all too clear. However, much credit for the successful integration must of course go to King Moha for his fine leadership and ability to stress the importance of a harmonious community.

A story is also told, some say it is a myth, that in the Far North during the early hours of the second morning of the storm, in fact just as the wind began to subside and the moon peeped intermittently through the dark clouds that were scurrying across the sky, a huge and terrifying figure was seen perched upon the uprooted trunk of a newly fallen ancient oak. Knowing what frogs are like, for as you have already heard they are prone to embellishing a good story, you may find the following a little hard to believe as it is said that the shape of this figure resembled the grossly misshapen form of a frog although it was at least ten times the size of a fully grown adult.

Whether it was a trick of the light as the lightning flashed, or the silhouette of a small frog made large by the long and eerie shadows of the storm, no frog could honestly say. The strange thing is that when the place where this figure or apparition had been seen was later inspected it is said that a noxious milky substance was found there that caused those frogs who went too close to it to have a stinging sensation in their eyes and a horrible feeling of sickness and dizziness. Those who actually came into contact with the milky fluid were violently sick and some are said to have suffered a quick but excruciatingly painful death.

The aftermath of the storm had left a vast area to the north of Seaxe as a swampy uninhabitable place where no plant life could flourish and what did grow was always distorted and usually died within a few days. The whole place thereafter was regularly shrouded in a grey impenetrable mist and the dank smell of rotting vegetation would sweep across Seaxe when a north wind blew as if reminding the local frogs of what lay therein. This bleak and desolate place was known as Waga and neither into it nor beyond it would any frog of Seaxe set hindleg or forelimb. It is beyond the swamps of Waga that the forbidden and dreadful lands known as the Far North can be found.

And so it was that the story of the Far North originated. It was not surprisingly thereafter regarded as a malignant place that could brew murderous storms and where evil and wicked giant frogs lived who were capable of killing other creatures just by spraying them with a slimy, disgusting and stinking liquid. Whether the tales that were told were entirely accurate there was no way of knowing and many would prefer to consider them as the sort of myths and fancies that frogs were more than a little expert in creating. Nevertheless, what it

...it is said that the shape of this figure resembled the grossly misshapen form of a frog although it was at least ten times the size of a fully grown adult.

had certainly instilled in the frog population of both Seaxe and all the creature communities that lay to the south, east and west of Waga was a great fear of what might lurk therein and beyond its swampy, smelly and misty boundaries.

It was certainly a fear so strong that no party of newscarriers would this day be journeying beyond the Near North frontier where it borders onto Waga to spread word of Moha's resignation as king of Seaxe.

Chapter Four

Bedlam in the Boathouse

The night before it was decided which seniors would be going where, in order to inform the other frog communities of Seaxe's need for a new king, a clandestine meeting was in progress in the Boathouse. This long disused tumble-down wooden building was situated in a sheltered inlet just beyond Lower Bridge some little way down the river to the south-east on the outskirts of the main community of Seaxe. Although the time was approaching midnight there was a great deal of animated discussion taking place and, from the general hubbub and raising of excited voices, it was clear that something of great importance was being debated.

"Are we all agreed then?" squeaked Geelan. His high-pitched voice barely audible above the noisy gabble of six very excited frogs. "Are we all agreed that we will confront Moha with our views which are, firstly, we don't support his and Mars' decision that we should have to journey far and wide in search of a new king; secondly, that we feel that the new king should be chosen from amongst the six of us sat here; and thirdly, that in future we should all be given much greater privileges as befits such senior frogs of our standing?"

Although Geelan squeaked louder and louder he was not heard as each of the other frogs was either shouting, croaking or bellowing simultaneously at the tops of their own voices in a vain attempt to make their own points known. As the hullabaloo reached its crescendo it suddenly died down leaving each of the six frogs spent and exhausted from their efforts.

In competition with Geelan's voice were those of Kejon, Brylil, Chrich, Lebish, and Josmi. As they sat back upon their hindlimbs each frog contemplated what they alone had said. They had as usual paid virtually no regard to what each other had proposed, apart from the odd word that may have filtered through their brains when out of physical necessity one had to pause for breath.

Such was the way in which all meetings of these six senior frogs were conducted. Not one of them had a great deal of respect for the other although this fact was rather well concealed in public. In this regard it was quite normal practice when one senior met another senior along the river bank for each to heap praise and congratulations upon the other recounting some wondrous deed or activity that could be attributed to their colleague (most of which, possibly all if the truth were known, had never even taken place). They would then part in extravagant gestures of friendship with much clasping of forelimbs and pats upon the back. To those who knew no better they could be excused for thinking that this group of Seaxe's senior frogs really were the very best of friends and that they shared great bonhomie and trust. In actual fact quite the opposite was the case.

No differently to all the previous occasions when they had met as a group, the six frogs, now quiet after their exertions, looked hesitantly around at each other. As usual none of the six had any definite idea as to precisely what it was they were to agree upon. Even more bizarrely, on this occasion, they had not even elected any of their number to be their spokesfrog in order to take the results of their deliberations to Moha. Nevertheless, and despite these failings, they all suddenly roared (except of course Geelan who squeaked)...

"*Agreed*!" and then they immediately put this matter to one side and continued to babble on into the early hours about a whole assortment of what they considered to be much more vital issues. These were in fact topics that were very close to their chests such as 'the best place to find the tastiest grasshoppers' and 'the joy of sunbathing on a late summer's afternoon as opposed to working' and also, and even more importantly 'the size of one's lily pad when compared to another's'.

It was actually arising out of these meetings that the popular frog phrase "He listens but he does not hear" was derived. Such a saying is often used by the local frogs of Seaxe to describe a situation where they have personally been given the opportunity to speak to one or all of the seniors on an issue that concerns them. They know in their hearts of course that this is only a token gesture as nothing will ever come of their representation or request. This is because although the senior or seniors appear to listen to what the locals have to say they actually make no attempt to hear what is being said to them. The exceptions to this rule are Moha and Mars who do try hard to support their fellow frogs and regard their high positions in the community as platforms from which they can help and assist their society and not as vehicles to feather their own nests or indeed to line their own lily pads.

The late night meetings in the Boathouse were unfortunately a fairly frequent occurrence. They normally took place a day or so before Moha's regular meeting with his seven senior frogs (that's the six now seated in the Boathouse plus Mars of course). I am sure you will be interested to know that Mars was never invited to attend by his six second tier colleagues as he was considered to be too close to Moha for their liking. In fact this group of seniors were keen to keep the existence of these meetings a secret from both Moha and Mars and believed all along that they had been successful in so doing.

Each meeting never failed to produce a great deal of hot air and excitement. They would discuss how better than Moha they could run the community and how Moha had grown old and was not now able to fully understand the needs of the modern day Seaxe frog. They would also discuss in great depth the development of profound, detailed and extraordinarily complex policies for each of their personal areas of responsibility and explain how they would wish to impose them upon their fellow frogs. The sad fact about their policies is that despite the many long hours and nights spent in their creation it was probably only the individual senior who had devised them who really understood what their own policy meant. Even so, there were occasions when it has been known for the particular seniors themselves to display a degree of confusion when asked to clarify certain rather complicated statements that are regrettably to be found in abundance in each of their respective policies.

You will, I am sure, already appreciate that a frog likes nothing better than to spend time 'dreaming up a scenario here' or 'mentally painting a picture there' or just allowing their minds to wander across a whole range of magnificent ideas none of which of course were ever likely to occur. This practice, however, was always considered by frogs to be a particularly valuable use of their time as well as being a very healthy exercising of their brain cells.

And so this meeting, like all the other similar meetings that had previously taken place in the Boathouse, had generated much boisterous enthusiasm and genuine passion. Many extravagant ideas had been proposed and some wonderful plans described. What was certain, however, was that no positive action would result, for, and it was indeed an unfortunate fact, there was not amongst this group an individual who could emerge as their leader or spokesfrog or who could represent them in order to take their best ideas to Moha where they could be clearly explained and appropriately considered for possible approval and application.

If the truth were known this was probably due to two simple facts. Firstly, and it really has to be said, none of these six seniors were of sufficient ability or intellect to act as the groups' leader. Secondly, and more importantly, whilst each of the six senior frogs recognised the need for a leader none would have been supportive of any of the group who assumed such a position. Sadly, although each wanted power, they individually knew that they were not competent to take on a leading role and, in this knowledge, could not bear the thought of any other member of the group assuming such a mantle.

This dilemma caused inertia in the group. Moha was of course well aware of the situation and had been so for quite some time. Mars knew too and both he and the wise old king pitied their fellow seniors' weakness.

Moha was always kind and gentle when the seniors arrived at his formal meetings and he gave them every opportunity to fully air their views. He dearly wanted them to develop and become strong and able frogs who would be held in high regard by the general community. Sadly, and try as he may, Moha could not encourage the six seniors to put forward the views that so regularly excited them in the Boathouse and, without exception, they would always leave Moha to make the important decisions (of which of course he was most capable of doing). To Moha's constant frustration he knew that once the six seniors were back in the security of the Boathouse they would again moan and complain about not being able to have a fair say in what went on in the community and that it was Moha who made all the decisions and that they never get a look in on the important issues. Interestingly they were of course always happy to take a share of the community's praise whenever Moha had taken decisions that were of great benefit to the community at large.

This then was generally how this group of six seniors behaved. They were not bad frogs or dangerous frogs or even (and you may be a little surprised to hear this said) subversive or mutinous frogs. They could perhaps be better described as sad frogs and rather disloyal frogs. They were however quite honest and caring frogs in their own way and as such the frog community tolerated them in their positions of trust as seniors. After all was said and done the local frogs of Seaxe always knew that if anything ever went seriously wrong then Moha was there to look after the community's well-being.

The truth about how the modern day Seaxe frog regarded their king was of course quite contrary to the view that the six seniors had formed. In the latters' 'considered' opinion Moha had lost touch with his community. However, this was of course very wide of the mark as the frogs of Seaxe loved Moha more and more with each passing day for they knew that he always had them at the forefront of his mind and that he held their respect and loyalty very close to his heart.

By the time the meeting had finished and the six senior colleagues of Moha and Mars prepared to leave the Boathouse, all their intentions to confront Moha on the matter of delivering far and wide the news of his resignation had evaporated (or more than likely had been forgotten). They had instead decided that the size of their personal lily pads, as compared to those belonging to less senior frogs, was a far more important issue and that this had to be on top of the agenda at their next meeting with Moha. They had deemed it an outrage that Geelan had recently spotted one of Mars' subordinates occupying a lily pad that appeared to be considerably more comfortable and desirable than Geelan's own. Geelan made it very clear that he required a sense of order to be restored and that he should not have to suffer the indignity of possessing an inferior lily pad. The six seniors found to their delight that they all agreed on this matter and it was thus a contented group, satisfied with their evening's endeavours, who surreptitiously made their way back home along the river bank an hour or so before the dawn was due to break.

*

At the moment the meeting closed a small bird slipped silently away from where it had been perched in its secret hiding place under what remained of the eaves of the Boathouse roof. The small creature had patiently sat in this concealed spot throughout the seniors' debate and had listened attentively to all that had been said. The silhouette of the tiny bird, unseen by any of the six senior frogs, now glided silently up the river north-westwards in the direction of the island that was situated in the middle of the wide stretch of water in the shadows of Horse Chestnut Wood. How gracefully the bird flew sweeping low over the water and then rising up and over the reeds and bulrushes that were swaying in the gentle breeze of the night.

When it reached the island the small bird landed softly in the branches of a small bush and then carefully looked all around to make sure no other creature had seen him arrive. Confident that his sudden arrival had gone unnoticed he hopped down from the branch on which he stood and on to an ancient tree stump which had been on the island's edge since any frog could recall. He then quickly darted into and disappeared amongst a mass of soft leaves and grasses which were piled up between the roots of the tree stump. In no time at all the little bird had burrowed its way through the leafy undergrowth before emerging into a large underground chamber.

This chamber was the king's residence where Moha lived and where many good kings of the Seaxe community had the honour to live before him.

The floor of the chamber had been hollowed out by a great many frogs who had long ago scrabbled with their forelimbs to loosen the earth and then pushed hard with their hindlimbs in order to propel the soil up and out of the burrow. Great care had then been taken to dispose of the debris created by these industrious workers by kicking the surplus earth and stones into the river so as not to indicate to any stranger that such a chamber existed.

The ceiling of the king's residence was naturally made and consisted of a mass of dead roots which over many years had twisted and turned amongst themselves to form an intricate and ornate design. These roots were smooth to the touch and they glistened like the sun on a fish's back whenever the daylight filtered in through the leafy entrance.

Many other roots had grown down from the ceiling and had penetrated the floor of the chamber. This had the effect of creating a number of smaller private areas around the circular chamber wherein Moha either slept; kept his food provisions; or accommodated close friends and visiting dignitaries who frequently came to stay in Seaxe as his guest.

The centre of the chamber was, however, quite clear of any such root growth and a large circular area with a smooth floor had been fashioned out of the earth. It was here that Moha held the regular meetings with his senior frogs as well as any other meetings of importance.

It was indeed into this area that the small bird had hopped and now patiently stood waiting to see Moha.

"Greetings, Peeyu." Moha heartily welcomed his friend. "What brings you here at this late hour?"

Moha looked across to where the small bird was standing and, although the chamber was in darkness, he could nevertheless see in his mind's eye a creature of great courage and beauty. For Peeyu was a kingfisher, the most magnificent and glorious bird to be seen anywhere within the river bank community of Seaxe. Peeyu was the son of Playa and this family of kingfishers lived in a nest dug high up in the river bank on the east side of the bridge which crossed the river at the opposite end of the community to the Boathouse. Peeyu's family had lived in this place for many generations and the bridge had become known as Kingfisher's Bridge.

*

Moha's friendship with Peeyu had begun within a day or two of his arrival in Seaxe to take up his kingship. It had been very early in the morning and the sparkling spring sun had just begun to rise on the eastern horizon. Moha had been ambling along the river bank getting himself acquainted with his surroundings when he suddenly caught a glimpse of flashes of brilliant blue and green darting in and out of the reeds along the water's edge. He was so taken by this wonderful display of colour that he carefully positioned himself in some long grass that had grown up behind a fallen tree to observe this fascinating sight. As he watched he saw that this luminescent splendour actually came from a small bird that dipped first this way and then that way before occasionally diving gracefully into the water, emerging each time with a small fish held tightly in its long black beak. The bird would then disappear away up the river for a few moments before returning once again to busily pursue its quarry amongst the reeds.

When he was a very young bullfrog Moha had often heard stories told of such a bird that reputably patrolled the river banks of far distant communities. Well-travelled frogs would speak of this creature in awe of its beauty and would regard its appearance as a favourable omen and a sign that good health would be bestowed both upon themselves and their families. These birds did not inhabit Somset and Moha had always hoped that one day he would be privileged enough to see one for himself.

It was therefore an enraptured bullfrog who looked on in total fascination as the small bird went about its business. Moha loved the way in which the sun glinted upon the bird's plumage and he was enchanted by the sapphire blue and emerald green flashes of its wings as the kingfisher went upstream. On its return journey, as it flew back along the river bank, Moha greatly admired the orange glow of the bird's belly which was beautifully offset by the shining white of his throat and neck.

It was on one of the bird's return journeys to search for fish that the kingfisher caught sight of a large and powerfully built bullfrog sitting perfectly still in the long grass by the water's edge. It only needed the blink of a frog's eye or the faint crackle of a broken blade of dry grass to catch the kingfisher's attention, so sharp were his senses.

Immediately he spotted Moha, the kingfisher swerved gracefully across the river and then vertically up and back over the water again circling the bullfrog first high and then low. Seeing that there was no danger the bird then dropped softly on to some bent reeds a few feet in from the bank and focused his keen eyes on the stranger.

Both felt a little apprehensive at first as they weighed one another up. However each was certainly admiring of the other as they instantly saw before them a magnificent example of their species.

"You must be the new king?" called the kingfisher.

Moha nodded in acknowledgement.

"I knew that you were coming," continued the beautiful bird. "Frogs have spoken of little else for months."

"It's good to meet you," said Moha. "But you have the advantage on me. I know neither your name nor whether you are a friend or enemy of the Seaxe frogs." And then, seeing a trace of disappointment in the eyes of the bird at the mention of the word "enemy", Moha quickly added, "Although I would guess from your courteous manner that you are indeed a very close ally of this community."

The small bird then suddenly sprang from its perching place and plunged into the water entering like an arrow. There was no splash and hardly a sound so splendidly and expertly did he dive.

Almost as quickly the kingfisher re-emerged with a wriggling fish in his bill and Moha watched as the luminescent blue and green flashed brightly as the bird zigzagged low over the river and away up towards Kingfisher's Bridge.

Moha sighed and carried on with his sojourn along the island's river bank. He had very much enjoyed meeting the small bird and hoped he hadn't offended him in any way. Whilst he walked Moha wondered if he would ever see him again although in that respect he didn't have long to wait for an answer as before he had ventured more than a dozen more hops he heard the same voice from just above his head.

"By the way I am Peeyu. Happy to make your acquaintance I'm sure. Sorry to dash off like that but we have a young son at home who needs his nourishment."

Moha liked the kingfisher but not only for his grace and beauty. He had also sensed a warm and friendly bird who appeared full of inner strength and honest conviction. The bullfrog was a wise creature and a very good judge of another's character. Time would of course tell us if his initial assessment of Peeyu was accurate, although I am sure you will be pleased to know that these two creatures became the very closest of friends throughout their lives. It was a friendship that flourished until it was brought to a most tragic end many seasons later up by Kingfisher's Bridge. You will no doubt hear more about that fateful day further on in this story.

"Hello again," said a delighted Moha. "I am pleased you have come back. Do you know the community well?"

"I should," replied Peeyu. "My father and his father right through to my great-great-great-grandfather have all lived in our home up by the bridge." Peeyu nodded towards the north-west. "You will hear that bridge called Kingfisher's Bridge. It's named after us. I can tell you all you need to know about the frogs of your community; the fish that swim in these waters; and the birds that fly overhead and nest in the nearby forest. That is of course if you don't know about them all already."

Moha was always keen to learn. He had grown wise knowing that you never stopped acquiring knowledge at any stage in your life. He would often be heard to advise the young frogs that another creature, whether it be a frog, fish, bird or whatever else you cared to name, was more than likely to know something that you didn't.

"I'd be more than happy to hear whatever it is that you wish to tell me," replied Moha. "When can we start?"

Peeyu proudly raised his beak and the light breeze gently stirred the orange feathers on his handsome chest and belly. He too felt he was in the company of a warm, friendly and genuine creature. He liked the new king and he was sure they were going to be the very best of friends.

"Okay then, I'll meet you here tomorrow just before sunrise," said Peeyu. "It's best that we meet alone and unseen by others." Then, noticing Moha look a little questioningly at this last remark, he added, "I'll explain why when I see you."

With that the kingfisher once more shot up in the air and then, just as quickly, darted down, imperceptibly parting the water as he dived. In a twinkling of the eye he was out again dashing back towards his family's home skimming low across the rippling river with yet another nutritious feast for his young son safely gripped in his long black bill.

What Moha heard the following day was a complete history of the river bank community ranging from frogs to voles and from birds to all manner of fish. He was told of noble deeds and great events of the past. He also heard of bad times and of storms and droughts.

Peeyu spoke with caution of the great danger posed by snakes and rats and of dogs and cats. He also told stories of far away lands that he had visited or of which he had heard other creatures describe.

Most importantly Peeyu advised of the secret bond that existed between the kingfishers and all the past kings of the Seaxe frogs and especially how the kingfisher would work alongside the king and keep him informed of matters of interest both within the community of frogs and of the other river bank creatures.

"A well informed king is a wise king," suggested Peeyu when their discussion was finally at a close.

*

And so it was that late that night, soon after the secretive meeting in the Boathouse had finished, Peeyu arrived in Moha's chamber full of the news of the six senior frogs' clandestine discussion.

Moha listened intently as Peeyu recounted the various debates. Sometimes the kingfisher would go into great detail on certain topics but on most issues he was only required to give Moha a flavour of what was discussed, When he had finished Moha shook his head sadly.

"What will become of these poor creatures when I am gone from here?" Moha spoke softly and sincerely. "They are not bad frogs but they act so immaturely for seniors. They should be working hard to gain the community's respect but still they argue about personal power and influence. They seem more concerned with the acquisition and demonstration of status than of being able to correctly use such a valued position for the direct benefit and well-being of our community.

"They also see respect as something that is theirs by right just because they have been promoted to senior positions. They do not appreciate that respect is a commodity that must be well earned and that it takes a lot of hard work and honest commitment to our frogs in order to gain such recognition. Long and sustained dedication to the task of senior is essential so that the frog community can see for themselves that they have leaders in whom they can believe and invest their faith and trust.

"My senior colleagues spend too much time squabbling over issues of little or no consequence and on matters that they perceive to be the trappings of their elevated positions. Such things in my view are unimportant. It is the well-being of the community at large and each and every frog within it that should be our prime concern. If either I or my senior colleagues are diverted from this goal then our frogs will have good cause to doubt and question our ability to govern effectively.

"They also spend too much of their time inventing new policies to replace existing policies. Unfortunately these new policies invariably end up saying much the same as the old ones but always at far greater length and with ever increasing complexity. The outcome of all of this misplaced endeavour is that generally these wordy statements finish up with so much description of what they feel needs to be done that the main objectives and targets are clouded and obscured by over-long sentences and incomprehensible prose. Our seniors must concentrate on preparing succinct and precise policies that contain clear strategies. They must also learn to set achievable and well structured targets and objectives within their strategies. It shouldn't be difficult for intelligent seniors to do this; and they are all, of course, intelligent frogs.

"However, I do know that they feel they have to create new policies that they think will stand as monuments of their personal contribution to the work of the community. They would instead be far better appreciated by our frogs if they just got on with the job and focused on setting clear and understandable targets. Targets which were capable of being successfully achieved or at least accurately measured if the end result fell some way short of original expectations. Their continuous fiddling with and revision of our policies, just for the sake of their own vanity, merely diverts them from concentrating on the more important matters in our community.

"Peeyu, my friend, I have sadly heard, on far too many occasions of late, one frog say to another when referring to the seniors' proposed new policies and strategies that "...all this policy is fine, if only we could understand it..." or "...it's all well and good for those with the right sort of brains but really I personally cannot see the water for the bulrushes...""

Moha's head was bowed as he spoke and Peeyu could see that the king found it painful to talk about his seniors in this way. They sat silently for a while respectfully allowing the gravity of Moha's words to register in their minds. Then Moha lifted his head and looked into the beautiful kingfisher's eyes.

"Thank you again, my loyal friend, for your news. I wish it were possible not to have to watch over my colleagues in this way but it is an unfortunate necessity of life that I must know what these six senior frogs are scheming so that I can carefully keep them from planning anything that may have dire or irreversible consequences for our community."

Peeyu nodded in appreciation on hearing Moha's words of praise. He loved the king for his kindness and wisdom and for the true and lasting friendship he had bestowed both upon himself and all the members of the family of kingfishers.

"Tell me, Peeyu, how is your young son? I saw him only the other day in the early morning light majestically diving for fish. He clearly has his father's grace coupled with the speed and agility of youth."

"Maccus is growing into a fine young bird," replied Peeyu, puffing up his chest in the way that all proud fathers are prone to do.

"His mother and I are pleased with the way that he listens to our teaching, but he has as yet a great deal more to learn. I hope that he will soon be ready to accompany me on my special work for you and your community. He is so keen to progress and is quickly earning his name which when translated means 'free spirit and strong will'."

*

As the two friends parted company, and Peeyu made his way silently back to Kingfisher's Bridge, Moha sat quite still and remained deep in thought for a while. He contemplated the future and, although he had received countless requests for him to reconsider, he felt sure that to resign now was the correct thing for him to do. He was certain that a change of leader in these modern times would ultimately be beneficial for the community of Seaxe. A younger king, he thought, with new ideas and the ability to cope with today's ever-changing environment, was what was now required.

After all, had he not also first arrived in the community as a young enthusiastic bullfrog with masses of energy to build a future full of hope and prosperity for the inhabitants of Seaxe? In the years that followed he developed his frogs throughout a long period of cultural reconstruction introducing many new ways that had, when required, both replaced and complemented tradition. The new wave of ideas that were now emanating from the Anurian Council were, in his humble opinion, probably much better suited to a younger leader who, in a similar way to the young King Moha of many winters past, would tackle such matters positively for the benefit of the community.

Although Moha was confident he had made the right decision he nevertheless felt a great anxiety about what might lie ahead. Try as he may he could neither eliminate this concern from his mind nor was he able to fully understand what it was that caused him to feel this way. It was therefore a deep furrowed brow that the old king took to bed with him just before the first chirrups of the dawn chorus announced the beginning of a new day in the tranquil community of Seaxe.

Chapter Five

Getting to Know the Six

As our story unfolds we will collectively refer to Geelan, Brylil, Lebish, Kejon, Chrich and Josmi as 'the six'. You will recall that this is the group of six senior frogs who had met secretively in the Boathouse and who of course featured prominently in the previous chapter. We already know what position of responsibility each of these seniors hold in the community but we don't as yet know what they are really like as individual frogs. It may be helpful, therefore, to look a little more closely at each of them in turn in order that we can get to know them all a little better.

You, the reader, will also need to appreciate that frogs are really quite complex little creatures who certainly have minds of their own when it comes to registering their likes and dislikes on matters which are of interest to them. Frogs are, generally speaking, a most loving and affectionate species and they like nothing better than to enjoy their time upon this earth chattering with their friends over a feast of tasty grasshoppers whilst perched comfortably on their favourite lily pad. They are also quite vulnerable little beings, perhaps in much the same way that either you or I may be, to temptations that may occasionally come their way. Again, and just like you and I, frogs have feelings that enable them to express love towards their friends and relations and pleasure when praised for something useful that they may have done for the benefit of the community. At the other end of the spectrum these little creatures are also capable of harbouring the more harmful emotions such as jealousy and hatred, and they can, unfortunately, even be enticed by the lure of greed and self gratification.

As in most creature societies that live upon this earth there is more that is good than bad in the hearts of individual frogs. You will find in this story a wide range of characters about whose morals you will have to personally make a judgement. Some such personalities you may recognise in people that you either know or of whom you have heard others speak. Be careful, however, not to see your fellow creatures as only one thing or the other, be it good or bad. We are all of us capable of change and, although we hope it is for the better, it is quite possible that for some it will be a change for the worse.

There are, unfortunately for us all, some creatures who have managed to transcend what we might understand as the normal boundaries of emotions and feelings. Creatures who are capable of calling on the forces of evil to pursue and further their desire for causing grief and pain to all who stand in the way of their achieving domination and superiority over their fellows. I must warn you that you will read about one such creature as you turn over the pages of this book. I only hope that you, unlike the experience of many of the kind souls in this story, have never met nor ever will meet a creature as evil and as wicked as the one they had the misfortune to encounter.

Let's now meet 'the six'. The order is not important nor is it significant. I expect, however, that if each of 'the six' were asked their preference in this respect, then purely out of vanity they would all wish to be named first rather than last.

*

Geelan

Geelan was an unusually short frog but he made up for his lack of height by being rather stout. He also had a surprisingly high-pitched squeaky voice which he regularly used to try to gain the attention of others.

Being of a particularly small and stumpy stature he unfortunately felt compelled to squeak rather loudly during debates, and even in general conversation, in order to put across his views. He also had a habit of bursting into uncontrollable fits of laughter at the slightest hint of humour, very often to the amazement of the speaker who may actually have been making a serious point at the time.

If Geelan's laughter could be described as ear-splitting, then the sound of his clumping through the undergrowth must be regarded as being akin to a military style in hobnail boots. When marching along, this stout little frog would intentionally land as heavily as he could on every hop in order to make as much noise as possible. In fact he was never happier than when the autumn leaves lay thick and crispy on the ground as on such occasions he would delight in the crunching sound his feet made as he bounded along with even greater vigour than usual.

Geelan's noisy disposition was his way of gaining attention. He genuinely felt that by speaking and laughing in a tone several octaves above everyone else, and by purposely thumping his feet along the river bank, it actually signalled that he was a very much more important frog than those about him. Thus Geelan's presence was instantly recognisable and, more often than not, long before he came into view.

Geelan was also a particularly bossy frog who saw in his senior role the need to exert his authority over those frogs of lower position and status. He had, in addition, unfortunately gained a reputation of being overly aggressive and dictatorial and had become widely regarded as being both extremely inflexible and totally single-minded. Regrettably these weaknesses in his character had caused many frogs to dislike him, either because they had been on the end of one of his tirades or they had encountered him stubbornly refusing to see their point of view (even when he was clearly in the wrong).

Geelan struggled enormously with the important responsibility he had for adequately resourcing his area of work and he was well known for his almost total lack of numeracy. In general conversation one frog would very often be heard to say, "Poor Geelan, he really cannot count beyond the number of his fingers and toes."

It was fortunate indeed that Mars was always there to support Geelan when it came to issues that required a logical and resourceful mind. Yet despite his almost complete absence of ability in this regard Geelan would always openly disagree with Mars' advice in public. How lucky this stumpy and ungracious frog was to have colleagues such as Mars and Moha who would patiently tolerate his ungenerous nature while he, having made yet another error of judgement, prattled on about being given bad or unclear advice upon which he had unfortunately relied in order to make his latest poor decision. The reality of it was that this discourteous and ungrateful frog was merely trying to divert attention away from his own poor decision-making by laying the blame at the door of someone else.

Oh dear, this does make Geelan sound like a very mean-minded frog indeed. You must be wondering if he has any good points at all! Well, I am sure you will be pleased to know that he did and at times he was a most engaging frog. Some would even go as far as to say that on occasions he was a quite entertaining frog. Given the opportunity Geelan liked nothing better than to pass the time of day with other frogs chattering on about matters of great inconsequence. On issues such as this he was a masterful frog and probably unsurpassed in the whole of the Seaxe community. He would spend many hours, with whosoever was passing or wished to stop and listen, discussing in great depth the ideas and notions of frog philosophers of days gone by, all of which were generally totally irrelevant to today's frog population. As he held centre stage his excitable nature and high-pitched squeaky voice enabled any frog who happened to be in the vicinity to know that he was there. This was of course a most useful signal as one could always avoid bumping into him if need be.

Geelan did, however, have a very unusual attribute that was rare in the frog community in that he could speak in a language that was foreign to the frogs of Seaxe. It would appear that his father came from a far distant land to the south-east of Seaxe wherein a culture was practised and a tongue was used that were quite different from that which existed in Seaxe. Geelan's father had been a dreamy frog and as a youngster Geelan's head had been filled with his father's tales of faraway places and of strange and mystical happenings. When telling his tales Geelan's father would speak in a language never before heard in Seaxe, although in time Geelan began to recognise the words and their meaning and thus he eventually became fluent in this rare dialect. Although no one in the community, save for Geelan and his long since dead father, spoke or ever had spoken this strange language, they did admire this stout and noisy frog for having the seemingly special ability of being (what we might call) bilingual.

In his role of being responsible for the young frogs of Seaxe Geelan was very patronising and condescending towards those in his charge. He always knew best (or so he thought) and he would generally attempt to exert his high position to influence acceptance of the messages that he personally felt should be put across. He was, unfortunately, invariably a great deal smaller than many of the older adolescents and they cared very little for his overly aggressive attitude towards them. This caused Geelan to become hugely frustrated and as a result he neglected his work with this particular group in favour of the very young in whose company he felt much more at ease (and a good deal taller too!). This group of infant frogs were also less inclined to answer him back when told what to do and Geelan much preferred to be in control.

However, little frogs do grow into big frogs so it was only really a matter of time before they too would observe and understand Geelan's attitude towards them and determine for themselves what they thought of their blustering mentor.

This stout creature lived in a very densely populated area of the community for he felt most comfortable being amongst a large number of his fellow frogs. What's more there was always an ear into which he could pour his thoughts on this and that be it welcomed by the recipient or not.

*

Brylil

Brylil was viewed by others as being somewhat of an enigma. Although he had always been involved in many aspects of frog community life and had on numerous occasions displayed a wide range of talents he was nevertheless largely unknown by his friends and colleagues. He was a frog who had seemingly always "been there", in the company of others as it were, yet when one frog said to another "...well what's he really like?", nobody ever had the answer.

Brylil lived alone in a heavily shaded area of the river bank. He courted neither the close friendship of female frogs nor that of male frogs. However he seemed to have a preference for both young frogs and elderly frogs and appeared to be far more comfortable in their company than in that of his contemporaries. Some would say, to the accompaniment of a knowing tap on their nose, that they thought they knew his preference for companionship. In reality of course they didn't.

If the truth were known about his choice of friends then it was only really Brylil who could say - and he had decided long ago not to make any declaration whatsoever on the subject. The guessing game continued, however, as it is a well known fact that given half a chance frogs will always participate in an interesting riddle or puzzle given half a chance.

Brylil was a kind and thoughtful frog who was generally well liked by the community. He was weak on making important decisions and in this respect always relied upon Moha's guidance. This was not a bad thing, however, as listening to the wisdom of the old king and acting upon his advice was always a most sensible thing to do. He would similarly arrange to regularly consult with Mars and also seek his assistance on difficult issues.

If Brylil had faults then they were rarely seen or at least well concealed. He was careful never to exceed either his authority or his ability and the mere thought of taking a risk made his hindlimbs go all wobbly! Much of what he did, therefore, was based upon the recommendations and suggestions of Moha and Mars. As a consequence of this wise counsel Brylil invariably made good decisions and was held in affectionate regard by the community of Seaxe. He was thus considered to be an adequately able and intelligent senior frog.

Brylil was also a very sincere and serious frog who cared greatly for the health and well-being of his community. This was both a strength and weakness of his as he often found himself so involved in another frog's problem that he could no more find a way out of the particular predicament the frog was in than the poor frog could itself. In such circumstances Brylil would hide himself away in the seclusion of his home and struggle desperately for a correct solution. Usually, after many hours and sometimes days of deep thought during which he would have explored many avenues and options, he would finally go to Moha or sometimes Mars for advice on what to do.

Moha would always find time to listen to all that Brylil had to say. He liked Brylil for his sincere and caring nature and he welcomed his workmanlike approach to solving problems. When they met in this way Moha would encourage his young colleague to think more clearly and to take each option a little further, or even consider other possibilities so as to examine the real benefits each solution had to offer. At the end of these consultations Brylil would come away satisfied that the matter being considered had been solved plus also being personally a little wiser for the experience.

Although Brylil valued Moha's help he did see in himself his own faults and particularly the weakness that prevented him from dealing personally with the more difficult situations. To seek the wise counsel of Moha (and Mars) he knew was a sound thing to do. He did, however, inwardly resent the fact that he was not able to reach such conclusions on his own and this annoyed him and made him feel inadequate. Even though these feelings ran deep inside his body Brylil managed to keep them well-concealed to the outside world. Moha was nevertheless aware of how he felt and the old king was greatly concerned that in this aspect of Brylil's character lay the young frog's Achilles' heel.

*

Lebish

What could be said of Lebish that Lebish had not already said of himself? If ever there was a frog who fancied himself as being 'the frog most likely to' then Lebish provided the prime example. The strange thing was, however, that in the community of Seaxe it was only Lebish who felt this way. Not only that but the vast majority of the local frogs were quite bemused as to how he had ever risen to the heights of senior frog status in the first place. Although many would regard Lebish as a seemingly intelligent and intellectual frog, and one who could certainly talk the fins off a fish's tail, to actually imagine placing him in the important role of a senior – well, never in a month of blue Sundays in February!

The promotion of Lebish to senior had actually occurred whilst Moha had been away from the community checking the northern perimeter of Seaxe to ensure that his frogs were safe from whatever lay beyond the swamps and desolate lands of Waga. Moha had in the past always undertaken such journeys on a regular basis, although of late they had been of greater frequency as he had found himself becoming increasingly anxious about what might live and exist in the forbidden Far North. He found that as the seasons passed his original apprehension of the Far North had turned to anxiety and from this to deep suspicion. Moha could not understand these feelings but they haunted his soul and he knew that some day he would have to confront the root cause of this deep-seated fear.

So it was that whilst Moha was away on one such mission Lebish had been promoted to his current role of senior. The Anurian Council, in their wisdom, had considered that it was not necessary to await Moha's return to fill this post which had suddenly become vacant following the unexpected and untimely death of the previous incumbent. Although, as you know, the appointment of seniors is the responsibility of the king, on this occasion the Anurian Council unfortunately felt that they needed to act quickly in order to fill this position. In their apparent haste Lebish was asked to step into this very important role.

Not one of the everyday frogs living in the community of Seaxe appeared able to explain either how the council found it within themselves to appoint Lebish, or, more suspiciously, how the allegedly accidental death of Lebish's predecessor had occurred. If the truth were known (and it is only you the reader and me the author who is privy to this most coveted of secrets) it is actually only Lebish who knows the full facts of the incident and he, interestingly, has never let it be known to anyone that he is the holder of such information.

What appears to have happened is that the former senior had been lured to Duke's Weir, which is situated on the north-east side of the Boathouse, by a bogus message that purported to indicate that should he arrive there at a certain time he would be likely to hear something to his advantage. Understandably, and with frogs being naturally inquisitive creatures, he was keen to know what this was all about. Accordingly he decided to venture downstream to the weir on his own whereupon he waited at the location the rendezvous was meant to take place. As he patiently stood on the river bank, looking out over the raging torrent of water as it gushed through the weir, he was unaware that the plump silhouette of a rather overfed frog was creeping up behind him. The next, and unfortunately the very last, thing he knew was that he received a violent push from behind which sent him somersaulting into the foaming currents of Duke's Weir, wherein the life was crushed out of this unsuspecting and hapless frog.

Some say, but only in a whisper far out of the hearing of strangers, that following Lebish's promotion a number of members of the council appeared to develop rather fatter bellies which were reputably the result of feasting on a recent supply of very succulent grasshoppers. It may of course have been quite coincidental but it is a well known fact that Lebish has dubious contacts in the acquisition of provisions and that he is particularly partial to top quality grasshoppers. Those who have seen it say that his personal store of grasshoppers is unrivalled in any frog community that they know.

As for the whereabouts of Lebish at the moment his predecessor was murdered... well... this is something that is not known for sure. Several hesitant and seemingly embarrassed councillors did come forward at the time to say they had seen him up by Kingfisher's Bridge and that he had been there all that day. This of course was for the purpose of confirming that Lebish had been many hops away from Duke's Weir when the tragic accident (?) occurred. However, had any frog seen the plump silhouette that had crept up behind the unfortunate former senior they would have been surprised at how similar it was in both shape and size to Lebish himself!

It's only a guess of course, because I wasn't there myself to actually witness the event, but I think... no, maybe I shouldn't speculate and jump to the obvious conclusion. Perhaps it's better to let you read on so that you can learn a little more about the character of our friend Lebish - then you will be able to make your own mind up on Lebish's possible role in this matter.

Moha had reluctantly accepted the decision to appoint Lebish, although he made it clear to the Anurian Council that it was not supported by him. He did in fact confidentially advise them that he considered Lebish to be unsuited to senior status and that in his opinion he was both sly and untrustworthy and in addition that he was inclined to be disloyal.

On hearing these words a number of members of the council were clearly embarrassed and shuffled uneasily on their hindlimbs as they felt Moha's keen eyes upon them. These signals of malpractice were not lost on the old king and he sensed only too well which of the councillors had been won over and corrupted by Lebish. Moha despised such members for their weakness and greed and for allowing themselves to be coerced into voting for the devious frog just to satisfy their bellies.

Although Moha was greatly angered by the whole sorry situation he regarded a handful of easily duped and fraudulent members of the council to be infinitely more straightforward to manage than the cunning and devious Lebish.

So it was from that day on, both through his own careful observance and through the ever vigilant eyes and ears of Peeyu, that Moha kept a very close watch over the antics and activities of Lebish.

*

Kejon

Of 'the six' Kejon was by far the strongest. He was both more powerful in body and resolute in character than his fellow seniors. Not surprisingly he was regarded warily by his peers as each of them recognised in Kejon such personal qualities that they did not, and would never, possess.

Kejon did however have a major weakness and this was his inability to cope with situations that suddenly occurred of which he did not agree or that he felt he could neither directly influence or control. In such circumstances, instead of sitting back and analysing the situation, he would fly off into a rage and storm up and down the river bank shouting and reprimanding any unfortunate frog who happened to be in his way. He would of course eventually simmer down, but by then, as you can imagine, the damage had been done and his lack of perspective and personal discipline had once again been exposed for all to see.

Despite this apparent flaw in his nature he was a good friend of Mars. They were both brown frogs of similar build and stature. They were also much more athletic and fitter than their senior colleagues and they shared many common interests. Their athleticism, when compared to that of their fellow seniors, was particularly striking as the others were rather lazy when it came to taking exercise and as a consequence were physically very much out of condition.

Mars had also long since learned how to cope with Kejon's explosive temper and so it was to him that others would go when they saw that Kejon was starting to rant and rave over some problem or another. If he was on hand then Mars would attend to his friend and soothe his wrath with kind words and gentle advice.

Kejon, for he was as proud as he was temperamental, both respected and envied Mars. He envied Mars most of all for his ability to listen to others and then being able to offer back clear, concise and greatly valued advice. He knew that although younger than himself Mars was far more mature and capable than he was ever likely to be. As already mentioned this caused Kejon to be envious, whereas other members of 'the six' in the same situation would have felt jealous of their more talented colleague. Kejon's envy, however, was based on his admiration of Mars and as such was therefore quite healthy. It actually made him evermore determined to improve his own performance and standing in the community.

Notwithstanding Kejon's recognition of his personal limitations you would never hear him admit that he was subservient in any way to any other living creature be it one of the other five members of 'the six', Mars, or even King Moha himself. Furthermore, although Kejon had accepted the hand of friendship that had been extended long ago to him by Mars, he was nevertheless always on the lookout for something to latch on to that would encourage the frog community to hold him in higher esteem than they did his more competent colleague. Kejon regarded this as perfectly acceptable behaviour and saw it as merely being part of his generally competitive attitude.

Thus the relationship between Kejon and Mars could be described as one that blew both hot and cold. It would be warm and friendly one day and then rather distant and chilly on another, especially if Kejon had spotted an opportunity for practising a bit of one-upmanship.

Kejon was rightly considered by the other five (of 'the six') senior frogs as being ahead of them in the community's eyes. As such they regularly kept a weather-eye open for some grain of a story that would detract from his higher recognition.

That he was moody and sombre there was no doubt. That he was sometimes rather a bully there was also no question. Allowances were, however, often made to excuse this type of behaviour on the basis that it was just Kejon's superior physical strength and athleticism showing through as natural aggression and that this could on occasions be rather awesome particularly to his subordinates.

There was, however, one particular flaw in Kejon's attitude towards his fellow frogs that was a major concern to many in the community. This was his inability to relate well either to female frogs or to those who were described as 'unfortunate' frogs. Female frogs he regarded as having one singularly important role and function within the community and this was that they play their biological part in the reproductive cycle of the frog population. Beyond this Kejon saw virtually no other good purpose for female frogs other than that they should be silent and have respect for him and the rest of the male members of the community. As far as the 'unfortunate' frogs were concerned Kejon found it difficult to set his eyes on anything other than what could be termed normal, fit and healthy frogs. He also wished that there were not quite so many frogs in the community who had come from the north during the great storms. He was not overly keen on accommodating frogs from other communities and he much preferred his own kind. It was no secret amongst his senior colleagues that if ever Kejon was given the opportunity he would send these 'foreigners' back to their own communities and restore Seaxe to its pure indigenous race. In this respect Kejon regarded Geelan with great suspicion and doubted the stumpy frog's integrity as a senior on the basis that he could talk in a strange tongue.

To find himself responsible for the elderly frogs in the community was something with which Kejon visibly struggled. Although many of the elderly were quite healthy and capable for their age there were also a great number who had grown frail with the passing of time. Kejon found having to care for the latter group a tiresome trial and he spent many hours pondering over how he could develop ways of side-lining such nuisances to enable him to concentrate on the fitter and healthier specimens.

It was in fact Kejon, with some advice from his close assistants, who first put forward the proposal that perhaps the old and less fit frogs could be sent away from Seaxe when they reached a certain age or degree of frailty. His idea was that communities could be selected or created in locations where it was generally sunny and warm and where the elderly could thus live out their days in well-earned comfort and tranquillity.

The wording of the actual proposal was of course framed and presented in a much more acceptable manner, which suggested that such an idea would certainly be of benefit both to the older frogs themselves as well as to those who they left behind. Kejon argued that the elderly and frail frogs could retire peacefully and with dignity to a stress-free life on some distant and safe river bank, whilst those in Seaxe, who would otherwise be required to care for them, would not have to spend great swathes of their valuable time attending to their every need and requirement. Kejon euphemistically referred to this novel approach to caring for the elderly and frail as his 'Fun in the Sun' proposal.

Kejon did not conceal the fact that he would like to see a lean and fit society of frogs in Seaxe which was free of any defect; pure of race; and where female frogs knew and understood their role and place in the furtherance of the species.

To the vast majority of Seaxe frogs the sound of Kejon powerfully and forcefully stating his views on the 'ideal' society actually made the toes on their hindlimbs curl up at the ends. Such talk was considered extreme and most found it rather offensive and distasteful. However, Kejon did have his supporters and such frogs were cautiously regarded by others and given a fairly wide berth whenever possible.

*

Chrich

Chrich was by far the eldest of 'the six' seniors. He had been in high positions for almost as long as Moha had reigned and was in fact the first senior appointment the king had made.

At that time, many winters ago, Chrich had been a fine green frog. His vitality and energy were unsurpassed by any other frog and his enthusiasm for caring for his fellow creatures knew no bounds. It was in fact his dedication to supporting others and his honesty when giving advice or answering questions that initially attracted Moha. Almost straight away a strong bond developed between the two frogs that was to last throughout Moha's time as king – well, unfortunately not quite right to the end as you will see as you read on!

It is difficult to tell whether it was the stress that inevitably accompanies the holding of high positions, or possibly the exhaustion that follows long and sustained hard work, but of recent years Chrich's efforts were clearly diminishing. Moha could see his old friend becoming more and more tired with each passing season and so he correspondingly reduced his demands and expectations of him.

It now seemed an age ago, but when Chrich was a young frog he had been widely regarded as the frog most likely to succeed. At that stage in his development the community were certain that it was only a matter of time before Chrich would hear of a kingship becoming available in a distant frog community and, with Moha's blessing and support, he would apply for such a position and be appointed their king. That this never occurred was a puzzle to the frogs of Seaxe but they put it down to the fact that Chrich was probably content to remain as their senior and devote himself to the good of their own community. Not only that, but as is usual with the passing of time, maybe his personal ambition was ebbing and his motivation to attain the highest level was not quite such a driving force now as it had once been in his more enthusiastic and formative years.

The real truth, however, was that although his fellows were right about Chrich's dedication to their community they were wrong in respect of his happiness to remain a senior. In much the same way as you and I may have felt, if we had been in the same situation as Chrich, he had always dreamt of being given the opportunity to become a king. However, in reality, he was very frightened about the prospect of taking on a position of such power and responsibility.

For all his wistful thinking about what might have been Chrich was nevertheless an intelligent frog and knew his limitations. He also took wise counsel from a close personal friend, a female frog named Katash, in whose judgement and insight he placed great faith. In deep and serious conversations the two friends would discuss many issues both of a business and personal nature. During these private 'tête-à-têtes' they would speak honestly and openly about each other's abilities and qualities and they had concluded long ago that Chrich would not survive as a leader of a community. They both knew in their hearts that although he possessed all the ingredients that were needed to be a first rate senior he did not, unfortunately, have the charisma and leadership qualities demanded of a king.

With such a vital element missing from his make-up Chrich was destined to remain a senior for the rest of his useful working life. That he had been successful in this role there was not a frog in Seaxe who would fairly say otherwise. Nevertheless, it forever remained a great mystery to the community at large as to why he had not progressed to the highest level.

Chrich was now a tired old frog whose best days were definitely in the long distant past. Given his absence of further ambition, and long before Moha had made his announcement to resign as king, he had set himself a personal target that he too would stand down from his senior position at the same time as Moha resigned. Although that moment had now arrived he felt an inner reluctance to carry out his original intention and he wondered if he should carry on for a little longer... just to help settle in the new king, don't you know?

Although against the wise advice of Katash, who dearly wanted to see her long-time companion retire gracefully and with dignity, Chrich determined that he would indeed continue after Moha had resigned.

As for how the other members of 'the six' saw Chrich it should be said that their views had changed substantially in recent seasons. In his earlier years, and largely due to the promise which Chrich had shown as a young adult frog, he had been quite jealously regarded by his peers. They viewed him as being of greater substance than themselves and this caused them to become envious of their more mature colleague and particularly so when they heard other frogs in the community praise him and say that they thought he would surely one day become some lucky community's frog king. However, now that his drive and ambition had visibly all but evaporated, they no longer felt any threat and they consequently heaped much praise upon him for his past achievements knowing that nothing more was to come from this once prolific and enthusiastic old senior.

*

Josmi

Josmi was the youngest of 'the six' and his rise to senior status had been nothing short of meteoric. It had in fact been so fast that apart from his closest friends and colleagues there were very few other frogs in the community who had even heard of him prior to his appointment as senior.

This young frog's greatest skill was his creativity. It was therefore most appropriate that he should hold the post where his time could be devoted to 'ideas and concepts'. Josmi in fact needed only the smallest germ of an idea for him to be able to create a vast range of scenarios and mental pictures of how one may devise and develop new schemes and methods of changing the ways of the past.

Josmi saw himself as a vehicle for change and he cared very little for the tried and well-tested ways of days gone by. Tradition, in his view, was far from ideal and he saw change and innovation as essential for the betterment of the community.

He was thus regarded by his fellow seniors as being rather unsettling and possibly even a little dangerous. After all they each had large parts of their own areas of responsibility that had been built up on past good practice and they felt confident that what had worked well previously would continue to do so in the future. (You may at this stage, and especially in view of the last comment, be thinking that such an attitude is contrary to what you have heard about the way the seniors spend much of their time as they do appear to devote a good deal of it constantly re-jigging their policies and their strategies. The truth of course about such changes is that the policies and strategies normally end up saying much the same thing as before, only in a rather more complicated and long-winded manner.)

At the regular meetings of 'the six' the other five seniors found it almost impossible to stifle Josmi's eagerness for change and they felt very uncomfortable whenever he focused on any of their respective areas of responsibility. They gave advice to their young colleague by saying such things as "...surely it is better not to rock the lily pad..." or "...do we really need change just for the sake of change...?" This was all to no avail however and such defensive talk was no deterrent to Josmi when he was on the scent of an interesting new scheme or in the mood for some creativity.

The other seniors therefore found it necessary to play a game with Josmi that involved diverting him from one idea to another so that he was never able to concentrate for too long on any one particular issue. By virtue of this tactic they were each prepared to suffer a little discomfort when Josmi alighted upon a subject in their area of work knowing that it was only a temporary intrusion as he could soon be influenced to turn his attention to something else. In this regard, and as soon as Josmi appeared to be getting too involved in a particular matter, they would advise him that some other even more important issue had suddenly risen to the top of their shared agenda that required his urgent and most excellent attention.

So it was in this manic and contrived environment that Josmi operated. His head had become so full of ideas and notions that his effectiveness was now negligible. In addition, and due to the joint manipulation to this effect by his colleagues, his personal agenda had gradually grown into one that was so long and inflated with top priority issues that he could never determine which was the most important and where he should most appropriately be allocating his time. It certainly wasn't in the best interests of his colleagues to help him with such an exercise and, on the occasions when he did ask them for some assistance with prioritising, they would simply say that to make such a judgement was way beyond their comprehension and such decision making was really more in keeping with a super-intelligent frog such as he.

Josmi found these outward signs of support from his colleagues hugely embarrassing, for he knew in his heart that he was not coping at all well with his workload. His skill and passion for change had become so thinly spread across a vast range of ideas that he had completely lost his focus on what was really required. He honestly believed that everyone genuinely wanted change as much as he did and that by not delivering his agenda he was letting the community down. Josmi's pride, however, and the never ending flow of flattering comments he constantly received from his senior colleagues, made it impossible for him to openly declare that he was actually struggling with his job and what he really needed was help.

This situation was of course perfect for the other five seniors who regarded poor Josmi as very neatly side-lined and therefore no longer a threat to their work activities. When he was not in their company they would often say with a little snigger, and quietly behind their forelimbs "...a change is as good as a rest... but more rest is better!"

*

Now that you know a little more about Mars' senior colleagues it is time we returned to the story. However, after all you have heard about 'the six' I hope you don't think too badly of them. Despite their failings (and we all have failings - don't we?) they do have some good points otherwise they would not have been appointed by Moha and thereby achieving senior status. The one possible exception, of course, is Lebish whose elevation to senior frog was tainted with intrigue and suspicion and who is the only one of all the seniors who Moha did not personally promote.

Chapter Six

The Beginning of the End

"Tell me more, crow!" This demand was coarsely uttered from the mouth of a huge and fierce looking toad. "Tell me more about this news of our gutless brethren from across the swamps!"

The crow shifted nervously from foot to foot as it stood before the ugly and intimidating creature. The frightened bird could neither stare into the eyes of the toad nor could it bear to be in its presence. It knew, however, that if it dared to disobey the toad and did not recount fully what it had seen and heard earlier that day in the land immediately beyond the swamplands to the south, then a certain and painful death would be his reward.

"The news, O Master, is of the community of Seaxe who are at this very moment looking for suitable candidates to replace the great King Moha who will be resigning from his kingship at the end of this coming winter."

The toad sat back and contemplated this information. As he did so a sinister leer slowly spread across his face. This, he thought, could be just the opportunity for which he had been waiting. The ideal reason to venture across Waga and seek fresh challenges in the south. The chance to get out of the dark and dismal Far North community of Tamsid which was an area in which he had reigned unopposed for many years. He had of late grown increasingly weary of these Far North frogs and of the monotonous lives they led in their bleak and colourless community.

This vile and evil toad had ruled over the frogs of Tamsid by creating fear and terror in the hearts of its inhabitants. In return these fearful creatures showed neither a purpose nor a passion for life and merely existed from day to day. The constant reminders that individuals and their families were under a threat of death if they

'Tell me more, crow!' This demand was coarsely uttered from the mouth of a huge and fierce looking toad.

disobeyed their king served to discourage either enterprise or creativity in the community. There was, therefore, neither enough interest nor spirit to inject any enthusiasm in developing new ways of doing things or changing the ways of their distant generations.

As a result the huge toad had become tired of his subdued and boring community and he now craved southern pastures, for he had heard others say that the lands and rivers to the south of Waga were inhabited by more receptive and ebullient frogs. In fact he had for a long time felt that they may be just the kind of frogs that he could manipulate and coerce by his cunning stealth to obtain his coveted ambition of overall domination of all frogs.

The desire to add to his kingdom the frogs who lived to the east, west and south of Tamsid burned like a raging fire within him and this obsession caused him to grow more and more angry and dissatisfied with his lot with every day that passed. What irked the toad even more was the fact that he was so limited in his ability to go out and conquer nearby neighbouring communities, since in the great storms (of which the tale has already been told) every Far North community had been entirely obliterated with the exception of Tamsid. The huge and ugly toad had therefore become almost totally overwhelmed by the urge to go rampaging into distant communities and literally take what he wanted. But now, as he listened to what the crow had to say, he could sense a more legitimate method developing in his devious and wicked mind of gaining a foothold in the south.

"How did you hear of this story?" inquired the toad, slowly easing himself up on to his powerful hindlimbs and leaning forward towards the crow. As he did so the noxious smell of the giant creature wafted over the frightened bird whose head was now spinning round and round with a mixture of the foul odour of the toad's breath and the unbearable heat that had built up within the main hall of the toad's palace. Pulling himself together, but avoiding the temptation to draw in a lungful of the toad's stench, the crow answered.

"Our magpie friends who regularly journey over the desolate lands of Waga speak of much activity in Seaxe. They have heard that the king of that community, the much loved King Moha, has decided to retire at the end of this winter. Their council are therefore in the process of sending messengers to places both near and far to tell of this news. These messengers will also be saying that tradition dictates that their new king must come from outside of the community of

Seaxe and that they are therefore seeking applications from such eminent frogs who are interested in succeeding Moha.

"Bring me the messenger!" ordered the toad. "Alive for the moment. I want to know exactly what is going on and all the detail of this mission."

"Yes, O Masterly one. As soon as I can," replied the crow.

"What do you mean... as soon as you can?" seethed the toad through very tight lips. "You will do it as soon as I say... *And I say I want the messenger right now*!"

These last words were spat out by the toad and the hapless crow reeled as the bad breath of his master enveloped him. The crow shook in his alarm at the severity of the toad's temper and, nodding nervously in his anxiety, he hastily backed out of the hall taking great care not to turn his head away from the direction of his king for fear of being struck down from behind.

*

Left alone in his palace the toad allowed a sly smile to creep across his mouth. This expression only served to enhance the menacing appearance that his community had grown to fear.

"I shall! I must! I will become the great ruler of all the frogs and creatures who live upon the river banks and in the forests! Nothing and no creature will stop me in my quest for total domination." These words were spoken in a low rasping and sinister voice by the massive toad. Fortunately there was no other being around to hear this diabolical vow, for if there were they would surely have died in fright at such a prospect.

The toad then ambled out of his palace and into the Tamsid daylight which revealed a land almost totally void of vegetation and which largely consisted of smelly swamps in which numerous black pools of slimy mud had collected. He gazed down into one such foul smelling pit and considered his reflection.

"Emled. You really are quite the most handsome of creatures." The toad turned his head from side to side as he screwed up his eyes peering deeply into the blackness at what he thought he could see.

"Quite irresistible to those witless female frogs and so envied by those pathetic male frogs," continued the toad. "Emled, my friend, you really are the most wonderful frog of all."

The toad would often sit admiring what he considered to be his reflection in these stagnant and swampy pools of slime. In reality all he could see of course was a vague and shadowy silhouette of himself and it was this that he truly considered to be a creature, indeed a frog, of great beauty with an equally magnificent physique.

What others saw, however, was quite the ugliest creature that had ever hopped upon a lily pad in the Far North - or anywhere else, come to think of it, according to the more widely travelled magpies of the Tamsid community. Nevertheless, Emled desperately wanted to see a handsome frog when he looked into the still and murky waters, because a handsome frog is what he craved to be.

Emled was, however, a toad! Not, unfortunately, what you might regard as an everyday sort of toad, the type of which you may spot sitting quietly minding its own business in the shallow waters of a secluded pond. Not a chance of that I'm afraid because this toad was quite the most evil and unsightly of toads that has ever lived!

The most peculiar thing about Emled and his wanting to be a frog was that he actually despised and detested all frogs. He thought, however, that in the eyes of others (and scarily, as you will find out later, this included humans) frogs were seen as rather endearing and cute little creatures and he similarly wanted to be viewed in this way. Although he was in truth well aware of the very different appearance between himself and a frog, even the largest of frogs, he was nonetheless determined to be regarded as a frog. And not any old frog, don't you know, but a stunningly handsome frog at that.

So Emled lived his lie. Always wanting to be what be wasn't. However, when he bothered to search his soul he knew very well that he was a toad - in fact an extraordinarily ghastly toad - who was truly evil and heartless; cruel and ruthless; extremely mean and with absolutely no thought for the well-being of others!

Although inwardly he cherished such features of his character, and prided himself on his wicked ways, the public face he attempted to present was quite different. To the frogs and creatures of Tamsid, therefore, he would make a display of kinship and support for his community. However, what he was really doing was attempting to dupe them into believing that he cared for them all and their families when in reality he cared only for himself.

Not surprisingly, in this environment, there therefore lived a confused community of frogs. On one day they might see their king, for all intents and purposes, offering some degree of support and indicating signs of friendship towards them. On another day, or maybe even later the same day, they might alternatively witness the full and savage fury of a seemingly insane king handing out spine-chilling and blood-curdling orders the like of which are too terrible to recount even in a story such as this.

When Emled was in the mood for wooing his community he would often be heard to express his favourite phrases, namely "Who cares... Emled cares... I care..." and "Frogs first". When the former phrase was spoken Emled always made a point of speaking the words "Who cares... Emled cares..." very loudly and with his forelimbs thrown extravagantly open in an attempt to reassure any listening frog that he really does have their well-being at the forefront of his mind. He would then drop his voice to a harsh whisper when delivering the third element of this phrase, and, as he did so, he would draw his forelimbs tightly across his chest as if clutching his heart, all for extra effect of course.

Quite what was the significance of his phrase 'Frogs first' no frog ever really knew, for whenever Emled was asked to explain its meaning he would simply reply, "Why, whatever you want it to mean of course."

How Emled despised his community - and now even more than ever before. He hated the fact that he could never be one of their kind no matter what he did. For all his undoubted physical power and creature cunning there was nothing he could do to alter the biological facts of nature. He was a toad and would always remain a toad.

So long had he craved to be what he wasn't that he often had vivid dreams in which he truly believed he was a loveable and handsome frog king. When, however, he awoke on these occasions and the realisation came that he was still a toad he was instantly filled with an all-consuming sense of hatred and bitterness and he detested his community even more.

Knowing deep down that he could never actually be a frog himself he had instead made it his aim to be the ruler of all frogs. If he couldn't join them he would beat them and he knew only too well that beating the frogs would be a much easier thing for him to do. His sheer size, stature and massively superior strength alone struck terror into the hearts of the Far North frogs. They had neither question nor answer to give him when confronted by the toad so menacing was his gaze and intimidating his physical presence.

The frogs of the Far North had long since become resigned to their situation and reluctantly accepted their miserable, dull and repressed existence. They didn't even ask questions as to why many of their kin had mysteriously disappeared during Emled's reign of terror, nor did they enquire after his regular and increasingly frequent extended absences from their community. They were concerned that if they ever did query the disappearance of friends or family members in Emled's presence, or within earshot of any of his multitude of confidants who appeared to have infiltrated every aspect of their community life, then they too might be the next to go out and never return home.

The Tamsid frogs, therefore, accepted Emled's word that the vast majority of their colleagues, who for some reason or other did not return to the community, were actually now doing good work in far distant lands. Emled would make this explanation more acceptable by adding that these frogs would, at this very moment, be spreading the news of Tamsid's recipe for a happy and contented community where every frog can achieve their ambitions and obtain a full and contented tummy into the bargain.

However, it wasn't until the frogs of Tamsid actually sat down and thought about their lot that they realised that although what Emled preached was clearly true for him personally, in respect of their own positions they seemed to be having a far from happy existence. And as far as full tummies were concerned, the only full tummy around was in fact the enormous one that belonged to Emled.

Despite this apparent contradiction in the way they lived, the Tamsid frogs collectively kept their heads down. They each of them certainly hoped that they would never be chosen to represent their community as an ambassador to spread the news of how wonderful life was in Tamsid, for they knew that this was the signal that they may go and never return. They couldn't be sure, of course, but some of the locals even wondered if these representatives had met with an untimely death. Although no Tamsid frog could either confirm or deny this terrible speculation, there were certainly none who would dare to ask such a question or risk querying with Emled the whereabouts of a close friend who had not returned from some mission or another.

I'm sure that you the reader would like to know what really happened to the Tamsid frogs who mysteriously went missing from their community without giving prior warning to their friends and relatives. In time, of course, this will all be made clear but for the moment you will have to be patient. I can only say at this stage that you must prepare yourself for some quite grisly and disturbing revelations, particularly when it comes to the disappearance of the young frogs of Tamsid.

Chapter Seven

Lebish Shows His True Colours

Lebish was already finding his task of visiting the Near North communities extremely tiresome. That he considered it a huge waste of his precious time to go hopping about the countryside, we have already heard. Almost as bad for Lebish, however, was the thought that he had left behind a number of his subordinates who had certain responsibilities and he was worried that they might take important decisions that may not meet with his approval whilst he was away. Lebish's style of managing meant that he insisted on personally having to give his seal of approval to every decision that was taken by the frogs in his charge.

Not only was Lebish worried about what decisions his subordinates may be taking but he was almost as equally concerned with regard to the inroads these particular colleagues might be making into his private stock of juicy grasshoppers. Lebish could only dream about the contents of his store and whenever he did so it caused him to fret about its likely depletion.

Throughout his sojourn to the Near North, Lebish had not been able to acquire more than a couple of skinny little grasshoppers and these he had found quite disgusting. Being starved of its normal substantial quantity of food Lebish's potbelly was not only rapidly reducing in size but it was also complaining very loudly. The hollow rumbling and severe hunger pangs served as constant reminders to the rotund senior that he was urgently in need of a jolly good feast. It also meant that he could not stop worrying about the probable feasting his subordinates would be doing in his larder and at his expense too.

It was whilst Lebish and his group of frogs were making for their tenth and final of the Near North's minor communities that great shadows suddenly spread across the river bank along which they were travelling. Lebish looked up towards the sky and he saw about fifty or more large black crows drifting high above their heads. The small group of frogs sat quite still and were fearful of what they saw. Crows are a natural enemy of the frog and when these little creatures are exposed on dry land then they are vulnerable to an attack from these sly and unprincipled birds.

The crows were as black as night and appeared much larger than any that the frogs had ever seen before. They also seemed to be acting very aggressively and looking for some trouble.

Suddenly, and quite unexpectedly, as Lebish and his companions huddled together upon the ground, some twenty or so of the crows dropped out of the sky and swooped down upon the small group of defenceless frogs attacking them most brutally and violently.

Lebish froze and shut his eyes as tightly as be could. He feared that his own death was imminent and he just hoped that it would be quick and painless. He heard great raucous 'caws' from the crows and croaking cries for help from his frightened companions. Lebish knew there was nothing he could do to help them. He had never been a fighter nor was he agile enough to make a quick escape. He just curled himself up and waited for the end to arrive.

As the pitiful pleas for mercy and the harrowing croaks of pain and fear from his colleagues slowly died away, Lebish realised that death had for some reason not come to him. He warily opened his eyes hardly daring to look at what could possibly have happened to his fellow travellers. What he then saw sickened him to his hindlimbs for all around were strewn the horribly mutilated bodies of his innocent companions. As his colleagues lay dead or dying Lebish wondered just what evil could commit such horror and cause such carnage.

Lebish stood quite still. He had momentarily lost all track of reality. He could feel the heavy thud of his heart palpitating and he thought that the very life within his body was trying to burst out of his skin. He also sensed a mounting panic building up in his head and he could neither think what was best to do, nor act decisively, so great was his fear.

Then, almost as if being shaken out of a deep sleep, Lebish suddenly became aware that standing right in front of him was a huge black crow. Lebish could see straight away that this was no ordinary crow, and, as he cowered low beneath the shadow of the evil looking

Lebish looked up towards the sky and he saw about fifty or more large black crows drifting high above their heads.

bird, the terrified frog again thought that his time on this earth was about to suffer a premature conclusion.

The crow towering above Lebish was in fact the same black crow who had been ordered by Emled to bring to him the messenger from Seaxe. Whereas in the presence of the massive toad the crow had trembled he now postured in such a way as to imitate the fearful manner of his master. He planned to make every effort to fill Lebish with the same sort of fear that Emled had instilled in him only a little earlier that day.

"Wh... wh... what do you want with me?" whimpered the extremely frightened Lebish.

"You and the news you are carrying are to be taken to our leader - Emled The Great of Tamsid!" replied the crow, who had taken an instant dislike to this overfed and paunchy little frog.

Lebish knew there was absolutely no escape from the predicament in which he now found himself so there was no point in wasting energy even thinking about such a course of action. He had at least gained some idea as to why his life had been spared and he was grateful for a reprieve whatever the circumstances. In typical Lebish style he turned his thoughts away from his slaughtered companions as self-preservation was now his prime concern.

"You can have whatever you want but please don't harm me," pleaded the now very humble frog. "I will help you in any way that I can." He then gestured towards his fatally injured colleagues and said, in a surprisingly matter of fact manner, "They are all frogs of little or no consequence. I, however, am a very senior frog from the community of Seaxe and I am sure I can be of useful assistance to your master."

The crow was by no means the sort of bird you would care to meet upon a darkened river bank late at night and certainly not one you would wish to have as a friend. However, it did have enough subtlety to appreciate a sly and devious creature when it saw one, and that is precisely what he thought of Lebish. How he would have preferred, and enjoyed, personally dealing with this despicable creep who clearly thought only about himself and showed no compassion towards his fellow companions. How much more satisfying it would be to pulverise this ignominious frog right now, rather than having the inconvenience of escorting him all the way back to Emled's palace.

If it hadn't been for the fact that to disobey his master's orders would certainly have resulted in a fate far worse than death for himself then Lebish would certainly have fallen to the beak and claws of the menacing black crow at that very moment. The crow, however, most fortunately for Lebish, resisted the temptation and reluctantly put the thought of murdering the fat frog to the back of his mind - at least for the time being that is to say!

"You will follow my flight to the edge of the great swamps to the north and from there you will be taken by the marsh frogs who will lead you across the stinking Waga." The crow referred to the marsh frogs in such a way that Lebish felt distinctly apprehensive about the prospect of meeting these creatures. "I will meet you again on the other side in the community of Tamsid whereupon you will then be taken to our master."

Notwithstanding the fact that he was in a rather unfortunate predicament, Lebish nevertheless began to feel a little more secure. His own life had been spared whilst those of his companions had been so violently taken. Now he was going to be escorted (albeit by some rather unsavoury characters) to be introduced to a king of a Far North community. Being somewhat overcome by what he viewed as his own self-importance caused Lebish to swagger and become overfamiliar towards the crow.

"Come on then, old Crow," motioned the newly confident Lebish. "Let's get going. Mustn't keep his eminence waiting or you'll be for it I'm sure." Lebish was gabbling on almost to the point of arrogance and quite forgetting the dire situation he was in. He even allowed himself to inject a deal of sarcasm into his voice, especially when he spouted the words "his eminence".

The angry crow instantly and very painfully jabbed the chubby frog in the chest with his beak, the force of which sent Lebish rolling across the ground.

"Consider yourself lucky that the decision on your ultimate fate has been suspended for the moment. However if you dare to repeat that sort of disrespect and insolence towards Emled then you can expect your head to become quickly detached from you shoulders. Just make sure you remember that it is only because you have some information which our king requires that has kept you alive so far. If wished by our master you will meet the same fate as that bunch over there." With that the crow gestured with its beak to where Lebish's fellow frogs lay decimated and sprawled upon the ground.

The crow then advanced towards the prostrate Lebish in what the frog considered to be a most threatening manner and said, "Now get up off your fat hindlimbs, you good for nothing lump of frog spawn, and make sure that you carefully follow the line I take. I hate to think what might happen if you get lost all alone in this frogforsaken place."

Lebish wasn't too keen on that thought either, so, uncertain as to whether or not he was about to get another prod from his aggressor, he warily hauled himself up and wobbled as fast as he could after the already airborne crow.

*

As Lebish hurried along he could feel his chest pounding as a result of the crow's painful strike. He had of course immediately obeyed the crow's order for him to follow on, but inwardly he vowed vengeance on his assailant.

How Lebish now regretted neglecting his body for so long. As he chased after the crow, keeping one eye on his escort and the other on the many obstacles on the ground, he found himself fast becoming out of breath. He wanted to call out for the crow to slow down but he didn't have sufficient energy to shout loud enough to attract the bird's attention. He certainly dared not stop because he greatly feared what might become of him if he was lost in these strange lands.

With regard to Lebish's physical condition he hadn't just let the importance of being such a senior frog go to his head. Unfortunately his elevated status had also had a very significant effect upon his tummy. From being a reasonably fit and active frog in his youth, Lebish had since then steadily grown into an extremely unfit and fat creature whose insatiable appetite for the most succulent of grasshoppers was plain for all to see as it had caused him to develop a very large and very round belly.

As a consequence of this rich indulgence it was now a totally exhausted frog, feeling very sorry for himself, that huffed and puffed his way across muddy streams; over the debris of fallen trees; and through great piles of soggy leaves and bracken in his quest to keep up with the crow.

Travelling all the while ever further northwards he noticed that the air was gradually turning cooler. The atmosphere was also quite oddly becoming much thicker and a rather unpleasant smell had filled his nostrils.

The poor fat frog once again contemplated his lack of fitness and promised himself a regime of regular exercise and a healthy diet if ever he was able to return to his nice comfortable home in Seaxe. If his life was to be spared he determined that in future he would be generous and share his great stocks of food with his fellow brethren rather than greedily keeping them all for his personal consumption. He would certainly never again think of using his supplies to endear himself to others in order to obtain rather dubious 'favours'. Yes, he decided, if he was given the chance to return home he would become a reformed character!

Well, I think we might all be getting to know enough about Lebish to make the fair assumption that the good intentions he harboured at this moment of great discomfort were really of very fragile substance. Although he may have meant what he was thinking right then it was only a hollow promise that was made in the hope that it would help to preserve his own well-being. In fact if his life was to be spared and he was able to return home to Seaxe then he would be more likely to make up for lost time, owing to his temporary absence in these bleak and desolate lands, by raiding his well-stocked larder and gorging himself to the point of bursting on the most juicy grasshoppers he could lay his forelimbs upon. There was, therefore, very little likelihood of his giving any thought to being generous or charitable once he had returned home to his stores of delicacies.

Lebish suddenly came to a halt. The overgrown area he had been travelling through had thinned out quite significantly over the last hundred or so hops and now what lay in front of him was a vast stretch of the most foul smelling swampland he had ever had the misfortune to cast his eyes upon. He could see no vegetation save for a few rotting ferns and the occasional withered trunk of a long dead tree. The crow which he had been following descended towards him and carefully landed on a firm piece of ground alongside the totally exhausted Lebish.

"This is as far as you go with me for the moment," leered the crow. "We are due to meet the marsh frogs here and it is they who will guide you across the swamps of Waga. You'll see me again when you get to the other side from where I will take you to your engagement with Emled." The crow allowed a wry smile to develop around the corners of his beak as he added, "Enjoy the marsh frogs – they will make excellent company for a slimy specimen such as you!"

Lebish knew that he was in no position to do anything but accept all that the crow had to say. However, the bird's mocking of him had heightened his secret vow of vengeance and of repaying him in full for the very undignified manner by which he had been treated. He therefore used this opportunity to find out a little more about his aggressor.

"Thank you, Crow, for being so kind and for guiding me so expertly across your beautiful countryside. But look, if we are to be such regular travelling companions, I cannot carry on addressing you as 'crow'. It does sound so unfriendly. Pray tell me what is your name?"

The crow cocked his head on one side. For some reason, and just for an instant, he thought he felt a chill run up and down his spine.

"It's really of no interest to a creep like you," retorted the crow as he again poked Lebish in the chest and exactly on the same spot as before. "But, if you really want to know, it's Gawk." He then thought for a moment before adding. "Although for your cheek you can call mc sir from now on."

On that note the coal-black crow flew up into the air to rejoin his compatriots. Lebish watched the madcap flock of birds as they whirled about cawing excitedly and making a great deal of commotion. They enjoyed nothing better than causing murder and mayhem to other creatures and particularly to those who were weaker than themselves. By their reckoning, today had been a very good day, and, to celebrate the fact, they continued to noisily and roughly congratulate each other on their slaughtering of the frogs from Seaxe until Gawk eventually decided to regroup his villainous band and fly off high into the sky, heading in the direction of the Far North.

"Gawk...! Gawk...!" Lebish hissed the crow's name through tightly clenched jaws. "You'll get what's coming to you... you see if you don't!"

*

Lebish sat perfectly still for a while. He was now feeling rather sore and very lonely. Added to that he was also extremely scared of whatever fate lay before him. The rancid smell of rotting vegetation and stagnant water filled his head and made it hard for him to think clearly.

"So this must be Waga," he muttered to himself. He had of course heard terrible tales of this frogforsaken land and had hoped he would never have to set hindleg or forelimb in such a place. "What a frogawful blot on the landscape this is for sure. Can there be any living creature who could possibly wish to live in a stench like this?"

"So our beautiful swamp doesn't meet with your approval?"

These words were spat out in a harsh whisper from just behind Lebish. In fact they were almost poured straight into his ears, so close was the owner of the voice. Lebish was so surprised by this unexpected intrusion into his solace that he very nearly jumped out of his skin. In his fright he spun around and then leapt backwards falling onto his hindquarters in the process as he literally came nose to nose with what he immediately considered to be an over-sized brown frog.

As Lebish sat upon the ground and gathered himself together he saw that the frog who had made him jump was actually accompanied by several other frogs of similar size and appearance. These latter frogs stood in a casual manner some way behind their spokesfrog. Lebish assumed that this group must be the marsh frogs that Gawk said would be accompanying him across Waga; at least he hoped they were for they all looked extraordinarily fierce and threatening. Although poor Lebish would not have chosen such creatures as friends he decided at that moment that he would rather have these ugly brutes as guides than be a victim of some violent attack by them.

The leader of the gang then spoke again. "Lost your tongue, little fat one?"

"N... n... no! Only you did rather m... m... make me jump," spluttered Lebish. "Have you been sent to escort me across your swamp... I ... I .... mean Waga?" he asked in his most polite voice. "I am of course quite mistaken about the environment in which I now find myself. It is clearly a most beautiful place, with, if I am not mistaken, the charming smell of autumn leaves permeating the air."

The leader of the marsh frogs advanced aggressively towards Lebish. "You are every bit the creep that Gawk said you were," he growled as he pressed his nose hard against the nose of Lebish, causing the tubby Seaxe senior to become dizzy under the influence of the smelly creature. "The swamps of Waga are barren and desolate; they are foul and they stink; they are also full of dangerous bogs into which fat frogs like you will disappear if you are left to your own devices."

As well as squashing Lebish's nose the intimidating marsh frog also prodded him harder and harder as he emphasised each word he uttered. This was becoming much to much for Lebish and he really did consider that he had suffered quite enough painful prods on that day alone to last him a lifetime. He thought, however, that right at this juncture it was probably best not to object too strongly. Instead he clutched his chest and let his much larger foe know that he was now in fact in quite a deal of pain. Not only that but he also wished to respectfully advise his escort that he had received similar treatment from Gawk only a little while earlier.

Unfortunately the gentle pleading by Lebish was to no avail whatsoever. If anything it actually had the effect of irritating the marsh frog which made the latter even more spiteful than before. The marsh frog looked disdainfully at Lebish and snarled...

"And as for 'escorting' you across Waga is concerned, don't think for an instant that you are in for any special treatment," continued the marsh frog leader. "You will be more pushed and poked across than 'escorted' as you so naively call it. Why you have even been spared is a mystery to me. However, that's for Emled to know and not for me to reason why."

Lebish thought about explaining to the marsh frog that it was probably due to the fact that he was such an important frog of very high standing within his own community that had encouraged the king of Tamsid to order his safe passage and seek an audience with him. However, he thought better of it as he desperately didn't want to upset this fearsome frog any more than he had seemingly done already.

"Do you have a name, sir?" enquired Lebish of the marsh frog. "Just so that I may at least know to whom I owe such a debt of gratitude for seeing me safely to the other side of Waga. As it is you and your fine colleagues who will be accompanying me I do hope that we can be friendly towards each other."

Lebish's patronising tone was lost upon the marsh frog as the latter's skills were more of the 'brawny' type rather than those that involved using a bit of brainpower. Quite oblivious therefore to

Lebish's impudent attitude, the hard-headed marsh frog decided to do a little boasting about his own position in the community of Tamsid, and, puffing out his chest, he said, "My name is Kaara. I am Emled's warrior lord and leader of the great army of the Far North marsh frogs. We are the strongest and fiercest frog fighters that you will find and woe betide any frog who thinks it can rise up and beat us."

Lebish assured Kaara that he didn't doubt the marsh frog's capabilities in that respect for a moment. He also apologised for never having actually heard of the community of Tamsid, but explained that this was probably due to the fact that his own community were far too backward in coming forward when it came to getting out and about and meeting their neighbours. Why, he himself had quite shamefully never even been allowed to travel this distance north before.

Kaara momentarily eyed Lebish a little suspiciously and then quickly turned around and rejoined his gang to discuss the arrangements they should make in order to convey their chubby charge to Tamsid.

Whilst this was going on Lebish rued his predicament. How he wished he had never been sent to this place. Wasn't it he who had personally advised the Anurian Council, and both Moha and Mars, that it was a big mistake to entertain this quite absurd mission. Unfortunately, and despite his good advice, it was now he personally who was bearing the full brunt of their ridiculous decision to spread information in this way. He would certainly be giving the powers that be in Seaxe a sizeable piece of his mind when he returned home. That is if he ever did return home!

Although feeling wretched, and full of anger and hate, Lebish was nevertheless managing to present a humble face on which he hoped Kaara and his gang of thugs would take pity. Inwardly his vengeance was ever mounting and his black list had now grown to three. Top of this list, of course, was the spiteful crow, Gawk; but he was now closely followed by Kaara. Third in line for the Lebish treatment, however, was Mars, and for him Lebish was planning something particularly nasty. And why not, pondered the fat senior? After all it really was all Mars' fault that he should now find himself in this disastrous situation. If only Mars had minded his own business and hadn't interfered in an area of responsibility that was of no direct concern to him then none of this would have happened. But no, Mars had to get involved and put forward the suggestion of sending newscarriers to all points south, east, west and, most unfortunately, to the Near North. But for Mars' intrusion, instead of all this pain and suffering, he would have been in the comfort of his own home tucking into his favourite meal of tasty grasshoppers. Yes, he thought, Mars will have to experience something far worse in return for meddling in his area of responsibility. In fact, come to think of it, he wasn't too sure whether he hated Gawk and Kaara to a greater or lesser degree than he did Mars.

"Now, you slimy good for nothing, keep your mouth shut and come along with us!" ordered Kaara. "Not a word out of you or you will find yourself sunk without a trace in a suitably smelly pit!"

With that the marsh frog leader hopped quickly into the swamps of Waga moving swiftly and deftly between its bubbling and steaming black pools. Kaara relentlessly forged a route over the treacherous landscape, only stopping every so often to check for signs of any possible danger from potential enemies. Not that Kaara had much to fear, however, as being part of the Emled empire acted as sufficient protection in the Far North. There were very few creatures who were either brave enough, or some may say, foolhardy enough, to attack members of his alliance and thus risk incurring the wrath of the evil toad.

To avoid being left behind, Lebish had to summon up stamina that he never knew he possessed. Additionally, and in order to help him keep within a reasonable distance of Kaara, Lebish had two large marsh frogs, one on each side, who were roughly bundling him along and who cuffed him whenever he showed even the merest hint of flagging. A third frog brought up the rear and this frog pushed and prodded Lebish continually, even when he gave no indication of slowing up.

This really was quite the most dreadful predicament in which Lebish had ever found himself and he vowed once again that certain frogs, and a particular crow, would pay dearly for this outrage.

Chapter Eight

Contenders To Be King

Back in Seaxe the local frogs were getting excited. Although it had taken a while for them to get over the shock and disappointment of Moha tendering his resignation, the community nevertheless accepted that a successor now had to be found. Many of his friends, and everyone in Seaxe (with the possible exception of several of the infamous 'six' seniors of course) considered themselves to be good friends of Moha, had asked him to carry on as their king. They assured their kindly old leader that he really was irreplaceable and that he still had many winters left before him in his high office.

Moha's mind was firmly made up however and now that he had made an announcement of such importance he was determined to carry it through. He had, after all, spent many long hours and nights weighing up the pros and cons of his decision. At the end of his contemplation he felt, on balance, that it really was the right time for him to stand down. He considered it wise that he should make way for a younger frog who would hopefully be both ambitious and full of good plans for the continued well-being of the Seaxe community.

A great deal of responsibility, therefore, now rested in the forelimbs of the Anurian Council, for it was they who would be called upon to undertake and organise the selection of suitable candidates out of whom their new king would be chosen. Without any shadow of doubt this was their single most important task. However, although this august body of frogs should have been capable of performing such a duty (after all the council of the time had of course been successful in their selection of Moha), the old king still strangely continued to feel concerned about the future. The chill wind from the north that had troubled the giant bullfrog over recent months now did so more regularly and it greatly frustrated him that still he could not understand the reason for his anxiety.

There was, therefore, a rising tide of emotion in Seaxe on which rode mixed feelings of excitement and sadness as well as waves of speculation and anticipation. What was the future going to bring and just who would be appointed king – the new king of Seaxe?

*

Once the news of Moha's resignation began to be spread far and wide the Anurian Council started to receive a number of registrations of interest from ambitious young frogs who wished to be considered for the role of king. There was Cabal, from the community of Solk; and Tanal, from the community of Nolk. These two fine frogs were in fact twins and had both risen through parallel careers to be the respective kings of their neighbouring eastern communities. From the west there came a serious application from a frog king named Denray who lived in Cowall; and from the community from which Moha hailed, namely Somset, a promising frog king called Truda had expressed his wish to be considered.

The southern region had produced a particularly strong candidate from the community of Surey who went by the name of Fara. This exceptionally gifted young frog had only been the king of his own frogs for some two winters but already he was showing the sort of promise that would enable him to very soon be able to take over the helm at a far larger community.

It should be explained at this point why it is that frogs who are already kings in their own lands should be applying to be the king of Seaxe. The answer is really quite simple and is due to the fact that Seaxe is what most everyday frogs would call a desirable place in which to live, and what other frog kings would describe as a prestige community to rule. In the lands that are known to the frogs in our story, which stretch as far to the east, west, south and near north as their imaginations will allow, the community of Seaxe is widely regarded as the largest and most important. It is therefore the community to which only the most genuinely gifted and talented frogs will legitimately be expected to apply when the prized position of its king becomes vacant.

It is not surprising, therefore, that each of the aforementioned candidates, namely, Cabal, Tanal, Denray, Truda and Fara, were all kings in their own communities. They were also very well thought of and highly regarded frog kings of which great things were expected. The fact that frog kings of such stature had demonstrated a wish to become the next king of Seaxe certainly recognised the high esteem in which this kingship was held.

So far there had been no interest shown from any of the Near North communities although, to be fair, it was still early days. Nothing of course had been heard from the Far North, and nothing was expected. What lay beyond Waga was considered by those to the south of it to be best left laying beyond the treacherous swamps and slimy bogs.

Even though no information had so far arrived from the Near North it was still expected that a suitable candidate would be forthcoming. Although the Near North frogs were not renowned for their charm or wit, and very often appeared dour, humourless and rather too serious in the way they viewed life, they did have some qualities that were widely respected by other frog communities. The Near North frogs were fairly regarded as being tough, gritty and determined. In addition it was always said, as a compliment, that when it came to an argument no frog was considered to be more stubborn than a Near North frog.

There was in fact a very fine prospect for the Seaxe kingship from this region who went by the name of Keba. This strong and resolute young frog had shown exceptional leadership qualities in his home community of Cabidge since being appointed as their king some five winters ago. He consequently, therefore, also had a good deal of practical experience to go with his other widely acknowledged talents.

Keba had, not surprisingly, been very interested in the possibility of leading the frogs of Seaxe, and, as soon as he heard that Moha was standing down, he had set forth with a team of close associates to journey south to signal his intention to apply to be king. What Keba had not reckoned on, however, was that from amongst his own personal assistants there was a traitor, who from time to time relayed information about events in Cabidge to his real friends on the other side of the swamplands of Waga.

This deceitful frog's name was Sliva, and, although similar in colouring to his colleagues in Cabidge, he was significantly larger in size and noticeably more strongly built. He was in fact a marsh frog and he had been sent many full moons ago to infiltrate the community of Cabidge and send back useful facts to Tamsid for Emled's personal attention.

News that Keba and his party were to be journeying south was accordingly transferred at the dead of night to Emled via crow and marsh frog. Although the wicked toad could do little about potential candidates from the east, west and south, due to their considerable distance from Tamsid, he certainly could do something about a far too useful rival from just over the other side of Waga.

And so it was, not long after the unfortunate Keba had set out for Seaxe, in fact he and his companions had travelled no great distance at all, that he found himself confronted by a very ugly bunch of quite the largest and meanest marsh frogs he had ever had the misfortune to set his eyes upon. Had Keba taken more notice of the single black crow, Gawk of course, who had been circling around high above them all that morning from the moment they had left the boundary of Cabidge, then possibly his suspicions may have been aroused and he and his colleagues might have avoided the ambush. However, their thoughts had been so firmly focused on the reason for their journey that they had understandably paid insufficient attention that day to their personal safety.

Gawk's job had been to track the Cabidge party. From his aerial vantage point he was to act as a guide for Kaara and his gang of mercenaries who were following out of sight some way behind. As soon as Gawk was sure that he had identified a suitable spot for an attack he was to signal as much to Kaara, who would then mount his onslaught on the luckless Keba.

As was quite typical of the way in which Gawk and Kaara operated when it came to perpetrating evil acts, this ambush was well set and quickly executed. Keba and his friends had no chance against such powerful and merciless opposition. The Cabidge frogs were entirely slaughtered by their aggressors and no sight nor sound nor reason for their disappearance was ever given.

The community of Seaxe had no idea that Keba was coming of course, so for them they had no need to show any concern for his not showing up. As for the frogs of Cabidge they deeply mourned the loss of their good king and his party and they grieved for many days and nights. However, they could do no more than assume that the party had been taken by a more regular foe as so often happens to frogs when travelling abroad. They certainly wouldn't have considered the possibility of the fate that had actually befallen Keba and company as, in quite the same way as the frogs of Seaxe, they had grown used to a peaceful and harmonious existence. There was certainly no need for warrior frogs in Cabidge nor were any of their community suitably equipped for fighting or fending off enemy frogs. As far as they were concerned they did not need to have any of the latter attributes as such aggressive and warlike attitudes and actions had long since been banished (at least from the south of Waga that is) by the spreading of the good work and teaching of Moha.

The like of the marsh frogs from Tamsid, and the savagery that so distinguished them from all other frogs, was quite alien to the more peaceful and friendly frogs of the Near North and those to all points east, west and south.

*

Meanwhile, in the community of Seaxe, a most unusual situation had occurred. In fact it was something that had never happened in its entire history. There had, quite astonishingly, been several firm applications from local frogs who wished to be considered for the position of king of Seaxe. That such a thing might have arisen had of course not even remotely been contemplated. The reason why, as you will of course know, is that by long-standing tradition the new king can only be selected from frogs who come from outside the Seaxe community. However, and not notwithstanding tradition, three such applications had been received by the Anurian Council.

The first of the local applications had come from Lebish. The second to arrive was from Brylil. The third from Geelan.

Lebish's application had of course been made just prior to his leaving for the Near North. In his own little world, where he had so greatly inflated his self importance, Lebish had no doubts about his justification for applying for this most senior position. After all he was, by his own estimation, a far more educated and able frog than any of his senior colleagues. He would most certainly include Mars in the latter category and Moha too for that matter.

Lebish also gave very little credence to tradition and particularly when it was likely to work against him. He therefore fully expected to be the first frog from within Seaxe to have bestowed upon him the community's greatest honour – that of becoming its king.

Whereas Lebish had convinced himself of his own ability to break the mould of tradition, Brylil's and Geelan's reasons for applying were quite different. Brylil was, as has been said before, a kind and caring frog. He was also, however, quite the wrong material to be king. He knew this of course but wondered privately that if the Anurian Council did break with tradition, and if he was appointed king, then he would always have Mars to help and support him on the difficult issues; and surely old Moha would not be too far away if things got really tough.

It could be said, therefore, that Brylil was rather chancing his forelimb, but, by his own reckoning, the worst that could possibly happen is that his application would be turned down. At least he felt comfortable in the knowledge that he would have tried and done his best. He was also confident that he would probably be better thought of by the community for having the courage and belief in his own ability to give it a go and for taking such a bold stance.

Geelan, on the other hand, had no really clear or genuine reason to be applying. Indeed he had made his application entirely on the spur of the moment and it had happened immediately he heard that Brylil was putting his own name forward. In fact as soon as the news of Brylil's application reached Geelan he quite lost all his senses. He dashed too and fro squeaking loudly and quite uncontrollably. His main concern was not his suitability for the job, it was more that he felt he might be missing out on something if one of his colleagues applied and he didn't. If they were going to put in for the kingship then why shouldn't he?

What the poor, misguided Geelan did not appreciate was that his application caused great mirth and laughter in the community. There was not another creature in the whole of Seaxe who would have given him a frog-spawn's chance amongst a hundred hungry ducks of ever being appointed their king. As a consequence of his rashness and rank stupidity he was for evermore regarded as being a clown who had no real understanding of his position. Without doubt he was already by far the weakest of the other seniors in every way. Unfortunately for Geelan he now gained the unwanted, but richly deserved, additional label of community jester and he was never again taken seriously by his fellow frogs.

*

The final day for applications from would-be successors to Moha had arrived. It had been agreed that on this day the Anurian Council would meet to discuss those individuals who wished to be considered for the kingship. It had also been agreed, that as the sun set and slipped beyond the western horizon, only those names that had actually been put forward by this time would be allowed as valid contenders.

The council sat in silence as they watched the sun begin its nightly descent. On the agenda for discussion were the names of eight frogs; five of whom came from other communities and three from Seaxe. The five outsiders were Cabal, Tanal, Denray, Truda, and Fara. The three locals were, as you know, Lebish, Brylil and Geelan.

The day had been bright and crisp, and so it was into a clear night sky that the assembled council gazed. As they watched the tip of the gloriously rich, red, autumn sun slowly disappearing, a strong, cold wind suddenly blew from out of the north. As it did so, low storm clouds began racing across the sky, and, lost in the darkness of their background, a great number of coal black crows glided silently towards Seaxe, their feathers ruffled by the brisk wind. Tightly grasped in the claws of the leading crow, and quite unseen from the ground, was a large villainous marsh frog whose mission was to deliver a very important message to the Seaxe Council.

The frog in question was Kaara and his guardian crow was none other than the unsavoury Gawk. Kaara hated being transported in this way and not just because he felt totally uncomfortable about not having his feet firmly on the ground or preferably swimming up and down in cool clear water. His main fear was that he had absolutely no faith in his carrier, for no frog in the Far North knew better than he of the cunning and wicked ways of the crows, and of Gawk in particular. He was well aware that he could just as well be dropped to his certain death as delivered safely back home. The only thing, however, of which he could be sure was that he would definitely arrive in one piece at his destination in order to convey his important news, as the message he was bringing actually came from Emled. It must be said that the black crows of Tamsid were every bit as fearful of the wicked toad as were the marsh frogs, and Gawk knew that a horrible fate would be his for certain if he did not at least ensure Kaara's safe arrival in Seaxe.

So, as the wind suddenly howled and the night sky was instantly blackened by the angry clouds which brought darkness prematurely to the community of Seaxe, the frogs of the Anurian Council huddled more closely together in preparation for the important task of considering who was to be their next king.

Just then, and from quite where no member of the council could ever explain, a large frog suddenly appeared in their midst. Kaara had of course been rudely deposited by his chaperone, and from rather too high for his liking, right into the middle of the gathering of Seaxe councillors. When Kaara's entrance had been mentioned after the meeting had finished those present said they just assumed that so large a frog had hopped into their meeting when none of them had been looking, such had been their level of concentration on the matter in hand.

Following his rather bumpy entrance, Kaara rapidly pulled himself together trying hard to ignore the pain he felt in his hindlimbs which had been caused by his heavy landing. He looked around at the sea of faces as all the eyes of the councillors were upon him. Not wasting any time at all in which he might be asked difficult questions, like "Who arc you?" or "Whcrc did you spring from?" Kaara decided to quickly announce his message.

"I bring news that Emled, great king of the Tamsid frogs, humbly seeks your approval to be considered for the position of king of Seaxe, being as it is the most prestigious of all kingships."

The members of the council, having already been startled at Kaara's sudden appearance, now looked around uncomfortably at each other. In the increasing gloom they now found themselves unexpectedly confronted by a rather too large and dully coloured frog, the like of which they had never seen before. If they found his sudden arrival threatening then they were equally intimidated by his gruff manner. They were also mystified as to why they had not heard of Tamsid, and, if they hadn't heard of this community, or their king for that matter, then how had he heard of them?

The Anurian Council was of course made up of equals, but it was acknowledged that whenever they required a spokesfrog or representative then it was the eldest frog who would perform such a role. Accordingly, as befits the time-honoured ways of the council, an old frog by the name of Jopik shuffled forward to address Kaara.

"Pray tell us more about this frog king of yours. I'm sure that I am right when I say that neither he, nor in fact your community, are known to any of us here?"

Kaara noticed that many heads were nodding at Jopik's words and he realised that this anonymity gave him an excellent opportunity to present Emled in the best possible light. He was quite certain that if he made a good job of praising Emled, and this resulted in the evil toad being appointed king of these undersized and weak-limbed frogs (Kaara's description), then there was every likelihood that he himself would be most handsomely rewarded by Emled with gifts of even more food and servants both for him and his family.

Kaara was also well aware that Gawk had silently perched himself on the lower branches of a nearby tree and he was therefore able to hear all that was being spoken. A word or comment uttered out of place at this stage would for sure be reported back to Emled, the consequences of which sent a tremulous shudder through the marsh frog's body.

"Why, I am very surprised that you have not heard of our leader!" piped Kaara. "After all he is indeed a most wonderful frog king." Kaara studied the faces of the councillors for a short while and he could see that he held their interest. They looked as if they were keen to hear some more from him so he thought he should oblige and not disappoint his audience.

"Emled has great strength, both of character and body, and he is charming in every way. He is quite the most handsome frog you will ever meet and his eloquence is a joy to hear. Our loving king devotes almost all of his time to caring for the well-being of our community and in turn his frogs give him their respect and loyalty. He is kind and considerate and..." Kaara went on for many long minutes spewing out as many phrases that he could think of which helped portray Emled in a quite dazzling light.

Whilst Kaara was warming to his task, Gawk looked on from his vantage point in the trees feeling more and more sick at what he was hearing. Even though he knew that the marsh frog was only repeating what Emled had ordered him to say, he couldn't help feeling a considerable amount of disgust towards his Tamsid colleague. Gawk also understood of course, that he was just as much trapped as was

Kaara by the power and evil influence of the wicked toad. He had, therefore, long accepted the fact that he, like the rest of the creatures in Tamsid, was ensnared for the rest of his life whilst Emled remained their king.

Whilst the words that were gushing out of Kaara made Gawk's beak curl, for he knew that Emled was cruel and callous in every way known to a frog, the crow leader was hopeful that if the toad was to be offered the kingship of Seaxe then this would result in him leaving Tamsid, possibly forever. Gawk certainly never underestimated Emled's ability to get whatever it was that he wanted and so the optimism with which he viewed the toad's chances of success in his application gave him some hope for his own future comfort and safety.

"...and finally, although I could go on at length," continued Kaara, "our king is a great friend of all the Tamsid frogs. He is, without any shadow of a doubt, a magnificent king in every way." Kaara then sucked in a huge lungful of air and puffed up his chest as he sat back contentedly on his haunches awaiting the reaction of the intrigued councillors. He felt more than a little satisfied with the way he had delivered his speech, and, as he surveyed his audience, he sensed some excitement and eager anticipation on their part at the thought of such a worthy candidate being interested in leading their community.

There certainly was a good deal of emotion in the minds and bodies of the council members that ranged from curiosity to being totally overwhelmed at the prospect of meeting such a fine candidate. Could all that they had just heard from this admittedly dubious looking frog be true? Why, not even Moha in his prime could better a frog with such fantastic credentials. Never in all their years on the council had they heard one frog speak of another in such glowing terms. It was a reference indeed to rival all references.

"You speak astonishingly well of your king," said Jopik. "There must be some reason why we have not heard of his great deeds before. Maybe it is because your community is so far away from here? Pray tell us from whence you have travelled?"

Kaara felt he had no reason to hide the fact that his community lay far to the north of Seaxe. He therefore said that his fine community of Tamsid could be found nicely situated beyond the swamplands of Waga in the Far North.

On hearing this news there was a concerted gasp from the council. Kaara was stunned, as what seemed to be going so well all of a sudden appeared to have gone horribly wrong. He knew it was linked to something he had just said, but then again all he had really referred to was where he and Emled lived. What could possibly be so bad about the Far North for it to have elicited such a dramatic response?

"Y.. y... you s... s... say you are from the F.. Far N... North?" stammered Jopik.

"Well yes!" replied Kaara. "But you all look as if I may be carrying some sort of plague. What can I have said that causes you so much distress?"

Kaara looked about him and saw what he would later describe to Emled as a "squirming bunch of tadpole-sized frogs". How he detested the sight of the Seaxe councillors shifting about nervously and looking at each other with fear in their eyes. Given half a chance, he told Emled, he would lick this pathetic lot into some sort of shape – and have great fun in so doing.

"Our knowledge of the desolate lands of Waga and what lies beyond is extremely limited." Jopik had steadied himself and had recovered sufficiently to respond to Kaara's question. "What little we do know, however, is enough to warn us that it is unsafe for frogs such as ourselves to venture further north than the area we know as the Near North. For us, therefore, the furthest north we would dare to roam is to the Near North boundary of Waga, and only then if it was absolutely necessary."

Kaara realised that he had to act quickly in order to restore the good position he felt he had earlier established in respect of Emled's standing in the councillor's eyes. Up in the tree Gawk looked down on the proceedings with a renewed interest. He was enjoying watching Kaara have a difficult time, and he allowed himself some sinister thoughts of what punishment Emled might have in store for his unscrupulous marsh frog colleague on their return to Tamsid if this mission resulted in failure.

"Why, you have nothing to fear from Waga," began Kaara. "Nor have you any need for undue concern as regards what lies on the other side to the Far North..."

Kaara decided that the best policy was to promote the Far North as much as he could without giving those assembled in front of him any cause to be suspicious by his going over the top. So he went on to inform the increasingly attentive and absorbed councillors that Tamsid was clearly mistakenly viewed by the good frogs of Seaxe. It was, he assured them, a most wonderful place where lily pads grew in abundance and where the grasshoppers were more succulent than could be imagined.

"In fact..." continued Kaara, "...you may find this a little hard to believe, but the sun always seems to shine in the Far North. As for the rivers, well, they flow so gently and are full of the most refreshingly clear cool water. Our frogs, as you would expect, flourish in these excellent conditions; and our numbers continue to multiply in a land where we have very few enemies."

Kaara could sense that he was gradually winning back his audience's enthusiasm, so he added, very pointedly and with sufficient emphasis to impress the council, "And all of this is of course attributable to our masterful leader – Emled the Great Provider."

"We have heard that terrifying storms roar continually throughout the Far North and that nothing but the hardiest of plant life is able to survive," said Jopik. "How is it that a community of frogs can live and breed in such a place?"

Kaara was not about to reveal how Emled's frogs obtained their supplies of food, nor was he going to let it be known what it was the marsh frogs most enjoyed doing during their leisure time. Suffice to say, you the reader will have a very good idea about both these activities and will not be surprised to learn that the marsh frogs happily combine the two. In fact the favourite pursuit of Kaara and his mercenary colleagues, under the direction of Emled of course, is to cross Waga and carry out raids in the Near North on unsuspecting frog communities and other vulnerable creatures. The marsh frogs then plunder the devastated community's stocks and stores before returning home to their own grim environment. In this way Emled is able to keep under control his murderous frogs' insatiable lust for both satisfying their bellies and spilling the blood of their innocent victims.

"Well actually I expect that what you know about the Far North is probably how it was immediately after the Great Storms of many seasons ago," said Kaara. "It is true that during that terrible time the whole of the region to the north of Waga was razed to the ground. When the storm eventually stopped there was hardly a tree, bush or blade of grass that had not been uprooted, wrecked or damaged in some way." The marsh frog paused for a moment or two to allow the images he had described to develop in the minds of the Seaxe councillors. He then continued before he could be interrupted. "But now of course the whole community has been rebuilt and revitalised under the strong and determined leadership of our wonderful King Emled. It is now a quite beautiful and happy place in which to live."

All that Kaara had said was a tissue of lies of course, but, in their understandable ignorance, the frog councillors were keen to hear good things about a place that they had long feared. In fact, and it must unfortunately be said, they were suitably impressed by what they had heard about Emled, Tamsid and the Far North, and they were now keen to end their conversation with their surprise visitor on a particularly high note.

"Thank you for bringing to us your news," said Jopik. "Please thank your king for the interest he has shown in our community and assure him that he will be given every consideration along with several other contenders who wish to be the next king of Seaxe."

*

Strangely, although not a great deal of notice was taken by the councillors at that precise moment, almost immediately Kaara left the meeting so the storm clouds lifted and the stiff wind dropped considerably. The sky in fact became much brighter, reflecting as it did the hidden sun's rays, and the end of the day turned into a fine and mellow late autumnal evening. The warm shades of pink, orange and grey in the distant western sky were ideally complemented by the gently whispering breeze that faintly stirred the leaves on the trees. Such a beautiful evening gave no warning of the dark days that lay ahead for the community of Seaxe.

*

The Anurian Council had business to do and they prepared themselves for a long night of discussion in which they would explore in depth the potential of each of the candidates. It must be said, however, although I am sure you will find this rather disturbing, knowing what you already do about Emled, that the council were in a somewhat buoyant mood having just heard from Kaara an account of a frog who they considered could surely on this description match the greatness of Moha.

As a decision making group they knew they had much to live up to for members of the earlier council, which had appointed Moha, had become celebrated frogs and regarded as being most able and wise members of the community for the foresight they had shown. They too wanted such acknowledgement and, from what they had just heard, they had now been presented with an opportunity to make a similarly brilliant appointment. For was it not true that in addition to the many wonderful qualities that Emled appeared to share with Moha it seemed that this place called Tamsid could, as a direct consequence of the actions of their king, boast enormous lily pads and far more succulent grasshoppers than could be found in Seaxe?

The talking continued far into the night and each of the frogs from outside of the community was examined in detail. The three contenders from within, namely, Lebish, Brylil and Geelan, were discarded at the start of the proceedings as no-hopers. Some sympathetic sounds were made in respect of Brylil and several of the members politely suggested that he may one day make it as a king in a very small and not too testing a community. However, and certainly for the moment, they felt he was really only a light-weight and that he really did need to acquire a great deal more experience before he could expect to progress to higher office. As for Lebish and Geelan, a number of the councillors said they felt quite insulted that either should have the nerve to apply and they wondered if sanctions should be taken against them to make an example of their outrageous and totally unacceptable behaviour.

After a considerable debate upon the subject, during which a great deal of heated discussion took place, the council finally decided that they would politely advise the three insiders that they had been unsuccessful and that on any similar occasions that may arise in the future they would expect Seaxe frogs to respectfully observe tradition.

The council, however, were impressed by what they had heard about each of the other frogs who had applied from outside of Seaxe. After lengthy analysis they eventually agreed that they would ask three of these distinguished frog kings to attend a special council meeting at which the contenders would be critically interviewed and asked many very searching questions.

The first of the three frogs to be selected was Truda. There was a good deal of interest in relation to this candidate, not least of which was due to the fact that he heralded from Moha's home community of Somset. The council felt that if this young frog had acquired the sort of qualities that Moha possessed then he would indeed have the potential to be a very fine leader.

The second frog to be selected was Fara. This frog, when the council compared the personal references they had received from each of the candidates' home councils (excluding Emled's of course which had quite literally been dropped in by Kaara), actually stood out from the rest. He appeared to be a very bright and rising star who had a great future as the king of a prestige community.

The third frog to be chosen for the special meeting – and you may need to steady yourself for this news by taking a very deep breath – was none other than Emled, king of Tamsid in the Far North.

That the council had found it within themselves to call Emled for an interview was something that for many years later would cause one frog to say to another "What ever possessed our wise and learned councillors to choose such a frog?" However, there it was. The council had determined their shortlist and interviews were to be set up and candidates accordingly invited to attend.

It should be mentioned at this juncture that it wasn't all plain sailing during the shortlisting process and a number of the councillors extended the debate on whether or not to stay with the tradition of not appointing their new King from within. Whilst it was clear that all those at the meeting were of the opinion that neither Lebish, Brylil nor Geelan were suitable prospects, they did wonder whether it would be possible for either Chrich or Mars to replace Moha.

Having set aside the tradition factor to enable them to have a fair discussion, and the council liked to think of themselves as open-minded and not prejudiced in any way, they first of all agreed that Chrich was perhaps a little long in the hindlimb and some way past his best to be able to cope with such a substantial responsibility. With regard to Mars, however, there was a good deal of support and particularly so from one of the most well-respected of councillors, a female frog named Lilgree.

Lilgree was in fact a rarity in the Seaxe community in that she had actually broken through the barrier of tradition herself several winters ago. Up until then it had never been known for a female to be elected to the Anurian Council or for that matter be appointed to the level of senior frog. This tradition had been founded on the basis that to be a leader amongst frogs it was vital for such important creatures to be physically strong in addition to having all the other important qualities. The reason that strength was such an important factor was due to the fact that in the days before Moha there were a great many battles between frog communities as they fought to acquire larger and larger empires. With the coming of Moha, however, there came a more peaceful existence where the subject of community boundaries was discussed and agreed rather than obtained through brute force.

Lilgree had therefore emerged from out of the ranks of a great many highly competent females who were now legitimately challenging their male counterparts for the senior roles in the community's management hierarchy. In fact, and as a reflection of the high regard in which Lilgree was held by her fellow councillors, she was genuinely acknowledged as the second most senior member of this esteemed body and a worthy leading representative whenever Jopik was otherwise engaged.

In Lilgree's support of Mars she had put forward a very strong case saying that his youth, vitality and enthusiasm were considerable aspects in his favour. She had further pointed out that when such excellent attributes were added to the wisdom and learning that Mars had clearly received from Moha then this all contributed towards making Mars an exceedingly fine prospect indeed.

Although they could see that there were a number of benefits in appointing Mars, the older council members felt that they were not yet ready to go against tradition. In truth their main concern was that if they appointed Mars and something subsequently went wrong then they would always be remembered as the councillors who blatantly snubbed tradition and that they may dearly pay the price for taking such cavalier action. It was, therefore, primarily the risk of damaging their personal credibility that prevented them from asking Mars to be king.

The council were of course able to console themselves in the knowledge that they did in fact appear to have a very good selection of external candidates, so they were not actually restricted to looking inwardly into their own community for Moha's successor. They were thus satisfied that having given all the candidates and all the possible options a good airing, their selection of Truda, Fara and Emled as the final shortlist was the very best decision that they could make.

*

If only the Anurian Council had at that time found the courage within their hearts to set aside tradition and go along with the sentiments and wise advice of Lilgree, then what follows in this tale about the fate which subsequently befell the community of Seaxe may never have needed to be told.

Chapter Nine

Emled Hears the News

You may have been wondering what fate had befallen Lebish. You will no doubt recall that when we last heard of him he was being propelled across the smelly marshes and swamps of Waga by Kaara and his band of mercenaries. We can now see what occurred during the period between Lebish's uncomfortable journey and the moment that Kaara dropped in on the Anurian Council with his message from Emled.

*

When Lebish reached the other side of the swamp he immediately collapsed in a heap on the first piece of firm ground he had hopped on for what seemed like an age. The quick march over the cruel terrain of Waga had totally and utterly exhausted him and all his energy was spent. He really could go no further and, as he gulped down huge lungfuls of the chilly and pungent Far North air, his head became strangely dizzy and he passed out into unconsciousness.

Lebish was suddenly and very rudely awakened from the nightmare he was having. He had been dreaming that he was being chased by huge dark brown frogs through a land in which he could make no progress as his feet kept sinking in slimy, sticky mud the smell of which was making him heave. Even worse than this was the fact that he was continually being swooped upon by large black crows who kept battering him with their beaks at every opportunity.

As he gradually came round Lebish felt a firm prod in the side of his body which, because of his dream, he assumed was a crow's doing. On opening his eyes, however, he was alarmed to see in front of him quite the most enormous frog he had ever encountered. This frog was not only quite unlike any other that he had seen but it was also unlike anything he could possibly have imagined. It was therefore an incredulous Lebish who now sat staring open-mouthed at this most awesome sight.

"Get up, you overfed, fat-bellied slob!" Lebish recognised the guttural voice of Kaara scornfully giving him an order. "You stand to attention in the presence of Emled, the Great King of Tamsid!"

"Wh... what... wh... who... Wh... where am I?" whimpered Lebish, who was so taken aback by what he saw that he had quite forgotten his grovelling ways as he stood in the shadow of this monstrous creature.

He then received a sharp poke in the neck from the nose of Kaara. "Where are your manners, you slimy, good for nothing pot-bellied no-hoper?"

Lebish soon gathered his senses, realising that he must now have crossed into the Far North and, standing before him, was none other than the much vaunted King of the Tamsid community.

"Oh! Oh! I am so very sorry, great king. Please accept my apologies for my rudeness but I am so tired from the journey here that I must have fallen asleep. I am but a worthless creature in your company. Just ask of me anything... anything at all and I will do my best to assist you."

Lebish was just going to tell Emled about his fully stocked larder back home, and how he would gladly supply him with the very best grasshoppers and worms that his community could muster, when Emled curtly interrupted him.

"For pity's sake!" Emled's voice boomed out and its force staggered Lebish. "There's no need for all this. You have nothing to fear from me." Emled was staring deeply into Lebish's eyes as he spoke these words and the frightened frog found it impossible to return the king's gaze.

Lebish could see great menace in the face of Emled and he struggled to keep his wits about him. He was, however, beginning to think a little more clearly although he continued to remain rather in a state of shock as he still could not quite believe that there could be a creature living the like of which now loomed massively before him. He quickly summed up the situation and decided that if they had intended him to die then he would have been slaughtered earlier by the marsh frogs along with the rest of his companions. Having survived this far he desperately didn't want to do anything silly that may upset this terrifying king.

"What do you want of me, O Great One?" said Lebish in his most demeaning manner. "I am but a very humble and insignificant frog called Lebish who comes from the distant community of Seaxe which is far to the south of here. If I can be of any help to you, please tell me."

Lebish was now back to his grovelling best and although Emled was sure that this pathetic frog was entirely at his disposal he was nevertheless sickened by the overtly submissive behaviour being displayed by this weak limbed creature.

"Well, Lebish my friend, I do believe you can be of some assistance to me," drawled Emled who spoke with an accent that Lebish found hard to understand. "But firstly I want to know all about the expedition that you are on. A little bird informed me that you are carrying some very important news."

The Seaxe frog had to concentrate on every word that Emled spoke so as not to misinterpret anything that he said. Lebish was, however, beginning to relax a little. He hadn't been slain so far and he now had the opportunity to spin out his existence by telling this king of Tamsid all about his reason for being in the Near North. This rather suited the podgy senior for if any frog could tell a story and make it last then no frog could do it better than Lebish. He didn't actually even need the little matter of self-preservation to encourage such a recital, although, in the circumstances, it did nevertheless help to sharpen his intellect. He therefore began by relaying to Emled in great detail every element of the purpose for his setting out on this mission.

The toad listened attentively as the words gushed from Lebish's mouth. Emled hated wasting time and he frowned deeply as the Seaxe senior used many sentences to describe matters where only a few lines would have sufficed. He irritatingly found that he was continually having to interrupt Lebish, by saying "Get to the point" or "You've said that a number of times already" or "Come along, we haven't got all day and all night, you know."

Actually Emled had to concentrate very hard on not allowing his frustration with Lebish to get the better of his naturally aggressive and violent temperament and let himself get out of control. Quite honestly, if it hadn't been for the fact that Emled required a special task to be performed by Lebish then the toad would have struck him down dead as soon as look at him.

Lebish, being Lebish however, was warming to his task, and, try as he might at the behest of the toad, he found he could neither express himself, nor tell his story, without going all around the lily pads and up and down the river bank several times at least before he got anywhere near the point he was trying to make.

Finally Emled felt he had heard sufficient to discover all he needed to know about the soon-to-be-vacant post of king of Seaxe. He would normally at this stage have ordered the demise of his prisoner but, as was mentioned a little earlier, he could see in Lebish a particularly shifty and deceitful creature who might well be of further use to him.

"Well, my fat friend, that is all very interesting. I suppose I could now let you go and play with my marsh frogs. Would you like that?" As the toad spoke he allowed a sly grin to drift across his face. The thought of being alone with Kaara and his crew clearly filled Lebish with horror and Emled was well aware of the effect that his words were having upon the increasingly anxious senior.

"Er… Well… I'm not sure that they would want me to join them, I… I'm far too unworthy for such company," stammered Lebish, not wanting to offend the marsh frogs but at the same time desperate to avoid being sent to the mercy of these murderous creatures.

"Maybe I could instead ask you to do a small favour for me then?" Emled said in a soft voice that was as polite as it was threatening. Lebish knew there and then that there was no way he was going to be able to refuse the king's request, whatever it was he wished him to do.

"Anything, O Great One… anything at all," Lebish responded enthusiastically, for he at last sensed he was to be spared a cruel death at the hands of Kaara and his marsh frogs and that a chance was being provided for him to get away from this stinking community.

"Well, my chubby little friend, if you have quite finished with your story, and I assume you have as half of my community hereabouts have fallen asleep listening to you drone on and on," Emled was still finding it difficult to conceal his frustration and annoyance with Lebish. However, seeing on Lebish's face the disappointment that his last comment had caused, the toad quickly added (for effect only of course), "I did personally, however, find it all very interesting and most informative."

Emled snorted, before continuing, enabling him to regain his self-control. "This is what I want you to do..."

Emled proceeded to explain just what it was that he required. He had seen very clearly in Lebish a sly nature and an untrustworthy streak and he knew that he could profit handsomely from such frailty. As the toad drew in a huge lungful of air before setting out Lebish's next mission, it seemed to the frightened frog that this terrifying monster had grown half as big again and he cowered in the shadow of Emled.

The evil king then told Lebish that he was to return to Seaxe and let his council know that during his travels he and his fellow compatriots had become totally disorientated in the thick mists that are a common feature in the Near North. Having completely lost their bearings for several hours it was not until the mist began to lift that they realised they had wandered a lot further north than they had intended. In fact they had roamed so far off their route that they actually found themselves on the Near North boundary of Waga. Emled told Lebish that he was then to break down into a grief-stricken state as he explained how he and his group had then been attacked by a brutish bunch of vicious frogs who battered and bludgeoned all of his companions to death. He was to say that the only reason his own life had been spared was because they knew he was the group's leader and these thuggish creatures wanted to know the purpose of his visit to their area. He of course refused to buckle under what was an intense and extremely painful period of interrogation and, due to his stubbornness, they decided to tie him up in some long thick reeds and rushes and said they would return later that day to finally extract the information they wanted.

Lebish was quite enjoying being given this mission by Emled for he could see star status being accorded him as he recounted this tale back in his home community of Seaxe. He therefore listened very carefully as the toad neared the end of his orders. Emled's final instruction was that Lebish was to conclude by saying that shortly after the return of his mean-hearted captors, and whilst he was enduring quite the most horrible torture that had brought him to the very brink of giving way to their demands, a quite fantastic thing happened. Suddenly, from out of the dense undergrowth that surrounded the area in which he was being held captive, an army of large brown frogs descended upon then and proceeded to fight a long and hard battle with the wicked frogs that had imprisoned him. The result of this fracas was that all of his captors were slain with none being allowed to escape.

The very last piece in Lebish's instructions was for him to say that his saviours were led by an awesome frog leader who was called Emled.

He was to describe this creature as a most magnificent specimen, who clearly possessed great courage and charisma, and, that by rescuing him, this heroic frog had probably saved the whole community of Seaxe from some catastrophic invasion by those that had murdered his fellow travellers. Lebish was to say he was certain that had he passed on the information regarding Moha's forthcoming resignation to such unscrupulous rebels, then they would almost certainly have used the opportunity to strike Seaxe when it was leaderless and at its most vulnerable.

Lebish really was rising to the occasion and he very much liked being asked to sing the praises of this grotesque and menacing creature if at the end of the day he was going to be feted for his own bravery. What's more he was beginning to spot another opportunity in that he felt he might actually gain some benefit from Emled for carrying out the king's orders. Puffing himself up into what he considered to be his most important and business-like posture he decided to pose a little question of his own.

"And what's in it for me ?" he inquired of Emled.

"What's in it for you!?" boomed the toad. "*What's in it for you!?*"

Lebish watched on in amazement and was petrified as the monstrous creature drew himself up to his full height and towered threateningly above the fearful frog. The toad's throat had turned purple and crimson in his all too apparent rage and his already bulbous eyes looked as if they were about to explode. Lebish instantly regretted his attempt at what he had considered to be a cunning bit of opportunism and was sure that the king, who now looked as if he was about to burst, would now strike him dead.

Instinctively Lebish threw himself to the ground and shut his eyes as tightly as he could, waiting for what seemed like an age for the end to come. And then, both to his surprise and relief, he heard Emled say in a reasonably controlled voice:

"I'll tell you what's in it for you, fat frog! It is that I will not flatten you where you lay by hopping upon your pot-bellied body." He then hissed, “And it is that I will not then throw your broken limbs to the crows as carrion for their dinner.”

“Oh s... s... sir. Oh m... m... master... Great King Emled,” Lebish stuttered feebly as he tried desperately to think of a way to avoid such a terrible death. “Wh... wh... what I really meant to say was... ‘and what about me?’ Did it sound like... ‘and what’s in it for me?’ Oh, I couldn’t possibly wish for any material gain from one so great as you. Just being in your honoured presence is sufficient reward for a frog as humble as I. I...”

“Shut up, creep!” the toad cut Lebish short. He had heard sufficient to know that the grovelling creature in front of him was lying through his glands. Emled was, however, quite astute enough to see through Lebish’s deceit and he knew that he could rule this shabby and contemptible frog by fear. Lebish, he felt sure, would do anything to preserve his own life and that certainly included betraying his home community.

The strange thing is that up until what followed next Lebish had no clear idea why Emled was asking him to relay this information back to Seaxe. If he had been asked to guess at that very minute what this was all about then he would probably have said that it was just another king with an inflated ego who wanted wider recognition. In truth he was just thankful he was still alive and he intended to stay that way come what may. When Emled spoke again, however, everything began to fall into place for the Seaxe senior.

“On returning to your home community you will sing my praises and say very clearly that if ever there could possibly be a replacement for your king, who had qualities which were equal to and probably in excess of those held by Moha, then you had just met such a creature on your travels; a frog who is known by the name of Emled.”

Lebish let the words sink in as he thought about what Emled had just said. “So this is what he is up to?” considered Lebish. “He intends to become our king. He wants to be king of Seaxe!”

“And furthermore,” continued Emled. “From now on you will be faithful only to me and act as my eyes and ears on all matters that occur in the community of Seaxe both now and after I have been appointed its king.” Then, noticing the look of surprise and realisation on Lebish’s face, he added, “For I will be King... You mark my words!”

Emled's colouring was returning to normal and he had assumed a less threatening posture. He was even speaking quite calmly again and in a cool and calculating manner. It must be said that Lebish was indeed very impressed that Emled could change so quickly from being a totally violent and openly aggressive, in fact almost manic, creature one moment into one that could certainly be described as 'capable of charming a contented frog off his favourite lily pad' the next. Such a rapid about turn in character also rather unnerved the tubby senior and he visibly shivered as Emled's attitude towards him became oddly amiable.

"Now off you go, my little friend," said Emled, "and I will be seeing you very soon. You will of course remember at all times that I expect your full and complete co-operation as well as your absolute loyalty?" Lebish saw a glint of something quite evil flash across the king's eyes as he spoke these words. "I would hate to hop upon such a worthy and useful frog, as you now most certainly are, by mistake."

Lebish shivered again at the prospect and he nodded vigorously in his acknowledgement. The wicked toad clearly had all the assurance he required.

Chapter Ten

The Council Decides

Emled's timing was perfect. Having extracted all the information he required from Lebish he was able to plan his bid to become the next king of Seaxe with precision.

The arrival of Kaara at the eleventh hour right into the heart of the council's deliberations, in order to declare Emled's interest in being their king, had been a brilliant ploy. It had clearly given the messenger a great opportunity to say wonderful things about this seemingly outstanding applicant from the Far North in a setting where it was guaranteed to provide maximum impact.

If this action could be considered to have been cleverly and shrewdly arranged, then the release of Lebish back to his home community, with exciting news of his rescue by an heroic leader from far distant lands, must regrettably be described as a masterstroke. In addition, and this point was hugely emphasised by the podgy senior, not only had Lebish been saved but this act of unsolicited bravery had in itself almost certainly prevented a deadly attack on Seaxe from an army of murderous rebel frogs.

In order to put himself in the best possible light, Emled had also designed Lebish's return to Seaxe to coincide with the day of the special meeting when the three prospective candidates to be king would be interviewed by the Anurian Council. Lebish accordingly arrived back during the middle of the morning of this day and the first of the interviews was to be held at noon.

The whole of the community had been very concerned for the safety of Lebish and his party. It was of course not uncommon for frogs to be lost on long journeys, as there were many aggressors who were their natural enemies (a cat or a duck for instance would kill them either for pleasure or for food). The Seaxe frogs had therefore become increasingly worried when their colleagues were several days late in returning. Lebish and his group had been chosen for the mission to spread the news of Moha's resignation both because of the diplomatic skills they had acquired and the fact that they were all recognised as seasoned travellers. As such they were regarded as being well-equipped for almost any eventuality that may have arisen on their travels.

It was therefore entirely understandable that when Lebish hopped into Seaxe on the day of the interviews he was immediately surrounded by a large group of garrulous frogs all wanting to know how he was and what had happened to the others who had set out with him.

Almost before he had time to draw a breath Lebish was hurried along the river bank to explain his trials and tribulations to the Anurian Council. They were already in session as it had been agreed that it would be useful to meet early that day in order to discuss how they should approach the interviews with each of the three candidates.

As he was ushered in to meet the councillors it was not difficult for them to believe the story he went on to tell, for it was plain for all to see that his body was indeed quite severely battered and bruised. That this was almost entirely attributable to the beak of Gawk and the forelimb of Kaara, and nothing whatsoever to do with beatings or torture allegedly inflicted upon him by the hypothetical rebel frogs, only you the reader and me the storyteller will ever know. Lebish was also most bedraggled and he had noticeably lost a good deal of weight both as a result of his exertions back and forth across Waga plus the meagre diet of scrawny Far North grasshoppers that he had swallowed with great disgust since departing from Seaxe several days earlier.

In short, Lebish looked a wreck and this enabled the horrific picture he painted of his torment at the forelimbs of the rebels to appear quite plausible to the councillors. Confronted as they were by the extremely sorry sight of an exhausted and bruised Lebish, the council had no reason not to believe all that he said. After all he did in fact give them a very convincing account of his unfortunate sojourn to the Near North boundary of Waga and the subsequent attack by rebel frogs.

It must however be said at this juncture, just for the record of course, that Lebish considered his performance in front of the council to be a masterpiece and the more impressed they became by his apparent bravery the more he played upon their gestures of sympathy towards him.

When he went on to describe how it was that this fine king of the Far North community of Tamsid had actually not only saved him but probably the entire community of Seaxe, then the councillors found their excitement almost impossible to suppress.

Could this be...? they wondered. Could this be the same king of whom they had so recently heard such great things? Could this be the same frog that they had called for an interview this very afternoon? As they listened, now totally and utterly enthralled and intrigued by Lebish's story, they realised to their delight that this frog king was indeed the very one that they had selected in their final three candidates.

Now it should be made clear that the councillors were all genuinely very sad when they heard of the tragic loss of a number of their colleagues at the forelimbs of the rebel frogs. It was however quite understandable, although not entirely excusable, that, on learning of the fantastic coincidence that Lebish's saviour was actually the very same frog king whom they had called for interview, they immediately put to the backs of their minds the terrible fate that had befallen their friends.

At this moment, therefore, with only a few hours to go before the interviews were due to take place, the impression the councillors were developing was that they were indeed lucky, if not privileged, that such a fine and worthy frog as Emled should honour Seaxe by applying to be its new king. How fortunate they felt, and what a great opportunity they now had, to be able to appoint a king who appeared not only to offer all of the qualities Moha possessed, but in addition had far superior physical strength that could protect their community if ever they came under attack from aggressors. Moreover, was it not a fact that Emled had already demonstrated his considerable power by defeating the rebel frogs, so preventing what could have been a disastrous incursion on their families and their homes in Seaxe!?

*

Lebish was indeed feted by both the council and his colleagues, and, for the rest of that day, he was cared for by several frogs who attended to his bruises, whilst being waited on by other frogs who brought him large and juicy grasshoppers. In fact, he was being spoiled to such a degree that even when he heard the news that his application for the kingship had been rejected and that he would not be given an interview it didn't trouble him overmuch. Instead, he merely lay back enjoying all the attention he was receiving and luxuriated in the feasting and fuss that surrounded him.

As he mused he saw ahead of him a rather pleasant existence. He was certain, from the reaction of the council to his contrived story, that Emled would be chosen as the next king of Seaxe. He was also fairly confident that provided he kept his glands clean and his fingers out of mischief then he should reap a rich harvest as the new king's right limbed frog.

Whilst he pondered over his future, Lebish grew sleepy from the rigour and excitement of the past few days and he drifted off into a deep sleep. In his dreams he retraced all the events of his journey to the Near North; across Waga; and into Tamsid. He saw evil monsters in the grotesque form of crows and what looked like distorted and misshapen frogs. He also felt their constant punches and pokes to his body and he could see bruise after bruise swelling up on his skin. He then had visions of himself giving commands to his fellow frogs by the order of a wicked king named Emled. As he exerted his authority he saw frogs scurrying hither and thither, obeying his every word, as they were frightened of what may happen if they did not do as he instructed.

As he continued to dream he also imagined that he saw the face of Mars and he heard himself saying "By the decree of King Emled the Great I am here to tell you that you will from this day relinquish your position as a senior frog in this community and you are now banished for all time from Seaxe, never to return!"

*

Lebish finally awoke from his heavy slumber feeling refreshed and once again ready to consume an enormous pile of his favourite grasshoppers. He was in fact just about to call for some service when he became aware of a great hubbub of croaking and chattering outside his leafy hollow. On looking out he saw that there were many frogs hopping to and fro in a very excited manner. He also noticed that the light was fading and that dusk was approaching, from which he deduced that he must have been asleep for many hours.

Lebish had, for the moment, actually quite forgotten about the interviews for his mind was much more focused upon his intended gorging of delicious grasshoppers. He called to a nearby frog and asked what was going on.

"Haven't you heard?" cried the excited frog. "We have a new king!"

"Oh... Oh of course," stammered Lebish as the reality of what was happening suddenly replaced all the dreams he had been having. "And who is it? Who is to be our King?"

"Why, it's Emled!" enthused the bubbly frog. "The council have appointed Emled from Tamsid! From what they say he is going to be a fine leader - maybe even better than Moha."

As the frog hopped away in great bounds back to his friends Lebish's expression darkened

"So it wasn't all a dream," he thought. "Our wise and learned council has elected a brutal and merciless creature to be our leader. Things are going to be different around here from now on, that's for sure. Still I should be okay as long as I keep on the right side of the king."

However, despite all his previous thoughts about what personal benefits might lay in store for him, Lebish felt for the first time a real and intense sense of foreboding about the future. What had he done by singing Emled's praises? He alone in the whole community was aware of the truth about their new king's deceitful rise to the most influential kingship in all of the frog communities south of Waga, but, unfortunately, what he knew he was unable to impart to another living creature. Such was his allegiance with Emled that if ever he broke his oath of being faithful to the evil toad then a certain and cruel death would be his punishment for sure.

Chapter Eleven

Moha Says Goodbye – Enter the New King

It is normal practice, following a frog king announcing his resignation, for there to be a period of several months to elapse between the selection of the new incumbent and the day the latter officially takes control of his new community. The principle reason for this is that it enables the old king to gently wind down his term of office whilst simultaneously making full and proper arrangements for the smooth hand-over to his successor. It also enables the king-in-waiting to have a period during which he can get to know his new community in a less formal and relaxed manner prior to officially taking up his duties.

Quite understandably the final months of Moha's reign were very subdued. The disappointment of learning that he was to resign had greatly affected the whole community, and every frog, if they had been asked, would have confessed that as a result of such devastating news their spirits had dipped as far down as the river bed itself. Unfortunately there was very little that Moha could do to raise his community's morale as it was clearly his standing down as king of Seaxe that was at the root of their extreme sadness.

It is true to say that the appointment of the new king did initially inject some excitement into the community but this had only been short lived. Spirits were temporarily lifted as frogs clamoured to discover firstly, who was on the council's final shortlist; and then secondly, to try and find out as much about Emled as they could when it was announced that it would indeed be him who was to become their new king.

The fact that no frog in Seaxe knew anything about this stranger from Tamsid, other than what Lebish had told them and of course what Kaara had rather dramatically imparted to the council, meant that gossip regarding his past exploits was at a minimum. In the absence of any actual evidence of the new king's credit-worthiness to be their leader the frogs of Seaxe made do with extravagant speculation of what Emled may have achieved. Unusually for frogs, who can normally be relied upon to make a good story last for many warm and sunny afternoons, such interest waned after a few days and it was not long before the local frogs got bored with fantasising and soon settled back into their general melancholy.

Moha, in the meantime, had sought close counsel with Mars. The old king had slept very little of late as he had devoted his energy to trying to understand just why he had for so long retained an overwhelming feeling of impending doom and particularly why this had of recent times markedly increased. He was gradually beginning to sense that his concern was centred on Emled himself, but he, like every other frog in the community (with the exception of Lebish of course), knew absolutely nothing about this apparent heroic frog's past nor for that matter had he even heard of his home community of Tamsid. So why did he feel this way? What possible reason could he have for his very real concern?

Moha had always placed great faith in what he would cannily describe as his gut reaction. Indeed he had made many of his best decisions based on his inner feelings even when this flew in the face of what others may have regarded as 'the logical thing to do'. In the years that followed his resignation, Moha often chastised himself for not having acted in such a way as to prevent Emled from becoming king of Seaxe. After all, his senses at the time had begun to warn him that, as a result of the appointment of this creature from the Far North, bad times would almost certainly lie ahead for the community he had nurtured and led so lovingly.

Of course if he had acted according to his feelings then this story may never have been told. It is also probable that those who subsequently suffered at the hands of Emled would not have done so in the way they did, as you will see when you read on. Fate, however, is a strange phenomenon, and maybe those who were adversely affected (and there were a great many) unwittingly acted as a sacrifice for the greater good of all the other creatures of the river banks and forests.

In so doing they almost certainly played their part in averting an even greater catastrophe. Moha, therefore, should in no way be blamed for the coming of Emled, for what follows illustrates just how difficult it is to assess the balance between good and evil. What is certain, however, is that the power of evil and its widely spread net of influence must never be underestimated - not in any circumstances!

*

Moha and Mars sat together in the king's chamber. The old king had also asked Peeyu to join them a little later but first he had words only for Mars' ears.

"Mars, my dearest friend, there is something quite terrible that I have to tell you." Mars could see great concern on the face of the kindly bullfrog and in the deep furrows that ran across his king's brow.

"I now feel sure that my main concern and sense of foreboding for our community's future well-being lies with Emled himself." Moha paused for a while as Mars displayed expressions of surprise and puzzlement. As soon as Mars recovered from his initial shock he continued.

"You well know that for many seasons I have felt a chill wind that has troubled me. It has been a coldness which has come out of the north from far across Waga." Mars nodded in recognition as he had indeed heard his friend speak of such a thing on several occasions in the past.

"It has always carried a warning, the meaning of which I have unfortunately never been able to fathom," continued Moha. "I still can't in any detail, but I am now sure that it involves Emled and that he will be the carrier of bad tidings for our community."

Mars thought for a while before responding.

"We could perhaps go to this place called Tamsid to try and find out a bit more about our future leader?" suggested Mars. "Although to do so would require crossing land that no other living frog in our community has ever dared to do."

"It can't be a frog that takes on such a task," replied Moha. "Leastwise, not alone. Without an escort to guide him across the swamps of Waga a frog would perish for certain in that foul place." Moha was again silent for a while before he continued speaking.

"Your suggestion that we arrange a trip to Emled's home community is an idea to which I have also been giving some thought. With this in mind I have asked Peeyu to join us. He will be here in a few moments. I am going to ask him to undertake this most dangerous mission. I am going to ask him if he will indeed carry out the task of infiltrating the community of Tamsid in order to find out what this seemingly magnificent new king is really like."

"Then I must go too," declared Mars, immediately on hearing these words. "It is too dangerous even for a brilliant bird such as Peeyu to travel alone. Let him guide me across the swamps. With his keen eyes we can plot our way through Waga and he can also keep a look out for any danger that may lurk therein, such as the murderous rebel frogs who attacked Lebish's party."

"In all honesty, my friend, I do not want to accept such an offer because I know that both your lives will be at risk. It will be hazardous enough for Peeyu, but at least he will have the ability to fly quickly away from trouble. The swamps and muddy pits of Waga will not be a problem for him whereas for you, dear Mars, such obstacles in a strange and pitiless environment may prove to be your downfall."

"My King, please let me go with Peeyu. Two heads will be better than one, especially in such an inhospitable place as the Far North. Peeyu and I always work really well together and if anything does go wrong then at least one of us may be able to return with the news of Emled that you require."

The old king looked down at his friend and colleague. He was full of admiration for the young and handsome frog who proudly stood before him eagerly awaiting his master's approval to accompany Peeyu on this most perilous of missions.

"That you are prepared to voluntarily give your life for the sake of our community is something that stands you apart from our other seniors. Your loyalty and devotion to your fellow frogs is unrivalled in Seaxe and it is greatly appreciated by me."

Mars felt proud to be described in such a way, particularly when it was Moha who said these fine words. He could also feel a warm glow running through his body which gently reddened the complexion on his chest and throat.

"I shall accept your offer to undertake this task although I do so with great reluctance," said Moha. " We both know of course that such a mission is necessary for the good of our community." Moha then paused before adding, "I do, however, have a feeling in my gut that the story Lebish told about being saved by Emled didn't altogether sound quite right. Why should he save Lebish for instance and not any of the others?

"I also feel rather suspicious of the sequence of events that occurred during Emled's application to be the next king of our community. The appearance of that large brown frog messenger from Tamsid at the meeting of the Anurian Council, just as they were about to consider potential candidates; and the arrival back of Lebish with news of Emled's heroic deeds, crucially and literally moments before the final interviews were to take place, indicates to me something rather more than mere coincidence. If I am not mistaken, my senses tell me that these events were planned and cleverly arranged to provide maximum impact in order to reinforce Emled's bid to be our community's next king. My senses also tell me that a creature who goes to such lengths may probably not be all that he wishes others to believe he is and may well want the position for all the wrong reasons. When all things are considered it does suggest that some greater force has been at work which has corrupted the appointment process and ensured that fate has been manipulated to favour the selection of Emled."

At that moment Peeyu arrived and Moha and Mars greeted him warmly. When the two frogs explained to him what they had just been discussing Peeyu was quick to give his full backing to such a mission. He needed absolutely no encouragement to volunteer to accompany his friend, irrespective of what dangers may lay ahead for both of them. Peeyu's love of Moha was equal to that of Mars' feelings towards their kind old king and they would both have moved a river bank if it was to support their great leader.

*

During the transitional period that followed Emled's appointment, whilst Moha saw out his days in Seaxe and the toad supposedly did the same in Tamsid, a wide range of Seaxe frogs began receiving missives sent to them personally by none other than Emled himself. To begin with each of the senior frogs in Seaxe, with the exception of Mars, had been asked to consider their current plans and policies and to think of ways to improve on what they had already achieved. A further and

At that moment Peeyu arrived and Moha and Mars greeted him warmly.

more detailed set of similar questions was then put to those frogs immediately subordinate to the seniors. Interestingly, in respect of this group of frogs, those who were responsible to Mars were not omitted from the exercise as had been their leading senior when the seniors themselves were questioned.

The responsibility for transporting backwards and forwards Emled's exhaustive array of questions and the multiplicity of replies given by the Seaxe frogs was actually carried out by the vast flying army of Gawk's black crows.

At first the questions appeared to be quite innocent and the local frogs merely considered them to be Emled showing a healthy interest in the work and organisation of their community. They felt it was understandable that Emled should carry out some preliminary fact finding so that he might gain a clear view, both of individuals who lived in Seaxe and of events that had taken place or were due to take place that had a bearing on everyday community life. After a while, however, the questions became more and more searching and increasingly frequent. Also, the fact that this activity was being stepped up, resulted in there being many more of the black crows barging their way into the community and the sight of these ill-natured and extremely unpleasant creatures arrogantly strutting about gave Emled's information gathering process a rather sinister touch.

There was clearly a mixed reaction by 'the six' seniors to this approach. Initially the mere fact that Emled was taking the trouble to ask them individually for information made virtually all of them feel rather important. At the same time they knew that Mars had received no such request. In addition they were also aware that Emled had not bothered, even out of courtesy, to ask Moha if he minded him making direct contact with the Seaxe frogs whilst the old king saw out his term of office.

There even came a point when 'the six' seniors actually regarded Emled's enquiries as somewhat of a contest and a gauge of their personal popularity with him. They each made an issue out of such contact and openly bragged whenever they were asked by Emled to do something or another. It was not long before this behaviour led to there being a great deal of jealousy and each of 'the six' seniors quickly grew to hate hearing that one of their peer group had received yet another request from Emled.

However, it was when 'the six' senior frogs became aware that their future king was also directing his questions to their own personal subordinates that the real problems began. The seniors felt very uncomfortable at this tactic of Emled's and they could not accept their being treated in this way. What's more they regarded this approach as being a serious attempt to undermine their authority.

Things did not get any better for 'the six' as very soon they learned that not only were their subordinates now receiving a greater number of missives from Emled than they were, but these lower ranking frogs had actually been told by the new king that under no circumstances were they to discuss their replies with their respective senior. Emled had made it quite clear that he wanted their own personal views on what was happening in Seaxe and that such views were not to be influenced in any way or be vetted by their seniors.

Of course this strategy of Emled's had the effect of encouraging the subordinate frogs to feel rather more important than they had previously regarded themselves. They soon recognised that here was an opportunity to shine in the eyes of Emled and who knew what might happen when he arrived to take over from Moha. There could, for instance, possibly be a reshuffling of senior positions and this might create the chance of promotion arising.

And so it was that a substantial number of hitherto satisfied frogs began to ponder upon the possibility of newly imagined future opportunities. In his deviousness Emled had manipulated the minds of these Seaxe frogs and engendered in them a lust for power that they had never before been encouraged to display. Emled had purposely engineered a rift to develop between the seniors and the next level down of frogs in the management hierarchy. This in turn had caused a great deal of mistrust and suspicion to arise between these two important groupings of frogs.

The plan behind Emled's approach was that the existence of such attitudes would enable him to benefit from being able to form useful relationships with those whom he would be rewarding with offers of rises in status or other personal and material benefits. Emled knew from his experience in Tamsid that he could pollute even the most well-run of communities with such a subversive approach. He was also well aware that within all creatures there is the capacity for being influenced or corrupted by greed especially when there is the possibility of obtaining something that one longs for but would never normally be able to acquire as of right or through legitimate means. Yes, unfortunately, this was even the case in the happy and peaceful community of Seaxe!

*

Frogs in Seaxe were therefore being very careful with what they said to each other and made certain of being constantly on their guard not to say anything that could be taken by a colleague and passed on to Emled's crows as "useful" information for the consideration of the new king. This was done so pointedly that even conversations between long time friends were both economically and cautiously phrased for fear of saying something which could be misconstrued to their disadvantage.

The general atmosphere of mistrust and disharmony that Emled successfully encouraged in Seaxe in the days leading up to the official commencement of his kingship was something that had never existed under Moha and the local frogs were finding it quite impossible to cope with these new feelings. With all the turmoil that Emled had injected, together with the fact that the senior frogs and their subordinates were totally engrossed in what each other was doing, meant that almost nothing was being done to support those frogs in the community who both needed and looked for leadership and assistance from their supposedly more erstwhile senior colleagues.

Standing apart from this unhealthy situation were Moha, Mars and Mars' faithful and very close subordinate colleagues. In the case of the latter they had always been extremely loyal to Mars and they had the greatest respect for him. When in fact they received the same messages from Emled that the other 'six' senior frogs' subordinates had received they firstly discussed together what it was that they thought they were being asked to do. Having debated the matter in a sensible and constructive manner they felt certain that Emled was for some reason setting out to subvert the community's existing systems and structures.

Unlike their peers in the other 'responsibilities' they decided to go to their senior frog and tell him that they felt uneasy about Emled's antics. Indeed they advised Mars that they were not going to conform with Emled's request for information about their respective roles in the community. Mars knew that to refuse the king-in-waiting in such a way would probably prove to be damaging to each of their personal futures, so he advised them to give the required information to the crows. However, he also said that if they wished they could discuss what they were going to say to Emled with him first. This they all did of course!

Such was the relationship between Mars and all those who worked with him. He always operated well with his subordinates and he offered them openness and honesty in all things. This was greatly welcomed and much appreciated and in return they gave him their full respect and loyalty. Virtues such as these are precious and so very rarely are they fully earned. They were in fact virtues that Mars' senior colleagues longed to acquire from their own subordinates, although unfortunately they would never know how they should go about it. They were virtues in fact that Emled would kill for!!!

*

It was whilst this turbulent state of affairs continued that Mars and Peeyu slipped quietly out of Seaxe and carefully made their way north towards Waga. The only initial problem they experienced in proceeding to the Near North boundary was to avoid being seen by the passing black crows who regularly flew overhead. Fortunately for the two Seaxe friends these birds were far too busy concentrating on the enquiries and information they were carrying back and forth to Emled to be worried about frogs and kingfishers hopping and flitting about below.

Crossing Waga of course was an entirely different matter. In the first place they could quite easily be spotted by the crows from the air even if the latter were not particularly looking for strangers. This was because they would almost totally be exposed in the barren swamplands which provided only minimal cover by way of its scant vegetation. Secondly there was always the danger of being confronted by the marsh frogs who were constantly patrolling in the area. We know only too well that these cold-hearted creatures would show no mercy to intruders and derive great pleasure from so doing.

So, in order to prevent their being seen, the two companions travelled by day in the Near North and decided to attempt to cross Waga by night under the cover of darkness.

They agreed that when they reached Waga, Peeyu would carry out as detailed a survey of the swamps as was possible in the twilight of the day. His job would be to find a safe route that Mars could take across the dangerous terrain whilst he led the way from the air. However, before Peeyu started out on his reconnoitring, they had to do something to conceal his bright colours which sparkled even in the grey murkiness of the dank Near North. So, with the help of Mars, he covered his beautiful plumage with the muddy waters of the swamps thus giving himself a dark and mottled brown appearance. This of course provided a perfect camouflage in the fading afternoon light of the grim and bleak environment of Waga.

Flying low over the swamplands, swiftly and unseen, Peeyu was able to mark out what appeared to be a safe route for them to take. Then, as darkness fell, the two friends set out on their journey across the dangerous landscape. Thankfully the night was cloudy and the mist not too dense so enabling the dull white glow of the moon to give just sufficient light to be helpful and fortunately not too much to expose their presence.

Their progress that night was understandably slow as the two companions needed great vigilance to both ensure safety underfoot as well as to avoid being seen by any of the swamp's more regular occupants. On a number of occasions they heard the distant flap of wings which indicated the approach of a black crow. This was the signal for Mars and Peeyu to lay flat upon the ground and rely on the darkness and their camouflage to mask their existence. In the gloom of the night the crows were themselves of course totally invisible. However, when the moon peeped through the breaks in the clouds, their passing overhead took on a sinister appearance with their wide spread of wings eerily silhouetted against the whiteness of the moon.

There were also several occasions when they heard the unmistakable guttural croaking of marsh frogs who were either on patrol or returning home after a late night session searching for intruders who they could ambush. One such party of marauders passed within a few yards of Mars, and, as he lay perfectly still hardly daring to breathe, he could clearly hear them boasting of an attack on some unsuspecting group of frogs. He then again had to take cover as another bunch of these villainous creatures passed by. This group of frogs were equally as boastful as the others but this time it was of their scaring of a skylark from her nest and their subsequent destruction of her new born chicks.

As he listened to the wicked bragging of the marsh frogs, Mars felt an anger well up inside his body the like of which he had never before experienced. His life in Seaxe, and the peace and goodwill that Moha had brought upon his community, had shielded him and his fellow frogs from such ill-doing and depravity. In later years Mars was to reflect on his first introduction to this malice and wonder if his community's earlier teaching ought to have included a better understanding of the type of malevolence that abounded in the Far North at that time. There is of course no easy or right answer as for each level of evil that is experienced so another even worse happening will be uncovered in the future. However, some comfort can be found in the words of the wise old Moha, who once said that goodness will triumph over evil even if it does take a generation or more for it to do so.

Peeyu had estimated that it would take a full night to cross to the other side of Waga and it was indeed just as the dawn was breaking that the two friends reached the drier land that marked their arrival on the far side of the treacherous and horrid swamp.

Physically exhausted from their exertions, and mentally drained from their need to be constantly vigilant throughout the night to the existence of danger, both Mars and Peeyu collapsed into a deep sleep as soon as they found a safe place in which to hide. Although not particularly comfortable their refuge of an old, rotting, hollowed out tree stump, which was totally covered by damp fallen leaves, provided a perfect place for them to stay whilst they regained their lost energy.

Several hours must have passed whilst they slept for by the time Mars warily peered out of their sanctuary he noticed that the sun had now risen high in the southern sky although he felt little warmth from its rays in the damp climate of the Far North. The young frog shivered as he thought about the previous night's endeavours and also about what might now lie in front of them in this frogforsaken land to which they had come.

Mars heard Peeyu stirring from his slumber and he turned to greet his friend. Peeyu sat up and began preening his feathers which were completely caked in Waga's mud. How he longed to dive into the clear, cool and refreshing water of the river that ran below

Kingfisher's Bridge and rid himself of this foul coating that was his disguise.

"We should eat," said Mars, as he turned and smiled at his friend. He knew Peeyu must detest being covered in Waga's sticky mud so he joked a little, in the way close friends can even in the most difficult of circumstances, about how handsome the kingfisher looked in his fine new brown coat. Peeyu smiled back and he felt the tension of their situation lifting a little by Mars' lightheartedness.

"You're quite right, we do need to eat. We must build up our strength and be fit to deal with whatever difficulties fate has in store for us," replied Peeyu. "It will however be too dangerous to be out in the open for too long so I'll fly around for while and check out our surroundings. Hopefully my beautiful coat should not attract too much attention."

Despite their predicament the two friends found time to laugh and Mars stepped to one side to allow Peeyu through the small opening they had made as an entrance to their hideout. It wasn't long, however, before the small bird returned to say that it was indeed safe for them both to go outside and search for food.

While Mars hunted for grasshoppers Peeyu flew from branch to branch high up in the trees in order to keep a lookout for any danger. When Mars indicated that he had eaten sufficiently the young frog returned to the shelter of the rotting tree stump. Peeyu then took the opportunity to dart across to a shallow dirty river he had seen earlier a short distance away that laboured between deep muddy banks. Here he dived a few times catching small greyish brown fish on each occasion. As was the case with the sustenance that Mars had found, the food Peeyu consumed was scrawny and tasteless. It did, however, provide some nourishment even though it was rather difficult to swallow.

When the two friends were rejoined back in their temporary refuge, and each had eaten enough grasshoppers and fish respectively for the time being, both agreed that it was quite the most disgusting meal that either of them had ever had the misfortune to put into their tummies.

Just at that moment there came a faint rustling from outside their hiding place. They froze as they listened to the sound of something coming towards them. The creature's movement was measured and purposeful as if whatever it was that was out there knew of their existence. The rustling then stopped and the next thing the two friends thought they heard was the distinctive sound of the flapping of wings.

"We must have been seen," whispered Mars. "Surely that's one of Emled's carrion crows."

"The wings don't sound like those of a crow," replied Peeyu very quietly. "But I wouldn't take that as meaning their owner doesn't intend doing us any harm. There can't possibly be many good souls in this terrible place."

"Unfortunately we don't have time to ask questions," said Mars. "You will have a chance to get away if you make a very fast exit and take our visitor by surprise. I'll be captured for sure but at least you may be able to get a message back to Moha."

"I won't leave you behind," assured Peeyu. "You are my very good friend. We shall stand together or fall together such as will be our fate."

The two friends looked deep into each other's eyes: their friendship now more powerful than ever before.

"Thank you for saying you will stay," said Mars. "But it is our duty to take back whatever information we can to Moha. I know from what we heard last night that a massive evil lurks both in and beyond Waga to the Far North. Whatever it is that Emled has built up it is certainly not what we should be importing into our community. You must therefore make your escape and give warning to our friends and colleagues back in Seaxe. After all, our prime responsibility is to Moha and our friends and colleagues back home."

"It's okay. Don't be alarmed. I mean you no harm." A voice suddenly came from outside of the entrance to their refuge. It sounded friendly and reassuring, and quite out of place in this land of apparent treachery and wickedness. The voice continued.

"My name is Krakow, I have been watching you ever since you entered the swamps of Waga from the Near North. You crossed that evil place most skilfully. To have come so far and with such great care suggests to me that you must have a very important mission to accomplish. If you have good intentions then I would wish to help you."

The owner of the voice did indeed sound genuine. Peeyu and Mars said nothing but they exchanged glances that suggested they both felt it would be safe for them to venture outside. They were most intrigued to see who it was that spoke with such a warm and friendly disposition.

Chapter Twelve

Krakow Tells the Story

Mars was the first to hop out of their refuge with Peeyu following close on his heels. As soon as they were out in the daylight Mars heard a sudden gasp of amazement from behind him.

"Krakow the Wise!" exclaimed Peeyu. "Is it really Krakow, the wise old blackbird and the holder of the 'Great Learning of the Supreme Qualities of Wisdom and Knowledge' of whom legends are told?"

Before them stood a very old blackbird whose feathers, although now sagging, were clearly once fine and strong. The bird's spindly legs supported a thin and seemingly frail body and, where in days gone by the bird's head would have been covered in a fine black down, there was now revealed a large bald patch that began just above the bird's beak and stretched over his head finishing halfway down the nape of his neck. The brightness of his eyes belied the bird's great age and Mars was immediately drawn towards him by a warmth that he could not explain. The blackbird shifted from one thin leg to the other and then replied modestly.

"I am certainly called Krakow, and indeed, as you will see from my appearance, I am old if not ancient when compared against strong young creatures such as yourselves."

The two friends allowed their heads to drop on to their chests as they felt a little embarrassed by the blackbird's response. Seeing their reaction the old bird quickly added to his reply by saying, "As for being wise and regaled in legends then that is not for me to say but it is rather for you to judge. I could indeed say many things that turn out to be quite untrue, although you may initially accept them as being correct. It may therefore be more astute of you to examine and

The brightness of his eyes belied the bird's great age and Mars was immediately drawn towards him by a warmth that he could not explain.

question me first in order to form your own opinion and not just take me for who I or others say I am."

Peeyu knew without doubt on hearing such words of wisdom, which were spoken so honestly and modestly, that this indeed was the Krakow of whom his grandfather had long ago told such wonderful tales.

That a creature named Krakow had existed at all youngsters such as Peeyu could never be certain, for grandfathers, as you will well know, are rather prone to telling stories to their grandchildren that take a little believing, if indeed they were ever true in the first place.

"It's not safe for you to be seen here," continued Krakow. "If you follow me I will take you to a place where prying marsh frogs and nosey carrion crows rarely come."

With that Krakow swiftly turned and skipped away in a manner that defied his great many years.

"Come on, Mars," urged Peeyu. "It will be safe. I know in my heart that this is the bird who is a friend of all creatures who are good and just. We shall be all right, I am sure of it."

Mars instinctively looked around for any signs of danger and, seeing none, joined his friend and hurried along after the old blackbird.

They had only been travelling a short while before Krakow began to slow down and then stopped by a tall oak tree. He turned and beckoned to Mars and Peeyu to join him. As the two friends came alongside their new found companion the old bird hopped up on to a network of exposed tree roots that wound around the base of the tree. He quickly, but cautiously, scanned the area thereabouts before diving down into the mass of fallen autumn leaves that were interwoven between the roots like a damp carpet. The two friends, who had already been surprised by the bird's speed across the ground, were now fascinated to witness Krakow's great dexterity. For no sooner had he touched down on the leaves than he was disappearing through a small gap that had been well concealed by some broken twigs. Mars and Peeyu then hopped up on to the roots and likewise jumped down and into the hole through which Krakow had just gone.

As their eyes got used to the change of light they found they were standing in a surprisingly spacious area that was actually quite well lit from the sunlight which filtered in through a small number of tiny holes in the tree trunk that were handily positioned a little way above the level of the concealed entrance. Whilst they reorientated themselves, Krakow busily pushed some leaves and other debris back into the opening so as not to reveal their presence therein to any unwelcome passers-by. When he was satisfied that he had made a good job of disguising this secret retreat he then returned to speak to his visitors.

"You can't be too careful in this evil land," advised Krakow. "It is only because I have always managed to stay one hop ahead of the villainous crows and murderous marsh frogs, who I am sure you are aware inhabit this land, that I have survived here for so long."

Krakow indicated to his guests to take some rest. He then looked Peeyu up and down and said in a very confident tone of voice:

"Now, my friend, let me see. If I am not mistaken I would say that beneath that veneer of swampy covering there grow the beautiful feathers of a fine young kingfisher. Furthermore, and if my memory serves me well, that kingfisher is a direct descendant of the graceful Mylor, whose home, when I last met him, was in the bank of the river that flows through Seaxe up by Kingfisher's Bridge."

Mars looked on in amazement as the old bird spoke these words with such certainty. Peeyu was nodding excitedly.

"That's right! That's right!" cried Peeyu. "Please say again that you are Krakow."

All Krakow had to do to confirm this fact with Peeyu was to smile benignly and offer his extended wing for the young kingfisher to touch. Peeyu was satisfied at that moment that he was indeed in the presence of the legendary bird.

"Mylor is actually my grandfather and it was he who spoke of you as being the wisest and bravest creature in all of the rivers and forests that are known to us. He said it was from you that creatures sought wise counsel whether they were kings seeking guidance on matters of great importance or merely a poor sad frog who had fallen upon hard times. My grandfather said that notwithstanding a creature's status in their community you would always find time to spare in order to give them wise advice or assistance."

Peeyu then paused for a while before continuing to speak, the expression on his face reflecting his incredulity at the chance of meeting with this legendary bird.

"But it was thought that you had perished in the great storms that came out of the north and which destroyed much of our environment," said Peeyu. "No one has seen or heard from you since then although you are always in our minds as many wonderful stories are regularly told by elders to their eager and intrigued youngsters of your great deeds and adventures."

Krakow smiled at his guests and they felt both welcome and safe in the company of this revered and much loved bird. He could sense that their mission was very important and he was not about to tease them by not admitting that he was in fact the Krakow of whom Mylor had spoken. In any event he wanted to help these courageous creatures who had travelled far to be in this forbidden land.

"I am of course Krakow and if ever I have given sound advice or taught the young the virtues of life then I am very happy to have been of some value to my fellow creatures. I have often wondered if I was missed by those that I left behind on the other side of Waga in the friendly lands to the south, I guessed that they had probably considered me dead and lost, as were many poor creatures on that terrible and wild night."

Krakow sat for a while and closed his eyes. He was not sleeping but instead he was deep in thought. He allowed his mind to return to the night of the storm. The two friends looked on. They would not interrupt him as he pondered. They understandably felt in awe of this wise old blackbird and knew they were in the presence of a creature who possessed great learning and supreme knowledge. They really did feel secure for the first time since they had set forelimb and claw into the swamps of Waga.

After a short while the wise old blackbird slowly opened his eyes and looked across at Mars and Peeyu.

"It would be dangerous for any of us, and especially for the two of you, to venture outside at the moment. There is a great deal of activity going on in Tamsid and marsh frogs and crows are everywhere. As you know, of course, Emled the wicked king of the Tamsid community is soon to be leaving this evil place to take over the kingship of your community. I pity the poor creatures who are your friends and colleagues and I really do wonder at how the council of Seaxe could possibly have seen fit to appoint such a monster to be their king. My senses tell me that your visit here, and the stealth you have employed to journey this far, is not entirely unconnected to Emled's new appointment. I would guess that someone who is wiser than any of your councillors has felt it necessary to find out more about Seaxe's future leader. Could that someone be Moha by any chance?"

The two adventurers were again taken aback by the insight shown by this old blackbird. They marvelled at his wisdom and the ease with which he was able to describe their reason for travelling to Tamsid.

Mars spoke for the first time since entering Krakow's secret hide.

"May I please introduce myself? My name is Mars and I am a senior frog from the community of Seaxe. We are indeed honoured to make the acquaintance of such a great and wise bird as you. You seem able to so easily deduce our reason for being here in a way that suggests you actually anticipated our coming."

"Most things in life, my young friend, are controlled by destiny and by a spirit much greater than the combined spirits of all the creatures that live upon this earth. I simply allow my thoughts to develop quite naturally and try hard for them not to be cluttered by any bias that I may have. For, just like both of you and all other living creatures, I do have preferences and prejudices that attempt to influence my thinking and obscure my vision.

"I also do my best to cast out any temptation that may come my way, although, an occasions, this is a very difficult thing to do as such enticement is often dressed in a so called friendly disguise. It is therefore quite easy to be deceived by seemingly innocent offers of favour or reward only to find out later, and sometimes much later, that there was more to the offer than was initially apparent. Such seducers and deceivers must be recognised in order to prevent them from taking advantage. My own way of dealing with such eventualities, and the advice I give to those that request it, is simply not to expect or accept any personal gain or benefit whatsoever in return for anything that you may do. In this way I have lived my life, neither being beholden to anyone nor them to me.

"Therefore, having cleared my mind in such a way, I try to apply logic to a given situation and anticipate a creatures' actions or reactions by setting out a range of possible future options. Having created this framework I find that I can then work backwards and forwards in order to fathom out the reason why something has happened, which then helps me to estimate, with some degree of confidence, the probable outcome of similar scenarios in the future.

"If all that has given me the reputation of having greater wisdom and vision than my fellows then I would say that it is certainly something that thankfully I can pass on to others through my teaching.

"I must now say to you that it is decreed by nature's laws, together with the spirits of the rivers and forests that guide me, that it is to a frog that I must soon pass on my wisdom and knowledge. Although I have been aware for some time of the species of the creature it is not until today that I have been certain of the individual. In my earlier days I always thought that it would be Moha who would come to me for the Great Learning, but he has grown older and wiser in his own way, and he has developed into a very fine leader of his community and a magnificent example to his kind. The burden of taking over the mantle of great wisdom and knowledge from me would have unnecessarily diverted him from all of his good work. I have therefore held on to this responsibility for longer than was ideal so that it could be kept safe until the right inheritor came along. That is why I have spent so many seasons alone in this wilderness wherein I have been able to live quietly and anonymously. With everyone assuming me to have come to grief in the great storms it has not proved difficult to live in almost total obscurity.

"Now my instincts tell me that although Moha was sure of the task he required from both of you when he asked you to travel to the Far North, he was also strangely aware, albeit subconsciously, that fate had destined that you, Mars, were to find me for some greater purpose. My head, my heart and all the senses that I possess tell me, my dear young frog, that it is indeed to you that my wisdom and knowledge is to be passed." Here Krakow briefly paused before continuing. "My most immediate role, however, is to help you in any way I can in respect of the mission that brings you here. I must then ensure your safe return to Seaxe so that you may fulfil the task which Moha has set to enable you to take back vital news of this evil and malevolent Emled.

"When your current mission on behalf of Moha is completed, and you have safely passed on to him the information he requires, you will return to me for your teaching. My hope is that between now and then there will neither be too many lives lost nor the innocent minds of good birds and frogs tainted with the multitude of evil thoughts and inclinations towards bad vices that Emled so revels in encouraging.

"Much now depends on you, young Mars, although you were never aware that such would be your ultimate burden when you initially set out for this frogforsaken place only a day or so ago."

Needless to say Mars was absolutely stunned by this news and totally lost for words. Although be had heard the last few sentences spoken by Krakow the words were understandably just swimming around in his head. He was, however, aware that Peeyu had moved a little closer and Mars felt the warm bond of friendship that had grown between them strengthen even more as they stood before Krakow the Wise. With his friend by his side giving him support Mars fairly quickly recovered from the shock of Krakow's statement. Even though what the old blackbird had just said had not yet sunk in, Mars did feel able to give Krakow a detailed account of the purpose of their mission.

"The reason we have come so far and risked our lives to cross Waga is that Moha is certain that the coming of Emled to Seaxe will bring bad times upon our community. He therefore wants us to find out as much as we can about this frog king before he arrives."

"Your king is wise to do his homework on Emled. I do, however, pity your council for their lack of foresight in not taking more time to research this evil-doer more thoroughly before taking the decision to appoint him as your king," replied Krakow.

Mars then told of how Lebish had returned from Tamsid with tales of Emled's heroic deeds and how the council had been overwhelmed by his description of the greatness of this huge frog. Peeyu also told Krakow of how one of the favoured frogs for the kingship, namely Keba from Cabidge, had surprisingly not applied for the post, only later for it to have been reported that he was actually lost whilst on his way to Seaxe to register his wish to be considered. He also added that many a succulent grasshopper had been wagered on Truda from Somset being appointed Seaxe's next king, although much to almost every local frog's amazement he too was overlooked in favour of Emled.

Krakow shook his head slowly from side to side.

"How easy it is to deceive those whose wisdom is only superficial," said the old blackbird. "I suspect that Lebish is a weak soul and that he has been promised great things by Emled as his reward for recounting such a tale. Yet in one such as this Lebish, who is seemingly so easily swayed and in whom must lie a seed bed that is waiting to be fertilised by greed and perjury, I am surprised that such defects were not already known to your elders. I am certain that Moha at least would have been aware of these potentially dangerous shortcomings."

Before replying Mars openly sighed at the thought of Lebish's deception for personal gain.

"Moha indeed knows a great deal about each of his senior frogs. He did actually suspect that Lebish's story was a fabrication and that is one of the reasons he sent us on this mission. It now appears that it was most wise of him to have done so. I am not seeking to make excuses for our council, nor am I trying to be wise after the event, but I do think that they may have been very susceptible to being mislead in their eagerness to appoint a king who, on the basis of their admittedly scant information, appeared to offer credentials that at least rivalled if not surpassed those of Moha himself. For many years the councillors who selected Moha as our king have been held in high esteem by our community for their wise choice. The current councillors quite understandably want to have a similar distinction and in Emled they must have thought they had what appeared to be the ideal replacement for Moha. They were indeed quite clearly presented with a larger than life frog with apparently the most outstanding attributes."

"There are many things you need to know about Emled that you must take back to Moha," warned Krakow. "I must however advise you that what I am now about to say you will find shocking, and, if even only a small part of it had been known to your council prior to their first hearing from Emled, then they would most definitely not have appointed him as your next king. Unfortunately, however, a frog councillor will not lose face by admitting to such a great mistake so I fear that it will be up to you two along with Moha to do what you can to prevent Seaxe from becoming a mirror image of this sad and brutalised community of Tamsid.

"In order to fully appreciate the enormity of the evil that permeates through every sinew and every tissue of life in the Far North, it is necessary for me to recount to you the story of Emled's rise to prominence in this region." The expression on Krakow's face had visibly darkened as he considered what he was about to tell his visitors.

"Although what I am about to say will take quite a while to tell, you do in fact have sufficient time to sit and listen as it is far too dangerous for you to venture outside at the moment during the hours of daylight. Even though you have taken great care not to have been seen during your secret journey, I would not be surprised if your arrival has in fact been noticed and that as we speak Emled will be aware of your existence in Tamsid. Therefore, after I have told my story and you have listened carefully to my words, you must quickly leave this place just as the dusk begins to fall in order that you can return to your community by noon tomorrow."

Peeyu and Mars settled down and listened attentively to what Krakow had to say. The old blackbird, however, remained standing throughout the whole time he spoke, hopping to and fro and gesturing extravagantly by spreading and closing his wings as he expressed particularly fearful moments from the past. He told terrible tales of great cunning and malice perpetrated by the evil Emled; and of wicked deeds, the like of which on hearing, that would make even the most hardy of creatures feel rather faint.

The two friends heard how the coming of Emled to the Far North coincided with the arrival of the great storm. This occurred at a time when Krakow had actually been visiting friends in the area that is now known as Tamsid. He recalled that the first indication of bad weather was some brisk and squally gusts of wind that stirred the branches on the trees. This, however, was no signal for the scale of what was to come, as almost immediately the storm rose to a level of such violence that it had not given the creatures in the community thereabouts time to take sufficient cover, let alone to return to the supposed safety of their own homes.

Being so exposed a great many lives were lost within minutes of the storm breaking and hundreds and thousands of creatures were seen to be sucked up into the air as a terrifying whirlwind snaked its way angrily through the forest.

Krakow was visibly moved whilst he told of great trees crashing to the ground as wind and jagged forked lightning ripped through the community. He had personally been sheltering at the time with his friends in the lower and thicker branches of a massive and ancient horse chestnut tree when there care an almighty and simultaneous roar of thunder and flash of lightning overhead. All the birds on the branches were thrown this way and that as the once proud horse chestnut literally burst apart from the savagery and suddenness of the lightning strike which had torn into the top of the huge tree. Krakow had escaped with only burns on his head and back, which, incidentally, had caused his baldness. His friends, however, were not so lucky and all were killed by the explosion as the tree disintegrated into millions of blazing embers.

Krakow then explained that it was as the storm raged that Emled had first appeared. The old blackbird's expression became very sombre and his voice dropped to a whisper as he cast his mind back to that terrifying time. He told of how a large thatched farmhouse had also been hit directly by a flaming thunderbolt which had caused it to instantly be set ablaze. The thunderbolt itself had already caused substantial damage but the subsequent fire all but destroyed the building.

It appears that as the family who lived on the farm fled for their lives the farmhouse's great oak beams began collapsing all around them. In the chaos the children of the family hastily collected all kinds of pets that they had kept in the house but unfortunately, due to the intense heat of the flames, they were unable to save them all. One such pet that had to be left behind was an especially prized possession. It was in fact a huge cane toad.

When Krakow mentioned this species of toad he could see a puzzled look appear on the faces of his audience so he advised them that this creature is considered to be one of the most deadliest and evil of toads that is known to exist. However, as it comes from far distant and much warmer climes than ours, it is thankfully a great rarity in the lands that are known to us.

This abomination was thought by the family to have perished in the fire so they did not bother to give a warning that such a potentially dangerous creature was out in the wild. The old blackbird said that he understood that even humans are wary of the cane toad and when in its presence they fear for both their own safety as well as that of their young and their pets.

Krakow had been speaking for quite some time and he held Mars and Peeyu spellbound by his grisly account of those terrible times. He then decided to sit down very close by the two friends and they instinctively knew that what he was about to say next would be worse than anything they had already heard so far.

"Whether it was by a sheer fluke, or the timely intervention of the evil hand of fate, the cane toad actually survived," said Krakow. The two companions from Seaxe looked amazed as they wondered how on earth any living thing could have possibly lived through such a ferocious and tempestuous happening. He paused for what seemed like an age before continuing. It was then that he delivered the most devastating piece of news to his eager listeners.

"I must tell you that the creature of whom I speak, this abominable and evil cane toad, is none other of course than Emled himself."

*

The two friends gasped on hearing the news that Emled was not a frog but a toad – and not just any old toad either but one of the most deadliest of toads that have ever hopped upon this earth. From what they had heard so far, and what they were soon going to learn from Krakow, they would find that Emled was quite the most evil, insidious and wicked creature that they would ever have the misfortune to meet.

"How could such a creature become a king of a frog community if he is not a frog?" asked Peeyu.

"My friend, you will find out in time that Emled is never quite what one expects him to be," explained Krakow. "He is rather what 'he' wants to be. My feeling is that his wish to be a frog, something which he plainly is not of course, has caused his mind to become unbalanced. He is constantly fighting his natural instincts to be able to act just like a frog and not like a toad. He cannot even bear the thought of being regarded as a toad. For some reason he is intensely embarrassed by his species and considers it to be second rate when compared to frogs. In truth it must be said that he has an insane craving to be seen as a frog."

"But how do the frogs in Tamsid view him?" enquired Peeyu. "Surely they must know the difference between a frog and a toad?!"

"What you must know, and despite the glowing references that Lebish may have brought back with him to your community, is that Emled is hugely feared and deeply hated by the vast majority of those that he rules. Although he is thus despised by those that should love their leader, as is the way of the Seaxe community for your good king Moha, he should also be pitied for his confused state of mind. He is so big and powerful, however, that no creature would dare speak to him on a personal basis or try to discuss his problems with him directly. Anyway, he would probably kill anyone who attempted to converse with him in this way. This even includes the despicable duo of Gawk and Kaara, of whom you will very shortly hear a good deal more.

"What this has meant," continued the wise old blackbird, "is that those who work closely with him have had to assume similar tendencies to his own in order to survive in his evil regime. In particular his senior frogs, and those others who hold important positions in Tamsid, have therefore had to become evil and cunning just like their master. You will especially see this in the creatures I have just referred to, namely, Gawk the crow leader; and Kaara, who is Emled's highest ranked warrior marsh frog."

Mars and Peeyu could see a great concern in the eyes of Krakow and the intensity of the way he described Emled's brand of evil sent shivers running up and down their backs. The old bird rested a short while before continuing.

"For those frogs who live within the Tamsid community their lives are dull and totally controlled either directly or indirectly by Emled. He has effectively brainwashed his community into following him and adopting his policies by introducing a fear factor into more or less every element of Tamsid life. Their mortal dread of becoming noticed or standing out from the masses has caused individuals in the community to become introverted and unwilling to act creatively in any way. Paradoxically it is actually this anxiety which has been instilled into them by Emled and his cronies that has caused the wicked toad to despise the very frogs he rules. For on the one forelimb he wants his frogs to be more interested in developing their skills and ideas, but on the other forelimb if they show signs of such personal initiative then he gets jealous and sees them as a threat to his own position. Many decent and well meaning frogs have disappeared as a result of their attempt at self improvement during Emled's reign of terror.

"There is however one particular trait in Emled that is possibly the most frightening aspect of all." Krakow lowered his voice at this point almost to a whisper and the two friends could see the pain and anguish in the blackbird's face as he thought of what he was about to tell them. They wondered what on all the river banks and forests it could be that worried him so. They didn't have long to wait as Krakow began telling them quite the most startling and indeed dreadful tale they could possibly ever wish to hear.

"I will come straight to the point although I know that you will find what I am now going to say absolutely unbelievable... It is that Emled actually meets with humans and appears comfortable in their company!"

If the two Seaxe friends had already been shocked by what they had heard so far then they were totally flabbergasted by this latest statement from Krakow. To creatures such as frogs and birds (and also generally speaking toads as well) the mere thought of mixing voluntarily with humans would be considered to be a total anathema. In fact there could not be a worse fate for a creature who lives free in the wild than for it to be in the hands of, or imprisoned in cages by, humans. Indeed the curse of curses that one creature could possibly wish upon another is for it to be trapped by humans and held for the rest of its life in captivity. Thankfully such a poisonous curse is very rarely issued, as it is believed that not only does it work upon the recipient but a painful end will also await the one who delivers this profane oath.

Peeyu and Mars were, therefore, not surprisingly left open-mouthed and incredulous on hearing this contemptible news. Seeing their amazement and disbelief that such a thing could be possible Krakow wondered momentarily if the two friends were up to learning more at this time about the evil toad. However, he decided that they should hear the real truth if they were ever going to be prepared to confront Emled head on, as he knew that one day they would surely have to do. Krakow felt that they should know their enemy and know him well. He therefore continued with his description of Emled's encounters with the humans.

"I have observed him on many occasions when he has left his palace at night and he has travelled far away from the sight of his community. I have followed him as he bounded over the land and through the forest until he reached and entered into the full glare of the grounds of brightly lit houses where no other right-minded creature would dare to be seen. I have watched him as he then sat in the lamplight croaking loudly until he succeeded in attracting the attention of the humans who would come outside and make all sorts of strange affectionate sounding noises to him. Emled is then happy to take food directly from the hands of the humans. He even further demeans himself by standing up on his hindlimbs, as tall as he can, as if actually begging for the scraps of meat which the humans dangle just out of reach and above his head."

Mars and Peeyu shuddered at the thought of the toad accepting food from the humans and lowering himself to the level of some domesticated creature.

"Is Emled not attacked by the animals who live with the humans?" enquired Peeyu. "Surely a cat or a dog would torment a toad in much the same way as they would harm a frog or an injured bird."

"Normally that would be so but you must not forget that Emled is no ordinary toad. Firstly he is very large and this can present an intimidating prospect to a cat or a dog. Secondly, and more importantly, he can excrete a poisonous thick white fluid via glands in his body that has a potentially devastating effect on any animal that comes into contact with it. I have on occasions seen the effect of this defence system and witnessed poor creatures suffering a slow and excruciatingly painful death, even from collecting just a tiny trace of this obnoxious substance upon their skin.

"This being so, animals who recognise the wicked toad tend to give him a very wide berth indeed and therefore do not venture within range of his poison. This of course means that he enjoys an almost guaranteed safe and trouble free existence and gives him the opportunity to stuff himself full of the food normally given to the human's pets. Thus the humans feed him and their animals leave him well alone."

As Krakow told his story it was becoming more and more easy for Mars and Peeyu to understand that it was by fear that Emled ruled his community. They too were beginning to feel very anxious at the prospect of ever meeting this evil creature.

"I'm afraid that you still haven't heard the worst," Krakow continued to speak softly as he carefully chose the words he used in order to accurately reflect his feelings. "What I shall now tell you is quite the most horrible tale you are ever likely to hear. Please believe me when I say that it is all true, for you will need to be aware of the scale of horror of which this abominable toad is capable when he comes to rule in Seaxe."

Mars and Peeyu again looked at each other, and, not for the first time that afternoon, braced themselves for whatever was to come.

What they then listened to was Krakow describing quite the most despicable act they had ever heard. It was so terrible that they could not have thought any creature to have been capable of such a thing. In fact the story Krakow told was way beyond their imaginations.

"The first time I encountered this evil it was quite by chance," began the wise old blackbird. "Some little time before it occurred I had been listening to two marsh frogs who happened to be chatting just outside this very tree trunk. They were talking excitedly about a new venture of Emled's which the toad had termed his 'Young Frogs Initiative'. It appeared that Emled was going to take a group of a thousand or so young frogs out on an expedition to teach them how to fend for themselves when away from the community. You must be aware that this was in the very early days of Emled's reign and so there was understandably a great deal of eager anticipation about such a new and interesting sounding scheme.

"Well, I was as keen as any creature to see what this so called 'Young Frogs Initiative' was all about. So, when it was arranged for the large group of young frogs to set out, I decided to follow. I did so of course from a safe distance, flying from tree to tree, and being extremely careful not to be spotted from above or below. You see, that with the notable exception of his night time excursions to rendezvous with the humans, which are always performed in secret and on his own, Emled hardly ever goes anywhere without being accompanied by an entourage of his leading and most villainous marsh frogs and sly carrion crows. Their job is to ensure the safety of their master and to give an early warning of any potential danger.

"As I hopped to and fro I noticed that some way ahead of the group several humans had seemingly concealed themselves in the undergrowth by the side of the path along which Emled and the young frogs were proceeding. I couldn't make out why the black crows who were circling overhead, or the vanguard of marsh frogs who were positioned some way in advance of the main group, were not giving warning of the very dangerous situation into which they were walking. Despite their cruel and malignant nature, marsh frogs and crows are no different to our friendly everyday frogs in that they would always avoid bumping into humans if at all possible. Nevertheless Emled appeared to be leading his group of juniors right into trouble and strangely, even though the crows at least must have spotted the humans, no warning signal was being given by the guards."

Mars and Peeyu were absorbed by what they were hearing and they wondered just what it was that Krakow was going to say next. Krakow continued.

"Emled and the young in his charge kept on hopping along the path getting ever closer to the place where the humans were hiding. I could see clearly by then that the humans were definitely lying in wait and I wanted to swoop down on them so that in the commotion they would surely reveal themselves to Emled and company who would then see the danger and flee for their lives. However, I just couldn't believe what I was seeing and for some reason I was frozen to the branch on which I was standing.

"The most amazing and frightening thing then happened. When the junior frogs came to the point where the humans were hiding, Emled suddenly, and without notice, leapt forward and left the group of youngsters stranded. The adult marsh frogs who had been patrolling to the front, sides and rear of the group also very quickly simultaneously dispersed and hopped away with their king. As the young frogs huddled together in their fear of being left all alone in an unfamiliar place, and totally unprotected by their elders, the humans jumped out from behind the bushes and cast a thin net over them. None of the poor young things escaped the trap, being transfixed as they were by their fear.

"Whilst their captors gathered them up, all that the young frogs could hear were the mocking sounds of the carrion crows who cawed raucously and loudly as they danced about high up in the surrounding trees clearly happy with what had just taken place.

"To imagine Emled had done such a thing on purpose seemed totally outrageous and I did hear that on his return to Tamsid he had made a great show of grieving the loss of such 'wonderful young marsh frogs'. He also gave a very plausible story of how they had been caught unawares by humans and that it was only due to his own strength and that of the adult marsh frogs that enabled the elders to make their escape. He openly wept as he said he so much regretted not being able to save the 'brave young things'.

"Emled then actually took the opportunity of this devastating event to point out to the community of Tamsid the importance of pursuing his 'initiatives' as how else would the young learn about the wicked ways of the outside world. He advised that the acquisition of such knowledge may help them to avoid such disasters in the future. He therefore promised to immediately organise more of his 'Young Frogs Initiatives' and that he intended to make them available to even greater numbers of the younger generation.

"Something inside my body caused me to feel uneasy about the situation and I felt I needed to be sure that what I had witnessed was in fact an unfortunate catastrophe and not some macabre pre-planned trap to ensnare the young frogs for some evil purpose. I therefore made a point thereafter of following his various 'initiatives' when he had arranged to lead the young of Tamsid out on some expedition or other. I have to say that on many more occasions further substantial losses were suffered and each time a different reason was given by Emled as to why the young frogs had not returned home with him. I have heard him tell of attacks by huge flocks of birds and even of one occasion when he had said the whole group of youngsters had fallen into a deep ravine which had all of a sudden opened up in the ground and then closed again swallowing them as if it were some monstrous beast from the bowels of the earth. The strange thing is that the real reason for the young frogs' disappearance was always the same, for it was the humans with their nets who actually took them away."

Peeyu and Mars were bewildered as to why such a thing should happen. They knew, as did all frogs, that humans do sometimes try and catch tadpoles in their small nets but this is on such a very small scale as to not be considered in itself a big threat to the future of their species. However, the explanation, when it came for this mass abduction of young frogs, sickened them to the centre of their hearts.

"I know you will probably be wondering why the humans attack and capture the young frogs. On the surface there doesn't appear to be any reason for doing this as frogs do not cause the humans any harm nor do they feed on plants or vegetation that the humans need for their own purposes. In fact, apart from the use of the small nets and the occasional capture of tadpoles and young frogs to be kept as pets, humans are not really considered to be a major problem. Some have even been known to spend a great deal of time watching and apparently studying the development of the frog species without doing them any harm whatsoever.

"The truth of the matter behind this large scale ambushing of the young Tamsid frogs is that the humans now regard the legs of these poor unfortunate creatures as something of a delicacy. They are therefore captured in order to satisfy the greedy bellies of the humans.

So, by taking the young of Tamsid straight into danger, it appears that Emled is in some sinister way in allegiance with the humans and that he is thereby assisting in the gross massacre of countless thousands of innocent young frogs."

The heads of Peeyu and Mars were spinning with this news. Their own legs felt like jelly and they were indeed feeling quite faint.

"Surely the population of Tamsid is being wiped out by his tyranny?" questioned Mars.

"You certainly would imagine that the number of young frogs in Tamsid would have been drastically reduced by these acts of gross barbarism but strangely the contrary is true. This is due to the fact that Emled has placed great importance on the development of young frogs. He has, not surprisingly, said that they must continue to be produced in ever increasing numbers as they are the lifeblood of Tamsid and that the prosperity for all the community depends upon them. This has resulted in an unprecedented rise in the amount of eggs being laid in the spawning season.

"The reality is, of course, that the production of more and more young frogs does not actually improve the prosperity of the community – it merely serves to inflate the belly of the evil monster Emled, who is rewarded for his collusion with enormous quantities of food fed directly from the hands of the humans. Hence the greater the number of young frogs born to the Tamsid community – the greater is the sacrifice offered to the humans by Emled – and of course the greater is the size of the evil toad's belly.

"He is, without doubt, quite the most callous and wicked creature ever to have set foot upon this earth. That he is shortly due to leave Tamsid is of course of some relief to this community, although it must be said that the leading marsh frogs and crows he will presumably leave behind are no better than he is. That his destination is Seaxe, however, is quite the worst possible news for you and your community and you must therefore return safely and give an appropriate warning to Moha. You will probably not stop him being crowned as your king but at least you will be aware of his evil ways, and, who knows, in time you may find the strength to deal with him permanently and rid us all of this malevolent creature."

Peeyu and Mars both felt physically and mentally drained by Krakow's story. They knew, however, that it was imperative that they should return quickly to Seaxe and give prior warning of what was to come. Despite their fatigue they began to prepare themselves for their long and potentially hazardous journey home.

"Mars, my young friend," began Krakow as he laid his outstretched wing upon the handsome frog's shoulder. "Once you have imparted all this fearful news to Moha you must return to me for the 'Great Learning of the Supreme Qualities of Wisdom and Knowledge'. You must understand the importance of successfully carrying out this process as it is on you and Moha, but particularly upon your young shoulders, that the future salvation of all frogs and all the other creatures of the river banks and forests depend.

*

Outside the great oak tree in which Krakow, Mars and Peeyu were secluded, the large figure of a toad slipped silently away into the long shadows cast by the late afternoon sun. The massive creature had heard all he needed to hear of the conversation that had taken place therein.

As fate would have it, a little earlier that day a common crow passing high up in the sky had spotted the two friends as they followed Krakow to the oak tree hide-out. The crow had decided to take this information directly to Emled in the hope that some special reward might be given in return for such a brilliant observation. This was quite typical of the culture that Emled had encouraged whereby to go behind the backs of, or to bypass altogether, one's more senior colleagues was considered to be a worthy thing to do. It was thought to be even better if the result of such action reflected poorly upon that individual's senior and indicated that the latter should have known better.

Emled had listened to the crow and he had been intrigued to hear about the unusual liaison that appeared to have taken place between an old and decrepit bald headed blackbird (as the crow had described Krakow); a kingfisher caked in mud; and a frog who was certainly a stranger to Tamsid. The crow clearly hadn't been bright enough to put two and two together and hadn't recognised the possibility of the blackbird actually being Krakow. Emled was that shrewd, of course, and he immediately made the connection that what the crow had seen may possibly have been the legendary and wise old blackbird.

Like many others in the Far North Emled had heard tales of the existence of such a bird, although in keeping with popular opinion he assumed Krakow to have perished, if ever he actually existed in the first place, during the great storm. The fact that he may still be alive and living right here in Tamsid made Emled both excited and extremely worried. He was worried because the appearance of this bird presented a very real potential threat to his plans to become an all powerful and great frog king. However, he was at the same time excited by the prospect of extracting Krakow's legendary powers of wisdom and knowledge and grabbing these supreme qualities for his own devious and corrupt purposes.

Emled had thanked the crow for being the bearer of what he considered to be moderately useful news that may or may not be of some value at a later date. There was no way that the cunning toad was going to acknowledge to the crow, who knew no better anyway, that he may have stumbled upon the legendary holder of great wisdom and knowledge. He therefore informed the crow that although the information was not as valuable as its purveyor had at first thought he would nevertheless be rewarded with a gift that reflected Emled's deep felt thanks. He then sent the crow away with a perfunctory gesture of thanks and a promise that his surprise gift would not be long in coming. In the meantime Emled told the crow that he must not impart a word of what he had seen to any other living creature.

As soon as the luckless crow had left Emled's palace the toad summoned Gawk. Emled then wasted no time at all in telling the crow leader of a problem that he had recently come across in the lower ranks of the bird's army.

"Gawk, I have some rather bad news for you. It appears you have a traitor in your ranks," said Emled. He then proceeded to tell Gawk that the crow whom he had just a short while before thanked for his news was actually the most deceitful and despicable creature he had ever had the misfortune to meet. Emled told Gawk that the bird had come to him telling tales about Gawk himself saying how he had seen the crow leader stealing provisions that were destined for Emled.

Although this wasn't of course the information that the crow had passed on to Emled, the evil toad was nevertheless well aware that Gawk did in fact make it his regular business to procure provisions in this manner. He had known about Gawk's thieving ways for a long time, but, rather than deal with it there and then, he had always felt that such information might be more usefully employed at some later stage. That moment had now arrived and for Gawk to hear from the fearful toad that one of his crows actually had the nerve to blab about his devious activities caused him to rock back on his claws. Gawk was quite certain that to be caught cheating on Emled in this way would mean a sentence of death for him, irrespective of his being an important cog in the toad's evil wheel.

"Y.. y... you surely don't believe the w... w... word of such a worthless piece of rotten flesh, O Master?" said Gawk, as he cringed in front of the massive toad.

"Such a thought never crossed my mind," lied Emled. "Your loyalty, my friend, is without question of course." Emled could see the crow's relief on hearing his hollow words of support. "I do however think that you should deal swiftly with such insubordination," he further advised.

Gawk accordingly took his leave of Emled and later that same afternoon he followed the aforementioned luckless crow as the latter made his way home to his nest. Gawk saw his ideal opportunity to 'deal' with the bird when it stopped and rested in the branches of a tall pine tree. Under the cover of the thick green foliage Gawk flew silently up from behind the bird and delivered a fatal blow with his beak to the side of the unfortunate crow's head. The bird was instantly dead and he only fell a little way before his lifeless body became entangled in the pine's web of branches. Along with the death of the bird, of course, went the knowledge of the existence of Krakow. This conveniently left Emled as the only one in the Far North who was aware that the legendary blackbird was not only still alive but that he was actually living on the outskirts of the Tamsid community.

Armed with the knowledge that the crow had passed on, and confident that Gawk would quickly and efficiently dispose of the wretched creature, Emled had slipped out of his palace soon after Gawk had taken his leave and quickly made his way to the area where the crow had said he had spotted the three strangers. The directions the crow had given Emled were very accurate and it therefore did not take the inquisitive toad long to pick up the scent of two of the trio, namely Mars and Peeyu. He could, however, trace neither a scent nor a sign of a blackbird, for Krakow had perfected the art of automatically covering his tracks.

Notwithstanding the absence of Krakow's own scent he followed those left behind by the other two strangers. Moving swiftly, and with surprising stealth for such a large creature, Emled arrived silently at the concealed entrance which was located in the foot of the old oak tree through which Krakow had taken Mars and Peeyu. Here he stopped and eavesdropped on the conversation therein. What he heard convinced him that if he was indeed to become the ruler of all frogs and creatures of the river banks and forests far and wide, then it was he who would have to acquire the 'Great Learning of the Supreme Qualities of Wisdom and Knowledge' that was currently possessed by Krakow. What's more he had to do so before the wise old blackbird passed them on to this upstart of a frog called Mars, who, coincidentally it appeared, came from the very same community where he himself was soon to be taking over as king.

Mars was indeed now potentially the wicked toad's greatest threat, both in his new kingdom of Seaxe and to his future plans to become the conqueror of all he surveyed.

Chapter Thirteen

Home Again

After hearing what Krakow had to say there was no reason for Peeyu and Mars to remain in Tamsid a moment longer. It was now far more important for them to relay to Moha what they had heard from the wise old blackbird as soon as possible. Of course quite how this information would be received and ultimately used back in Seaxe was something of which they were not yet clear.

By the time Krakow finished telling his story and had provided a nourishing meal for his visitors the first signs of dusk were approaching. The autumn sun had dropped down beyond the distant horizon although the western night sky remained bright and clear. As was the case in the Far North as soon as the final traces of direct heat from the sun disappear, so the thick mist rolled in from the foul smelling swamps of Waga. Very soon only the brightest of stars in the cloud free sky could be seen as they tried to penetrate the gloom. And then, almost before you could count up to ten, so those bright stars too were also eliminated from view.

Under cover of the thickening mist Krakow carefully escorted his friends to the Far North border of Waga and he wished them well for a safe journey back to Seaxe. From there Peeyu and Mars followed a similar path to the one that had brought them across the rancid swamp. Having a better knowledge of the evil that lay within Waga made the two companions even more vigilant and they took the utmost care to avoid being seen from the prying eyes that they knew were all around and above them.

They were much relieved when finally, having crossed Waga without incident, the trees of Horse Chestnut Wood came into view. They knew then that they only had a few hours left of their homeward journey to complete. After the bleakness of the landscape they had so recently left behind in the Far North the familiar sight of Seaxe, with the autumn colours of the forest and hedgerows bathed in the early morning sunshine, really gladdened their hearts. The thought of protecting their peaceful and beautiful community somehow seemed even more vital than before. They therefore picked up their pace and headed straight for Moha's chamber to pass on to him the news they had learned from Krakow the Wise.

When the two friends entered Seaxe there appeared to be a great deal of activity and frogs were busily chattering to each other. A young friend of Mars saw him and hopped quickly across to where the two companions were standing.

"Mars, you must hurry to the Boathouse," said his friend very excitedly. "Emled is there and he is meeting with all the seniors this morning. You should also be there right now."

Mars was understandably surprised, as firstly, he was quite unaware of Emled's intention to hold such a meeting; and secondly, as far as he knew, like him the toad had been in Tamsid only the evening before.

"Do you know why he is here?" Mars politely asked his friend.

The young frog was shocked by Mars' reply as he had assumed that his senior would have been well aware of Emled's arrival and the purpose of his visit.

"Do you mean to say that you didn't know that he was coming?" the young frog asked.

"I'm sure I would have remembered such an important event. Maybe there has been an oversight somewhere along the line or the meeting may only have been arranged at the last minute. I have actually been away from Seaxe for the past couple of days on community business so I was probably otherwise engaged when the information about the meeting came through."

The young frog nodded and instantly put the thought that Mars may have been intentionally overlooked out of his mind. He smiled at Mars and said he was pleased to have been of assistance. When he was safely out of the hearing of the two friends Peeyu turned to Mars and whispered very softly.

"Something smells about Emled being here! What's he up to, I wonder? We need to find out, but first of all we ought to go and see Moha to give him our news. After that you must go and see what is occurring in the Boathouse."

On that note Peeyu and Mars made their way swiftly to Moha's chamber. Moha was visibly greatly relieved to see his good friends.

"My dear friends. How good it is to see you both again… safe and sound, I trust? I was so worried that something terrible might have happened to you… are you both well? Tell me about your journey? By the way have you heard that Emled is here in Seaxe right at this very moment?"

Moha's questions came out in a rush, so worried had he been for his two friends' safe keeping and so pleased he was that they were now standing before him. He could see that they were in a good state of health although they were certainly fatigued from their exertions of the past couple of days. They were also understandably rather muddy and grimy although this somehow added to the excitement of the adventurers' return.

"I do know that Emled is here," said Mars resignedly, "although I quite literally heard only a few moments ago. I gather he is in the Boathouse with our senior colleagues. I know that I should go there straight away but I do have so much to tell you that is more important and it really cannot wait."

Moha beckoned to his two brave friends to follow him. He then led them to a quiet and secluded place deep within his chamber where it was impossible for any ears to listen in on their conversation. Once there, and having made themselves comfortable, Mars and Peeyu proceeded to tell the loveable old bullfrog about Krakow plus all that the wise old bird had told them about Emled and the tyranny the evil monster ran in Tamsid.

Moha did not interrupt Mars or Peeyu whilst they told their story. Apart from a great many gasps, sighs and sharp intakes of breath, Moha stayed silent until Mars indicated that they had told the king all they knew. When they stopped talking Moha sank back on his hindlimbs. The anxiety that he had harboured for so long and that he had felt had its origins in the Far North, although he had not understood quite why that should be so, was now fast becoming clear to him.

"He has already begun to bring his evil and cunning to our community," said Moha grimly. "You will know about his attempts to undermine those frogs in senior positions by encouraging their subordinates to give their views on how they feel their whole area of responsibility could be better run. This would generally speaking not be a bad thing to do if it were not for the fact that he does it in such a way as to encourage the subordinates to tell mischievous tales about their more senior colleagues. The sad thing is that whilst Emled is systematically destroying any respect that our junior frogs may have held for their seniors, these subordinate frogs think that they are gaining the evil toad's goodwill and support.

"Emled started this ploy a few weeks ago and now the seniors are hopping around like mad things trying to over-compensate for any of their misgivings that may have been made known to Emled by their subordinates. It makes me cringe to see our senior colleagues fawning like this and acting in such a shallow way towards the frogs for whom they are responsible.

"Do you know out of all your senior compatriots only Kejon has spoken to me since Emled's appointment as Seaxe's future king. However, even he found it hard to express his true feelings although I could see that he did not like what Emled was doing. I could also sense that he was too frightened for his position to do anything about it. Kejon is a tough frog and, from what you have told me about Emled, I hope his toughness does not prove to be his downfall in the face of this evil toad."

The two frogs and the kingfisher sat in silence for a little while. They were comfortable in each other's company and they quietly reflected at their ease on all that had occurred. Moha was the first to speak again.

"Emled gave me no warning of his intention to visit our community today. He arrived quite unexpectedly and he has not even had the courtesy to come and tell me that he is here, I guess that was done on purpose in order to begin to undermine me in a similar fashion to the way he has already undermined Kejon and the other seniors."

"The main difference," replied Mars, "is that after he formally takes over as the king of Seaxe he can expect to have no further communication with you, whereas with the seniors, he will need to work with them until either he or they resign their positions or even eventually die."

"What about you, Mars," asked Moha, "I can't believe that Emled arrived without knowing that you were not here. His insidious crows have been everywhere and into everything since he was appointed. They have quite literally had their nosey beaks into all of our business.

They would surely have told him that you were out of the community at this time. As far as I know he has certainly not made a fuss of being unable to find you nor has he shown any wish to have you at his meeting with the other seniors. It's almost as if he knew you wouldn't be here. Do you think he could have seen you in Tamsid?"

"That's a possibility of course," said Mars. "Although we did keep ourselves under cover almost all of the time we were away. Surely Emled would have had his marsh frogs or crows attack us, or at least capture us, if he had been aware that we were in the Far North. It would be unlikely that he would have run the risk of allowing us to return with the sort of information that we have just passed on to you. After all we have told you of enough of his evil doing to discredit a boat load of wicked toads?"

"Now that I know what I do about Emled I wouldn't put any form of behaviour beyond this cunning toad," warned Moha. "Come on, Mars, I think it is high time you gave the king-in-waiting a big surprise by presenting yourself at the Boathouse. You may then find out a little more about why this meeting has been arranged. For some reason I have a sneaking suspicion that he doesn't expect you to be there."

With these encouraging words from his king, and with a profound sense of purpose, Mars hurried along to the Boathouse. He hopped along the river bank as far as Lower Bridge and from there he swam across to the small building where the meeting was taking place.

From outside the Boathouse Mars could hear the voices of his senior colleagues, although he could not make out what was being said. He waited for a while before going into the meeting and during this time not once did he hear anyone other than his senior colleagues speaking. Mars wondered if he had missed Emled and he very much hoped that the evil toad had not already left the meeting and started on his journey back to the Far North.

All heads turned as Mars entered the Boathouse. To Mars' delight Emled was there. Or at least Mars assumed that the hideous beast who slouched before 'the six' seniors was in fact the wicked toad.

The look on Emled's ugly face was a sight to behold. At first he had looked genuinely astonished to see Mars but the handsome young senior was sure he very soon detected an expression of anger and, for some reason he thought, hatred on the face of the toad. However, just as quickly as these emotions appeared so the demeanour of the monstrous toad reverted back to a fairly blank expression as he regained his composure.

Mars' senior colleagues were also amazed to see him although not in the same way as Emled nor for the same reason. It appeared that Emled had told them that Mars might be along a little later although he had added that it was more probable that he would not make it at all.

The emotion that was most noticeable on the faces of his fellow seniors, however, was that of acute embarrassment. Mars' arrival had clearly caused them to feel awkward and he wondered if what they had been saying to Emled was something they would rather not say in front of him.

Mars turned to face Emled and looked him straight in the eyes. This was of course the first time he had actually seen the toad, who now dragged himself up slowly and laboriously from his sitting position and rose to his full height. He was indeed an awesome figure and Mars felt strangely intimidated and threatened by the toad's massive frame. As he stared up at the face of Emled, Mars wondered how it was that any frog could have mistaken this huge and ugly toad for one of their own species.

After a moment or two, although it seemed like an age to Mars, the handsome young frog averted his gaze and quickly cast his eyes over the body of Emled. The toad really was so unlike any frog in their community or anywhere else for that matter. He had a very dry skin that appeared to be covered in unsightly warts, and his colouring was strangely lifeless being a dull mixture of brown, swampy green and a lacklustre red. In addition to being a great deal larger than any frog that Mars had ever seen, he noticed how Emled's body was hugely out of proportion to his hindlimbs and forelimbs, all of which appeared to be much too short for a creature of his size. Compared to the toad's massive torso his arms and legs looked peculiarly stunted. This strange and ugly combination made his overall appearance even more abominable and sinister.

Mars again raised his eyes and stared straight back into those of Emled and the young frog instantly sensed the menace that lay within this grotesque beast.

As far as Emled was concerned he had never met another creature who either dared to, or for that matter could bear to, hold his gaze. Mars, however, did this much too well for his liking and seemingly without fear. Although inwardly admiring the young frog for his courage he felt strangely unnerved by Mars' apparent strength and spirit.

It must be said that Mars found the presence of this monster, who was so different from those over whom the toad sought to reign, a totally bizarre situation. In his own mind there could be absolutely no mistaking Emled for a frog. Yet it appears, however, that this diabolical toad had somehow deceived not only the frog community of Tamsid into believing he was one of their own species but he had also tragically succeeded in doing the same to the Anurian Council of Seaxe.

"Please accept my apologies for not being here when you arrived in Seaxe," said Mars to the toad. "I have actually been away from the community for a couple of days on private business for Moha. I hope that you were not too inconvenienced by not being able to find me."

Emled appeared to Mars to accept this statement as the toad merely flicked a forelimb in casual acknowledgement of Mars' explanation. The toad knew full well of course where Mars had been and so he had no need to enquire as to the nature of his 'private business' for Moha. Emled also felt quite confident that his credit in the eyes of the other six seniors would be enhanced by his apparent coolness in not needing to check just what this business had been about. It did, however, rather indicate to Mars of course that Moha's view was accurate and the toad probably did know of his own and Peeyu's presence in Tamsid the day before. If the initial expression on Emled's face was anything to go by then he had clearly not expected them to return so quickly – or maybe at all for that matter!

"Take a seat among your colleagues. You will soon pick up on the conversation. I really don't have enough time to repeat the discussion so far." Emled spoke softly in an accent that was very different to that of the Seaxe frogs. Mars shivered at the sound of his voice and he wondered if the same tone had been used by the evil toad when sending the many thousands of young Tamsid frogs to their certain death at the hands of the humans.

Emled motioned to Chrich to continue with the discussion that had been in progress prior to Mars' arrival.

"And lastly you, Chrich. What can you tell us about your experiences in this community? Are you happy with the way things are or do you feel that some change is required?"

Chrich turned towards each of his senior colleagues, with the exception of Mars, as if looking desperately for strength and support from them. He didn't find it, however, as one by one they each dropped their eyes or averted their gaze, purposely not wanting to catch his attention. Chrich suddenly felt very alone. Everything had gone swimmingly up until then and all he had wanted to do was endorse what the others had said before him. Now this nuisance Mars had arrived and, unfortunately, speaking out about his own experiences and thoughts had become a different matter altogether. However, although Chrich was in advancing years he was still an old campaigner and he knew that he must say what he had intended to say despite the embarrassment it would cause him now that Mars was in attendance. He stammered badly over the first few words but then he got underway. As he spoke he chose to look in the direction of Emled although he was focusing on any part of the toad's body rather than directly into his eyes.

"I... I... I really d... d... do also think that Moha has f... f... failed all of us here and indeed f... failed our whole community," began Chrich hesitatingly. "He has avoided taking action on issues that all of us in the senior frog group feel should have been positively dealt with long ago."

Chrich was now gaining confidence as several murmurs of support came from Geelan, Lebish and Brylil.

"We have asked him any number of times to address many issues that require change and improvement but such appeals have all been to no avail. On countless occasions we have asked Moha to..."

And so the tired old frog continued. He went on and on about what he felt Moha had not done but never once did he specify quite what he meant in detail. Not once, for instance, did he give an example of what he alluded to nor did he attempt to clarify what he meant. It was all purely rhetoric aimed at reducing Moha's standing and credibility as king whilst obviously simultaneously trying to say things that he knew Emled wanted to hear. It was quite clear to Mars that from what Chrich was saying he was only echoing what the others had already said.

'The six' senior frogs sat in a semicircle facing in towards the vast bulk of Emled who had positioned himself a little way removed from this group and just outside what would have been a completed circle. Even though he sat back on his hindlimbs in a lazy sideways slouch his body mass was none the less intimidating. Chrich was at one end of the senior's semicircle and Mars correctly deduced that they had taken it in turn to talk and that the old frog had been the last of them to be asked to speak on the subject of Moha's past work in the community.

Mars' frustration with Chrich did not go unnoticed by Emled who had been looking out of the corner of his eyes at the young frog whilst Chrich had been rambling on. Mars had sat down next to Kejon on the far side of the semicircle to Chrich.

"Now then Mars, I would be very interested to hear what you have to say. You will probably have picked up on the general feeling of your colleagues. You may of course wish to say nothing at this stage seeing that you have only just arrived. I would quite understand if you decided to remain silent." This last sentence came as something of a threat and all those present sensed that Emled actually wanted Mars to say nothing and that he was in fact daring Mars to speak.

Mars was close enough to Emled to catch a waft of the foul smelling breath that came from the mouth of the rank toad. His head swam a little as he tried not to breathe in for a moment or two in order to avoid the stench. When he was sure that the smell had drifted away he turned his gaze from Emled and looked directly towards his six colleagues. His initial comments were, however, directed at Chrich.

"Thank you, Emled, for offering me the opportunity to speak," said Mars. "And yes I do have something I wish to say."

Mars could see by the way his colleagues were shuffling about that they were very uncomfortable that by choosing to speak he was clearly going against the wishes of Emled. They also anticipated that he would give a contrary view to the one that they had just corporately espoused.

"How can you say the things I have just heard?" began Mars. "You owe everything you have to Moha. In fact all of us here and all of our friends and colleagues owe Moha a great debt of gratitude for the love he has given us and the trust and faith he has invested in the community throughout his time as our king. He has been a very fine leader and it is hard to believe that there is any other frog who could possibly take his place or emulate his greatness."

Mars then looked back again at Emled. He was aware that his comments were likely to be considered as anti the toad so he thought he had better ameliorate his views somewhat – at least for the time being!

"I do not mean to be disrespectful to you, Emled, but it is my honest belief that it will be a major challenge for any creature to follow Moha and be successful as our king. Even the mightiest of contenders for his crown will find it a monumental task. And despite what you may have heard today in this Boathouse from my colleagues I guarantee that you will hear only praise and reverence from the community of Seaxe at large."

Showing respect to the evil toad made the words stick a little in Mars' throat. However, it was too early to try and explain to his colleagues just what kind of devil creature they had in front of them. Mars knew that the time was not yet right to make such a declaration as the mood of his erstwhile colleagues was seemingly one of support for Emled at the moment.

Something else Mars had noticed when he had been speaking was the way that Emled had himself shifted about uncomfortably when he had said the words "...for any creature to follow Moha..." Mars wondered if Emled had sensed that he had realised he was not a frog but that he was in fact a toad. Mars was thus conscious of the fact that he now had to tread extremely carefully as he knew that Emled would stop at nothing to keep secret his true identity. Mars again looked towards Chrich.

"You, more than any of us here, know just how much Moha has given our community. You have been his friend for many years, maybe even his closest friend. Just think a little about what you have just said." Mars then pointed with his right forelimb in a wave, first at Chrich and then sweepingly at the others.

"Each of you, with the exception of Lebish, has been personally appointed by Moha. He has cared for you and nurtured you throughout your rise to the status of senior frogs. He has encouraged you to be good frogs and to take care of those for whom you are responsible. He has borne the criticism on his own shoulders when you have not performed adequately and he has been happy for you to take the plaudits when things have gone well. That any of you should now see fit to slander his name and reputation is unforgivable."

Emled rose up from his lolling position. "You seem to see things so very differently from your colleagues, Mars. All I have done is to ask each of the seniors what they think of the way the community has operated and have they any suggestions for making things better. I could not anticipate how they were going to answer. However, it does appear to me that they have honestly expressed their opinions and, interestingly, they have all said the same thing, which is that Moha has largely been ineffective and negative and that he doesn't listen to what others have to say. I must say that I really do find it quite fascinating that all this is quite contrary to the way you have seen Moha's style of management. Why do you think that is so?"

"My view of what I have just heard from Chrich, and what I assume the others have also similarly said, is that it is utter rubbish!" Mars was by now becoming extremely angry. Trying very hard to keep his cool he turned to his senior colleagues and said to them. "Come on, if you are so keen to run Moha down, let's hear of some actual examples of his bad management! Let's put some flesh on the bones because all that I have heard from Chrich so far is a whole load of generalisations that relate to nothing in reality and appear to be spoken only for Emled's benefit."

There was a gasp from Geelan and then silence. Not surprisingly none of the seniors volunteered an example. Mars watched them as they all anxiously squirmed and wriggled, being, as they were, quite unable to look either Mars or Emled in the face. For one moment it looked as if Lebish was about to say something, but then Mars (and only Mars) noticed Emled flash his eyes at the fat frog and give a barely imperceptible warning shake of his head which indicated that Emled did not want him to speak. The sly senior immediately slunk back on his hindlimbs, said nothing, and averted his gaze to the ground.

Sensing an unwelcome tension in the atmosphere that he felt could prove detrimental to his plans to discredit Moha, Emled hurriedly interrupted the embarrassing silence. "I personally don't think it is important to give examples. It is much more relevant and meaningful to say how you feel."

"Quite right! Quite right! Well said, Emled!" squeaked Geelan, whose presence in the Boathouse at a meeting of this level seemed even more out of place than ever before.

Emled was clearly irritated by Geelan's noisy intervention and he gave the over-excited frog a most threatening glare as he slowly turned his head to face the short stout senior. The glare then became something of a cross between a grin and a grimace as Emled realised the level of fear that his initial look had instilled in Geelan. A fear in fact that was also experienced by all of those who sat in the Boathouse. A fear that would be indelibly printed upon the minds and memories of each of the seniors.

"Thank you, Geelan. Thank you for your support. It really is very much appreciated." Emled lied through his foul mouth as what he would have preferred to do was stamp upon this bothersome squat-bodied frog.

All the seniors, and Geelan in particular, felt their inner emotions quickly change from downright fear to a feeling of relief. None of them, except Mars, of course, who knew a great deal more than they did about the toad's evil ways, quite understood why they had been so frightened by Emled's menacing expression. They therefore put the thought to the back of their minds for the moment, as Emled's current demeanour had become almost friendly again towards Geelan whom he now openly and roundly thanked for his noisy support.

If each of 'the six' seniors had been asked there and then to explain their initial feeling of fear, they would have been hard pressed to give an accurate answer. They would probably only have been able to say that they had been extremely frightened for some reason or another. They would certainly have said that they felt strangely intimidated by Emled, but whether this had anything to do with his size; his odd shape and colouring; his dry warty skin; or indeed just the menacing glare he had given Geelan when he unintentionally let his thin veil of friendship and goodwill to all frogs slip momentarily, they just couldn't be sure. It would not be long, however, before each of the seniors experienced the same fear again and on many occasions thereafter. They would then look back on that fateful day in the Boathouse and wonder why they had not read more into that exchange of glances between Emled and Geelan. They would indeed wonder at how they allowed themselves to ignore the obvious malice that had even then lain within their evil king-in-waiting.

Emled felt that the time was now right for him to summarise the discussion. He certainly didn't want to give Mars any more of an opportunity to gather support for Moha after he had so successfully instilled in each of the other 'six' seniors a strong sense of feeling against the good old king. He also sensed that Mars knew rather more than he should about his own style of leadership back in Tamsid and, although he felt confident that the young frog would not be able to convince the council of Seaxe that they had made a mistake by appointing him as their king, he desperately wanted to prevent Mars from saying anything that might tarnish his seemingly unblemished record.

Emled considered that on the whole his strategy was working out quite well. He knew that Moha had been much loved by his community and that he could never legitimately match the qualities that the old bullfrog possessed. He had therefore devised a plan whereby he would seek to pollute as many of Moha's qualities as he could and in such a way that the frogs of Seaxe, with the benefit of corrupted hindsight, would reverse their high opinion of their once great and much vaunted king.

His debate with the seniors in the Boathouse had been very much aimed at Moha's ability to make the right decision, particularly when the subject under discussion at the time had actually been beyond the powers of 'the six' senior frogs to come to a collective agreement. On so many occasions in the past Moha had sat and listened to a babble of confused chatter from his senior frogs on what line to take in order to deal with a certain situation. Moha had always encouraged discussion and debate during which he tried to pass on his own very clear thinking to his colleagues. Unfortunately these discussions very often ended with Moha having to make a decision on behalf of the group whereas he would have much preferred the seniors themselves to have achieved a clear and satisfactory consensus. Such was the nature of 'the six' senior frogs, however, that sadly they were never able to reach agreement collectively on important business matters.

Now Emled was attempting to utilise 'the six' senior frogs' shortcomings to his own advantage, and, by portraying in their minds Moha's genuine attempts to help his colleagues reach positive and collective decisions as being acts of almost tyrannical proportions, he sought to undermine the excellent work of the good old king. He wanted these naive seniors to believe that Moha was not actually trying to help them but that he was really being manipulative under a disguise of kindness. The unfortunate thing was that Emled appeared to be succeeding in his devious ploy.

"I want to thank all of you for being so open and honest," said Emled. His face almost expressionless, save for a faint trace of disdain for those who sat in front of him that went entirely unnoticed by the senior frogs. "I want to thank you in particular for saying to me how you feel about the way you have worked with Moha and what you really thought of his leadership. It has taken great courage for you to be able to speak to me in such a way and I am grateful for your trust.

"I feel so sorry for all of you having to endure what must have been a most difficult and suppressive regime," As he spoke Emled looked at each of the seniors in turn but carefully avoided any direct eye contact with Mars. "I sense that you found it impossible to express your true feelings to Moha. What I want you to understand, however, is that with me you can come and freely voice your concerns. I shall encourage all frogs within the community to bring their problems out into the open, even though for others such revelations may be uncomfortable. So please, in future meetings of this kind, say what you feel, and, if you disagree with either me or your colleagues, then speak up so that we can openly and critically discuss all options before we corporately arrive at a decision. I want, and indeed shall insist upon, open and honest governance at all times. In fact I want you all to feel empowered in a way you may never have experienced before."

Mars watched his senior colleagues as they puffed up their chests in self congratulation. They were clearly happy with regard to the way the meeting in the Boathouse with Emled had gone. It was evident that the seniors had considered the opportunity to bad-mouth Moha and enthusiastically depreciate his good points in front of Emled as a means by which they could get into the evil toad's good books; or so they thought. Emled had encouraged them to talk in this way and they had risen both willingly and obligingly to the bait.

If only 'the six' had known then how their actions were actually viewed by Emled. Although he was evil and bad in almost every way imaginable, he genuinely despised weakness of character and deceit in others; even, perversely, when it worked to his own advantage. In the way he had so easily exploited 'the six' he could see both these traits demonstrated very clearly in each of them.

Then there was Mars. What was Emled to make of him? On the one forelimb he admired Mars for the stance he had taken against his colleagues but, on the other, he knew that the threat he posed to his wicked plans must be extinguished before too long. What a shame, he thought, that Mars' qualities could not be re-focused to his personal advantage and utilised in order to further his evil strategy.

"I shall now call this meeting to a close as I have urgent business that requires my attention back in Tamsid. We shall meet together again in two weeks' time when I formally take over from your present king." On that note the massive toad hauled himself up and left the Boathouse, barely acknowledging the seniors as he took his leave. Geelan, not unexpectedly, was being excruciatingly humble by his fawning of their future leader. As Emled passed by he caught a glimpse of Geelan bowing and scraping as if in divine reverence of him. For a moment the evil toad considered again the pleasure he would derive by stamping on this sickening and miserable tadpole of a frog.

Emled exited from the Boathouse and made his way along the river bank before heading north through Horse Chestnut Wood. As he did so it was evident that a substantial number of large brown frogs and huge black crows began appearing from out of the undergrowth, or from high up in the trees, and followed in his wake. It was extremely rare for Emled to travel alone and his murderous entourage were as usual accompanying him on this excursion. They both protected and spied for their evil leader and in addition reported anything which they considered might be of some use to him for a future purpose.

One thing that had come to the attention of an especially sharp-eyed marsh frog, whilst he was keeping watch on the Boathouse from his position concealed within a thick clump of reeds by the far river bank, was that just as Mars had arrived at the meeting he spotted the unmistakable bright green and blue flashes of a kingfisher as it darted to and fro along the river. He was most interested to see the bird alight on the roof of the Boathouse and then quickly disappear under the eaves where it had remained for the duration of the meeting. The marsh frog had informed Gawk who made a point of personally following the kingfisher when it finally flew off from its secret perch a moment or two before Emled himself had departed.

Gawk tracked the small bird as it deftly skimmed the ripples on the gently flowing river. The beautiful bird was totally unaware that it was being followed, so, as was usual, he made his way back to Moha's chamber to report on the events that had taken place at the meeting. Gawk of course reported this news to Emled on their arrival back in the Far North. Emled wondered to himself if the kingfisher could be the same bird that had recently been in Tamsid with Krakow and Mars.

"It sounds to me as if we have a spy in our camp," said Emled. "I think there is really only one solution to such a problem - don't you?" He then looked at the crow leader and Gawk could see the malice in his eyes. He instinctively knew what was coming. "Gawk, I want you to eliminate this troublesome bird! I want him dead by the time I arrive in Seaxe to take up my official duties in two weeks' time!"

Such instructions were a joy to the ears of Gawk. There really was nothing that he liked better than to carry out Emled's most murderous orders.

"I shall personally deal with the arrangements, my Master. Consider the job done!" he replied with a grin almost as menacing as Emled's.

Chapter Fourteen

The King is Dead – Long Live the King

It was now the day before Emled was due to arrive and take over as king of Seaxe and great celebrations had been arranged to mark the end of Moha's reign.

There could be no greater love for a leader than that shown to Moha by the everyday frogs of Seaxe. He was indeed quite overcome with emotion by the numerous expressions of gratitude and good wishes for the future that he received from his fellow creatures. Despite their sadness they were determined that they were going to give him a splendid send-off and do their best to make Moha's last day as king of Seaxe a happy one that would be remembered for all time.

Whilst frogs sang and danced upon the lily pads and river banks; and birds whistled merrily in the trees of Horse Chestnut Wood, Moha moved amongst his loving community thanking all the creatures therein for their past friendship and support.

The day was planned to end with the council, who would be represented by Lilgree on this occasion, formally thanking Moha on behalf of the whole community. Unbeknown to the old king, Lilgree was going to present him with a special gift which was to be awarded in honour of his reign and as a measure of the esteem in which he had been held.

Moha had never been one to court grand occasions and he had always been rather shy of accepting accolades for his achievements. He regarded it as more than sufficient reward to see his frogs happy with their lot. He needed neither favour nor personal tribute as an acknowledgement of the benefits he had heaped on his community during his many years at the helm.

It was therefore with some embarrassment, as the sun was setting on the river banks of Seaxe, that he stood before his community listening to Lilgree speak of his many wise decisions and the lasting glory and peace he had brought to their community. It was with even greater humility that he accepted the kind gift of a most beautiful lily pad that Lilgree said would always be his to sit upon for as long as he lived whenever he visited Seaxe. Everyone said that they sincerely hoped that such occasions would be many and that he would in fact return to see them as soon as possible.

Moha's acceptance of Lilgree's kind words and of the community's wonderful gift was typically modest. He said he would indeed return some day to Seaxe and that he was sure that when he did so he would find great enjoyment in sitting upon his lily pad. Moha added that on such occasions he very much hoped that all his friends would come along and join him in doing what frogs most love to do, which is to have a jolly good chat and swap wonderful stories in the warmth of the late afternoon sunshine.

As Moha bade his frogs farewell the cheering, croaking and general stamping of hindfeet upon the earth was quite deafening. It had indeed been a send-off that would stay in the minds of the loveable old king and his adoring friends in Seaxe forever.

*

Moha was to start out on his journey to his native Somset that evening and it was with great sadness and mixed feelings that he stood for the last time at the entrance of his home preparing to go on his way. Mars appeared at his king's side also looking sad, and, Moha thought, a little forlorn.

"Come now, my friend," Moha spoke softly and in a soothing tone. "It really is time for me to leave this place and move on to make way for a new era. I can't continue as king forever and it is only right that I step down at some time to enable a younger king to take over. Just you be sure to remember the wise words of Krakow."

Mars looked into the eyes of Moha and found inspiration in their great depth of wisdom.

"I am so sad that you are leaving," said Mars. "I am sad for our community and I am sad for me. I know that it is wrong to feel this way for myself but I can't help the emotions that are churning up inside my body."

"You will cope, my friend," assured Moha. "We both know that the immediate future will bring troubled times to our community and that it is upon your broad shoulders that the burden for caring for our friends and colleagues will fall. Although your task will be immense, and there will for sure be moments when you will wonder if the road ahead is too formidable, you must never weaken or allow yourself to doubt your ability even in the face of the greatest of adversities. You have the strength to succeed and, providing you don't weaken, you will succeed."

"There seem to be so many obstacles and such a great evil in front of us that will surely prove more powerful than me. Can I really tackle such opposition on my own?" asked Mars.

"You will find that goodness will always eventually overcome badness no matter how high the odds may be stacked against such a victory or how troubled the waters that run in the river through our community. You may, in time, feel all alone in this world, but the good that you exude will attract others of like mind and body who will gather around you, thereby enabling you to combine your strength and their support to overcome even the greatest of evil." Moha spoke these words most passionately and with such great belief in his young friend that Mars suddenly felt a surge of inner strength well up inside his body. He knew, of course, that it would be difficult to maintain such a feeling as there would always be some self-doubt. He would nevertheless have to consider such negative thoughts as cautionary only and regard them as reminders that he should take even greater care to make good and accurate decisions. He knew that he must remain positive at all times and he was ready to accept the challenges that lay ahead.

The shadows cast by the harbingers of evil were there for Mars to see. The well of goodness that was within and throughout his community was deep, although it was understandably naive and largely unaware of the powers of evil. At the moment what lay between these two extremes was Mars' main concern. Where, for instance, did the other senior frogs want to operate, and did they themselves appreciate the difference between good and evil? For they, like the rest of the community, had only ever experienced the powers of goodness and the benefit of peace during Moha's reign. They unfortunately knew nothing of the other and darker side of life, except what they had heard when they were young in stories of the Far North.

The two close friends sat perfectly still for a while both contemplating the gravity of the situation that the community of Seaxe now faced. The old bullfrog instinctively knew that it was not he who was destined to lead the good frogs of Seaxe and, for all he was aware, possibly all the other communities south of the frogforsaken swamps of Waga, against the evil that was about to descend upon them. What he did know, however, was that despite his youth that responsibility was to be carried by Mars. As they shared each other's company, for what was to be the last time for many a long day, the old king felt strangely in awe of his young companion. He was indeed proud to be standing by his side.

"Do you know, Mars, my dearest and trusted friend, that not one of our senior colleagues has come to wish me farewell. Along with all the fond memories that I will cherish of my beloved community, that sad fact will stay with me for ever."

*

In the way that Moha preferred, and especially after all the formal celebrations that had been arranged for him, the old king said his final goodbye to Mars quietly and in private. He then made his way briskly down to the island's edge from where he entered the water and swam strongly across to the main river bank. Moha looked back just once and raised his right forelimb to Mars. As he did so he briefly wondered when he would next return to Seaxe. He then turned away and hopped off in a south-westerly direction towards Somset.

*

Moha also wondered where Peeyu had got to as his kingfisher friend had said that he would accompany him for the first part of his journey. The old king hoped that all was well with his feathered friend as he knew that only a matter of great importance would have prevented his joining him in order to say farewell personally.

"Must be some problem or other with the family," thought Moha. "I'll send him word of my safe arrival when I reach Somset."

With that thought on his mind the kindly old giant bullfrog continued on his way to Somset and back home to his roots.

Chapter Fifteen

Emled the King – The Dawn of a Dark Era

After the magnificent occasion and the festivities that marked the end of Moha's reign as king of Seaxe, the arrival of Emled was what could best be described as a much more sober affair.

It was difficult to say what was the greatest cause of the depressed atmosphere that hung over Seaxe on Emled's first day as king. Whether it was the inevitable sadness and considerable sense of loss that was felt by the community in respect of Moha leaving, or if it was the fact that Emled asked for no special fuss to be made as he took up his new position, no frog could really be sure. It must be said, however, that the arrival of the new king was rather an anti-climatic affair and not the type of joyous occasion one would normally expect to mark such an important event in the life of a frog community.

There were two things that were particularly noticed by the good frogs of Seaxe on that first fateful day of Emled's reign. Firstly, the sheer size and appearance of Emled came as a huge shock to all those who had not seen him before. Apart from the seniors, and of course the members of the Anurian Council who had appointed him, only a very few others had actually even managed to get a brief glimpse of their new king on his two previous visits to Seaxe. On those occasions, both when he came for his interview and when he arranged the surprise meeting in the Boathouse, he had made a point of having as little contact as possible with the local everyday frogs. Of course in all the excitement, and with frogs loving to expand upon stories and be extravagant with reality, the community's expectation of Emled was of a well-built, muscular and handsome frog who would be an ideal replacement for Moha.

What of course the frogs of Seaxe now saw in their midst, however, was a massive creature with quite the most ugly features they had ever set their eyes upon. They saw a leader who was unquestionably covered in the unsightliest of warts and whose skin was both dry and extremely dull in colour. They saw something that vaguely resembled a frog but whose limbs were totally out of proportion to the rest of its body. They in fact saw in Emled a creature that was quite unlike themselves and they wondered just how such a being could ever have been appointed as their king. It was also said, by those who had ventured too close to the new king, that he gave off quite the most awful odour that they had ever had the misfortune to breathe in through their noses.

The second thing that the frogs of Seaxe noticed was the sudden influx of a great many new frogs. These frogs were in fact a good deal larger than the locals and their colouring was a particularly dismal brown. The early rumours were that these were marsh frogs and that it was understood that Emled had considered it to be a good idea to introduce these individuals from Tamsid into the Seaxe community. He had apparently said that it was in order to enable the locals to come into contact with other cultures and thus broaden their own horizons.

Emled had also been reported to have said that he thought it would be an excellent idea if some of the local frogs could do an exchange with the Tamsid frogs and go and live in the Far North for a while. He was certain, he added, that when the frogs of Seaxe saw the wonderful life he had created for the inhabitants of Tamsid it would enable them to see how their own lives and well-being could be greatly improved.

However, as time went on, the integration of Tamsid frogs soon proved to be not so straightforward and a number of unfair practices were seen to be introduced into the Seaxe community. For instance, it appeared that the Tamsid frogs were being given preference on accommodation plus they were also being allocated supplies of food that were far superior to those being made available to the locals. It was also evident that Emled was creating a number of highly desirable new jobs that were on the face of it being offered to all the community, but, very suspiciously, the only frogs successful in acquiring these positions were those frogs who came from Tamsid.

Emled described this latter issue as a most strange occurrence and quite coincidental. In his view only the right frog for a job would be appointed. In fact he made a great show of saying that he would personally never discriminate between one frog and another whether it be on the grounds of their place of origin; if they were young or old; or even on the basis of whether they were male or female.

It must be said, however, that at the end of the day whatever criticism one may have aimed at Emled for what certainly appeared to the local frogs to be a very prejudicial employment policy, it was certainly not possible to accuse the evil toad of inconsistency. This was because when it came to deciding who got the jobs it was Emled alone who had the final say an such matters. The good frogs of Seaxe were soon to learn that when it came to taking important decisions their new king neither sought nor welcomed advice, and, although he would publicly say that he wished to hear what the community wanted, he always found such comments to be a great source of irritation unless of course they were in complete accord with his own way of thinking.

The aforementioned new posts that Emled created were at a level just below that of the current seniors. In fact for each of the seniors a new post of 'Adviser to the Senior Frog with Responsibility for... (followed by the full title of each senior)' was now set up and immediately occupied – by a Tamsid marsh frog of course!

The Tamsid frogs were also very much more aggressive in their general attitude towards others and it soon became blatantly clear to the Seaxe frogs that it was not really a good idea to cross such a frog or even vaguely suggest they stop doing something that may be causing annoyance, such as their persistent bullying which was a common feature of the marsh frogs' behaviour. In fact during the first two weeks of Emled's reign a number of the local frogs had been cuffed around the head by the much larger marsh frogs for no reason at all. On most such occasions the local frog would just hop off as quickly as he or she could and rub their bruises some safe distance away. However, for those who had stood up to their more powerful aggressors, a far worse fate awaited and several young frogs had already been maimed or killed in such skirmishes with their Tamsid neighbours.

When any of these occurrences were reported to Emled he would simply let out a heavy sigh and say how he wished the two cultures could co-exist happily. He would then go on to say that he was nonetheless certain the experiment was worthwhile giving his assurance that in the long term the community would benefit, although the harmonious bonding of the two quite different groups of frogs may yet take a little time.

As for the senior frogs their initial euphoria was beginning to wane somewhat. They had originally seen in Emled, or so they thought, an opportunity to make their own decisions. It was an unfortunate fact but 'the six' seniors really did live under the misapprehension that they had not been given sufficient freedom to act under Moha. The truth was that on their own they were individually not sufficiently able to cope with important matters or make assessments of tricky situations. Moha, however, had a great ability to give all of the seniors their head in discussions and then he would take their best suggestions when coming to a decision. To have ever expected a consensus to be reached by 'the six' without such guidance would have been quite unrealistic. With Moha's careful nurturing, therefore, they did as a group produce many good ideas and he had been sure that in time they would develop into a useful and corporate team.

It really was most unfortunate that each of 'the six' had such an inflated opinion of themselves as this had always prevented them from being good team players. Emled, of course, had been sufficiently aware to immediately spot this weakness and was keen to exploit it for his own benefit.

Despite their initial hopes, and quite contrary to what they had originally been given to believe, it was fast becoming clear to the seniors that not only was Emled personally determining policy and practice in the community but their own contributions were being almost totally ignored. They were also getting increasingly suspicious of the activities of their new 'Advisers'. However, when any suggestion was made that all was not well with their 'Advisers', Emled was always very quick to remind them that one of the issues they had initially raised with him that they had said was a big problem under Moha was that they had never been given enough high level workers to achieve the sort of targets they had been set in their respective strategies. Emled said he was therefore so pleased to be able to create the new posts of 'Adviser' which he trusted must be the answer to their prayers.

Although at first 'the six' were overjoyed that their wishes had apparently been granted, and they initially had thought that Emled was much more aware and sympathetic to their needs than Moha had been, the complexion on this matter was rapidly changing.

Unbeknown to 'the six' the introduction of the 'Advisers, was something that would have happened anyway, for Emled was keen to ensure that he knew at all times what was occurring in the community. He also wanted to make certain that none of the seniors... 'took it upon themselves to take matters into their own hands and start making awkward personal decisions'. The creation of the 'Advisers', therefore, was an ideal ploy to satisfy his concerns and keep control of such matters. On the one forelimb he would be seen to be apparently satisfying the wishes of the seniors whilst more sinisterly, on the other forelimb, he was actually installing his marsh frog lieutenants into the higher echelons of the Seaxe management as his personal spies.

It was also now becoming evident to the seniors that not only was Emled not confiding in them on important issues on which they felt they should be making an effective contribution, but the devious toad was seemingly bypassing them altogether and operating directly through their marsh frog 'Advisers'.

*

Four weeks after Emled's arrival he suddenly announced his second formal meeting of the seniors. There had been no advance notice and each of the seniors had been simultaneously told by their 'Advisers' late that morning that they must present themselves at the Boathouse at noon. You will recall that at the first such meeting that had taken place, some two weeks prior to Emled commencing his new duties, it had been agreed that this second meeting should have occurred on his first day as king of Seaxe. Unfortunately, and due to his "many commitments" on that day, he had decided to cancel the meeting. He then explained that as he had to spend some time "getting to know his way around" in order to "meet his new friends in the community", the next meeting would take place later during that first week. Four weeks had in fact gone by, and many important decisions had been made personally by him, before he actually bothered to call the next meeting.

This delay had caused 'the six' senior frogs a good deal of anxiety but they felt powerless to do anything about it. They were greatly frustrated by Emled's lack of urgency for them to meet together.

The Boathouse had again been arranged as the venue because Emled felt that as they were used to meeting there they should continue to do so for the time being. That was to say at least until he had found somewhere more appropriate and suitable. In much the same way that he openly criticised any former action and decision taken by Moha, or any arrangement made in respect of the community's policy and practice, he had made it quite clear publicly that the Boathouse really would not do for such important occasions. He had therefore promised the seniors that he would personally organise something better.

By speaking in this way he had of course completely ruled out any possibility of a corporate decision being taken on this matter that may have included some suggestions by his senior colleagues. This was a method of decision-making that the seniors were going to find practised more and more in the future.

If the truth were revealed then the seniors would have known that all Emled had said about improving their meeting facilities was a lot of meaningless hot air – and foul smelling air at that! He had in fact so far not given the matter a moment's thought and he intended wasting none of his time on the issue in the future either, "That useless bunch of no-hopers can make do with what they have got," he had said to Kaara. "I've got much bigger and more profitable items on my agenda to which I must attend before I can be bothered about their personal comforts."

'The six' seniors therefore had to make last minute changes to their arrangements for that day in order to be able to assemble on time in the Boathouse, albeit with significantly less excitement and anticipation than had been the case at their first meeting with Emled. Had that really been only six weeks ago? It seemed like a lifetime! In the heavily subdued atmosphere only Lebish was showing any signs of optimism and he chattered away cheerfully as the seniors awaited the arrival of their new king. Unbeknown of course to the others, Lebish had his own dark reasons for thinking that the future under Emled was going to be juicy grasshoppers and cosy lily pads all the way.

As 'the six' seniors shuffled about nervously, the appointed time for the meeting to start passed by and still Emled had not arrived.

They were already rather anxious as they did not know what issues were even going to be raised or discussed at the meeting. They had previously been used to suggesting items to Moha prior to the regular high level management meetings taking place and the old king would ensure that all such matters of concern or interest were given a fair hearing. When later such a process was mentioned to Emled he simply dismissed it with an extravagant wave of his forelimb and he said that he did not intend to do business in that way. They began to sense that with Emled, and despite his so called 'open' approach, things were going to be very different in Seaxe from now on.

'The six' seniors therefore waited, suspended as they were in a high state of concerned anticipation, not knowing what to expect from their leader.

Finally, and about two hours late, Emled arrived. Behind him, and much to the surprise of the seniors, came their marsh frog 'Advisers'. Emled then placed himself in front of 'the six' seniors who sat before him in a semicircle. The 'Advisers' took up positions directly behind their respective senior.

The seniors were clearly thrown off balance by the presence of the 'Advisers'. In Moha's time these high-level meetings had been primarily for the king and his senior frogs. It was only after discussion and agreement that others had been invited to attend. They therefore looked anxiously behind themselves, as well as at each other, before turning to face the monstrous figure of Emled who had sat down very heavily and was now sprawled out in front of them.

Not one of 'the six' seniors felt able to question Emled about the inclusion of the marsh frog 'Advisers' at their meeting. They were all, however, greatly and visibly agitated by their presence; a fact that the evil toad noticed and found most amusing. Indeed it was with some degree of difficulty that he managed to conceal his pleasure and satisfaction at causing them so much discomfort. He accordingly thought that he shouldn't allow the moment to pass without making some comment or other.

"I can see that you are all a little... shall we say surprised at my asking your 'Advisers' to attend this meeting," said Emled.

The seniors all nodded, somewhat relieved that their concern had at least been acknowledged by the king.

"As you know it is my view that the management of this community has in the past been far too secretive and that the voices of the ordinary frogs of Seaxe have not been heard," continued Emled. "I therefore feel that by encouraging a wider cross-section of the community to attend these meetings on a regular basis it will serve to demonstrate my commitment to changing the bad practices of the previous administration."

A noisy and raucous babble of support erupted from behind the seniors. "Quite right!" said one of the marsh frog 'Advisers'.

"Too true!" said another.

"Something must certainly be done about it!" piped a third who sat immediately behind Brylil.

It must be said that the seniors didn't know which way to turn or what they should say. The mere presence of their 'Advisers' had already caught them off guard. That their 'Advisers' should now be so vociferously showing their support for statements made by Emled, and in an environment from which they would normally be excluded (unless formally invited of course), greatly added to their mounting discomfort.

"Well, what do you think?" Emled looked impassively at the seniors. "Do you consider openness to be a good idea? I want the whole of our community to feel they have a part to play in our community's future. No frog is to be denied the opportunity to have his or her say!"

Quite honestly the seniors didn't know what to think. If the truth were known the only feelings they possessed at that moment in time were those associated with being threatened and intimidated. For in front of them the vast bulk of Emled seemed to have grown even larger and more imposing; and behind them the hot breath on their backs and the unmistakable smell of rotting vegetation in their nostrils signified the nearness of the marsh frogs. All this only served to heighten their anxiety.

Lebish was the first to speak.

"You are of course quite right in what you say. Our decision-making has for far too long been confined to only the king and the seniors, and, very often, only to Moha himself. We have, as you correctly say, not listened to the community and we have consequently lost touch with them. Why only the other day..."

"Thank you, Lebish!" Emled had cut him short. He had heard more than enough gossip from Lebish recently to last him a lifetime. However, aware of the effect that his abruptness had on Lebish, and noticing that the pot-bellied senior had been left open-mouthed by his interjection, Emled added, "...and thank you for such a helpful contribution. Yes, that really was very helpful indeed."

Lebish closed his mouth and puffed up his chest. He tried to look proud to have received a compliment from the foul king, although in truth it was more relief than pride that was coursing through the veins of the churlish senior.

It appeared that none of the other seniors was going to make a contribution. They were all as confused as each other as to just what was going on and they had all been totally wrong-footed by the attendance of their 'Advisers'. This of course suited Emled very well indeed. He neither welcomed opposition to his views nor for that matter did he wish to entertain any suggestions, particularly when they did not accord with his own way of thinking. Feeling rather pleased with himself, and confident that he had taken the wind out of the sails of the seniors, he was just about to continue with his brow-beating of the Seaxe 'six' when Kejon decided to speak.

The stubborn senior had been getting angrier and angrier as he sat watching and listening to the antics and rhetoric of the evil toad. He hadn't liked anything that he had seen or heard so far and he certainly did not enjoy what he considered to be an intentional intimidatory tactic employed by Emled to post his despicable marsh frogs right behind the seniors. His temper had finally reached boiling point and he just had to let off steam.

"I really must comment on what appears to me to be happening to the way we, or should I say you, are managing our community!" Kejon's tone was fierce and his manner heated and excited. He breathed in deeply and continued. "I have personally tried very hard over the past couple of weeks to speak to you about important matters affecting my area of responsibility. However, not only am I physically prevented by your 'personal aides' from seeing you, but I am told by these thugs that your advice is that I should discuss such issues with my 'Adviser' because you do not want to be bothered with trivia!"

"But, Kejon," interrupted Emled. "You know that I am always available both to you and to every other frog in the community. I want you all to understand and realise that I believe in being accessible to all my frogs and at all times of the night and day. I sincerely want to hear what individuals in my community have to say. Surely you know by now that I support openness in everything that we do." Emled spoke in a most sickeningly patronising manner that only served to infuriate the angry Kejon.

"Well that's not the way I see it!" retorted Kejon very sharply. "That's not the way I see it at all!"

At this point Kejon's senior colleagues were pitched somewhere between downright fear and being frightened beyond their imaginations. They had never seen Kejon so full of rage and they found themselves cowering low upon the ground as if trying to duck under the thickening and increasingly tense atmosphere. They wondered and feared for whatever may be coming next as Kejon continued to voice his disapproval.

"It seems quite obvious to me that we, the seniors, are being excluded from important matters and from making decisions which might in any way influence the future of our community," shouted Kejon in a very loud voice. "Why is it, as I have already said, that I am being told to speak to my supposed 'Adviser' on matters that are really more appropriate for you and I together with our senior colleagues to discuss and determine. I want to know what role do you now see for us? What for instance is our place in your future plans? And just what function do you anticipate will be performed by our so called 'Advisers'.

"That really is a lot of questions, Kejon," replied Emled. "I wonder how I can answer them all to your satisfaction."

The toad was clearly peeved by Kejon's ebullient intervention. He had neither planned for, nor had he anticipated, that any of the seniors would query his motives. Even less had he expected any one of them to have the gall, or indeed gumption, to take such an aggressive stance against him. In his own mind Emled had considered that even if the seniors had felt moved to flag up a contrary view then the mere presence of the 'Advisers' would instantly quell such thoughts from actually being put forward.

"I'll be satisfied if you can tell me just what it is you stand for and what role you have in mind for us seniors. In addition, if you could set out for us your vision of the future for our community then I am sure we could then work out how it is that we may best support you."

The other five seniors were now finding it quite impossible to cope with this confrontation. Indeed they were so affected by the intensity of the situation that they could neither speak nor move. Not one of them possessed the fire and aggression of Kejon and they knew that he was not given to backing down even in the most difficult of circumstances. With this in mind, and sensing the enormity of Emled's indignation, they fully expected a catastrophic ending to this challenge by their stubborn but brave colleague.

"All right! ...Okay!" retorted Emled. The toad was now finding it even harder to keep his temper under control. For two tadpoles he would have jumped upon Kejon and crushed the life out of him under his own bodyweight. It had also not gone unnoticed by any of the seniors that as Kejon had stood up in order to make his points more forcefully, so the 'Adviser' directly behind him had likewise risen at the same time. This was not done in support of his senior, however. It was actually done as part of the protective barrier that constantly surrounded the toad, for each and every marsh frog is trained from a very early age to defend their master from any aggressor. That Emled could have personally dealt with Kejon if he had attacked the king there was absolutely no doubt of course. Nevertheless it was the natural instinct of a marsh frog to react in this way, as Kejon, in this thunderous mood, appeared to pose a threat to the massive toad.

"You really will find it impossible to be constructive if you allow yourself to be provoked in such a way when in all honesty there is very little about which you need to get excited," continued Emled, seemingly getting himself under some semblance of control although inwardly he felt like slaughtering Kejon. "Now let me see if I can deal with your questions in a manner becoming adult frogs so that I may help you to understand a little better how I want this community to operate in the future."

Kejon could sense Emled's air of condescension. He was also aware of the movement behind him and that his 'Adviser' was now standing up. In fact the marsh frog was standing so close that Kejon could literally feel the hot breath of the loathsome creature upon his neck. Whilst he did not rule out the possibility of an attack from this marsh frog, he did hope that surely such a thing would be out of the question in a civilised community like Seaxe. He nevertheless had a feeling that all was not well and that maybe he should show his annoyance somewhat less openly and aggressively.

"I would be grateful if you could," replied Kejon, who had now settled back on his hindlimbs in a less provocative manner. "I'm sure we would all like to hear what you have to say." Although the tough senior appeared to have quietened down, and was seemingly giving

Emled his complete concentration, he still sensibly kept a wary eye out for his 'Adviser' who had decided to remain standing, having been ordered so to do by a barely perceptible signal from the wicked toad.

"One of the reasons I applied to be king of your community," began Emled, "was because I felt that it could provide me with the opportunity to acquire the experience of a new culture. Indeed a culture quite different to that of Tamsid. I also thought that the frogs of this community might in turn benefit in some small way by me introducing to them some of the customs of the Far North. It does seem a pity that for so many years the communities to the north of Waga have been so poorly regarded by their eastern, western and southern neighbours, even though no foreign frog has ventured across these swamplands to find out for themselves what life is really like in a community such as Tamsid.

"Of course life is harder in the Far North. The air is much cooler and at times, particularly in the long dark winter months, the food may be less nutritional and more scarce than it is here in the warmer southern communities. However, and as a consequence, we have bred a very hardy line of frogs as you will of course see represented by the excellent specimens behind you. The frogs of the Far North have also learned to cope with adversity the like of which you will never have faced here in Seaxe.

"I also hope that I can bring the type of leadership qualities of which you are apparently in desperate need. Almost everywhere I go I hear tales of Moha's poor past management of this community and of his habit of taking decisions that did not reflect the wishes of the frogs of Seaxe. Why, you all said as much to me at our first meeting before I formally took up my position here." As he spoke these last few words he gestured with his forelimb at each of the seniors in turn as if defying them to dispute what he had just said. They could not of course deny that they had voiced such an opinion about Moha. However, each of them now wondered, with the possible exception of Lebish, just what had made them speak so disparagingly of the giant bullfrog who had so successfully and quite magnificently brought their community so much peace and happiness.

From behind the seniors came a number of jabs in the their backs from their 'Advisers' who acknowledged the statements being made by Emled with comments such as...

"You did say that didn't you?" and "You are surely not now going to say that you lied about Moha's appalling management?" and "You must admit you did say that he was a poor king? Your words not mine!"

The seniors were confused. They certainly had defamed Moha. And yes, they must admit that they had unanimously bad-mouthed the kindly old bullfrog despite the fact that it was he who had made it possible for them to reach their current prestigious positions in the community. What they were not now sure about was whether they had willingly said such things because they believed them to be true, or whether they had been influenced in some sinister way by Emled and actually encouraged by him to slander Moha.

Before the extremely perplexed seniors could begin to sort out and rationalise their mixed up thoughts, Emled continued with his monologue.

"You say you want to know about you futures and what I require of you. Well, I will tell you." Emled leaned forward in order to press home his points. As he did so a sudden disgusting waft of his foul smelling breath drifted slowly over the seniors causing them to feel distinctly nauseous.

"I want you all to practise the principles that I hold dear to my own heart. I want you to be kind and courteous to your fellow frogs. I want you to encourage openness in debates that will enable the whole community to contribute towards the development of our policies and strategies. I want you to carefully nurture the young and give respect to the elderly. Finally, but not conclusively, I want you to ensure that those who are less fortunate than yourselves are also made to feel that they are useful members of our community."

Total silence followed these words as Emled raised himself up to his full height. He now towered above the seniors. They were all momentarily stunned both by the toad's attractive oratory and by the awesome size of his massive and grotesque body. He then spoke again.

"Above all else I want you to care for your community in a way that reflects your king's feelings for his frogs. *After all, who really cares? ...Emled cares! ....I care!*" To the astonishment of 'the six' seniors, who it is safe to say were by this time totally mesmerised by the proceedings, Emled boomed the latter statements with a force they would not have believed possible of a normal living creature.

There then came a sudden burst of clapping and a croaking from behind the seniors, the noise of which shook them back to their senses. They felt that they had been in some kind of hypnotic state whilst Emled had been talking during which they had been powerless to respond and only able to sit seemingly transfixed while he stated his personal values and vision.

"Well said!"

"Hear! Hear!"

"Great words from the king!"

"Long live the king!"

"Three croaks for Emled!"

The 'Advisers' cried out their support for their evil master roughly jostling, pushing and prodding the seniors as they did so.

'The six' seniors were sandwiched between Emled and the excited 'Advisers'. There really was no way out for them and quite literally no room to turn. Gradually, and one by one, they too began to stand up and croak their support for the monstrous king. First Lebish; then Geelan; and then Brylil and Josmi together. Although their chanting and cries of support for Emled were a little muted, and initially somewhat reluctant, they soon became much more animated following a fair degree of physical encouragement from their 'Advisers'.

Chrich had taken a few moments longer to get into the swing of things. He fleetingly saw pictures flash through his mind of happy times when Moha had been king. He wondered if it could be only four weeks since Moha had left for Somset – it now seemed such a long time ago! He was still thinking of mellow late autumn afternoons sat upon a gently bobbing lily pad when he too found himself chanting along with the others.

Kejon was the last to participate. He was feeling very grumpy and he certainly did not like being pushed into doing something against his will. A couple of particularly sharp digs in the back from his personal 'Adviser', who then nodded his head in the direction of Emled, clearly suggested that Kejon should join in the celebration of the king. Although momentarily annoyed, the stubborn frog also began clapping and croaking with his colleagues. For Kejon, his participation was more to prevent him from appearing overtly disrespectful or even anti the new king. However, he definitely did not like what was happening – not one tiny bit!

"Thank you! Thank you!" cried a jubilant Emled. "Thank you for all your wonderful support." He paused briefly as if to catch his breath. "Now let's close the meeting on this high note. We really have made progress today and we have done some excellent work. I'll let you know as soon as possible when we shall be meeting next."

With that he left the Boathouse.

Lebish, Brylil, Josmi and Geelan were all well and truly caught up in the perverse emotion that Emled had created. A cocktail of fear, relief, confusion, elation and desperation filled their minds and bodies. They chattered nervously, and somewhat incomprehensibly, as they excitedly patted each other on the back in mutual congratulation.

"What a marvellous king," squeaked Geelan.

"What a powerful leader," croaked Brylil.

"He really knows how to make a point," chirped Josmi.

"You really do know where you are with this king. That was a very useful meeting. Such a lot of good work carried out. Emled said that we were excellent." This came from an overly enthusiastic Lebish whose eyes and belly were now firmly focused on a rich and flourishing future. "This is all so much better than the constant patronising we used to get from Moha."

"Moha!... Who's Moha?" shrilled Geelan, who then burst into uncontrollable laughter at his own individual and pathetic brand of humour.

Chrich and Kejon looked at each other with an equal mixture of confusion and embarrassment as they listened to the gibble-gabble of their joyous senior colleagues. Neither spoke. They didn't need to. They merely stared into each other's eyes and wondered what on earth was happening. All they had in fact heard from Emled during the meeting was him setting out his personal credentials. The group had collectively made no decisions, nor, for that matter, had they discussed policy or raised any important issues. As meetings go this one had been totally absent of business. Instead it had rather been crammed full of dogma – and Emled's own sinister brand of dogma at that.

They could not of course openly come out and say so as the 'Advisers' had lingered after Emled's exit. This was of course to ensure that they missed nothing of how the seniors had responded and especially what they may have said to each other about the king. Any points of interest noted by the 'Advisers' would be reported directly back to Emled.

Kejon and Chrich slowly blended in with their feverish colleagues and now gave the appearance of joining in the excitement. They were, however, both greatly troubled as to what was seemingly occurring in their community. Whether or not either of them, singly or jointly, would have the strength to do anything in respect of their concerns is something about which we will have to wait to find out later in this story.

Chapter Sixteen

Mars Receives a Message

I am sure you will have been wondering why the second meeting in the Boathouse, an account of which you have just read in the previous chapter, did not feature Mars. With all that had gone on at that meeting, and especially the way it had been conducted, surely Mars would have had something to say. It's for certain that he would not have put up with the bullying behaviour of Emled's marsh frog 'Advisers'.

Well, the truth of the matter is that Mars was actually not present at the meeting and, in order to find out the reason why this was so, we will have to go back to a time during the week prior to when Emled was due to arrive in Seaxe to officially take up his new role as king. It is also a fact that there was no sign of a kingfisher in the vicinity of the Boathouse on the day of that second meeting and that is something else that needs to be explained.

We need in fact to go back to a point in time just five days before the evil toad descended upon Seaxe and whilst he was still back in his home community of Tamsid seeing out the remainder of his time there as king. (What was actually happening in Tamsid, and all the ghastly events that had gone on there in the past – in addition to the incidents involving the sacrificing of thousands of innocent young frogs to the humans – are too numerous to tell here. Maybe one day they will be the subject of another story? One can only hope that those grim tales will be told before Emled finds out that the truth about his dark deeds is known and he tries to put a stop to the veracity of his wicked ways being revealed.)

On this day Mars had been taking a few peaceful moments' rest in a quiet and secluded spot deep amongst the bulrushes. As he relaxed, half submerged in the water, he reflected on all that was occurring in his friendly community of Seaxe. The sun had just peeped over the eastern horizon and the air still held the coolness of the night as the warmth of the new day's sun had not yet had time to embrace the surrounding countryside. This was a place to where Mars often came when he wanted to think. It was his very own secret niche and, as far as he knew, he was quite alone this morning.

Mars was deep in thought. He felt so sad that Moha was leaving. He was not only losing a good and trusted king but also a much loved friend.

All at once his peace was shattered as a dozen or more huge black crows suddenly swooped down and around him cawing hysterically. They flew so close that their flapping wings almost flicked in his face.

The suddenness of their arrival and their ear-splitting shrieks caused Mars to dive for cover. He quickly and expertly slipped under the surface of the river and swam down towards the river bed. He then made his way into a very tightly knit clump of bulrushes and, with the security of the reeds and rushes around him, he carefully let himself rise up through the roots until he was able to just peek out above the level of the rippling water.

It was then that he saw, circling directly above... the unmistakable shape of Gawk. Mars recognised the unsavoury creature from the many recent visits this detestable crow had made to Seaxe wherein he had acted as Emled's go-between carrying messages back and forth to the seniors and their subordinates. Gawk had also caught sight of Mars although there was no way he could reach or touch him, so dense was Mars' cover of reeds and rushes.

"Hey, frog!" yelled the raucous crow. "I've got a message for you! Get yourself out of the water and on to the river bank!" he ordered.

Whilst Mars remained where he was he knew that he would be safe from any physical attack from Gawk or any of the other crows for that matter. Gawk wouldn't dare risk landing on anything as flimsy as a lily pad or a bendy reed for fear of falling into the water. He was no swimmer and he would almost certainly drown.

Nevertheless Mars felt rather vulnerable. He was by himself and some distance from the main community. None of his close colleagues knew that he was there and with it being so early in the morning there were no other creatures around to witness what was happening. If he agreed to Gawk's demand and he did get out on to dry land then he would be leaving himself totally exposed and open to an assault from which he would have little chance of escape.

"I can hear you well enough from here, thank you," replied Mars. "Anyway I would rather stay where I am if you don't mind. It's far too chilly for me on the river bank at the moment. I shall therefore remain in the water until the sun warms things up a bit. What is it that you want?"

Emled's instructions to Gawk were in fact that Mars should not be harmed at this stage, so, although he didn't know it, the young frog was not actually in any physical danger. Mars was of course not aware of Gawk's orders so it was a very wise precaution that he took to avoid giving the crow even the remotest opportunity to strike him.

Gawk was annoyed. He was not used to creatures disobeying him. As he hovered above Mars he flapped his wings in an even more aggressive manner, the anger welling up inside him. In his frustration the black crow again swooped low over the reeds just flicking them with his tail feathers.

"Emled wants you... and he wants you immediately!" screamed Gawk. "You are to come with me straight away and travel to Tamsid." In his anger Gawk spat these words at Mars.

"But why such a rush?" replied Mars calmly. "Surely I can discuss any issues with Emled when he comes here to be king. After all there's only five days to go and I have a great deal to do in preparation for his arrival."

"If Emled says he wants you immediately he means just that. It doesn't mean when you are ready or sometime never. Now do as I say and get out and on to the bank!"

Mars noted the anxiety in Gawk's voice. He felt that the crow was probably telling the truth and that he didn't just want to get him out of the water for any other reason than to take him to Tamsid. He also sensed that Gawk was very concerned and he guessed that it was this unsavoury bird's personal responsibility to ensure that Emled's orders were carried out to the letter. It was clearly Gawk who would receive a tongue lashing from the foul toad if he didn't successfully deliver Mars as instructed.

It was also evident that Gawk was not accompanied on this occasion by any of the marsh frog thugs who may have been able to bully Mars and physically force him out of the rushes. Mars therefore knew that he was safe for the moment as none of the crows, and least of all Gawk, would risk getting their tail feathers wet in order to pluck the young frog from his secure haven.

"Okay, I'll come," said Mars. "But you must give me time to let my colleagues know what is happening. They will wonder where I have got to and will worry if I am away from the community for any length of time. I'll meet you at the Near North border of Waga just before the sun reaches its highest point today. It's then or not at all!" With that Mars darted below the surface and swam strongly away through the reeds. He neither listened to Gawk's reply (which was lucky for it contained many foul oaths) nor did he allow himself to be further exposed to any possible danger of an attack from the crows.

Gawk seethed with anger. At first he tried to follow Mars and, flying as low above the river as he dared, he could just make out the silhouette of the athletic young frog as Mars swam deep below the surface. However, the reflection on the water of the brightly rising sun soon made such an exercise impossible and Gawk quickly realised that he would have to resign himself to Mars' ultimatum.

Gawk knew that he would lose face by not having succeeded in coaxing Mars immediately back to Tamsid and he didn't much like the thought of being embarrassed in such a way. He yelled at his bunch of fellow crows to fall in behind him and, with a flap of his wings, he led them off in the direction of the midday meeting place where he would rendezvous with Mars. He had decided that to fill in the time before noon, and in order to restore some personal credibility in the eyes of his murderous gang, he would allow his mob of mercenaries to invade some unsuspecting creatures such as young birds in their nests. Nothing like some wanton death and destruction to raise their spirits, he thought; plus it would probably help them to forget his none too successful coercion of Mars.

*

When Mars got back into the main area of the community he told Moha and Peeyu of his encounter with Gawk. After weighing up the possible consequences the three friends decided that Mars should meet with the crow as planned. It did after all appear to be a genuine message that Emled wanted to see him, although what it could possibly be about was a complete mystery. On balance it seemed important to find out just what it was that Emled was up to and accordingly Mars met with Gawk at noon at the Waga border.

In fact Gawk made a point of joining Mars quite some way in advance of the appointed meeting place in order to give the impression to the waiting marsh frogs, who had also assembled there, that he had personally brought his charge all the way from Seaxe.

Mars noticed that the band of accompanying crows were in particularly high spirits. He was also certain that several of them had the dark stain of blood upon their feathers. Mars' disgust of these despicable birds increased as he watched them hopping and jumping on the ground and squawking in mock attack clearly re-enacting whatever abomination it was that they had just performed.

As had clearly been pre-arranged, as soon as Mars and Gawk reached the Near North border with Waga they were instantly joined by the marsh frogs whose job it was to escort the Seaxe senior across that smelly place.

"'Bout time you lot got here!" sneered Kaara who considered the task to be of such importance that he ought personally to supervise this leg of Mars' journey. "Our king will not be a happy soul to have been kept waiting so long for his visitor."

"We met with a little difficulty from our distinguished guest," retorted Gawk, angrily gesturing with his beak towards Mars. "Nothing that I couldn't handle though," he falsely added.

"I expect Emled will be the judge of that," replied Kaara mockingly. He was clearly enjoying the discomfort that his comments were causing his crow associate. Although marsh frogs and crows willingly assisted Emled in his evil doings, and actually committed many atrocities together on his behalf, it was a well known fact that there was no love lost between them. They were allies in crime but in all other ways they really hated each other. This certainly made for a somewhat fragile relationship to say the least.

The trek across Waga was fairly straightforward and Mars was hurried along at a very fast pace. Accompanying him he had three brown marsh frogs as his escort with one on either side and one bringing up the rear. The speed did not worry the young frog at all as he had always kept himself very fit. His escorts however were neither as young nor were they particularly fit. Mars was thus aware of a great deal of huffing and puffing, not to mention croaking and complaining, from each of his three close attendants; they also appeared to be more than a little put out at having to make up for time already lost due to Gawk's inability to present Mars in line with Emled's instructions. As far as Mars could see the creatures under Emled's control had to carry out all his demands at double quick time.

When Mars arrived in Tamsid the first thing that caught his attention was the general level of activity in the community. There really appeared to be an exceptional amount of 'to-ing and fro-ing'; as well as a great deal of 'coming and going', although, as Mars soon began to realise, most of it seemed to be rather aimless. There certainly appeared to be an enormous amount of verve and energy expended as frogs dashed from one place to the next or hopped rapidly off one lily pad and on to another. However, almost as quickly as they left their original base they would very soon end up where they started again. Mars was rather amused by what he saw and thought it looked a little like two hops forward and three hops backward with no creature actually making any progress at all.

Mars wondered if he could be wrong in his assumption that the hustle and bustle seemed to be more for show than to achieve any real purpose. However, the positioning of large brown marsh frogs at strategic points in the community who looked as though they were watching every Tamsid creature's movement, and who also appeared to be moving on anyone who stopped for any longer than was necessary to draw breath, rather answered Mars' question. He was then certain that all the frogs in Tamsid were purposely being kept continually on the move, with those frogs who had business actually going about their business and those frogs who had no particular business of their own being actively encouraged by the supervising marsh frogs to find out what the busy Tamsid frogs were doing.

To Mars it really did look like a giant work creation scheme with no frog being allowed to stand idle. The young frog senior thought that in some ways this could be a good thing as if every creature was busy then no one could say that they were bored. However, the local frogs of Tamsid, that is to say all those excluding the larger brown marsh frogs, looked extremely harassed and sullen and seemingly resigned to this rather pandemonium style of living.

The difference between the marsh frogs and the local Tamsid frogs was primarily in their size although there was also a variation in their colouring. The marsh frogs were considerably larger and more powerfully built than their local brethren. In terms of colouring the difference was not so striking as both were a fairly dull and mottled brown. If one looked a little more closely, however, it was possible to detect traces of light ivory and jet black ebony stripes along the sides of the local frog.

There were also a great deal more of the common Tamsid frogs than the larger marsh frogs, although it looked fairly obvious to Mars that it was through these latter thugs that Emled ruled and controlled the locals.

It is again quite another story to go into the way in which the Far North evolved following the great storms which, of course, heralded Emled's arrival in Tamsid. Suffice to say, at this stage, that the race of frogs in this community had developed in two main strains. Firstly, there was the pure-bred marsh frog of whom it has already been said is a very large specimen indeed. Secondly, there is the local Tamsid frog who is a cross between the pure-bred marsh frog and the original indigenous species of the area now known as Tamsid. These latter frogs, although noticeably smaller than the marsh frogs, are nevertheless still significantly larger and much more powerfully built than the everyday frogs of Seaxe and the other frogs to the south of Waga.

In the frog society of Tamsid there was clearly a strict class distinction between the elite group of pure breeds and the mixed race of the common Tamsid frogs. However, and quite regardless of their size or the roles played within the community by these two quite different strains of Far North frog, there was one significant and binding similarity that they shared. I refer, unfortunately, to the hateful and fulsome natures they possessed which had been conditioned within these creatures by their vile and poisonous leader Emled!

The bottom line, therefore, on all the extremely undesirable inhabitants of this Far North community is that whilst there was certainly a prevailing attitude in Tamsid of 'them' and 'us' between the common frogs and the pure breeds, when it actually came to a confrontation with an outsider then for the latter a frog from this evil place would be described as a marsh frog whether the creature was large, huge, brown with black stripes or, for that matter, sky blue pink with yellow spots. They were therefore all regarded as equally mean and callous particularly when on the move and on the rampage under the leadership of Emled and Kaara.

Mars was soon brought to a halt outside a cavernous opening which had been formed by an uprooted oak tree that had fallen to the ground during the great storm. Some of the tree's roots which had been attached to the top side of the fallen tree had been ripped from the ground, but those roots to the side and bottom of the trunk had remained embedded in the earth. The resulting gaping hole was, as a consequence, shaped like a huge archway. Mars guessed that this must be Emled's palace, as nowhere since he had arrived in Tamsid had he seen a more imposing or impressive form of accommodation as that into which he was presumably now going to enter.

The area around the fallen tree was also very obviously being guarded by a substantial number of large and fierce looking marsh frogs who were making no attempt to conceal the nature of their presence. Mars also noticed a great many crows' nests which had been built high up in the tallest trees. It was clear by the number of untidy and dishevelled clumps of twigs that were liberally spread amongst the upper branches that Emled also had an aerial patrol to complement his troops on the ground.

The biggest give-away, however, as to who could be the occupier of this vast place was the unmistakable smell that emanated from the gaping hole. Mars recognised the stench as being the same as that which had wafted around the Boathouse at the seniors' first meeting with their new king. It was surely the appalling fetor of the odious toad!

From deep within the hole came a rustling of leaves and a laboured and impatient grunting. Then he appeared from out of the shadows. At first it looked like a distorted silhouette which had been enlarged and thrown out of proportion by a trick of the light. Then Mars realised that it was no distortion, it was Emled! Much larger even than Mars had remembered from their meeting in the Boathouse. He was massively huge in body, both in height and breadth. He also wore quite the fiercest expression on his ugly face, which was every bit as frightening as any frog could possibly imagine even in their wildest of dreams.

"Mars! Mars! My dear sweet little friend. How good it is of you to come all this way to visit me in my humble abode. Gawk must have had some difficulty finding you as I expected the pleasure of your company much earlier." Emled's sickly sweet manner belied the evil of which Mars knew he was capable.

"There was no difficulty. No difficulty at all," replied Mars. "It was due to me not being able to leave straight away as it was necessary to advise my personal colleagues that I was going on a trip to Tamsid. I can't just hop off a lily pad and disappear without a word of explanation. They now know that I have come to see you."

Mars was aware of Gawk's discomfort. The crow had positioned himself about halfway up a tall tree to the side of Emled's palace, and here he skulked, listening to what was being said below and hoping against hope that no mention would be made of his apparent inefficiency. On hearing Mars' explanation for his late arrival, Emled turned his head around slowly until his eyes found Gawk. Even from the safety of his high perch Gawk felt afraid as the toad glared at him with an expression that could best be described as malevolent. Gawk's legs felt as if they had turned to jelly and he wobbled a little before regaining his balance.

"I see," was all Emled calmly said. His eyes however told an altogether different and much more sinister story as they pierced into the body of the hapless crow.

Mars again looked around at the over-active Tamsid frogs who, judging by their forlorn and downcast expressions, were clearly unhappy with their lot. Mars was also struck by Emled's reference to his huge palace being his 'humble abode'. As far as Mars was concerned Emled's accommodation could more appropriately be described as 'extravagant' and 'regal'. However, when he saw the conditions in which the ordinary local Tamsid frog lived then Mars thought that in their case 'humble' may well have been an improvement on what they currently endured. The impression Mars got from his early sightings was that the common Tamsid frog lived in meagre and extremely basic accommodation. In fact most of it appeared to be makeshift and temporary although it had clearly been that way for a very long time. What a difference there was between the way Emled lived compared to the quality of life afforded to those over whom he reigned!

"You make it sound as if I have come here out of choice," said Mars respectfully. He knew it would be wise to keep his head and stay cool. He felt there was a great deal of hostility in the atmosphere and much of it was being directed towards himself.

"Oh, my dear frog, I merely sent my colleagues to suggest that you come and see me. If you agreed to come then they were to escort you safely across the delightful Waga to ensure that you did not get lost. Seeing that you are here I assume that you have personally chosen to accept my invitation. I trust therefore that you are happy to be here." Emled's manner was almost plausible although he could not completely hide the fact that he really despised Mars and that he was so very full of jealousy and hate for the handsome young frog who now stood proudly before him.

"Well, I am here now," said Mars. "Whether at your bidding or my wish it makes no difference. Beyond that, all I know is that you want to discuss certain matters with me which I assume you consider to be important."

Despite the emotions of jealousy and hate that permeated every part of Emled's huge body, he could not help but admire the unruffled and confident way in which Mars conducted himself under what the toad knew was a great deal of pressure. However, there were two things that Emled desperately wanted from his young visitor, although, for obvious reasons, they would not be discussed on this occasion. Firstly he yearned to have something that was actually impossible for him to acquire... this was his desire to be a frog. He longed to look like Mars and be handsome and lithe and be able to boast of an athletic physique. That this could never happen generated a loathing for Mars that twisted every sinew in the toad's evil gut causing him spasms of great pain.

The second thing that Emled wanted was something Mars himself had not yet acquired but the wicked toad knew that he was soon to receive. This was, of course, the 'Great Learning of the Supreme Qualities of Wisdom and Knowledge' that Krakow the wise and legendary blackbird was shortly going to pass on to the young frog.

*

If we again cast our minds back to the occasion of the meeting between Krakow and the two young adventurers, Mars and Peeyu, then you will recall that Emled had in fact overheard the entire conversation that had taken place in the old blackbird's hide-out. He now realised, therefore, that to be a truly great and all powerful king he would need to acquire the sacred qualities of wisdom and knowledge that Krakow possessed. Seemingly having found the secret hiding place of the legendary Krakow with such ease, Emled had no doubt whatsoever that extracting these qualities, from what the toad regarded as merely a weak and bald headed old blackbird, would be equally as simple. In fact, he thought, it would be as easy as tricking a hundred young frogs onto the dinner tables of the humans.

What Emled had not reckoned on, however, was that the insight and awareness which had enabled Krakow to live so long and survive undetected in such an evil and dangerous place as the Far North would not desert him when it was most required. For, although the old blackbird's guard may have been momentarily down when the chance sighting of himself, Mars and Peeyu had been made by the passing crow, his keen senses and razor sharp wits soon warned him that his life was in extreme danger.

When Krakow had returned to his hide-out at the base of the tree, after escorting Peeyu and Mars to the Far North border of Waga, he became aware of a strong and pungent smell to the side of the trunk just below the holes which allowed the sunlight to filter through. He immediately sensed danger on the ground so he flew up to a low branch in order to assess the situation. He scanned the whole area and as far as he could see there was no other creature in the vicinity that could cause him harm. The strong odour again wafted up to him and it was then that he recognised its owner.

"Emled!" he muttered to himself. "That foul and odious beast has been here."

To be on the safe side Krakow assumed the worst and suspected that Emled had knowledge of Mars and Peeyu being in Tamsid and that he had probably followed them, or had them followed, since they entered the Far North. The consequence of this hypothesis, thought Krakow, was that it was now almost certain that Emled would also be aware of the existence of himself and that the devious toad would very likely have eavesdropped on his conversation with the two young friends from Seaxe. If his assumptions were accurate then Krakow considered it a certainty that Emled would return as soon as possible and torture him for the valuable qualities he possessed. Krakow knew that his own death would inevitably follow such an encounter. However, rather than be worried about his personal welfare, the wise old blackbird was far more concerned about the greater evil that Emled would be capable of inflicting if ever he was to add the 'Great Learning of the Supreme Qualities of Wisdom and Knowledge' to his own vile brand of wickedness.

Krakow had therefore immediately decided to abandon his tree trunk home although, before he actually finally vacated this refuge, he did spend a little time busily dragging in various pieces of foliage which he deposited in a rather dark area just inside the entrance. To the casual observer it would have appeared that he was merely doing a spot of nest building or the like. However, what Krakow was really up to we will shortly discover! As soon as he finished this task he fluttered up to another hiding place he often used which was located high in the thick strong boughs amongst a small group of ancient oaks. From here he had a panoramic view of the whole of Tamsid and its surrounding area and southwards as far as the swamps of Waga.

Sure enough, as the sky began to darken, the massive silhouette of Emled slowly appeared in the shadows of the trees as he slithered towards Krakow's now deserted hide-out. The wise old bird watched as the toad crept closer and closer and Krakow was surprised how little noise he made for such a large and cumbersome looking creature.

Emled had then stopped and Krakow at first thought that he appeared to be listening for something. Then a very strange thing happened, for the slimy toad began to whimper and make the sound of an injured bird. Krakow shuddered as he suddenly realised what Emled was up to. He was in fact imitating the plaintive cries of a distressed bird in order to lure Krakow, who he must have thought was still inside the tree, out into the open. The noise was so realistic that Krakow thought that had he been in his hiding place he probably would have gone outside to offer assistance. He didn't like to dwell on what might have happened next had he done so.

As Krakow watched from the safety of his perch in the tree he noticed Emled becoming increasingly impatient as it was slowly dawning on him that his cunning plan was not working and that Krakow was not being tempted from his home. It was not long before the toad's patience finally cracked and he hopped up and down most heavily and violently in and around the concealed entrance to Krakow's refuge. Very soon, and after he had broken many twigs and kicked away a mound of dead leaves with his hindlimbs, Emled found what he had been looking for – it was the way in! He of course wasted no time by politely knocking and waiting for an invitation to enter. In his anger, and spurred on by the insatiable desire for the power he felt that the qualities of wisdom and knowledge would surely give him, he crazily battered down the entrance and burst his way in tumbling over and over as he did so down the slope that led to Krakow's main living area.

A second or so after the toad had disappeared through the entrance there came a hideous scream of agony from within. Moments later Emled reappeared with a number of holly leaves and hawthorns sticking into various parts of his body. In the event of something like this happening, the last thing that Krakow had actually done before vacating his tree trunk home was to collect a bundle of the most prickly holly leaves and spiteful hawthorns that he could find in order to prepare a welcoming carpet just in case Emled did decide to drop by unexpectedly. Emled had obliged superbly and he had quite literally fallen head first into the trap.

Krakow smiled as he looked on from above the toad. It was good to see the evil creature getting a little of his own medicine for a change. Emled wriggled first this way and then that way in order to extricate the painful barbs that were stuck firmly into his body. After several very torturous minutes of burning pain and anguish, that must have seemed like a lifetime to the toad, Emled finally pulled out the last of the spikes that had pierced his skin. For a while he ruefully rubbed each of the tender spots with his forelimb. His underparts were extremely sore and painful and, try as he might, he could not find a comfortable sitting position.

Up in the trees Krakow smiled again at his handiwork. Emled's suffering was only relatively minor, when compared to what many others had endured at the forelimbs of the rotten toad, but it was nevertheless good to see the wicked creature on the receiving end for a change. The only pity, thought Krakow, was that he was the only one there to witness this most enjoyable occasion.

Then Krakow heard something which chilled him to the bone and made the very feathers on his back stand up on end; for, from directly below him, came this blood curdling cry from the evil toad.

"Blackbird! I know you can see me! I hope that you can also hear me! Believe me when I say that you will regret the day you were born when I catch up with you! If it takes me until the end of time I will track you down and find you! And when I do I shall personally enjoy crushing every bone and shredding each and every sinew of your scrawny body from your beak to your claws! No creature has ever gotten the better of me and lived to tell the tale whether they be

A second or so after the toad had disappeared through the entrance there came a hideous scream of agony from within.

frog, bird, animal or human! You will be no different and if need be your so called wisdom and knowledge will perish along with you so leaving me supreme amongst the frog communities to the north, south, east and west!"

Emled's voice had grown louder and louder as he issued his threats, and, as he screamed his final oath, Krakow felt the very branches upon which he now perched shake from the toad's tremendous roar.

"*Can you hear me, old bird?! I shall not be thwarted in my quest for absolute domination!*"

As Emled's madness gradually subsided he stood still for a short while gulping in huge lungfuls of the stale Tamsid air. High up in the trees, and hardly daring to breathe for fear of giving himself away, Krakow watched with relief as the toad eventually turned and rather painfully limped his way back to his palace.

The wise old blackbird knew that time was very much against him. It was now more urgent than ever that he should meet up with Mars in order for him to pass on the 'Great Learning of the Supreme Qualities of Wisdom and Knowledge' to the young frog. He must certainly not allow himself to be captured by Emled, at least, he unselfishly thought, not before he himself had liaised with Mars.

Krakow was fairly certain that if Emled really made an effort to catch him and employed the full force of the frogs and crows at his disposal then he would be found sooner rather than later. However, Krakow was banking on the likelihood that Emled would in the first place be too embarrassed to describe his painful and humiliating encounter with the old blackbird; and, in the second, that he would not dream of disclosing the fact that the legendary Krakow was still alive, for fear of encouraging the likes of Gawk or Kaara to attempt to obtain Krakow's qualities for themselves.

Whatever happened now, Krakow knew that he could remain in the Far North for not a moment longer. The problem was, how could he effect his safe escape across Waga undetected by his potential assailants?

*

As Emled now stared down at Mars the thought of his painful and inglorious visit to Krakow's tree trunk home was very much at the forefront of his mind – not to mention his rear end! Memories of the stinging prickles and thorns caused the foul toad to automatically rub those parts of his warty body which had been most severely spiked in the old blackbird's trap.

For the moment, as Mars looked deep into Emled's eyes, the young frog could see that behind the toad's leering expression many evil and dark thoughts lurked therein. He also thought it strange that the obnoxious creature should be touching himself in such a peculiar fashion and with such an anguished expression on his face.

"Well, are you going to tell me why I am here?" asked Mars. At first Emled appeared not to hear and Mars could sense that his mind was elsewhere for the moment. "I really would like to know why you have had me brought here."

"Ugh! Oh yes! Yes of course! Most certainly!" Emled shook himself quite violently as he tried desperately to dispel the painful memories from his mind. "Now, where was I? Business and refreshment – we can do both together." Emled was slowly regaining his composure. "Come on inside, my friend, and let's delay no further."

Emled beckoned the young frog into his palace and gestured to Mars for him to walk in front of him. Mars felt rather vulnerable with Emled directly behind, but he was fairly certain that he would not come to any harm particularly as he had told his friends back in Seaxe where he was going. For this reason, plus the fact that he was to have the black crows and marsh frogs as his travelling companions, it made it highly unlikely that he would encounter any insurmountable problems on his journey.

Once inside the palace Mars found it extremely difficult to breathe for the air was thick with the rank smell of the toad. There was no ventilation and the heat in this vast underground chamber was highly oppressive. Mars felt light-headed and dizzy in this ghastly environment and it took him a while to get acclimatised. He nevertheless told himself to keep steady as he tried to clear his head. Whatever Emled had to say needed to be listened to with care. He had not been brought here for the sake of his own health. He felt that Emled was up to something and he was sure he was about to find out what it was.

"I can see you are impressed with my little home," Emled could clearly see that Mars was not at all comfortable in the heavy and smelly atmosphere and his statement was intended to tease the Seaxe senior into an angry reply.

"I am sure it is very much to your taste," replied Mars, "It is... how can I best put it.... very you."

Emled wasn't sure whether Mars was paying him a compliment or not. Out of sheer vanity he decided it was the former.

"Now then, young Mars," began Emled. "I am glad we have been able to get together at last for a confidential chat because I need to tell you that I am not happy with your current role in Seaxe. I really am not happy at all."

Mars considered saying something but thought better of it. He decided not to interrupt and waited for the toad to continue.

"I am sure you will understand me when I say that it is quite natural for any new king of a community to want to make changes to the way the previous administration operated. I must say to you that I am no different to others in this respect.

"There are many adjustments that will need to be made and I feel that it would be most unfair of me if I did not advise you personally where such matters directly affect you. I will therefore not beat about the lily pads so I shall come straight to the point." Emled paused for a moment as he could see Mars' brow was furrowed with concern at what he was hearing. The handsome young frog, however, kept calm and again waited for the toad to continue.

"Whilst I personally admire you for your ability, plus the marvellous work you have done for your community, I must be truthful and say that I don't require the role that you currently play in Seaxe to be part of my future administration. Please understand this is not intended to be a personal attack on you. It is the role you play that I want to focus on, not you or your undoubted ability."

Mars was more than a little surprised at these statements as he knew full well that the responsibility he had in Seaxe for acquiring and allocating a regular and ample supply of fresh food to the locals, as well as ensuring a safe and healthy environment for all in which to live, was an essential element in the successful management of any community. How could Emled possibly operate without such a key factor being covered in his own administration?

"I expect that you are wondering what will happen to your role?" Emled rightly assumed. "It is of course a very important job. The control of fresh food supplies in particular is vital in any community if it wishes to prosper and make positive progress." Emled could not hide the emphasis he had put on the phrase "control of fresh food supplies" and this fact did not go unnoticed by Mars.

"In my view this function is so important that I have decided to take it under my personal charge. I must therefore say to you that as I will be assuming this responsibility your current post will unfortunately become redundant. It is therefore with much regret that I have to advise you that with effect from the day I take over in Seaxe your services will no longer be required and, as a consequence, there will be no place for you in my management team of senior frogs."

Mars was shaken by the toad's remarks but he kept as cool a head as he could in the circumstances and tried to restrict his response to rational questions.

"Are there any other changes that you foresee?" Mars asked politely, seeking a little time in order to collect his thoughts. "What for instance will happen to the roles of my senior colleagues?"

"Well, for the moment I intend to make no other changes, although many more adjustments will be made after I have settled in. That information, I am sure you will appreciate, must remain confidential until I am ready to make the appropriate announcements. For the time being I am quite happy that each area of responsibility is adequately covered by a group of very able and most intelligent frogs." Emled's cynicism regarding his actual opinion of their 'six' senior Seaxe colleagues was not lost on Mars. "It is really only the issue of the management and control of fresh food, oh and yes, a safe and healthy environment of course," the callous toad added as an afterthought, "that concerns me at present as I honestly feel this needs to be something that is dealt with at the very highest level."

"Do you have any other role for me to play?" asked Mars.

"Well, as I am sure you can imagine, I have, of course, given this matter a great deal of thought. You are clearly a most able young frog and I have no doubt you will be very disappointed that your current position is going to be deleted. I personally feel that you will be greatly affected by my decision and, as I will not have a suitable alternative senior post to offer you, I am absolutely certain that you will find it quite impossible to accept a role of reduced responsibility. My advice, therefore, is that it will be best for all concerned if you were to take your leave of Seaxe and find yourself a new community in which to display your talents. You have an assurance from me that

I will provide you with a first-class reference so you will have no difficulty in acquiring a senior role elsewhere."

Mars knew that it would be unwise to argue with Emled. The toad had set out his game plan and there was no point in trying to change his mind. From what Mars had heard about the devious creature it was no surprise that he would want to have personal control of the community's food supplies. One need only compare the comfort he enjoyed in his palace, as against the poor conditions which the ordinary frogs of Tamsid had to endure, in order to appreciate what such 'control' in the forelimbs of this fraudulent creature would really mean for the community of Seaxe. Despite the overwhelming heat inside Emled's chamber, Mars shivered at the prospect.

"I trust that I shall have time to return to my home and at least be able to say goodbye to my friends?" asked Mars.

"But of course you can," said Emled. "You surely don't think for a moment that I could be so heartless as to deny you such a thing? I am not cruel or insensitive. I do so hope you can see that?"

Mars felt sick to the pit of his belly at the toad's attempt at charity and compassion as he tried to convince the young frog that he was really a kind and benevolent creature.

Hiding his disappointment Mars held his head up high and, looking straight into Emled's eyes, said, "Thank you for allowing me to return. I shall say my goodbyes and be away before you arrive in Seaxe. I can only say that I wish all my friends and colleagues well for the future. My heart will always be with them whatever fate may have in store."

Mars controlled his emotions in order not to say what was really on his mind. This was not the time or place to tell Emled what he really knew about him. Mars just hoped and prayed that the appropriate time would not be too long in coming.

"Good. Well said, my friend. I'm sure that you will soon find a comfortable lily pad on which to sit in some far away community," said Emled, strongly emphasising the words "far away".

"Now, I expect you know your own way back across Waga," continued the toad. "I presume you won't be needing my frogs to assist you?" Emled spoke in a way that purposely sounded more like a statement than a question as he was attempting to trick Mars into revealing that this was not the first time he had been across the border and into the Far North. He of course knew of Mars' and Peeyu's meeting with Krakow, although Mars could not be certain of this fact. The young frog's reply was therefore cautiously framed as he sensed that all was not as it seemed.

"I'm not exactly sure," replied Mars. "I guess if I retrace the route by which I was brought here by your assistants then I should be able to get back safely through the swamps. Some help would however be appreciated, if it could be spared."

Although Mars was confident he could negotiate his way across Waga by himself, he thought that if he were to be accompanied by one of Emled's marsh frogs then there was little chance of him 'mysteriously' disappearing with the excuse being given by the wicked toad that he must have lost his way.

"I can't actually spare any of my frogs at this moment in time as I have a great deal of matters to conclude here in Tamsid before I leave in several days' time. I'm sure you will be all right if you do in fact retrace your footsteps. You're quite capable of doing that!" Again there was more than just a hint of sarcasm in the toad's remarks. Then, as an afterthought, he added, "Oh, and good luck for the future, wherever that may be."

Emled actually had no intention of harming Mars as he travelled back home. He had thought about doing so but he considered it would be counter-productive to his credibility and popularity with his future subjects in Seaxe. After all he was aware that Mars was much adored by his home community and it would appear rather suspicious if the young frog were to be murdered during his return trip. No, Emled considered, it would be best for Mars to leave on the terms that he had just explained. Then, as soon as he arrived in Seaxe to take over as king, he would make it clear to the Seaxe community at large that Mars' departure was on the basis that the position which the young frog had held unfortunately did not fit into his future plans for a more prosperous and better cared for community. He would also make it known that it had consequently been mutually agreed between them that it would therefore be better for all concerned, and especially for Mars' future career prospects, if the young frog senior were to move on. Yes, that's how the toad decided he would phrase it.

Mars made his departure from Emled's palace and began his journey back to Seaxe. All the way home the leering face of the toad played upon his mind. The vile king of Tamsid, soon to be crowned king of Seaxe, was now content that he had rid himself of the one frog whom he felt could have upset his plans. He knew that after Moha then it was Mars who had been the most popular frog in the community.

Emled had decided that he had heard far too many good things said about the handsome young frog during his brief visits to Seaxe. The toad was also very concerned that had it not been for tradition then Mars may well have been appointed as the king instead of him. Such was Emled's jealousy of Mars that he could not have tolerated the young frog living in the same community as himself especially knowing the level of support which Mars enjoyed from many of the Anurian councillors and, more importantly, virtually all the everyday frogs of Seaxe. As far as Emled was concerned Mars had to go and he was therefore pleased that he now considered he had effectively removed the one potential thorn in his side. (And you can be sure that since he fell into Krakow's prickly trap Emled knew only too well how painful a thorn in the side can be!)

As for the other seniors, Emled was certain that they posed no such threat. They would be like tadpole eggs in his hands!

However, there was still the little matter of Krakow to which he had to attend. He also desperately needed to keep the old blackbird and Mars apart. Although he felt he had gone a long way to ensuring that they would be separated by forcing Mars away to some distant community, he couldn't be absolutely certain that they would not somehow manage to meet again. Emled scolded himself for his self-doubt – surely a bald-headed old blackbird would be no match for a huge and powerful adversary such as he. The toad puffed himself up as he considered his own self-esteem. He was determined to be totally confident that he would first of all catch the legendary bird; secondly, he would squeeze from him the qualities of wisdom and knowledge that he so desired; and thirdly, he would enjoy crushing the very life out of Krakow and then throwing his broken body as carrion to the crows.

Chapter Seventeen

Massacre at Kingfisher's Bridge

Mars was in fact escorted as far as Tamsid's Far North border with Waga although at the time he was not aware that he had a travelling companion. This was, however, more for Emled's peace of mind than for Mars' well-being as the evil toad did not want to risk the occurrence of a repeat meeting between Krakow and Mars. Although he hadn't as yet been able to confirm whether or not Krakow had left the Far North, Emled wasn't prepared to take any unnecessary chances.

Mainly for this reason, but also because Emled did not want to lose face by giving Mars the satisfaction of knowing that he had in fact been provided with a personal guide, the toad had instructed the marsh frog he had selected for this task to stay some way behind the Seaxe senior and to keep well out of sight until he was certain that Mars had entered Waga and was once again on his way back to his home community.

During the arduous and hazardous trek back across the swamps and bogs of Waga, Mars continually kept a wary eye open for any form of danger. Faced with just one or two marsh frogs he felt he would be capable of holding his own. However, against a gang of the murderous thugs he would have no chance. Fortunately Mars completed the long journey without any incident worth mentioning and he reached the Near North border as the sun was setting. Just enough time, thought Mars, to call in on Peeyu and let his friend know that he had returned home safely and of course to tell him why Emled had wanted to see him.

Although exhausted from his exertions, and understandably disappointed at the loss of his senior position in the community, Mars' spirits were surprisingly high. He was at least going to have a pleasant end to the day by seeing his kingfisher friend. Since their experience of carrying out the mission to Tamsid, which of course led them to meet Krakow, the two companions had become the very closest of friends. It was Moha who had in many ways brought them together and they both felt that the good old king had helped form the bond of friendship and trust that now joined them.

As Mars approached Kingfisher's Bridge he was suddenly seized by an overwhelming sense of foreboding. Around him he could see that there had recently been a great deal of activity, for on the soft earth of the bank there were the familiar prints of frogs. Indeed it looked as though a substantial number of frogs had passed that way. Not only that, judging from the size of the prints, these creatures appeared to be considerably larger than the local frog inhabitants of Seaxe.

Mars was immediately concerned. It was unusual for there to have been any signs indicating the presence of frogs in the vicinity of Kingfisher's Bridge as the locals rarely ventured that far up the river. The reason being that the area there had rather sparse vegetation for cover and the banks were too steep to climb. It was thus perfect for kingfishers but not so for frogs.

It was therefore a worried and cautious Mars who slowly drew near to Peeyu's home. Although he was certain that whatever frogs had been there were now gone, as he could hear neither a croak nor a rustle of movement, he nevertheless advanced with great care. It was then that he saw the devastation!

The whole area in which Peeyu and his family had lived for many generations had virtually been totally destroyed. The firm bank in which the kingfishers had built their nesting hole had been smashed beyond recognition and great piles of the earth had tumbled down into the river. The water, which normally ran so clear beneath the bridge that a fish could be seen sitting on the river bed, now resembled a muddy brown soup.

At first Mars thought (and hoped) that he had come to the wrong place. But then he saw something that made him cry out in anguish. For there, lying amongst the debris of the broken bank, was the motionless body of Peeyu. Although Mars could see that he had been savagely slain he could not believe that so magnificent a creature could be dead yet still look so beautiful. Mars searched the surrounding area for any sign of life. He knew that Peeyu had a family. There was his wife, and his mother and father, as well as the son of whom Peeyu had spoken so proudly and with such love. In his sadness Mars recalled how Peeyu had told him that his young son was a kingfisher after his own heart but with the dash and daring of his grandfather. He had been so sure that the youngster would grow to be a fine strong bird who would be a credit to his species and to the community of Seaxe.

Mars sobbed at the thought that the kingfisher family and Peeyu's dreams for his son's future had now all perished in the devastation on which he sadly gazed.

As the young frog gradually gathered his emotions, and braced himself to accept the worst possible news that there were no survivors in this apparent massacre, he heard a faint noise which came from within a tight clump of reeds in the water just below where he stood on the bank. At first he did not give any indication that he was aware of another creature's presence and he pretended to concentrate on his search for any signs of life. Fully expecting the noise to have been made by one of those responsible for the death of Peeyu he prepared himself to either leap at the murderer or, if necessary, jump far out into the river and swim to safety.

With the noise coming from behind him Mars crouched down low making ready to turn and spring at his assailant. He listened hard for any further sounds of movement that would signal the intentions of the aggressor and when the latter was going to launch his attack. There then came a strange sound which wasn't one of movement and certainly wasn't what Mars had expected to hear. In fact, rather than posing a threat, it sounded to Mars more like the creature was distressed or perhaps injured in some way. Mars stealthily climbed down the crumbling bank towards the reeds taking great care not to make even the slightest sound that might alert the creature, who was apparently concealed within the foliage, of his approach.

From the sounds of despair that were now clearly audible to Mars he assured himself that he was not personally in any danger from attack or that he was being lured into some form of sinister trap. When he reached the foot of the bank he called out for the creature to identify itself. At first there was no answer although the whimpering immediately stopped. Mars therefore called out again.

"It's okay to come out. You need not be afraid unless of course you are one of those who have killed my friend and his family. My name is Mars and I am a frog who lives in the community of Seaxe just down the river."

Very slowly a long black beak came into view as it poked its way through the tall reeds. This was then followed by the luminescent glow of the orange and blue head and the brilliant white neck of a beautiful young kingfisher.

"Hello. My name is Maccus. I'm the son of Peeyu. I know you are a friend for my father has often spoken of you."

Mars did not know whether to laugh or cry out loud. Peeyu's young son had been spared from the havoc that had been wreaked on his family and his home. Peeyu's only son. His very own pride and joy.

"You'll be safe with me," said Mars reassuringly. "Let's get away from here and when you are ready you can tell me all that has happened."

When they reached the outskirts of the main centre of Seaxe the two companions found a quiet spot and stopped. Maccus had hopped beside Mars all the way as his right wing had been damaged and he was thus unable to fly. To spread his wings in flight caused him a searing pain and he needed to rest his injury.

Maccus then told of how he and the whole family had been sitting in their nesting hole when they had suddenly heard a pandemonium of noise outside which came from above them on the river bank. Peeyu had apparently gone to see what was going on. At first it had seemed to be just a lot of crows tumbling about in the manic way that they so often do, pecking at each other when on the ground and then flying high in the air only to tumble back down to earth locked in a rough embrace. Peeyu had watched them for a few moments thinking what crazy and unpredictable creatures these birds were, when, all of a sudden, what can only be described as a flood of huge brown frogs appeared all over the river bank. It was in fact a massive army of the creatures and they emerged from out of the reeds; from out of the water; and from the bank above the kingfisher's nest.

Peeyu had never before seen the like of these frogs in Seaxe but he instantly recognised them as the same type he had spotted on his travels across the swamps of Waga. They were the dreaded marsh frogs and he and his family were now totally surrounded by them.

As soon as the crows and marsh frogs saw Peeyu standing at what they unfortunately correctly guessed to be the entrance to his nest they

Very slowly a long black beak came into view as it poked its way through the tall reeds.

mounted an attack which was so sudden and ferocious in its execution that the kingfishers had absolutely no chance of escape. The crows came first and Peeyu had fought valiantly to fend them off. He was hopelessly outnumbered of course but nevertheless he had battled hard to give his family time to get out of the hole and flee to safety. It was however to no avail. The crows were far too artful in the craft of ambush and Peeyu was soon pecked to death by the insidious creatures.

As soon as Peeyu fell so the marsh frogs joined in the assault. They clambered all over the river bank frantically digging and scrabbling at the soil in order to open up the kingfisher's nest. Once they had succeeded in their evil quest, and the whole bank had been turned over, they did the job of finishing off the frightened family.

Maccus had in fact only been spared because his assailants must have mistakenly thought him also to be dead. He said that the last thing he could remember was being savagely attacked by a group of crows during which he had been dazed by a blow to the back of his head. He must then have been slung into the air and left for dead as he woke to find himself deep in the clump of reeds in which Mars had discovered him. He had then stayed there for what seemed like an age, for although he could see that the massive brown frogs had gone he was too scared to move or call out for help for fear of the crows spotting that he was still alive.

"This is without doubt the work of Kaara and Gawk acting under the orders of their foul toad leader," said Mars. "If it is the very last thing I do in my life I will avenge the death of your father and your family and I will rid this world of the monster known as Emled!"

Mars spoke these words with great passion and commitment for he was thoroughly determined that he would not now rest until he had achieved this heartfelt but dangerous promise. Then Maccus said something which Mars had not expected from one so young.

"If that is your vow then I shall be at your side every hop of the way. They are now my enemy too and so we shall seek vengeance together. It is what my father and grandfather would have wished."

Mars knew at that moment that this beautiful and brave young kingfisher was indeed everything and more of what his father had so proudly boasted. There most definitely was a strong and courageous heart that beat under that magnificent plumage of youth. Mars looked deeply and lovingly into Maccus's eyes. He had absolutely no doubt of the young bird's conviction. Without any shadow of a doubt, and despite the brutal assault by Emled's evil disciples, the wonderful spirit of the kingfisher family still lived on in Seaxe.

"Yes, my friend," said Mars with pride. "Together it will be."

Chapter Eighteen

Life Goes on in Seaxe – Or Not, As the Case May Be!

For the frogs of Seaxe life was changing dramatically day by day. It was becoming clear to every frog, and not just the seniors, that the decision-making process was now totally in the hands of Emled. This was despite the fact that the monstrous toad would, whenever the opportunity arose, personally lay great emphasis on his self-acclaimed 'open style' of management which, according to him, allowed all frogs to have their say on all issues.

It had also become plain for every frog to see that the role now being played by the seniors was really only a token gesture to the past. It was strikingly obvious that orders given by Emled, regarding important matters in each of their respective areas of responsibility, were being directly carried out by their marsh frog 'Advisers'. However, whenever any of the 'Advisers' were asked what authority they had for taking a particular course of action (which wasn't very often as they were always extremely aggressive when approached by any of the local frogs), they would of course say that they were merely acting on behalf of their seniors. Nevertheless, and quite irrespective of what they might have said, the truth was that the seniors were effectively sidelined and in reality only did what they were told to do by either Emled, or more embarrassingly, by their own 'Advisers'.

The seniors themselves soon became quietly and reluctantly resigned to this regime, although their acquiescence appeared to be rather more bought by Emled than given voluntarily. It had, for instance, become common knowledge in the community that the king had provided substantial and palatial accommodation for each of the seniors. It was also understood that Emled frequently allocated to them as many succulent grasshoppers as they could eat. The devious toad would support this generosity (most would say unnecessary extravagance) with a wave of his forelimb and say that it was barely sufficient reward for the seniors in return for their unstinting dedication to the betterment of the community. He said he hoped those aspiring to reach senior positions would regard such well-deserved benefits as an incentive to work hard.

The reality of the situation was that the seniors were of course totally mystified by such statements as they were really doing very little that had any impact whatsoever on community life and certainly nothing that could be described as remotely worthwhile. However, in terms of their personal treats, the way they saw it was that they were doing very nicely thank you. Their tummies had never been fuller (except possibly Lebish's) and, as for being comfortable, they had quite literally never had it so good. In any event they were certainly not going to complain or rock the lily pad by making an issue out of the loss of their respective power bases. After all is said and done, what is a little power and authority when compared against a life of luxury.

Thus Emled had bought out the Seaxe seniors. If ever they did have any serious intention of taking a stance against him, or voicing a contrary opinion, they would certainly not do so now. There was no way they were going to risk losing their newly acquired lifestyle – not even if it meant that their fellow frogs might suffer at the mercy of the vile toad.

The seniors of course continued to meet as a group, albeit only whenever summoned to do so by Emled, to what the toad called his 'Team' meetings. But this again was merely tokenism as all the seniors did at these get togethers was sit back and hear what Emled intended to do. They quickly realised that the king wanted no contribution from any of them and all he in fact required was that they obediently nod in agreement with whatever it was he had decided upon. Emled was therefore happy that by their attendance, and automatic acceptance of all his decisions, democracy was seen to have been satisfied. And satisfied was very much the word that could best be used to describe 'the six' seniors' expanding bellies.

At the 'Team' meetings there was always a lot of noisy support for Emled which principally came from the 'Advisers'. The latter actually took great delight in painfully nudging the seniors to encourage them to join in the cheering whenever they thought it appropriate - and, faced with such poking and prompting, cheer the seniors most certainly did!

*

The only difficulty that Emled had encountered from any of the seniors since taking over in Seaxe had surprisingly come from Josmi. Josmi, you will recall, is the senior frog responsible for 'ideas and concepts'.

In his very own way Josmi was oblivious to the darker side of the evil toad. This was because he always had his mind firmly focused on new projects and improved methods of doing things, and, in many respects, he was regarded as rather absent minded. As a consequence the wicked ways of Emled and the devious activities of the 'Advisers' were not matters that were immediately obvious to him. In fact, the new regime notwithstanding, he still considered that there was an opportunity for him to make an important and valuable contribution to the well-being of the community.

Josmi therefore became even more crammed full of novel ideas and, as such, he was almost bursting with new schemes whenever he met or bumped into Emled. The giant toad very soon began to detest the sight and sound of the enthusiastic senior. In fact it got to a point where he could not even bear to have him in his company. For two scrawny grasshoppers he would have squashed the life out of the irksome senior but he knew that to do so would be unwise. Nevertheless, Emled determined that Josmi had to go and so he set about devising a bona fide reason for ridding himself of this aggravating frog.

Trying hard to think of something more acceptable than jumping up and down on Josmi's head, Emled suddenly thought of a scheme that he considered to be both clever and rather amusing. Why not send Josmi to Tamsid and install him there as the king of the community he had himself once ruled so tyrannically. In the first place it would definitely get Josmi out from under his feet, and that would for sure be a relief. Secondly, it would almost certainly guarantee that poor Josmi would get the stuffing knocked out of him by the frogs of

Tamsid, and the malicious toad pondered that eventuality with much delight.

This plan of Emled's for the unfortunate Josmi was quite easy to arrange for since he had left Tamsid the position of king had remained vacant. In fact as far as ruling Tamsid was concerned this was actually still in the forelimbs of the toad, and, although clearly some great distance from his old community, he effected this control through his evil lieutenants Kaara and Gawk. Therefore, even though he would be labelled as the king, Josmi would merely be a figurehead as Emled was certainly not about to relinquish the control he held on Tamsid. The toad's master plan had long been to be conqueror, of first Tamsid; then Seaxe; and finally the rest of the frog communities as far as any frog could see.

Josmi was therefore very speedily dispatched to the Far North and immediately installed as the new king of Tamsid. The frogs of Seaxe, and in particular the senior frogs, were shocked and amazed. How on all the lily pads in the river, they thought, could such a young and inexperienced frog as Josmi be elevated to this high office? He hadn't been a senior for five minutes and now, here he was, the king of a community and in the Far North at that.

It is fair to say that there was a general air of disbelief and bewilderment in the local population of frogs in Seaxe, and not a little jealousy from his senior colleagues. The seniors did of course wish him well for the future but each of them secretly hoped that he would fail and make a right royal mess of his new role. They didn't of course know it, but the chances of Josmi ever making a success of his kingship role were remote - in fact they were nil if the truth were made public. Josmi was going to have about as much say in the running of his new community as he would have done in Seaxe had he stayed at home.

Emled had now, therefore, successfully got Josmi out of the way and out of his warts. In so doing he had given the frogs of Seaxe the impression that he was the type of king who would support them whenever possible. How else then could a frog like Josmi have achieved the highest position in a frog community if it hadn't been for Emled putting in a good word on his behalf? Knowing Josmi like they did, the senior frogs of Seaxe had to admit that Emled certainly had a point!

*

Such was the way in which major decisions were being made. Emled ruled his senior group absolutely and, through the 'Advisers', he ensured that his dictates were carried out accurately and speedily.

A number of significant changes had also been introduced and, although they may not have welcomed many of the new ways, the everyday frog couldn't help but be impressed by Emled's ability to 'get things done', for it appeared that no sooner had he made a suggestion than it would be implemented. Indeed the local frogs were so impressed by the precipitous manner by which he put matters into action that they quite forgot about the 'open style' discussion they might otherwise reasonably have expected on the pros and cons of important issues.

It was in fact not long before one frog could be heard observing to another that "Emled takes no time at all to make decisions and carry them through to implementation... such an ability should be applauded". Another would then possibly remark, "However most of what is achieved does rather appear to benefit him personally." Again with regard to the outcome of Emled's decision-making, and seeing yet further benefits bestowed upon the king, other frogs may have been heard to say, "Well, that decision was all right for him but what about us? I thought that he said he cares about us!"

Such references were certainly made in respect of the accommodation that Emled had organised for himself immediately on his arrival in Seaxe. Although he had made a public declaration that he was a sincere carer for his frogs, and, in addition, a great investor in their well-being and comfort, he nevertheless quite insensitively set himself up in a most palatial home on the island despite there being far greater and more urgent needs within the community. Not only was this clearly a blatant disregard for the needy and unfortunate frogs of Seaxe but Emled actually used the very fit and able local frogs, whose energies and endeavours should have been targeted on helping the community's more unfortunate frogs, to build his lavish residence.

On his first day as king of Seaxe Emled had ordered a great many of the most fit and able local frogs to dig and scrabble around in the mud in order to burrow out a huge chamber for him underneath the roots of a fallen tree on the island. Day after day they laboured, digging deeper and deeper until an enormous cavern had been created.

At his request a further slightly smaller area was then excavated at the far end of the main chamber which was ostensibly to be used for storing his food. He then decided that it would be a good idea to line the floor of his chamber with leaves. So he ordered more of the locals to go out and collect bundles and bundles of leaves that had to conform to his precise specifications in that they were neither too damp or too dry; neither were they to be too soft or too hard. He advised the poor exhausted leaf gatherers that it was so important that a king should be comfortable in his 'little home'.

Some of the frogs who helped dig the second chamber thought it rather large even for the mightiest of appetites and imagined that you could probably use such a store for all of the community's needs. How perceptive they were, even if at that stage they did not know it. As the self-appointed controller of the community's resources Emled would indeed be making substantial and regular use of his cavernous store room, both to the satisfaction of his own tummy and the tummies of those he chose to 'reward' or 'favour'.

Having completed the palatial residence on the island Emled then gave further orders to the Seaxe frogs instructing them to dig another hole for him. This one was to be down by the waters' edge and the toad's special requirement was that it should be positioned so that it naturally filled with fresh water each day. The purpose of this facility was to enable Emled to satisfy the pleasure be derived from submerging himself in cool water, particularly during the summer months when the days got a little too hot for his liking, whenever he felt the need to lower the temperature of his warty and unsightly body.

All of this activity took a great deal of time but, while the project was underway, Emled appeared to regard it as both his and the community's main priority and hardly anything else was given any consideration whatsoever.

As for the Seaxe frogs who had previously lived on the island, and there were a great number, many of whom had been there for several generations, Emled had simply told them that they must move out and build new homes for themselves over on the main river bank. He had been dismissive about their preference to stay where their families had lived for so long and he backed this up by saying that it was clearly more appropriate for the king to have a home that was separate from the mainstream of the community. He explained to them how important it would be for him to have somewhere that was peaceful so that he could have the necessary tranquillity in which to think through the many decisions he needed to take in order to improve the lives of all the creatures in Seaxe. Their "initial slight discomfort", he strongly advised, "was a wonderful sacrifice which would ultimately be of benefit to all of the community".

In truth, Emled cared not a tadpole's eyelid for the frogs he was dispossessing from their natural habitat. In fact many of those he uprooted in this way were immediately ordered to work on the creation of his palace. The families of such frogs were therefore left both without a home and without the strongest male member of their household to build their replacement accommodation. To cause such suffering was totally unjustifiable and clearly served to demonstrate what it was that Emled regarded as most important. It was obvious that he placed his own self-gratification above the comfort of those he ruled. So much for the supposed 'caring' attitude of the new king!

As a final word of encouragement to the frogs of Seaxe to get on with the job of building his palace, Emled told them that the king's home should be a place where members of the community would wish to visit. Furthermore, he added, it should be pleasant and inviting, and, if that meant rather luxurious to some of the more cynical frogs' way of thinking, then so be it, Emled said he would just have to grin and bear the spiteful comments and simply put up with such sad and narrow-minded attitudes in the line of duty.

This all sounded quite plausible when the toad said it, but in truth the chance of any ordinary frog crossing the river and clambering up on to the island in order to see Emled was very slim indeed. Indeed, and as soon as he took up residence on the island, if any of the local frogs wanted to see him they had to register their request well in advance with one of the toad's 'personal aides'. These latter posts were actually a new innovation and had not been part of Moha's administration. Their job was to attend to the king's many pressing engagements and organise his schedule and all of his appointments. No frog was in fact allowed to see Emled without first going through the 'personal aides'. Even then it was only possible to see the king if these frogs thought it to be appropriate – and on most occasions they refused such permission. It was also evident that when Emled travelled around the community he would almost always be accompanied by his entourage of 'personal aides'.

It was not long before it became apparent that the only Seaxe frogs who were ever allowed to go over to the island to see Emled were those to whom he had personally extended an invitation. It was also becoming clear that those who were invited were generally of a certain type in that they were usually the younger frogs, almost exclusively female frogs, and, in the case of the latter, some might say only those females who were rather on the attractive side.

When any of Emled's 'personal aides' overheard a conversation in which one local frog had asked another why it was that only young and attractive females ever got invited to the king's palace, they were informed, in no uncertain manner, that Emled thought it a disgrace that Moha had never in the past promoted any female frogs to senior positions. As a result he was now personally, and very thoroughly, having to vet all appropriate females in order to correct this travesty of justice so that he could indeed appoint them to high positions in the community when the right opportunity arose.

This was of course a laudable policy but one that was not yet much in evidence as all of the vacant or newly created posts that had arisen since Emled's arrival in Seaxe had actually been filled by male frogs. To make matters worse, in the case of the 'Advisers' and 'personal aides' to the king, not only were the successful applicants male but they were, of course, also large brown marsh frogs. It was clear that Emled still needed to do a great deal more 'vetting' of the female frogs of Seaxe before he would be willing to put what he preached into practice.

As was to happen more and more with the pronouncements made by Emled they were merely turning out to be empty rhetoric. Sudden waves of enthusiasm engendered in the community by big statements of what he was going to do would soon be followed by massive tides of deflation as yet another promise would fall by the wayside. There would always subsequently be a reason why things couldn't be done and of course it was never his fault. Blame was nearly always apportioned to what Emled described as Moha's poor management. On such occasions the fulsome creature would sadly shake his head and excuse his inability to make sufficient progress by saying that it would take several long winters to eradicate the mistakes and negligence of the past.

To all intents and purposes the island had therefore become both a refuge and a fortress for Emled. On it he had built his palatial home, or rather the common frogs of Seaxe had built it for him. He had also removed all the local frogs who had previously lived there and in their place he had installed many of the marsh frogs whom he had brought with him from Tamsid. To further give the appearance of a 'no-go area' for the everyday frogs of Seaxe, Emled had the island's boundaries regularly patrolled, both day and night, by the mean-looking brown marsh frogs.

Although it was highly unlikely that any of the peace loving Seaxe frogs would have attempted to cross over to the island uninvited, the marsh frogs made a great show of warding off any creature who came within croaking distance. This meant that a considerable area around the island was now off limits for the locals. Such restrictions had never been imposed within the memory of any of the Seaxe frogs and they found it hard to understand Emled's motives in doing so now. On the one forelimb they had a new king who had personally told them that he was accessible to all; and yet on the other forelimb he isolated himself from the community with a protective barrier around him of water and extremely aggressive marsh frogs. It was not surprising, therefore, that they were becoming increasingly confused with the new regime.

Emled's excursions across the river to the main bank were also becoming less frequent. During the early days of his kingship he had made a point of being seen out and about amongst 'his frogs'. Gradually this practice had reduced and now, just eight weeks since he had taken over from Moha, the only times he left his palace were on the occasions when formal community meetings had been arranged in the main central area of Seaxe by his 'personal aides'. Sinisterly, these meetings were specifically organised in order to enable him to deliver yet another of his pronouncements on some important topic or another.

The personable and seemingly friendly approach of the first few weeks had now been replaced by pre-arranged and structured meetings to which only selected groups of frogs were invited. These meetings became the means by which Emled began his structured assault on the minds of the ordinary frogs of Seaxe in respect of the previous administration, whereby he sought to disabuse any fond memories that the community may still have held either for Moha or the happy days of the old king's reign.

Emled also ensured that the remaining seniors (now of course only numbering five since Josmi had been dispatched to the Far North) were excluded from these meetings so that he only had the ear of the common everyday frogs of Seaxe.

Emled's intention was to speak to all the community in this way and, whilst they were gathered in front of him, he would say how sorry he was that they had endured the rule of such an uncaring and thoughtless king as Moha for so long. He told them that during the days and nights he had spent amongst his new community he had heard many heart-rending accounts of their previous poor treatment. There had been stories, he said, that had moved him deeply. There had also been times when some of the tales of great suffering that he had listened to actually caused him to have long and lonely troubled nights, during which if he had ever eventually drifted off to sleep it was only after he had wept a torrent of tears.

Emled said that never again must the good frogs of Seaxe have to endure the pain and anguish of the past. He promised that he would personally see to it that no trace of the previous administration would be allowed to remain. In fact, he said, he wanted any frog who witnessed such activities of the past still being practised to feel able to personally come and see him and say just who it was that had perpetrated such unforgivable acts.

Emled called this approach his 'Croak Blower's Charter' and he said that any frog who came forward with such news should not be regarded as a telltale or a sneak but rather they should be seen as doing the whole community a great service. To expose such problems, as well as rooting out the purveyors of quite unacceptable past practices and attitudes in our community, he added, is a noble and splendid thing and must be seen as a benefit to all.

*

Now frogs are not necessarily the brightest of all the beings on this earth but they are generally regarded as trusting and very friendly towards their fellows. Some may describe them as being somewhat gullible in this respect although in some ways this is a rather endearing feature of these amiable little creatures. There will, however, always be exceptions to the rule as is so clearly and unfortunately illustrated by the marsh frogs. Frogs are also not renowned for having great powers of memory.

When all these ingredients are combined it will not be surprising for you to hear that with the passing of time the fond memories of Moha began to evaporate in the minds of the Seaxe frogs. For a wicked and devious creature such as Emled it was not too difficult for him to then fill this space with his own evil brand of dogma. Emled was of course very much aware of the psychology of the everyday frog and he cunningly used their weaknesses to his advantage.

It was not long, therefore, before one frog was saying to another how much they had been abused by the old regime and how welcome it was to have a kind and caring king like Emled in charge of their well-being. Converting any doubters to his way of thinking was also getting easier by the day for the evil toad, and this was largely due to the fact that if any local frog held a contrary view or spoke badly of him such an individual was immediately reported by way of the 'Croak Blower's Charter'.

Occasionally at first, and more frequently as time went by, Emled sadly had to report that some frogs were finding the new culture quite beyond their ability to cope. It was therefore necessary, he suggested, for frogs who had been referred to him through the 'Charter' to be sent away to a rather beautiful place where they would be assisted in their full rehabilitation back into the community. It had gone quite unnoticed in the new culture that was being introduced to the good frogs of Seaxe that such frogs never actually returned home again.

As for the exclusion of the senior frogs from the organised meetings in the community, Emled advised the locals that he considered this to be an essential element in his 'open' approach to their management. He said that he did not want the everyday frog to feel intimidated by the seniors. He advised that with the seniors present at the meetings the common frog might not feel able to raise issues that may reflect badly on their more highly ranked colleagues. Emled made it very clear that he wanted all frogs in the community to speak from the heart and be able to say what they really felt. After all, the toad would say, how else was he to know what needed to be put right if his community was not able to tell him what is wrong. As far as he was concerned they could say anything they liked to him because, and Emled always made a point of working this phrase into his speeches when he addressed the community, "*Who cares? Emled cares! I care*".

When Emled spoke these words (or his rallying call as he privately liked to think of it) he would dramatically raise his forelimbs and open them wide as if embracing his audience. He would then speak the first two statements of '*Who cares*' and '*Emled cares*' very loudly with forelimbs outstretched. And then, when he spoke the third statement of "*I care*", he would clasp his chest tightly with his forelimbs and drop his voice to a rasping whisper leaning forward towards the assembled masses as he did so in order to gain greater effect.

It would be very unkind of me to describe the everyday frog in the Seaxe community as having been brainwashed by Emled as this may give you the impression that they are a weak, feeble-minded and poor example of their species. This would of course be quite unfair for, as I have already said, they are kind, gentle and loving creatures as well as being trusting to the point of being gullible. That their good nature was being preyed upon by the wicked toad, who it must be said possessed a far greater intellect and intelligence than they did the foundation of which was based upon pure unadulterated evil, was in truth no real fault of their own.

Emled, therefore, was unfortunately finding no difficulty at all in succeeding to win them over by his dogma. A dogma that we know was based on terrible lies and great deceit. How else was it that the poor vulnerable frogs of Seaxe could ever have been encouraged to talk of Moha and their life under the kind old king as something that was horrible and oppressive and definitely best forgotten? And how else is it that they could now be ruled by such a wicked creature who had more evil in one of the warts upon his gruesome body than was possessed by the whole of the community put together.

Unfortunately, however, and it has to be said, the evil that was Emled was gradually being injected into the Seaxe community by virtue of his menacing presence and his organised onslaught on the innocent and pure minds of the everyday frogs. Through his constant bad-mouthing of Moha, and the widespread use of the 'Croak Blower's Charter', the foul toad was beginning to build up a good deal of support for himself from a community that was quickly forgetting how good it had been when Moha was king.

Had Moha and Mars been able to witness what was now going on in Seaxe they would have been greatly troubled. They would have been even more concerned by what they may have heard, for Emled had introduced a chant at the end of each of the organised meetings that he 'suggested' the locals might wish to join in. At first the Seaxe frogs were a little reluctant for they had never been asked to do anything like this before and they felt that they were almost being persuaded to worship their new king. Emled, however, advised them that it was quite normal and a good way to develop a community spirit. In their confused minds they couldn't recall Moha ever suggesting or asking for such vocal support – or did he, they wondered – it really was getting rather difficult to remember the old days?

Nevertheless, with a little cajoling and encouragement from the large brown marsh frogs who made a habit of 'getting amongst the audience' (as they liked to describe their bullying ways) at such gatherings, the local frogs soon began to join in the chanting. I am sure you will be interested to know the words that the frogs were encouraged to chant. They were as follows:

Who cares?
Emled cares.
Who cares?
Emled cares.
Hail the king,
Long may he reign.
Who cares?
Emled cares.
Emled cares for us all.

The chanting would initially be led by Emled who, as he rose at the end of each meeting, would throw open his forelimbs in a mock embrace and shout "*Who cares? Emled cares! I care*". Then, as he made to leave the meeting, the marsh frogs in the audience would puff themselves up and croak very loudly "*Who cares? Emled cares! Who cares? Emled cares!*" These disciples of Emled would look all around them and wave to the local frogs to join in until every frog without exception had also begun to chant. Then, when they were certain all those assembled were participating, the marsh frogs would conduct the audience in the completion of the chant.

Now, whilst it is true that all frogs do like to croak along together, and particularly so when there is some festivity or other to celebrate, they were quite unused to chanting. Without knowing exactly why, the frogs of Seaxe felt very uncomfortable carrying out what appeared to them to be a rather ritualistic practice.

Had you been able to observe at one of these meetings you would have noticed that when the chanting stopped it was always followed by an eerie silence. You would probably have remarked at that stage that the local frogs looked a little stunned at what they had done. You would certainly have noticed that no frog ever spoke to another frog about this form of supplication, for it was as if they were both numbed and embarrassed by their having taken part in such a strange ritual.

Things were thus changing substantially in the once happy community of Seaxe. Gone were the glorious days of Moha's reign which were rapidly being replaced by a form of suppression and control the like of which these kind and naive creatures had never experienced. It was now a community where their every movement was watched and noted; and what they said was reported and recorded. Some of the local frogs even wondered if their very thoughts were being monitored in some way, although they didn't like to dwell on such ponderings just in case they were true.

Most of the watching was of course being carried out by the marsh frogs and crows. However, the introduction of the 'Croak Blower's Charter' had disturbingly meant that one could not now even trust a close friend, as comments made quite innocently by way of idle chitter-chatter could be reported directly to Emled which might lead to one being sent away for 'rehabilitation'.

*

This new culture was based on a system that Emled described as 'openness and honesty' where all frogs would be enabled to positively contribute to the work of the community. He also insisted that within the system he wanted every frog to be trusting and courteous towards each other at all times.

What price this new culture? What price this culture which was in truth run by fear and intimidation? Although no frog would dare to say such a thing, too scared were they of the recrimination that would certainly follow, it did appear that the only real beneficiaries of the new culture were Emled, his favourite female frogs, and the ever increasing number of aggressive marsh frogs who continually dominated and bullied the indigenous frogs of Seaxe.

Moha and Mars would indeed have been saddened by the way things had developed in Seaxe. Life for the everyday frog had changed out of all recognition. Emled, of course, would say that it had changed for the best, but I wonder what you, the reader, thinks. Would you have liked to have lived under the rule of Emled within his new culture where his principles of so called 'openness and honesty' were practised or would you have preferred the old days when Moha was king? I know what I would choose!

Chapter Nineteen

Emled Has a Dream

About nine months had passed since Emled had become king of Seaxe. During this time the community had become thoroughly manipulated to suit the wicked toad. Fun and laughter were things of the past. The previously happy and contented frogs had become dour, sullen and downcast. It was of course indisputably a fact that they were now busier than ever before. Indeed they were far busier! However, if any frog had been able to take a little time out from his or her unrelenting daily chores then they would almost certainly have wondered what all this industry had actually achieved. In truth every frog was occupied with doing something or other all of the time, although the output and what they had to show for it was, in all honesty, negligible.

Emled's philosophy was that it was better to keep every frog's mind and body fully employed even if the resulting end product was worthless. In this way the frogs would have very little spare time in which to reflect on just how much of little value they actually produced. This of course meant that in the small amount of supposedly 'free time' the frogs of Seaxe were allowed, Emled was able to occupy this space by arranging his large gatherings whereat he could concentrate and focus his brainwashing and manipulative techniques on the poor wretched local frogs.

It was in these early months of Emled's reign that the seniors expressed an interest in knowing more about their new king's policies and strategies. It was, therefore, under what can only really be described as fairly gentle pressure that Emled was encouraged to set out his priorities so that the community could see clearly what issues he regarded as most important and those that he considered to be of lesser importance.

Not surprisingly in this exercise, Emled had determined that the well-being of the young frogs of the community should be the area requiring his most urgent and undivided attention. Not, he would say, that he didn't think that the adult frogs and those members of the community who were designated as 'unfortunate' frogs were equally as important. Far from it in fact! However, he would go on to explain, the young frogs are after all the life-blood of the community so it is vital that he should spend time nurturing the youngsters to ensure that a firm and resolute foundation could be laid for the future.

We of course know that the major reason why Emled concentrated on the young frogs was because he used them to ultimately engorge his fat belly by sacrificing the poor innocent creatures to the humans in return for their satisfying his insatiable lust for mounds of prime red meat. However, there is also another reason why he preferred the company of the young which, for a king who should care equally for all his subjects, is in its own way almost as sinister as the first. This is the fact that Emled actually detested frogs who were old or infirm, or upon whom some misfortune had fallen.

You see, inside the body of Emled there burned the desire for everlasting youthfulness, beauty and strength. This caused him to not even be able to look at the old, infirm or unfortunate frogs without being filled with abject fear of seeing what he himself might someday become. He shielded himself from these visions by only having in his close company the most perfect young specimens he could find.

It was, in fact, not long after Emled announced his massive declaration of interest and support for the youth of Seaxe that scores of the young frogs actually began disappearing. Just like the youngsters of Tamsid, Emled had taken them out on his field excursions, that is to say, the so called 'Young Frogs Initiative'; and again, just like the young of Tamsid, many never again returned to their homes.

Emled, as you would expect of this wicked and perverse monster, was always full of excuses for their demise. He would come back alone from these 'excursions' and speak of ferocious attacks by wild cats or sudden storms that had blown out of nowhere and which had whisked the young frogs away to their certain death. He did, however, on each such occasion make a point of reassuring the community that a strenuous programme such as the one he had set for the young frogs must be expected to incur a few casualties. To lose more than this would really be down to fate and he described such catastrophes as terribly bad luck. Although fate was seemingly not in Emled's favour when it came to his youth strategy, he advised that he knew what he was doing and, if any frog had any doubts, then they would be welcome to take a trip to Tamsid where they would see the fruits of his youth programme in a most successful and well run community.

That there was of course nothing to see in Tamsid by way of positive benefits did not concern the evil toad. He well knew that in the first place no frog from Seaxe would dare to travel through Waga to see the Tamsid experience; and secondly, if they did attempt to get across that smelly bog, then they would without any shadow of a doubt be murdered by the patrolling carrion crows and villainous marsh frogs.

Another thing that Emled knew was that if visitors did drop in unexpectedly on Tamsid they would find very little evidence there of Josmi being in charge or acting in a kingly manner. In fact Josmi had got off to a rather 'damp squib' sort of start in Tamsid for on his arrival he was given no festive welcome nor were there the usual scenes of the whole community coming out to greet their new king. Normally, on such occasions, the river banks would have been lined ten frogs deep at least; and, as for getting a better view from a well-positioned lily pad, then that would definitely be out of the question as the best sites would have been booked many weeks in advance.

The fact was that there were only a few creatures who even knew he was coming and these were Gawk, Kaara and a small group of Emled's 'personal aides'. Emled had left several of the latter behind in Tamsid with a mandate to oversee affairs and provide him with regular reports on what was going on in his old community. These frogs were as evil and wicked as any of Emled's closest allies and they were quite capable of managing Tamsid and suppressing Josmi's enthusiasm whilst Gawk, Kaara and Emled himself were away in Seaxe 'knocking the local inhabitants into shape' as the toad privately liked to describe their activities.

Once Josmi had been safely tucked away in an isolated but comfortable burrow some distance from the main centre of the Tamsid community, the 'personal aides' slowly put the word around that the new king had arrived. They informed the local frogs that king Josmi would be introducing himself in due course, once he had settled in to his accommodation, and they were sure that every frog would be interested to know that he had many magnificent ideas to explore with them. The 'personal aides' also advised that Josmi and Emled were going to experiment with the merging of cultures, as the new king had been brought up in a vastly different community to that of Tamsid. They added that it was certainly going to be an interesting experience seeing if frogs from other communities could cope with the enormously successful way of life in Tamsid.

When the local frogs of Tamsid did eventually get to see Josmi what they in fact witnessed was a zany character who was so full of ideas and notions about how to run a community that he was on to his next innovation even before he had finished the last. They would find that on one day Josmi would be excitedly addressing one particular group of frogs where he would be setting out his vision of the future; and then on the next day he would be found describing his vision to another group in an entirely different way but with just as much enthusiasm. Knowing Josmi as we do we can appreciate that he wouldn't have done this to intentionally mislead his new community. It really was just down to the fact that overnight he would have had so many more wonderful and creative new ideas that his vision would have automatically changed to cater for the latest concepts.

In truth Josmi's mind was now way out of control. That he had from time to time in the past dreamt up some very good ideas could not be contested. However, in Seaxe he had been well supervised by Moha who had been well able to sift the rather eccentric young senior's best suggestions from the many erroneous ones. Now in Tamsid, where he was being left entirely to his own devices, Josmi was viewed by his new subjects as being as nutty as a horse chestnut tree and as hard to understand as a monkey-puzzle tree.

Notwithstanding these rather unkind, but nevertheless, unfortunately, quite accurate views of Josmi, he was tolerated in his new community largely because the Tamsid frogs were intrigued to know what he would come out with next. Quite honestly they had for so long been devoid of humour and fun in their community that they regarded Josmi as providing some light relief and quite enjoyable entertainment. In fact new phrases were being introduced into the Tamsid vocabulary at Josmi's expense that were applied to actions that had little substance, meaning or use. Indeed phrases such as "That's a Josmi!" or "You're telling me a Josmi, aren't you?" or even, when describing a complete and utter calamity, "What a Josmi!".

Apart from obtaining their own amusement from him the Tamsid frogs paid quite literally no heed to their new king. In any event when it came to the actual management and daily running of the community it was the 'personal aides' of Emled, together with Gawk and Kaara, who were very clearly still in charge. As a consequence, and despite Josmi's many brilliant new ideas, not a lot had changed since Emled's departure. In fact nothing much had changed at all.

The 'personal aides' merely encouraged Josmi to come up with more and more ideas and notions which they assured him they would personally see were applied to the community. Sadly, of course, none of Josmi's concepts were ever introduced in Tamsid, although he was quite unaware that this was the case as he was permanently kept so busy being creative that he never had time to assess the effect his suggestions were having on the local frogs. Nevertheless, in his blissful ignorance, Josmi was happy doing what he did best which was to dream up new ideas one after the other and subsequently not having to worry if they actually worked in practice.

So Josmi was happy concentrating on his wonderful new ideas and concepts; and the frogs of the Tamsid community were in turn mildly amused by his antics. He did sometimes think how differently his new colleagues behaved, compared to his friends and colleagues back in Seaxe, for he couldn't recall having even one of his new ideas contested or questioned since his arrival in Tamsid. However, Josmi wasn't going to dwell too long thinking about the 'whys' and the 'wherefores' of such matters as time was precious and he certainly didn't want to waste such a valuable commodity by worrying about such trivialities.

Well, that's quite enough of Josmi for the time being. We will return to him later in this book to see how he progresses(?) in Tamsid. For the moment, however, we really must be getting back to Emled in order to see what evil he is planning.

*

It was indeed on an early autumnal night a little over nine months or so into his reign in Seaxe that Emled was to be found sitting in his palace on the island. He was restless and unbearably hot and sweaty and for the life of him he just could not get to sleep. He therefore decided to venture out into the night and head for one of his favourite spots.

The weather had been unusually warm for the time of year and on this night the air hung thick and humid beneath a heavy cloud cover. Even though he was now out in the open the toad still felt uncomfortably hot and sticky. The sky above him was littered with huge banks of rolling clouds that moved slowly across the moon bringing, whenever they did so, almost total blackness to the land. Then, all of a sudden, as the clouds moved on, a bright full moon would again peep out from behind its cloudy shroud and light up the earth with its soft white beams.

Emled shuffled his way to the far west side of the island from where it was just about possible to see the silhouette of the topmost part of Kingfisher's Bridge. The evil toad always allowed himself a sly smile whenever he saw or thought about the bridge as it brought back memories of the massacre of the kingfishers that he had ordered. He made a mental note on this occasion to rename the bridge as soon as possible. Maybe 'King Emled's Bridge' or possibly 'Emled the Great Bridge', he mused?

It was on this far west side of the island that Emled had arranged his hole to be dug in which he could wallow to his wicked heart's content. This pit, you will probably recall, was supposed to fill up and replenish quite naturally with water from the river. Over time, however, it seemed as if even the river didn't want to associate itself with the poisonous toad as strangely it had stopped taking the old water out and putting fresh water in. The result was that the pit had now become a sloppy muddy mess which stank to the very tops of the tallest trees of the rank and evil toad.

On reaching this gruesome place Emled laboriously eased the lower half of his massive bulk into the smelly liquid. He then sank lower and lower until only his thick neck and monstrous head were visible. As he felt the cool foul smelling mud reduce his body temperature he stared at his own reflection in the blackness of the pool. In reality all he could see was the outline of his head as it was quite impossible for the black slime to reveal any features whatsoever. Nevertheless the toad believed he could see every detail of his face and each time the moon bathed the surrounding countryside with its mellow white light he gloried in his own reflection. However, although the face that Emled saw in his mind's eye was actually that of Mars, the evil monster convinced himself that it was his own face that was looking back at him. Therefore, being extremely satisfied with what he thought he saw, Emled turned his head first to one side and then to the other constantly admiring the handsome creature he imagined he could see.

An owl suddenly swooped nearby and the scream of the poor animal it grabbed in its talons shook Emled from his reverie. At that moment more clouds gathered across the moon causing the toad's outline to totally disappear and the blackness of the pool to return. A grisly and angry toad leapt out of the putrid pit cursing Mars as well as the whole of the frog community of Seaxe. How he despised the creatures he ruled and how he loathed Mars for the strength of his mind and the beauty of his body. He knew that Mars possessed the attributes for which he craved, and which he, the all powerful and all conquering toad, would never admit to not being able to own.

Emled decided to make his way back to the palace. The exertions of the walk and his anger at being so rudely interrupted by the sounds of the night had at last made him feel tired and he now felt very sleepy. Once inside his residence he sat himself down on a pile of damp leaves and fell into a deep slumber.

It was not, however, a peaceful rest for the unsavoury and warty toad. In fact he spent an extremely disturbed and troubled night throughout which he constantly saw pictures of his past flash in and out of his mind.

Any creature on the island, and even those on the river bank or high up in the tallest trees of Horse Chestnut Wood, must have heard the fearful snoring and snorting that emanated from inside the malevolent toad's palace that night. As he saw his life passing through his subconscious the many wicked and sometimes painful scenes that he trawled from the depths of his evil memory caused him to toss first this way and then that way. And, each time he changed positions, his snoring would be violently interrupted by a great deal of spluttering and croaking as he screamed obscenities and curses at those he saw in his dreams.

The horrendous sounds coming from the obnoxious toad's palace so frightened the regular creatures of the night that they were too scared to come out of their burrows and nests choosing rather to stay close by their kith and kin. They had quickly grown to realise that when the king was angry the only safe place to be, if you could call it safe, was tucked up at home in their own beds.

In the most vivid and painful of his nightmares Emled saw a great fire burning all around him. He was engulfed in flames and there was no way out for him. He could hear creatures screaming and screeching as a fierce wind blew the tongues of fire deeper and deeper into the forest. There were also cries that he recognised from humans with whom he had lived but Emled could not see them through the billowing smoke that was choking his throat and stinging his eyes. He wanted these people to hurry and rescue him but he knew that the flames were too high and the fire too hot for them to get back into the farmhouse.

The huge glass aquarium in which Emled had been held captive was becoming hotter and hotter. Even the pool of water in which he had almost completely immersed himself was beginning to get more than just a little uncomfortably warm. He started to imagine that he was going to be burnt to death or boiled alive if someone didn't come and save him very soon. For the toad, there appeared to be no means of escape.

Then, from out of the sky, there came great white forks of lightning. The old farmhouse in which he was being kept had already been hit by a fireball and had immediately burst into flames. The family who had held him prisoner for so many years had only been able to get themselves out just moments before the wild flames took control. They had time neither to gather their valuables and belongings nor to think of the toad. The young child of the house who had fed Emled throughout his captivity would become distraught at the loss of his pet but there really was no way that anyone could re-enter the blazing inferno.

As yet more streaks of lightning dived into the surrounding woods they were accompanied by one of such immense ferocity that as it struck deep down into the heart of a huge oak, which stood close by the farmhouse, it caused the top half of the tree to immediately explode into thousands of burning fragments. The lightning then raced down through the devastated tree's trunk and into its roots causing the bottom half of the massive oak to split in two with one section falling backwards into the roaring forest and the other forwards onto the blazing farmhouse. As the enormous piece of timber hit the building it plunged right through the weakened and fire damaged wooden structure sending masses of glowing splinters and embers far up into the stormy night sky.

A sudden deafening roar was all Emled could recall as the tree tore through the farmhouse and crashed its way into the first floor bedroom in which his aquarium had been kept. Emled was shocked by the cacophony of noise as the house was being crushed by the falling oak. He shut his eyes very tightly waiting for the final few seconds of his life to expire. The next thing he knew was that he was aware of the sensation of being thrown through the air and, as he tumbled about in his glass prison, food bowls and all manner of paraphernalia hurtled painfully into him. Then, with an enormous bump, the cramped world in which Emled had lived for so long landed very heavily and the toad feared that this signalled that his life was now at an end. He kept his eyes firmly closed as even he was afraid of what he might see, feeling sure that he was dead.

But the end hadn't come for the toad, and, as he slowly opened first one eye and then the other, he realised that by some fluke he had been thrown clear of the devastated farmhouse and he had actually landed far out into the middle of the lawn. He was also, much to his amazement, still alive.

As he looked back at the farmhouse he could see flames leaping out of every window and a huge gaping hole where the oak tree had evidently crashed through the roof. He could also now see a dozen or so people hugging each other and crying in despair. There were some who were trying to extinguish the flames and others who were clearly desperate to save someone who was seemingly trapped inside the burning house.

The toad was filled with hatred for the family who had kept him imprisoned in his glass cage for all those years. The people who had pressed their noses against the sides of the aquarium prying into even his most private of activities. The very people who had tapped on the glass and woken him up from his precious sleep at all hours of the night and day whenever they wanted some entertainment.

Emled cursed them as he pulled himself together. "Suitable punishment in return for their cruelty towards me!" he muttered to himself.

Gathering his wits together Emled looked around before deciding to quickly make for the far end of the garden where no flames were burning and where there were no trees or bushes that could still be set alight. There he wriggled into an old and disused coal bunker where he remained throughout the night until he could be certain that all the humans had gone from the area.

The storm raged on and Emled listened to the rain as it lashed down upon the corrugated iron roof of the bunker. He crouched low every time a roar of thunder broke out in the troubled heavens and he screwed up his eyes as the simultaneous bright white flashes of lightning illuminated his refuge. The ferocity of the claps of thunder indicated that the centre of the storm was still above the farmhouse and each time the clouds exploded, so the floor of the small brick bunker in which the toad sheltered shook, as if in fear of imminent collapse.

Many hours later, and as the storm began to subside, Emled sat quite motionless and concentrated on the now distant thunder he could still hear rolling around in the clouds. The lightning had stopped although he could still see faint traces of brightness on the far horizon as the storm ripped into and brutalised some far off communities. The rain, however, continued to fall heavily and this pleased the toad as he knew that in such weather it was very unlikely that any of the humans whom he detested so much would be out and about.

When he emerged from the bunker and looked towards the farmhouse what he saw made him laugh out loud. Where only the day before had stood a large and very beautiful thatched period farmhouse, all that now remained was a smouldering burnt out wreck of blackened beams and skeletal mounds of bricks and misshapen iron supports. The air was thick with the smell of burning and long grey wreaths of smoke trailed up from the ruins and disappeared into the darkness of the wood.

Emled again cursed the people who had imprisoned him and he felt glad that fate had dealt them such a savage blow. He thought it went some way towards repaying them for the undignified manner in which he had been treated whilst in their charge.

The toad then climbed upon the charred stump of the very same ancient oak tree of which such a substantial part had fallen onto the farmhouse during the storm. From this vantage point he surveyed the devastation around him.

A sudden gust of wind blew from behind Emled in the direction of the remains of the farmhouse and the toad took the opportunity to fill his lungs with some clean cool air. He was free! Free from his enforced captivity! Free for the first time since he was torn from the grip of his mother's hands so many long and hate filled years ago! He was indeed now free to make his mark in the wild, and make his mark he certainly intended to do! His whole body was so full of loathing and bitterness at having been cooped up for so long that he now wanted to exact his revenge on all other living things!

"*I am Emled!*" he shouted from his tree stump platform. "*I am Emled, the most powerful of all the creatures of the river banks and forests, so beware!!*" As he boomed out his warning he emitted from the glands on his body a stinking milky fluid which spread all over and down the sides of the stump. The evil that was Emled had arrived, and, as he bellowed out his coming, he began marking out his territory with the foul noxious discharge.

Although no living creature was within range to hear his words, two adult frogs a good distance away saw what they thought was a large misshapen frog sitting upon the stump of a tree. Clearly in need of company, and being keen to check if they had found a friend or relative who had also managed to live through the storm, they hurried across to the place where they thought they had seen their fellow survivor.

Alas, by the time they got to the tree stump the toad had left to go trundling through the forest in search of food as the excitement of freedom had given him a great hunger. All that now remained on the spot where they thought they had seen a frog was a whitish slimy fluid which, on closer inspection, stank more than anything they had ever had the misfortune to smell before in their lives. The two frogs hopped quickly away with waves of nausea rushing through their bodies and their eyes stinging painfully from the vapour of the revolting milky substance.

The toad turned over and over in his sleep as in his dreams he recalled the storm and the traumatic moment he was given his freedom. The expressions on Emled's face contorted his features into an even more ghastly and frightening sight, as galloping through his mind raced further pictures of the death and destruction he had inflicted on all creatures that he had met in the early days following his escape into the wild. How he had enjoyed seeing smaller and less strong creatures suffer as he bullied and beat them. And what delight he had gained from witnessing the shock and fear he meted out on larger beasts such as cats and dogs when he lured them close enough so that he could coat them with his evil smelling and poisonous body fluid.

Most of all, however, he loved to dominate the local frog population of Tamsid. When he first saw these small creatures he had looked at his own reflection in the bogs more carefully and wondered why he appeared to be so different when compared to them. He knew that he had been brought to the farmhouse from a faraway land and he wondered if that was the reason for this striking contrast.

It almost goes without saying that the local frogs were equally surprised when they initially saw Emled as they had never before seen such a creature. At first they thought he bore a slight resemblance to their own species and that he may possibly be derived from some previously unheard of giant race of frogs. However, when they looked a little closer, they could see that he was quite unlike a frog. They had then wondered if the creature was diseased in some way, for he stank dreadfully and his face was so hideously ugly. They could also see that his body was grossly misshapen and covered in the most unsightly warts imaginable.

For his own part Emled thought the frogs were rather pleasant to look at with their small smooth-skinned bodies and a much greater natural athleticism than he could ever possess. He desperately wanted to look just like them and he refused to believe that he was not of the same species. He was, however, quite sure he could see many similarities between himself and the much smaller creatures and he therefore convinced himself that he must simply be a larger version of their kind. As for the differences he put these down to personally being blessed with greater beauty and a more muscular physique. He was indeed, he assured himself, a far more handsome and magnificent specimen than could be found elsewhere within his new found community of rather under-sized frogs.

It suited the inherent wickedness of Emled to force himself upon these small creatures for he knew full well that none of them could ever impose their will upon him. Thus, he soon found that he could very easily dominate the local frogs as he wished by virtue of his immense size and superior strength. This fact gave the toad a great deal of pleasure and he nominated himself as the king of their community knowing that he could rule unopposed in his new domain.

And so it was that Emled came to arrive in the community of Tamsid in the region known to frogs as the Far North. With absolutely no opposition either to his physical power or wicked ways he was freely able to practise his evil doings with impunity. Whether it was by destiny or by a perverse quirk of fate that such a creature should set hindlimb or forelimb upon this earth, it is not possible to say. However, come he did, and, as far as Emled was concerned, he was here to stay forever.

The only thing in fact that the toad actually missed from his years of captivity was the food the humans dropped into his aquarium. He pined for the delicious tasty morsels that they fed him and in particular the succulent pieces of red meat cut from prime steak that he used to occasionally be given as a special reward. Emled had soon worked out that to get such a treat he had to hop about in his glass prison in an undignified manner in order to satisfy the humans' amusement. After he had performed sufficiently they would dangle the steak above his large head so he almost had to beg to be given the meat. He abhorred having to act in such a demeaning fashion but he could not resist the juicy red raw steak. Occasionally, and usually just as he was about to snatch the food from the fingers of the humans, they would tease him by withdrawing the meat only to dangle it a little higher over him. He hated this trick more than he could describe and he promised himself that somehow, one day, he would get his own back on his captors.

Although he craved the delectable meat his captors had fed him during his captivity, the thought of recapture and again being confined to the small glass prison made Emled extremely wary of humans. However, his longing for the tender red meat caused him to watch out for their presence, and, when the opportunity arose, to follow them from a safe distance in the hope that they might drop pieces of food or leave some behind whilst picnicking. He would thus stalk humans and forage around in the area they had sat, in the vain hope that he would find something worthwhile to eat. Occasionally he was lucky and he would then greedily gobble up any acceptable scraps. More often than not, however, all that would be left behind were either a few greasy wrappers with tiny pieces of spicy potato stuck to the insides, or a number of small papery objects that were burnt at one end and stained yellow at the other which tasted quite disgusting.

It was about this time, and quite by sheer chance, that Emled stumbled upon a way of obtaining food from the humans. Indeed as much food as he could eat. It was good food too and quite as delectable and delicious as any of the sustenance he had ever received during his captive past.

This event occurred whilst he had been in the company of a large group of frogs. They had been out in search of grasshoppers, some distance from their home, in order to replenish the palace stores for the toad's personal consumption. As they foraged along the river bank, several humans suddenly sprung out from behind some bushes and spread a thin meshed net over the entire party of frogs including Emled.

As the excited humans took stock of their catch they selectively stamped an all but the young fit frogs and then they put the latter into large cardboard boxes. They were confused as to what to make of Emled. At first one of the humans shouted, "Keep 'im, 'e might be worth a few quid! He looks like one of them cane toads, you know, those poisonous blighters from Australia." Then, as one of the men attempted to pick him up, Emled automatically emitted the milky fluid in order to protect himself. His potential captor then cried out, "Cor, get a whiff of this! There's no way I'm grabbing 'old of this 'orrible beggar!" With that the man gave Emled such a powerful kick that it sent him cartwheeling into some long grass a good five or so metres away.

The toad sat in the shelter of the undergrowth ruefully rubbing the bumps and grazes on his body. At first he had been really scared as the thought of returning to captivity made his flesh creep. But then, as he watched the humans fill their boxes with the frightened and wriggling young frogs, an idea entered his mind. In fact a quite wicked and mischievous idea that encouraged him to think that he could convert this tragic situation into one that might just work to his own advantage.

Emled therefore decided to follow the humans to see where they were going to take their quarry. He scurried along behind them through the dense undergrowth of the forest's floor, carefully avoiding the well trodden path the humans were taking so as not to be seen. It was a long hike for the toad but eventually they came to a large house outside of which there was parked a small van in the driveway. The men then proceeded to put the boxes containing the young Tamsid frogs into the back of this vehicle. On the side of the van were written the words:

NEIL ADCOCK
PRESTIGE RESTAURANT SUPPLIER
Grenouille et l'escargot nos specialités

Emled had no idea what any of the words meant of course, but he was clever enough to realise that the men had purposely set a trap to catch the frogs and that for some reason or other they particularly wanted the young frogs. (For you the reader the translation into English of the French words on the van reveals that Neil Adcock is actually a purveyor of frogs' legs and snails to fine restaurants.)

When Emled eventually returned to Tamsid unaccompanied by the frogs he had led out earlier that same day he explained that they had been subjected to an attack by a group of crazed humans. Assaults by humans were not uncommon of course, although no frog in the community had ever experienced an occasion where an attack had resulted in the loss of over a hundred frogs at one time. Emled took care not to mention the fact that the humans had murdered all of the party except for the young fit frogs, as he considered this knowledge to be the key to his profiting in the future from this terrible situation.

Still harbouring thoughts of personal gain Emled decided to lead another party of frogs back to the same area a few weeks later. When they got near to where the ambush had previously occurred Emled ordered the group to stop, as he considered this to be an ideal place to dig for grasshopper grubs. As the Tamsid frogs busied themselves with their labours the evil toad slipped away to the actual place where the men had previously lain in wait.

Then he suddenly heard "There's that 'orrible smelly blighter we saw last week! I'm gonna smash its 'ead in this time! That filth 'e sprayed me wiv made me guts rotten for days!"

Then another of the humans cried out, "No 'ang about a mo'. Maybe 'e's got some more frogs wiv 'im like 'e did last time."

As the men ventured towards him Emled hastily turned and hopped quickly off in the direction of the frogs he had left searching for grubs. The toad had no idea if his plan would work and he knew he was taking a big risk by showing himself in the open to the humans. However, he had lived in their company for so many years that he felt he had a pretty good idea as to what motivated them. As far as Emled was concerned, greed was at the top of the human agenda – and Emled himself knew a thing or two about greed.

As he hurried along Emled stopped every now and then to make sure the humans were only following him and that they were not actually trying to catch him. Had it been the latter then the toad would have realised that his plan had not worked and he would very quickly have needed to dive for safety. Satisfied that the humans were indeed tracking him, and that they were clearly not intending to cause him any harm, Emled led them all the way back to his party of frogs.

When Emled reached a point several metres from the frogs in his charge he darted into the dense undergrowth and then peered out from between the grasses to see if his strategy had worked. The poor unsuspecting frogs had been concentrating so hard on their digging that they were totally unaware of the approaching humans. Then, to the frogs' surprise and to Emled's delight, the humans raced past him and flung out their thin meshed net so trapping every one of the unfortunate creatures.

Emled smiled the most evil of smiles as he watched the humans again carry out a massacre of all the frogs save for those that were young and fit.

From that moment on an unholy alliance developed between the evil toad and the brutal humans. Emled would thereafter regularly lead groups of exclusively young, fit frogs out into the forest for the sole purpose of their being captured by the humans and, for all he knew or cared for that matter, to their subsequent death. All that really concerned Emled was that the humans welcomed his presence and that they continued to reward him for his endeavours with chunks of lean red meat.

As a consequence Emled also became a frequent visitor to the house where he had first seen the humans packing the boxes containing the young frogs into the back of the small van. Whilst the community slept he would surreptitiously creep away from Tamsid late at night under the cover of darkness and sit beneath the bright porch lights of the human's house croaking as loudly as he could waiting for someone to hear his call. Without fail, as soon as the humans realised he was there, they would bring him out a plate of delicious red meat upon which he would gorge himself whilst they looked on, apparently charmed by his presence.

On one occasion, however, when he had turned up a little earlier than usual, he found to his surprise that the humans had already put some food out for him. Although this wasn't the normal routine he just assumed that they must have gone out for the evening and, anticipating that he might turn up that night, they had left him a nice little treat as a reward for his latest delivery of healthy young frogs. As he was greedily gobbling up his first mouthful he started to gag and he spat the meat out in disgust for it was vile and not at all what he was used to. What on earth was going on, thought Emled. What were these damn humans playing at? Why, it was only the other day that he had delivered five hundred of the finest young frogs he could find and this is how they treated him. Were they now trying to poison him?

Suddenly, from behind him, there came a high-pitched yelping and a Labrador puppy scampered excitedly up to see who was eating his food. Emled wasn't alarmed by the animal or even worried about being bitten as the rank smell which emanated from his body was normally sufficient to warn other creatures of his own poisonous and protective skin and body fluids. This being the case most animals would thus generally give him a wide berth. The puppy, however, wasn't so aware or experienced in the ways of the world and, although startled by the smell, he naively thought the toad was a potential playmate.

As the frolicsome pup nuzzled his new friend, and even though he was clearly not a threat to Emled, the wicked toad sprayed the unsuspecting animal with his poisonous milky fluid. In his surprise the Labrador puppy jumped back and began licking the noxious substance off his fur. Within seconds the pup was writhing in agony upon the ground and vomiting violently. The distressed animal then rushed across the lawn to the fish pond where it tried to wash the foul taste of Emled's excretion out of its mouth. Unfortunately this only succeeded in washing the venom deep into the poor creature's intestines.

In great pain and with racking fits of convulsions the puppy finally lurched forward into the pond and very soon it was quite dead.

Emled grinned his evil grin at the sight of the dead pup. He had enjoyed killing the animal and especially seeing it suffer. After all, it had been the root cause of his taking a mouthful of that ghastly food. In Emled's eyes that was sufficient for it to be given such terrible treatment. Much better, thought the evil toad, that the nuisance should be disposed of permanently.

The toad then took his leave of the house and garden and did not return again for a few days. He suspected that the humans would just have thought that the puppy had simply fallen into the fish pond and drowned. What he certainly didn't want to do was to give them any reason to think that he had played any part in the poor animal's death.

Normal service was resumed in due course when Emled next visited the house. The puppy's bowl had gone and when the toad gave his familiar croak the front door opened and he was very soon again being fed with chunks of juicy red steak.

Emled gloried in his depravity. He was being well treated by the humans in return for his regularly supplying them with hundreds of young frogs. The toad was also confident that if at any time another creature attempted to spoil this arrangement then he would be quite capable of dealing with such problems, as the Labrador puppy had found to its cost. The ugly creature was therefore very happy with himself and he patted his fat stomach and licked his lips having just gluttonously consumed yet another great pile of red meat.

It was therefore a full and contented toad who made his way back to the palace that night and the only thing on his mind was the planning of his next delivery of young frogs to the humans.

*

In his dreams, during this long and restless night's sleep, Emled saw all these visions of the past and many more wicked cameos besides. It was therefore an extremely tired and very angry toad who eventually blinked his way out of his palace the following morning and into the bright early autumn sunshine. The turbulent dreams had rekindled his evil flame and had whetted his appetite for creating further havoc. As a consequence it was an even more menacing and malevolent toad who now stepped out and into the Tamsid community.

However, before pursuing further malice, he had a huge belly to fill. All that dreaming had made him quite ravenous and the gnawing pangs of hunger in his gut just had to be satisfied.

Chapter Twenty

In a Westerly Direction

On the evening of the massacre at Kingfisher's Bridge, Mars and Maccus had travelled due west out of Seaxe. The young frog had already said his goodbyes to his closest friends and colleagues, explaining as he did so the reason why he had to leave. Although they were all very upset they nevertheless said they understood that in the circumstances it was both necessary and wise for Mars to leave Seaxe. They realised and accepted that it would have been impossible for him to have remained in his home community having had his area of responsibility taken away from him so unfairly and seemingly irrationally by the new king.

Some of Mars' friends said that they were not surprised by Emled's action as he was clearly jealous of the young senior's outstanding abilities and strikingly handsome appearance. They also said that they had sensed in the new king a great envy and a deep resentment towards Mars with regard to the fact that he was always so warmly received by virtually all of the community. This would, without doubt, have caused Emled to have viewed Mars as a substantial threat to his desire to dominate and rule the local frogs of Seaxe.

They all wished Mars good luck for the future and said that they would have preferred to be going with him rather than staying behind under the reign of Emled. If it had been possible Mars indeed would have gladly taken as many of his friends and colleagues as he could for he had greatly enjoyed their loyalty, support and companionship during his time in the community. He advised them, however, that they should stay in Seaxe as the local frogs would in time need all the help and assistance that they themselves could offer their kin.

Without yet being able to impart what he had learned from Krakow regarding the true identity of Emled, Mars gave warning of the dark days that would lie ahead under the reign of Seaxe's new king. He spoke too of the anxiety that Moha himself had felt about the future and how the kindly old bullfrog had thought that such concerns had something to do with Emled and the Far North. Mars advised his friends that now, more than ever before, the ordinary frogs of Seaxe would need their more erstwhile colleagues to provide for their protection and well-being.

In addition, Mars respectfully suggested to his friends that he thought the remaining six seniors would not be capable of seriously influencing the outcome of potentially major and unwelcome future issues as such events impact upon the community; and, furthermore, that his senior colleagues would unfortunately become more and more like puppets of the new administration. Mars said he was concerned that any ideas or initiatives that the seniors currently had in mind would more than likely be driven out of them at the earliest opportunity. He added that, sadly, only Kejon showed any real signs of strength in this respect and he feared that the stubborn frog might, as a result, soon fall foul of Emled.

Noticeably absent from the frogs who came to say their goodbyes to Mars were, interestingly, his 'six' senior colleagues. Neither one of Brylil, Lebish, Josmi, Geelan, Kejon or Chrich could bring themselves to face their departing colleague. Whether this was because of the embarrassment they felt at the way they had all succumbed to Emled's influence, or the fact that they had quite openly and purposely blackened Mars' contribution and role in the community by describing him to Emled as 'dangerous to the future development of the community', it is difficult to say. They had, however, made a great play of the fact that Mars had always been a staunch supporter of Moha. They said that they felt this would most certainly prove to be a problem for Emled as their senior colleague's loyalty would, forevermore, be with the old king; and not, as it ought to be, with Emled.

What was very clear, particularly to all those who cared to look critically at the situation, was that 'the six' seniors saw an opportunity to give Emled their whole-hearted support on a matter that they most definitely had in common with the evil toad. This was of course the fact that they were all so deeply jealous of Mars that, whatever their reasoning, they were just happy to see the back of the handsome young frog.

What a terrible and debilitating emotion jealousy can be! Although they were naively not yet aware of the potential of their behaviour, the immense jealousy that 'the six' seniors held for one individual frog was going to have severe repercussions on the lives of many thousands of creatures in Seaxe, as well as on the lives of tens of thousands of creatures from other communities both near and far. Whilst they blatantly showed their personal pleasure at having been party to the concerted effort to oust Mars from the community, one can only but wonder at their feelings regarding the locals who stayed behind to endure Emled's reign of terror. What price indeed personal gratification? Maybe it is only 'the six' seniors who can answer that conundrum?

Having set out in a westerly direction Mars and Maccus decided to make for the community of Cowall. Mars knew their king, whose name was Denray, having met him many seasons ago when he had visited this western area with Moha to attend a convention of frog community kings. Mars considered Denray to be a fine, strong and resolute character and he was sure that both he and Maccus would be welcomed into his happy and friendly community.

The lands to the south and west of Seaxe were well known for their beauty. The climate of warm sunshine and regular falls of refreshing rain resulted in those regions enjoying ideal conditions for both frogs and all the other creatures of the river bank. Flowing rivers and quick growing luscious vegetation, full to bursting with rich nutrients, meant that the frogs in the south and west were most amply provided with the succulent insects on which they thrived. It will be no surprise for you to learn, therefore, that these frogs were widely known for their friendly and happy nature.

As Mars prepared for his departure he remembered Krakow's wise words advising him that he should return to Tamsid in order to take on the 'Great Learning of the Supreme Qualities of Wisdom and Knowledge' . Although in his heart he knew that he should go straight back to see Krakow, his head told him that it would be too dangerous to attempt such a journey at the moment. He was absolutely certain that Emled would have posted extra patrols in the swamps of Waga and along its boundaries. He was also sure that his movements would be carefully watched to ensure that the route he took out of Seaxe was anywhere as long as it was not in the direction of the Far North. Mars consoled himself with the sincere promise that he would indeed seek to find his way to Tamsid and re-unite with the wise old blackbird as soon as possible once he had settled in his new community.

So it was with high expectation, tinged with the sadness of leaving their friends behind, that Mars and Maccus travelled in a westerly direction to carry on their lives in their newly chosen community.

*

They had been travelling for fully two nights and two days during which time the air had become markedly warmer. Mars and Maccus were both tired and in need of some sleep, so, when they came across a quiet pool of water that had formed in a sharp bend in the river, they decided to stop and rest for a while.

Maccus's wing had almost healed and he was now able to fly in short bursts without feeling pain. In a day or so he was confident that he would be restored to his full strength.

The two friends spotted a pleasant and safe resting place in the pool so they carefully hopped the short distance from the edge of the river bank into a tall clump of thick-stemmed reeds. Maccus perched some half way up on a broken stem whilst Mars found a comfortable position towards the middle of the reeds and settled himself down on the firm platform of a large soft lily pad.

*

High in the tall trees that grew beside the river bank along which Mars and Maccus now travelled, a lonesome bird sat unseen and unheard. He had watched over the progress of the two young friends since the moment they took their first steps out of Seaxe. Although he too had travelled in the same direction he had chosen an aerial route and had flitted from tree top to tree top. Throughout the journey he had taken care not to reveal his presence to either the two companions or to any other creature thereabouts.

The bird had kept a particularly wary eye on the trail behind Mars and Maccus for he had half expected Emled to have sent out a party of the murderous marsh frogs to hunt down and probably kill the young frog. Although the bird had not anticipated there being any danger arising out of the south or west, he was very interested to see how the young frog and the kingfisher would cope with navigating their safe route out of Seaxe and far away to Cowall.

All in all the bird was pleased with the skill displayed by the travellers. He had been impressed by the attention they had given to covering their tracks and also by their vigilance as to checking what lay ahead. The former task was the responsibility of Mars, whilst ensuring a safe onward route was the province of Maccus. The young kingfisher had constantly been alert, speeding ahead to establish a safe path and then darting to the left and right to make sure there was no danger that might appear from the sides. He would regularly then return to Mars and convey his information, and by this means the two friends made steady and safe progress on their journey.

Thankfully Emled had not actually ordered any of his villainous followers to chase after Mars. The watching bird, high up in the trees, was nevertheless pleased with both the meticulous way by which Mars concealed their tracks and the attention to detail that Maccus displayed in verifying that the way ahead was clear. You could never be too careful when out and about in the wild and it was a natural instinct for such creatures to be on their guard in case of danger. With Emled on the loose the forests and the river banks were increasingly an unsafe place for creatures to venture out alone. Mars did not of course know that neither Emled nor his marsh frogs were in pursuit of him, and the watching bird continued to be satisfied with the two travellers' diligence to avoid detection.

As far as the way ahead was concerned, Mars and Maccus could have been excused for thinking that as the lands they were travelling to were peaceful and friendly it was therefore highly unlikely that they would meet any danger on the way. Such an attitude, especially in the current circumstances, would of course have been very irresponsible. Happily the two friends took nothing for granted and they were committed to regularly checking their chosen path in case any danger lurked thereon.

This thoughtful approach was just as well because shortly before dusk on the first full day of their travels, just when the two companions were thinking about settling down to rest for the night and when the concentration of less mindful creatures might have been wavering, Maccus spotted a family of wild cats some fifty metres or so ahead and directly on the path that Mars was taking. These animals appeared to have already picked up the scent of the approaching duo and the mother cat and all four of her well-grown kittens crouched close to the ground making ready to pounce on whatever prey was now coming their way.

It was of course Maccus who had been the first to see that a trap had been set when he spotted a large bushy orange and white ringed tail poking out from under a dense thicket of low growing shrubs a short distance ahead of Mars. The tail was flicking impatiently and Maccus could sense that its owner was preparing to spring on his approaching friend. When he looked a little more closely he could see the rumps of four smaller cats, all of which were wiggling excitedly not quite knowing what was going to happen only that they thought it would be fun copying their mother's actions.

The kingfisher rapidly assessed the situation and quickly returned to Mars to warn him of the imminent ambush. The two friends had no need to speak in this situation and a mere exchange of glances was sufficient for Mars to get the message that all was not well ahead. Maccus motioned to Mars for him to slip quietly into the water. This Mars did and he then swam strongly and silently out into the middle of the river just beyond the tightly packed reeds and rushes that had grown thickly along the edge of the river bank.

The tinkling of the gently running river was sufficient to cover any sound that Mars may have made which could have alerted the family of wild cats to his presence. Maccus flew overhead along the course of the river and, as soon as he was sure that Mars had swum far enough to be completely out of harm's way, he motioned to his friend that it was safe for him to emerge from the water and climb back on to the river bank.

The kingfisher then took a final cautious look back at the cats and he was relieved to see that they had now abandoned any thoughts of an ambush and that the young kittens were all, once again, enjoying a rough and tumble under the watchful eye of their mother.

*

As Mars and Maccus settled themselves down in the shelter of the thick clump of reeds they decided that they had travelled far enough that day and, with the onset of dusk, it would be a good place in which to bed down for the night. This would then allow the two hungry companions an hour or so to forage for food which would comfortably see them through until morning. Anyway, by Mars' estimation, they were now only a couple of hours journey time from the community of Cowall. A nourishing meal and a good night's rest would enable them to arrive there by mid-morning the next day feeling relaxed and refreshed.

High up in the tallest of the forest's trees the solitary bird had also decided that it was time to rest. It had been a long while since he had undertaken such a long and arduous journey and his old bones ached in a way they hadn't ached for many a year. Nevertheless he allowed himself a wry smile as he considered how well he had coped with his exertions. "Not bad for an ancient bird like me," he thought. "There's still a little life left in this old and frail body."

The old bird nestled down in a long since vacated rook's nest. Although he was well out of the sight of the two weary friends who were bedded down far below him, he was nevertheless still able to keep an eye out for their well-being. As soon as he was happy that they had eaten their fill and were definitely settled for the night, the ancient bird had a final cast around to satisfy himself that no danger or perils of the darkness were loitering in the shadows of the forest. Happy that all was well he then slowly closed first one eye and then the other before he too began his much needed night's sleep.

*

Mars and Maccus awoke early the following morning and, to their great surprise, they found they had an unexpected visitor.

"Krakow!" exclaimed Mars. "Krakow! What a wonderful sight you are for sure." The young frog was so excited by the appearance of his friend. "How did you find us? What are you doing here? How...?"

"Slow down, my fine friend. One question at a time," pleaded the wise old blackbird. "But first of all please introduce me to your travelling companion. Correct me if I am wrong, but he does appear to have the unmistakably fine feathers of a certain Peeyu. Am I right?"

"You are of course quite right," replied Mars. "I have the honour to introduce to you Maccus – grandson of Playa, great-grandson of

Mylor and the much loved son of Peeyu." Then Mars lowered his head a little as he added, "The late Peeyu, I am so sad to say."

Krakow greeted Maccus warmly but then he turned to Mars with a heavy crown and with his beak tucked down upon his breast feathers.

"I heard there had been some trouble at Kingfisher's Bridge, although I was not able to find out the detail as very little information is being allowed out of Seaxe at the moment. It appears that Emled's odious marsh frogs and crows have created a virtual ring around the community through which only creatures and information having the prior approval of Emled are permitted. The word, however, is that it was that foul toad Emled who ordered his most cold-hearted carrion crows and mercenary marsh frogs to carry out the attack. I only know that there were reports of some deaths but I know no more than that."

Clearly sensing the worst Krakow then asked, "Tell me, were any others apart from this fine young fellow spared the evil that is the trademark of this abominable toad?"

Maccus then spoke up and explained what had happened. Krakow was deeply saddened by what he heard. The kingfishers of Kingfisher's Bridge had long been known to him and he was greatly affected by the terrible story told by Maccus of the carnage and destruction carried out by Emled's killing party.

Krakow stood quite still for what seemed like a long time and the two friends could see, as the wise old bird looked wistfully into the distant landscape, that he was allowing himself a few moments to grieve for Maccus's family. Then, breathing in a lungful of the crisp morning air, he turned towards Mars and looked deeply into his eyes.

"It is now time for you to take on the 'Great Learning of the Supreme Qualities of Wisdom and Knowledge', my friend. There is absolutely no time to lose. I must pass on what I know to a younger creature without delay if the inhabitants of all the forests and rivers to the east, west, south, Near North, and even the frogforsaken Far North, are to be saved from the evil that has descended upon the land in the form of this hideous toad. It is essential that a creature from amongst us shall rise up and challenge his dominance!"

Mars looked startled by Krakow's last few words. "Do you mean it is I who must personally challenge Emled? Surely I would pose no threat to his superior size and strength? After all it is said that he has been known to fight and beat both cats and dogs and to even kill such animals in single combat. What chance would I have against an adversary such as he?"

"It is clearly not by means of your own physical power that you will be able to challenge the toad," advised Krakow. "You will, however, need to find a way to destroy him in order to return Seaxe to its former happy and peaceful state. This will therefore have to be by virtue of shrewd judgement and your ability to devise a fine strategy that will defeat and rid us of this diabolic monster.

"In the 'Great Learning' that has been passed down through the ages," continued the old blackbird, "in fact, as far as I know, since time began, it has been prophesied that an evil of great magnitude will one day come amongst us. Exactly when and in what form has always been a mystery, but what has been known is that once this evil does arrive the holder of the 'Supreme Qualities of Wisdom and Knowledge' will rise up to lead a fight against the malignance and destroy it.

"In my heart and soul and with all my senses I know that it is you, young Mars, who has been chosen for this most daunting of tasks. As the current holder of the 'Great Learning' I can pass on to you all the wisdom and knowledge that I possess, but you will personally need to add to this the learning you have already experienced so far in your young life. It has also been foretold that when the holder of the 'Great Learning of the Supreme Qualities of Wisdom and Knowledge' has successfully defeated the evil, that we now know of course is Emled, then he or she will be recognised as the undisputed leader of all the creatures of the river banks and forests. When this day comes it will be you, my friend, who will be crowned as the king of Seaxe and the king of kings. You will restore that community, which has become so very sad and dispirited under Emled, to its former glory and revive the happiness and laughter that was known both there and throughout all the frog communities during the reign of Moha.

"Although you will not yet realise the fact, I can honestly advise you that you have been born for such a purpose," assured the wise old blackbird confidently as he laid a wing tip upon Mars' broad shoulders. "Inside your fine young body supreme qualities of leadership and vision have been developing since the very first day that you came into this world. The power that lies within you has been quietly waiting for the arrival of some gross malignance such as Emled. Now that this evil has come it is time for your powers, which represent all that is good upon this earth, to be released so that they will rise up and obliterate the malevolence that the toad has brought upon our land and rivers.

"It is therefore you, young Mars, who will find a way to save our fellow creatures and upon whose fine shoulders the future of so many will depend. Such is the prophecy of our forefathers who hopped and flew upon this earth many generations ago."

Mars suddenly felt overwhelmed by the old blackbird's words. In truth he was not at all sure how he ought to feel on hearing that it was he who had been chosen to stand up against all that was bad. That it was he who was to have the responsibility of defeating and eradicating the malevolence wrought by the foul ignominious toad. And that it was he who would lead the creatures of the forests and river banks out of the darkness of evil and back out into the bright light of goodness and virtue.

The young frog steadied himself as he allowed his thoughts to wander through a future that was not yet at all clear. He could think of many questions for which he did not have an answer. He could also imagine many obstacles over which or around he could not make out a path. And worst of all he could sense the ultimate in danger from which he could see no ready means of escape.

As the wise old bird looked lovingly at Mars he could read in the blackness of the young frog's eyes, and in the deep furrows that had appeared on his handsome brow, that his friend was greatly troubled at having this enormous responsibility thrust upon him. Krakow nevertheless allowed himself a smile in appreciation of the young frog's honesty and humility regarding his recognition of his own limitations.

"Mars, my dear friend, you have been chosen because you are perfectly equipped to acquire the necessary 'Great Learning'. These qualities, which have been developed over many generations, are not just randomly passed on without a great deal of thought being given to the credentials of the recipient. Such a unique and valuable gift has to be handed down to a creature who has been selected for the undoubted ability and potential he or she has shown. These 'Supreme Qualities' then need to be thoroughly learned and appreciated by their new keeper, as well as being both carefully nurtured and improved upon as time goes by.

"I have been the holder of these 'Supreme Qualities' since they were passed on to me by my father who in turn received them from Lyle who was the great-great-great-grandfather of one of your finest Anurian councillors. I speak of course of Lilgree. As the current holder, and in quite the same manner as my predecessors, I only have the 'Supreme Qualities' temporarily until the time is appropriate for me to also find the right creature on to whom they must be transferred.

"It is essential that the knowledge be fully learnt and the gift of wisdom well-developed whilst in the hands of the holder. Therefore, great care and attention must be given to the process of passing them on.

"It has always been said that there will come a time when these powers will be used for some great cause. That moment now appears to have arrived and the new holder of the 'Supreme Qualities of Wisdom and Knowledge' will have the responsibility of defending the powers of good against the powers of evil. Whether or not the 'Great Learning' is as yet sufficiently advanced to overcome the massive force of evil that now faces us will very much depend on how you, young Mars, combine the acquired 'qualities' with your existing strengths.

"Should the powers of which I speak fall into the wrong hands of course, such as those that belong to the purveyors of evil, then they will surely be used to further advance, unchecked and with no real opposition, the spread of wickedness and malice."

"Will you help me to fight this evil?" asked Mars.

"I can pass on to you the necessary 'Great Learning' but beyond that I shall be unable to personally assist you, for without such powers myself my own life will be spent. I am already old and nearing the end of my days upon this earth and in recent times I have been greatly concerned that I would become ensnared by Emled and killed for the 'qualities' that I possess. Had he known of my existence in Tamsid before I spoke to you and Peeyu then he would most definitely have done all that was physically possible to hunt me down and steal the precious powers. It is therefore vital that I pass on the 'Great Learning' to you before I either die of quite natural causes or perish at the monstrous forelimbs of the wicked toad. With the powers of good, that have been created and developed by our most venerable forebears, harnessed to the powers of evil, this infernal toad would be the master of all he surveyed and thus able to bludgeon his way through the lives of all the good creatures on this earth without fear of contradiction or opposition.

"We must now find a place where we can work together that is safe from Emled and his cronies. I suspect you are making for Cowall. If that is so, it will be perfect for my teaching."

Mars acknowledged the fact that they were indeed heading for Cowall and very soon afterwards the three companions set out on the short final leg to that friendly western community. Even though they did not have far to go Krakow kept a wary eye on what may have been surreptitiously approaching them from behind, whilst Maccus regularly flew ahead to check that their intended route was free of perils.

*

As the inhabitants of Cowall went about their early morning chores it was with much surprise that they witnessed the arrival of the three strangers. The sight of a handsome young frog; accompanied by an old but distinguished looking bald-headed blackbird; together with a beautiful kingfisher who was apparently recovering from an injury to his wing, caused a great deal of excitement amongst this happy community.

A message was urgently transmitted to Denray and he immediately made his way through the large crowd of local frogs that had already gathered to meet the three visitors.

Denray straight away recognised Mars from the time the young frog had accompanied Moha to the convention of frog kings that he had hosted some time ago. Denray had thought then that he had seen in Mars a frog of great potential. Although of course extremely surprised to see Mars turning up unannounced in his community, the friendly king nevertheless greeted Mars warmly, but he sensed that all was not well.

When Krakow was introduced by Mars, the wise old blackbird was greeted by Denray with a mixture of disbelief, wonderment and great affection. Although he had never met Krakow he had heard many tales of his marvellous deeds, and, in keeping with almost all other creatures who had never seen the legendary old bird, Denray had often wondered if the tales he had been told were merely myths and folklore of the forests and river banks.

Maccus was then presented to Denray, and Mars explained the devastation at Kingfisher's Bridge and the reason for the young bird accompanying him on this journey. The king of Cowall had looked upon the beautiful kingfisher with genuine sadness. He then spoke softly and comfortingly to Maccus saying that he was sure that in time he would recover from this tragedy and that he must try hard to remember the happy times he had spent with his family in their home. He said that he too had suffered similar pain in the past but he found the fond memories of happier days helped ease the ache in his heart. Denray gently put his forelimb upon the head of Maccus and said that he was welcome to stay in Cowall and live among the many families of kingfishers who inhabited and thrived along by the river banks for as long as he wished.

When Denray had finished greeting the three new arrivals, and the growing crowds had given them many wishes of goodwill and friendship, the king apologised to his community but said that he must take the visitors to the privacy of his residence as they were clearly in need of rest. The king also guessed that the travellers were carrying news of great importance and he was keen to know as soon as possible just what this might be.

The locals were understandably a little disappointed that they were losing their new-found friends so quickly after their arrival but Denray assured his community that they would be able to talk with them again as soon as the newcomers had rested and refreshed themselves. This pleased the frogs of Cowall because, as you know, frogs like nothing better than to sit upon a lily pad listening to a good story; and, what was certainly clear for all to see, was that behind the appearance of the handsome frog, the bald-headed blackbird and the beautiful kingfisher, lay a very fine story indeed.

*

When they sat together in Denray's residence it was only necessary for the three travellers to recount the events of the past nine months or so as Moha had visited Cowall soon after his return to Somset and he had of course spoken to Denray about the arrival of the toad.

The King of Cowall heard of the deceit, corruption and oppression that Emled had brought upon the frogs of Seaxe, and his expression became more and more serious as the tale of horror unfolded. Mars saved the worst till last, however, and when Denray finally heard about the atrocities that Emled had inflicted upon the young of both Tamsid and Seaxe, his blood really began to boil.

"This unprincipled and barbarous toad must be stopped before his unbridled evil spreads any further. Even as we speak he may already be planning to invade our neighbours. It is surely only a matter of time before he comes to plunder the peaceful communities of Surey and Somset and even our own fair Cowall. We all have frogs who are somewhat naive yet kind-hearted souls who will be susceptible to such power and influence. He will surely try to coerce such creatures and convert them to his way of thinking. We must do all we can to protect our frogs and our communities. I will help you in any way that I can. Please be certain of my full support. I am also sure that Truda, the king of Somset, will join with us to fight this evil as Moha will surely have told him about the arrival of Emled."

Krakow looked into Denray's eyes and he could see in them all that was kind and good. He was confident of the king's support but he needed to know the answers to two questions.

"Denray, there are two questions that I must put to you and to each of which there can only be one acceptable answer if the battle against the march of evil is to be won. I must advise that as you are already a king in your community you may find what I am going to say to be rather difficult. So please think very hard before you reply. Whether or not I ask you the second question will depend upon your answer to the first."

Denray nodded, indicating that he was quite happy for Krakow to continue, and he waited for the wise old blackbird to begin. Krakow could see that Denray was prepared for his questioning and, although he had never met him before, he knew that he was in the presence of a truly honest and sincere king. Krakow then put the first of his questions to the king of Cowall.

"Can you accept that a frog of lesser status to you, in either his or her own community, could actually rise up and lead kings of other communities without first having attained such high status themselves?"

Denray thought deeply before answering. Frog communities were almost always very orderly in their approach to seniority and the route to becoming a king was structured and carefully planned. As you will already be aware, it is the accepted tradition that a frog is expected to first of all attain the level of senior status in their home community before they can apply for a kingship elsewhere. An application is then made for a vacancy that may have arisen in another community as they cannot gain such a promotion in their own.

Denray had therefore to consider whether it was possible for a frog who had only been promoted to a level no higher than a senior, to be then elevated to the supreme position as leader of all frog kings and their communities. In effect a king of kings.

"For a frog to attain such a position of great prominence," began Denray, "and if he or she were to gain the support and respect of frog kings and members of their communities, then that individual would have to demonstrate that they have peerless abilities and a great understanding of the ways of all the creatures of the river banks and forests. I could not say that this is impossible but it must be very unlikely that such a frog exists. Indeed, for a frog to prove so worthy would require an achievement greater than that performed by any living frog or even of the great frog kings of the past. If you could describe such a frog, or assure me that a feat of this magnitude is possible, then yes I could accept that such a creature may rise to be a leader of kings."

Krakow acknowledged that he was satisfied with Denray's first reply. He then proceeded to put the second question to the good king of Cowall.

"It is clearly not possible for a frog to achieve such a feat on their own. It is much more likely, indeed it would be necessary, for the creature to receive the support of others in order to reach and perform successfully at so high a level. Therefore, on the basis that I am correct in my assumption that there exists a frog who is capable of rising from the rank of senior to become supreme leader of all frogs, would you feel able to give this individual your undiluted support? In doing so you must accept that this creature will be regarded, even by your own community, as the most exalted of all frogs?"

Denray again thought hard before answering as he wanted to be sure that he spoke from the heart as well as from the head.

"If the frog of whom you speak is able to command the loyalty and respect of all frogs, no matter whether their status is that of a king or the most unfortunate of frogs, then I would also pledge my loyalty and my life to support such a creature. On that you can depend."

Krakow was pleased with what he had heard for these were exactly the answers he wanted to hear. He moved close to the side of Mars who had remained silent throughout the discussions and spread out his wings to embrace the young Seaxe frog.

"Denray, my friend, this is the frog of whom I speak. This is the frog who has been chosen to lead our fight against the powers of evil. This is indeed the frog who will become leader of all frogs and who will prove his worth by ridding the land of the evil toad that is Emled."

For a moment Denray was stunned. He had listened carefully to the questions posed by Krakow and he had answered them thoughtfully and honestly. During the course of their discussion reference to a leader of all frogs had been purely hypothetical and Denray had therefore not been able to picture the chosen one in his own mind. Now, to actually have that very frog standing less than half a hop away, and to learn that the frog is Mars, really came as quite a shook.

Denray was silent for a moment or two. Then a smile appeared on his ruggedly handsome face which was very soon followed by a huge beam.

"If it is to be you, young Mars, who will lead us against Emled and be the saviour of all the creatures of the river banks and forests, then I will most certainly give you my support. I will also do all I can to gather in the assistance of my neighbouring communities. We must totally eliminate this evil and that means it is essential we work together corporately and focus on this one common goal. You do indeed have my fullest support! I will be by your side every hop of the way!"

Chapter Twenty-One

The Face in the Pool

Emled lurched about in his palace. He was becoming more and more bored. Life in Seaxe during these first nine months was proving to be nowhere near as exciting as he had first imagined. Maybe he had overdone the rough stuff with the seniors? Whatever the reason the remaining group of five leading senior frogs had turned out to be a mealy-mouthed bunch of feckless frogs. Whilst Emled certainly didn't like opposition or his orders disobeyed he also despised, nearly as much, weak-kneed frogs who bowed and scraped whenever he so much as croaked. Surely, he thought, one of them at least had a little bit of gumption or fight left in him.

It was perfectly true, of course, that four of the five senior frogs who remained in Seaxe, namely, Chrich, Brylil, Geelan and the slimy Lebish, had not a tadpole egg's worth of courage in their spineless bodies. Sadly, of late, not even Kejon could summon up any spirit. However, it must be said that he had lost his will to battle on out of choice, whereas the others, in all seriousness, never had any to start with.

Although he would never admit to it Emled actually missed having someone like Mars around whom he knew would have made life more interesting by confronting him on many of the decisions he had made since taking over as king. Mars would have provided him with much needed sport and Emled's face broke into a vicious grin as he thought of the fun he would have had slapping Mars down in front of his friends and colleagues whenever challenged by the young frog. How the evil toad would have enjoyed the opportunity of openly demonstrating his power over the community by publicly flattening Mars who he knew to be, after Moha, by far the most popular frog in Seaxe.

Unfortunately, of course, it was Emled himself who had driven Mars out of the community and he therefore only had himself to blame for that situation. That fact notwithstanding he soon turned his thoughts to other things as he didn't like to dwell for too long on any mistakes he may personally have made.

Having totally exerted his power and influence over the frogs of Seaxe, Emled had decided that the time was now right to search out Krakow in order to obtain the much revered 'Great Learning of the Supreme Qualities of Wisdom and Knowledge'. It was high time, he thought, that he seriously began his quest for total dominance over all the frog communities and to expand his empire beyond the boundaries of Tamsid and Seaxe.

Emled was supremely confident, and he had every right to be, that he would have no problem with over-powering and taking control of the majority of frog communities. Even without acquiring the powers from Krakow he knew that he could bully and bludgeon his way into most communities with his callous army of carrion crows and marsh frogs. What he wanted, however, was for this to be just the start, as his real ambition lay far beyond merely frogs. What the wicked toad really craved was total control over all the creatures of the forests and river banks. And he meant to get it!

Not only was Emled getting bored but on this particular day he was also getting very hot and bothered. The day had started out sunny and warm but during the course of the afternoon it had become increasingly cloudy. The thick bank of cumulus nimbus that had begun piling up during the middle of the day now acted like a huge heavy blanket locking in the warmth and consequently making the atmosphere uncomfortable and muggy. To find some way of cooling down Emled decided to go across to the west side of the island and have a soak in his slimy pool.

Interestingly, Emled had only ever been to this smelly spot at night time when it was dark and when most frogs were fast asleep in their beds as he hated being disturbed whilst bathing his warty body.

I am sure you will remember that when Emled went to this muddy pit on the night he had his bad dream it had indeed been dark, save for the moon's intermittent soft white beams which cast long shadows across the countryside and coated the gently rippling river with sparkling glitter dust. It was therefore only possible, on that occasion and in such light, to see the broad outline of shapes reflected upon the surface of the foul slime, and, when Emled had gazed into it, all he could see in reality was a large misshapen silhouette of himself. As there were of course no features visible on the silhouette, Emled saw what he wanted to see staring back at him from the blackness of the pool's reflection – that is to say the handsome face of Mars.

Now, in the light of the day as the massive toad leaned over the edge of the pool and peered at his reflection, Emled saw not the features of a handsome frog but instead, and quite clearly, the incredibly ugly and menacing face that was indeed his own.

Emled was startled and terribly shocked by what he saw and he jumped back in his surprise. The agitated toad sat still for a moment trying to collect his thoughts. He was aware that his body had broken out into a cold sweat and he noticed that he was trembling quite uncontrollably. He couldn't believe what he had just seen. He convinced himself that it must have been a trick of his imagination and so he decided to have another look into the pool. This time he crept slowly towards the rancid pit and hesitatingly raised his head so that only very gradually did he reveal his true reflection.

Again Emled saw the face of a horrendously distorted monster staring back at him. The ignominious toad began to shake as his whole being was filled with great emotion, ranging from fear at what he saw to a burning anger at the realisation of his own ugliness.

He began to cry out loud and he shook with huge, violent and piteous sobs. Then jealousy and hate began to consume him and his sobbing suddenly stopped. The look of anguish that had been on his face only moments before gradually changed into an expression of unimaginable fiendishness and malevolence.

As he stood by the stinking pool he cursed Mars and blamed the young frog for his own ugliness. He could not believe what he had seen in the putrid pool. He could not believe that he could be so hideous.

"So... Mars... You have dared to steal my handsome face! It was here when I last looked into the water and now it has gone! You shall pay dearly for this crime and I shall have back my good looks! Be sure that when I have squeezed the life out of you I shall rip your face from your body and take back what is truly mine. My beauty will then be returned to me – its rightful owner!

"I shall crush you for the recovery of my beauty and I will destroy that bald-headed excuse of a blackbird for the 'Supreme Qualities of

...Emled saw not the features of a handsome frog but instead, and quite clearly, the incredibly ugly and menacing face that was indeed his own.

Wisdom and Knowledge'. I shall then, without doubt, be the most irresistible and magnificent creature ever to have stood upon this earth. *I shall be all powerful and have absolute domination over all living creatures.*"

The evil toad's oaths and threats began with a coarse whisper but ended with a booming growl that reverberated around the island as he cursed the very souls of Mars and Krakow. This was no time to be within range of this evil abomination and all sensible creatures laid low and kept well out of sight whilst the raging king vented his fury.

Chapter Twenty-Two

Meanwhile Back in Seaxe (Emled Sets a Task for Lebish!)

Life in Seaxe was continuing in very much the same vein as it had started under Emled. The mass flurry of activity which Emled had ordered on his arrival was still evident. Less clear, of course, were the results of the local frogs' labours as there was nothing much to show for their substantial efforts except, perhaps, tiredness and confusion.

The seniors were now all totally superfluous to requirements although Emled had decided against openly announcing that they were officially redundant. He quite perversely considered that this might give the locals the impression that he was uncaring so he opted instead to keep them engaged under their original titles. In reality this was only a token gesture as the impotent senior frogs neither contributed to decisions regarding the community as a whole nor did they even have any say in the running of their own respective areas of responsibility.

It was Emled, and Emled alone, who made community-wide decisions on policy and strategy and, as far as the seniors were concerned, he sought neither advice nor counsel from them. With regard to the way he communicated his decisions within each of the various areas of responsibility, he had taken to doing this through the seniors' respective 'Advisers'. In fact the management of the community of Seaxe was now completely and utterly in the control of Emled and his marsh frogs.

To ensure the total confusion of the seniors, whilst at the same time trying to give the local frog community a feeling that the seniors were being usefully and gainfully employed, Emled had set in motion a structured programme of Senior Management Development (or

SMD as he described it). The intention of this scheme was that it would supposedly enhance the seniors' performance and improve their contribution to the community.

The way in which the SMD operated was that each senior spent a brief period in one particular senior position at the end of which they all rotated in order to take on a different senior role. The effect of this exercise was exactly what Emled wanted in that no one senior ever mastered any specific area of responsibility nor were any of them able to absorb enough knowledge about it to be of any useful value in the overall management of the community. They merely dipped and dabbled into their ever-changing roles, never spending long enough in one responsibility for the experience to be of any material or practical use. The seniors were therefore now rendered totally valueless.

And what of Lebish, the pitiful Lebish, who thought his early association with Emled would result in him being given a position of power and influence? As you the reader well know, Lebish had been more than a little hopeful (in fact he had been absolutely certain) that he would be awarded a position in the new administration that would enable him to lord it over his senior colleagues. More importantly, he assumed he would be given a legitimate opportunity to enable him to get his own back on Gawk and Kaara for the way they had pushed and prodded him around when they first took him to see Emled.

In certain respects Lebish and Emled were somewhat alike in that they were both greedy and deceitful and only ever considered their own needs. Lebish, however, lacked the sheer cunning and wickedness of Emled and he was definitely not in the same league as the foul toad when it came to matters of evil-doing and cruel deeds.

Emled had nevertheless noted the activities of Lebish and he had seen absolutely nothing to change the opinion of him that he had held from the moment they first met. At that time of course he had considered Lebish to be a rather despicable pot-bellied frog who would tell rather nasty tales about his friends and colleagues just to get a pat on the head from the king. Emled still regarded the podgy and untrustworthy senior as a very slippery and dislikable creature and, when the fat little frog came up to him with a tale he had made up about Gawk and Kaara planning a royal *coup d'état*, then Emled thought it was high time that Lebish was taught a severe lesson.

Emled guessed straight away that Lebish's story about his crow and marsh frog leaders planning to overthrow him was a falsehood.

Whilst he certainly would not have willingly entrusted his own life to his two principal partners in crime he nevertheless considered that it was highly unlikely they would ever seriously contemplate a mutiny as they both enjoyed a rather too grand existence under his dictatorship. They also knew that if Emled was not there to ensure that the crows and marsh frogs worked together then the two species would immediately be at each other's throats.

Before the arrival of Emled the crows and marsh frogs had constantly fought the most hateful of wars and this state of affairs had spanned many generations. They were natural enemies and would rather have torn the hearts out of each other than combine their evil ways. However, when Emled appeared on the scene in the Far North, he soon realised that it might be beneficial if the two most wicked and evil species of creatures, in either the forest or on the river banks, could be harmoniously recruited and formed into a single army under his sole command. He reckoned that with such a following he would one day achieve his dream of total domination and that he would become master of all he surveyed. The real truth, of course, behind the current seemingly 'friendly from a distance' relationship that now existed between the crows and the marsh frogs was their common fear of the evil toad. In fact the major reason the two species tolerated their apparent merger under Emled was the knowledge that unspeakable torture, and a death so terrible that it was beyond even the most wicked crow or marsh frog's imagination to comprehend, would be their instant reward if any of them caused problems in the ranks.

There were of course several other factors that bound these two abhorrent species and these included the passion they both shared for causing murder and mayhem and the obsession they had for the good things in life – and particularly if the latter had previously belonged to some other poor unfortunate creature. I don't really think that I need to say much more on the subject of which wicked activities these vile creatures most enjoyed, as you know well enough by now the type of evil beings that Emled had recruited into his fulsome army.

The toad decided that it would be fun to tell Gawk and Kaara of Lebish's little story. It was no surprise of course that when they heard what Emled had to say on the subject they both wanted to immediately go out and kill the fat frog. Emled said that he quite understood their feelings, and he of course supported their wish, but he had a better plan for Lebish's demise that would be much more fun than simply battering the sly frog to a pulp.

What Emled had in mind was to play a game with Lebish that would initially make the chubby frog feel more important than his fellow seniors but which was planned to ultimately backfire on him so causing the devious frog to be ostracised by his peers. Emled accordingly called for Lebish who of course appeared almost before you could say 'grasshoppers'!

"Ah Lebish, good of you to come," announced Emled as the badly out of condition senior hurried into the king's palace looking extremely flushed and puffing very heavily. "How are you, my friend?"

Emled's greeting was delivered with an accompanying sneer for he held the deceitful Lebish in the greatest of contempt.

"Oh thanks for asking, sir. I'm..." replied Lebish. But he was cut short by the toad who really had no interest whatsoever in the fat frog's state of health.

"Good! Good! I'm so pleased," interrupted Emled who had far more interesting matters on his mind than to waste time listening to Lebish ramble on about his personal health.

"Lebish, I have a very important task that I want you to carry out on my behalf. It's a job that I can only entrust to a frog of your standing who has such an excellent track record in this community. It is however a task that you must perform alone and therefore it is not to be discussed with any of your colleagues. It is in fact so important that you must only communicate with me on the subject."

As he listened to the toad, Lebish began to puff up his chest as a feeling of massive self-importance ran through his veins. In his excitement he filled himself up with so much air that he made the blood rush to his head and he became quite dizzy and actually staggered a little, so overwhelmed was he by the king's apparent new-found faith in him.

"I shall be honoured to do anything you request of me, sir. I am of course your most loyal and humble servant." Lebish's reply was full of bowings and scrapings and in fact at one stage he bowed so low that he actually bumped his nose on the ground.

"That's what I like to hear from my most valued confidantes," lied the toad. "Now, what I want you to do is to give some thought to developing a new hierarchy of management that is better suited to our community and which will improve the way we do our business. Having been here for a little over nine months I can see very clearly that what we currently have is barely adequate for the new challenges that lie ahead for the modern day frog community. I therefore want to see quite radical change and I am particularly concerned that we focus on such vital areas as the development of our youth policy as well as offering realistic opportunities for our female frogs. We really must be seen to be actively doing something positive for these valuable sections of our community and to encourage the young and female members to participate on equal terms with their adult and elder male colleagues in the overall direction and policy making in Seaxe. Do you feel you are able to take on such a task?"

"Y-y-yes... yes of course," blurted a stuttering Lebish. "In fact I have quite by chance only just recently been giving some thought to this very matter," lied the untrustworthy senior. "We obviously think along the same lines."

"What a wonderful coincidence," replied Emled, with more than just a hint of sarcasm in his voice which was totally lost upon the over excited Lebish, "I trust you can start right away on this task as I need to have your proposals in two days' time."

"Yes! Yes, of course!" bubbled Lebish. "I am so pleased that you have asked me to take on this responsibility rather than any of my colleagues. Although they all mean well, and of course they do try hard within their limitations, I honestly don't think that any of them are up to a task of this significance. Whereas I, on the other hand, am perfectly suited for this job. I shall be honoured to carry out your wishes. I am sure you will be pleased with the results. I really have so many ideas. I..."

As Lebish babbled on Emled was gently but firmly ushering the fat frog out of the palace. The onlooker would have seen the massive frame of the toad bearing down on his much smaller visitor who, although backing out towards the exit, nevertheless continued to gush out his description of what he was going to do to satisfy Emled's request. Just as he reached the way out Lebish caught his foot on a small tree root causing him to stumble backwards into the bright sunshine and roll over several times as he did so.

Lebish gathered himself together and blinked in the brightness of the day. He noticed how fresh the air felt and how good it smelled compared to the dank and stench-ridden home of the king. As he slowly struggled to his hindlimbs and began to dust himself down he hadn't noticed that Brylil happened to be passing by just as he made his inglorious exit from the palace. Brylil, who of course knew nothing of Lebish's summons to meet with Emled, clearly thought something was wrong and that his fellow senior had been pushed out of the palace by some aggressor or other.

"Are you okay, Lebish?" enquired the genuinely concerned Brylil. "That was a nasty tumble! Anything I can do to help?"

"N-n-no! Not really! I merely tripped upon a root or something as I came out of His Majesty's palace," replied an embarrassed Lebish who suddenly felt very foolish as he could see that it must look as though he had just been thrown out of Emled's residence. In his haste to dispel such thoughts from the mind of Brylil, and quite forgetting Emled's instructions to keep the matter secret, he quickly added, "I have actually just had a quite wonderful meeting with the king and he has entrusted me with a special task."

"What's that about then?" asked Brylil, who immediately felt a mixture of anger and suspicion welling up inside him.

Lebish was busting to tell Brylil. In fact he wanted to let all the seniors know about the work that Emled had asked him to do on the proposed new management structure. "They will be so insanely jealous of me," he thought to himself. "None of them has ever been personally charged with anything remotely as important."

"Oh! Oh! Just a special one-off job that the king has asked me to do. Can't talk about it though... Emled's express orders... It's top secret, don't you know." Lebish took to whispering the last couple of statements as he considered that it gave the conversation more of a mysterious feeling.

The effect on Brylil was that it only served to enhance his interest and he really was becoming very angry with Lebish.

"What do you mean... special one-off job that's top secret?" demanded Brylil.

"Well, the king has asked me to do something that he feels only I am capable of performing," replied Lebish, in a very boastful and rather condescending manner.

Brylil was clearly extremely put out by what he had just heard and he tried hard not to lose total control of his temper. Lebish, although he was pleased with the initial reaction of his colleague, was now beginning to wonder if he had indeed said too much. Maybe it would have been better not to have risked upsetting the other seniors. At least not until after he had completed the task Emled had set for him.

Sensing that he was not going to get a full and straight explanation Brylil considered it appropriate to rebuke his sly colleague.

"I must say to you, Lebish, that I am not happy about this state of affairs and I shall have to think how I respond to what I regard as a clear case of favouritism." With that comment Brylil turned his back on the podgy senior and scurried away in the direction of the community's main centre.

Emled had been standing just inside the entrance to his palace and, although out of sight to Lebish and Brylil, he had overheard the entire conversation between the two seniors. He had known with the utmost confidence that Lebish would never be able to keep a secret of the fact that he had been asked to carry out a special project for the king. He also knew that once the other seniors got to know about it then this would for sure create a high degree of jealousy amongst the so called senior group. They would certainly want to know what was going on and just what it was that Lebish had been commissioned to do.

When Brylil in fact told his senior colleagues later that morning what he had heard they did indeed want to know what Lebish was up to. They accordingly agreed to confront the podgy senior that very afternoon on the matter. Firstly, they wanted to know what Lebish had been asked to do, and secondly, why it was he who had been selected to do it.

In truth they were actually more interested in knowing the answer to the latter question as it was so long since any of their number had been asked by Emled to do anything that could remotely be described as useful. It concerned them to think that if Brylil had not been hopping past the palace at the moment Lebish had come tumbling out of the entrance they might never have known about this matter. They all considered the situation to be most undemocratic and more than just a little unsatisfactory. A question was also raised, and not surprisingly by Geelan, that there was a possibility that Lebish could be receiving some special favours for doing whatever it was that he had been asked to do.

*

A special meeting was therefore arranged in the Boathouse at noon and the five senior frogs duly assembled. A sixth creature was also there but this one chose to attend in secret and he would remain unseen by the Seaxe seniors whilst they debated their problem. Thus, in place of the bright and beautiful feathers of Peeyu who used to perch in his hiding place just under the eaves of the roof of the Boathouse, there now sat the sinister black feathered figure of Gawk who had been sent by Emled to listen in on the senior's discussion and then to report back to him on all that was said.

The five frogs sat in a small circle. Although Lebish was not sure why the meeting had been called, he did, however, feel a little uncomfortable. None of the others had bothered to talk to him since he arrived in the Boathouse and he had the distinct impression that they were making a point of actually physically distancing themselves from him. He also couldn't help noticing that the circle was rather lopsided with all of his colleagues congregated on one side with himself sat noticeably apart on the other.

A tense and rather nervous silence fell upon the group as Geelan, Brylil, Kejon and Chrich glanced at one another and, in so doing, took obvious care not to make eye contact with Lebish. Finally, after what seemed an age, Brylil spoke.

"It is with some concern... some very great concern actually... that this meeting has been called. On the strength of information I personally obtained this morning it was agreed that we should get together to discuss the issues surrounding what is potentially a very disturbing procedural matter."

Lebish couldn't help noticing that several heads were nodding in agreement with what Brylil was saying. To his mind this clearly indicated that all of his senior colleagues appeared to know what was going on and that he was the only one evidently who didn't. It then dawned on him that maybe it had something to do with himself. The quite deliberate way in which his colleagues were averting their gaze to anywhere but towards him was suspiciously stand-offish. And what was it that Brylil had said... something about information he had personally obtained this morning? Yes, this meeting must surely be about his earlier conversation with Brylil outside the king's palace.

The podgy frog started to put two and two together and he began to suspect that there was a distinct possibility that this meeting had been set up to discuss the rendezvous he had that morning with Emled.

He shuffled about rather anxiously as for the first time since his arrival in the Boathouse the others were now all looking directly at him.

"Hang about! Hold on for a moment! What is going on here? Am I being picked on for some reason?" Lebish asked all of these questions in a burst of excitement. He could hear himself shouting and his voice had risen to a higher pitch than normal. "If I am being picked on then I demand to know the reason why... and pretty quickly too, might I add!" continued the blustering senior.

"Oh! So you are now giving out orders as well as being in the king's good books!" squeaked an overly aggressive Geelan. "Maybe it's you who should be telling us what it is all about!" Geelan was also speaking an octave or two higher than usual. In fact, he quite frightened himself by his own boldness both at the sound of his words and the effect they appeared to be having on Lebish.

Lebish was incensed with Geelan and he advanced towards him in a very threatening manner. Geelan found himself sidling up a little closer to Kejon and in fact to a position just slightly behind the tough and muscular senior. Brylil could see that the situation was starting to get out of hand and although inwardly he quite liked the idea of seeing a scrap between Geelan and Lebish he thought it politic to intervene.

"Lebish, my dear fellow," began Brylil with more than a slight hint of sarcasm in the tone of his voice. "We are merely concerned about this task, or whatever it is, that the king has asked you to undertake. We are clearly not sure, unless you are able to advise us, why it is you he has selected for this matter instead of any of us. We need to know what is going on. I am sure you will understand our anxiety and natural interest as it is such a long time since any of us have been asked to do anything remotely worthwhile."

The tubby frog sat back on his hindlimbs, his feeling of discomfort rapidly being replaced by a smug sense of satisfaction. He was the centre of attention and he had some information that the others desperately wanted to know about. He was fast beginning to enjoy himself and he threw his head back a little and looked down his nose at the others in a very patronising fashion. He toyed with the idea of teasing his colleagues by playing a game with them and seeing if they could guess what task it was that Emled had set him. However, he thought better of it when he caught the keen eyes of Kejon peering at him in a searching manner indicating that he at least was not going to be fobbed off with any half-baked answers.

"I... er... I... I have been given a job by the king and he has told me not to discuss it with anyone. I am sure you will appreciate that it really is more than my life's worth to do so," burbled Lebish in a manner that could best be described as a rather strange mixture of pleading and aloofness.

The others knew that if they were in Lebish's position they too would also be scared of disobeying the evil king. One or two of them, if not all of them, shivered as they thought of the consequences of breaking Emled's confidence.

However, they were not in Lebish's predicament, Lebish was, and they were all both too angry and too jealous to worry about the fat frog's fate. He had apparently been considered more capable than they by the king and just for that Lebish deserved whatever punishment the king might wish to inflict upon him.

"We know all of that!" said Chrich angrily. "But that doesn't make it any less of a reason why you can't tell us what you have been asked to do. After all if you didn't want us to have any idea of this secret arrangement then you shouldn't have alluded to it when Brylil saw you falling out of the palace this morning."

"That's quite right," said Kejon who had not taken his gaze away from Lebish during the past few minutes. Irresistibly drawn by his voice, the fat senior turned his head to reply to Kejon. As he did so, he found himself looking directly into the coldest of eyes. Lebish felt small and vulnerable and his hindlimbs had gone rather wobbly. Kejon was in no mood for a variation of the truth. He wanted the facts and, from his expression, anything less was likely to result in Lebish receiving a fearful clip around the side of his head.

"Now come along," continued Kejon. "This meeting is being held in private. There is absolutely no way that Emled, or anyone else for that matter, is going to know what you tell us. We will certainly not disclose to the king anything that you say, if that is what you are worried about."

"Yes!" cried Geelan, emerging from behind Kejon in a second attempt at being brave. "For all we know you might have been asked to say horrible things about us in much the same way as Emled got us to say bad things with regard to Moha. You may even have become the king's sneak for all we know."

"Oh dear. Oh dear. Oh dear," said Lebish, managing with some difficulty to wrestle his eyes away from the piercing and hypnotic stare of Kejon, "Do you really imagine that I would stoop so low?"

As he looked around at the other seniors, and he considered their feeble attempt at interrogation, Lebish's self confidence (well pure arrogance really) began to return. Kejon was an entirely different proposition, however, and he was determined not to be drawn back towards a direct conversation with him.

"Okay," began Lebish. "Now let me see. I will have to think very carefully how I can give you sufficient information without contravening the king's orders. Perhaps, and if I may be excused not going into too much detail at this moment in time, I can say to you that the king has asked me to consider the overall management of our community. For reasons that only he alone knows he said that he regards me as the most appropriate senior to carry out an objective assessment of our current strengths and weaknesses in order to provide him with an informed view of a proposed improved management structure."

"But why you?" blurted Geelan again. "I know as much as you do about our community, maybe more. Why didn't he pick me? I could have done the job every bit as well!" Geelan's squeak had become a squeal such was the stout little frog's intense pent up jealousy and anger. This condition actually occurred quite frequently as Geelan exposed these emotions whenever anyone appeared to be given or awarded something that he thought should be his. Then, realising that he had just blurted out what all the others had been thinking but were careful not to admit, he lapsed into deep embarrassment and dropped his chin upon his chest. Not for the first time (in fact probably nearer to the hundredth) Geelan's inappropriate and light-weight contribution to matters concerning the senior group was exposed in an all too obvious fashion. His fellow seniors were really becoming quite used to concealing their very real embarrassment for their flaccid and rather too noisy colleague.

"Believe me, my dear friends, when I say I would rather it was any of you who had been asked to perform this task." Lebish wore a soulful expression as he lied to his fellow seniors whilst at the same time he was doing his artful best to make out that he had been terribly put upon by Emled. "Unfortunately, however, it is I who the king has charged with this responsibility; and it is therefore I, however reluctantly, who will have to carry it through to its conclusion."

Lebish realised that his explanation had not encouraged his colleagues to remove the pointed and angry looks that had been on their faces for quite some time. In fact he was sure that their expressions were actually hardening and getting more and more grim. He knew he had to find some way of pacifying them, so, thinking quickly, he decided to offer what he considered to be the perfect escape from the difficult situation in which he now found himself.

"It really is too much of Emled to expect a frog as humble as I to be able to cope alone with such a huge task," sighed Lebish heavily and resignedly. "It's quite unfair to burden me with an exercise of this complexity. I would certainly, therefore, greatly welcome any suggestions or ideas that any of you might have that I may usefully incorporate into my report back to our gracious leader."

Lebish was quite excelling himself in the patronisation and nose scraping departments and, to his delight, not to mention immense relief, this peace-offering proved to be a good move. The seniors accepted the fat frog's proposal with relish. They considered that it gave them an ideal opportunity to make an effective contribution to Lebish's exercise. It also appeared to offer them a direct route through to Emled by which they could each demonstrate to the king that it was not only Lebish who was capable of developing important recommendations regarding the future management of Seaxe.

They accordingly nodded approvingly at Lebish's suggestion and agreed that he had indeed been given a difficult task. The general consensus of the seniors, as they chattered happily at the conclusion of what had for the most part been an extremely acrimonious meeting, was that at least they would now be able to give Lebish their full support on the matter. Lebish said how grateful he was for their much-valued assistance and he added that with the task now being a team effort he was confident that he would be able to prepare a more meaningful and informed set of proposals for Emled's attention. He added that he was indeed greatly relieved to have been able to bring this matter out into the open for it had troubled him greatly to have been personally charged with such an onerous responsibility.

If Emled had heard the last couple of statements from Lebish he would have been somewhat disappointed. His plan was based on the assumption that the sly senior would find the opportunity to lord it over the others quite irresistible. He was sure that if Lebish had the chance to demonstrate that the king apparently considered him to be more able and intelligent when compared to the other seniors, then he would find it impossible to pass up such a propitious occasion.

In his plan Emled had anticipated that by Lebish acting in such a fashion it would induce his fellow senior colleagues to distance themselves from him and regard him as somewhat of an outcast. The evil toad had not reckoned on Lebish being so astute in the art of diplomacy as to think of being so accommodating to his peers by encouraging and seemingly welcoming their contributions.

However, Emled need not have worried unduly, because although Lebish had indeed indicated to their faces that he would welcome suggestions from his colleagues, what he actually did was to totally ignore their ideas and instead concentrated only on what he personally thought was best for the community - or more accurately, should I say, what was best for himself.

*

When Lebish arrived back in the king's palace two days later he was full of his own self-importance - as well as being extremely full of the juiciest of grasshoppers. This latter condition was due to the fact that as he had sat pondering on the task that Emled had set for him, focusing very hard on which of his ideas would provide him with the most lucrative personal gain, he had continuously gorged on a massive supply of insects from his well-stocked larder. It was therefore a frog with an over-inflated ego as well as an over-inflated belly that now paraded, or more aptly lolled, before the king.

Emled was not at all disappointed with Lebish's proposals for a new management structure. They were after all quite simple. At the top of the fat frog's list of suggestions was that he should personally be promoted to a new post of deputy to the king. In other words he would become the second most important member of the community, after Emled of course. In this role he had given himself a clear responsibility for all decisions made in respect of the crows and marsh frogs. In doing this his intention was of course to put himself in the ideal position whereby from this level of seniority he could quite legitimately avenge the pain and suffering previously inflicted upon him by both Gawk and Kaara. He made a promise to himself that he would devise a suitably horrible punishment for these two unsavoury bullies.

Lebish had also mooted raising the status of the seniors' 'Advisers'. In order to do this Lebish had proposed a formal reversing of the current roles of these marsh frogs with those of his fellow seniors. He explained to Emled that this merely recognised what was happening in reality as the 'Advisers' were clearly operating at a much higher level than were the seniors. Emled commented that this move would of course make Lebish's senior colleagues officially subordinate to their 'Advisers' and how would this be viewed both by the seniors themselves and the community at large? The podgy frog retorted that it was no more than his colleagues deserved as they had allowed themselves to become lacklustre and demotivated and he considered that really they offered very little of substance these days.

As well as awarding himself a number of other personal benefits, such as an enormous and beautifully proportioned lily pad in a most idyllic position just off the island, Lebish had also proposed a small palace for his use near to the king's own residence. Nothing too grand of course, and certainly not as fabulous as the king's own palace, he assured Emled, but a frog of his proposed standing would need to be seen by others as having acquired the privileges as befits a frog of such importance. Lebish was keen to add that to go with the accommodation he would naturally require many frog servants and of course the pick of the grasshoppers when it came to distributing the community's supplies.

"Excellent advice! You have done a wonderful job my friend! And in such a short time too! Quite remarkable and very impressive, might I hasten to add!" Emled heaped his empty praise upon Lebish for the deceitful and greedy little senior had fallen quite magnificently into his trap. "Just tell me again why it is that you feel you could perform well as my deputy and quite why it is that you do not think that I should let any of your fellow seniors, or Gawk and Kaara for that matter, compete for such a prestigious position?"

Lebish was warming to the task. He really did feel that he had finally won the king over to his way of thinking. How importantly he regarded himself, standing as he now did before Emled and discussing matters of a most lofty nature.

"Well, my king, or can I say… dear Emled?" Lebish was becoming extremely familiar with the toad and, although he found it hugely distasteful, Emled swallowed hard and grimaced his approval before encouraging Lebish to continue.

"You and I are so alike," burbled the tubby frog. "We think along the same lines and we are both creatures of great vision. My colleagues try very hard to do well but they are so limited and they have very little to offer that is either new or interesting. Whereas I on the other hand, as I think you have already indicated by asking me to carry out this management structure exercise, have so much more ability. I am of course also much better versed in the ways of the community and I have an in-depth understanding of what it is that individuals most want. This of course enables me to accurately focus on what is required by way of future development and be absolutely confident that I am right in my judgement.

"I think that in addition you will also find that I am greatly respected by the common frogs of the community, and, whilst I don't normally associate with those of the lower order, they nevertheless greatly admire my undoubted leadership skills and high intellect."

The expression on Emled's face had changed from firstly, being one of satisfaction that his plan had worked so well; to secondly, being one of amazement at how highly Lebish thought of himself; and finally thirdly, to being one of utter contempt at the slimy senior's total disregard and betrayal of his fellow colleagues. Lebish, however, took the toad's leer to be a smile of support, so, just for good measure, he decided to add a closing comment.

"As far as the way that Moha ran this community when he was king is concerned, I must say that I firmly agree with all the things you have said about the old regime. And as for Mars, well, I believe you were absolutely right in expelling him from Seaxe. He was a troublesome frog at the best of times and always considered himself better than everyone else. I think it was because he was much too close to old Moha. You certainly displayed a great deal of foresight when you got rid of him for he could well have proved to have been a thorn in your belly."

Emled looked down at the fawning frog and felt sick at the self-importance and disloyalty that was spewing out before him. Although it was in fact he who had personally encouraged such an attitude in the minds of the local frogs in respect of Moha, now that it was coming so enthusiastically and with such relish from the slimy Lebish it suddenly made Emled feel rather nauseous. He wondered how a creature could be so naive, as Lebish was apparently being, to think that what he was saying could possibly endear himself to anyone let alone the king of Seaxe. How on earth could Lebish imagine that his own bad-mouthing of Moha and Mars would encourage the king to promote him to a position where respect and loyalty were paramount. Not even the wicked toad would have taken such a risk! The thought struck Emled as being both amusing and potentially very dangerous.

There was no way of course that Lebish's plans for himself would ever come to fruition. However, on the other forelimb, Emled's macabre plan was working out wonderfully well and he was now preparing to really enjoy himself at the expense of this devious and sly frog.

"Lebish, my fine chubby friend," said Emled, in a sickeningly sweet and curiously amiable fashion. (He wanted to say something a good deal more insulting but, for the moment at least, he held himself in check.) "You really have done very well and you have more than repaid the faith I had in you by presenting me with a picture that in the circumstances I could not have drawn any better for you myself. I think you are quite right, we really do think alike; or more appropriately should I say, that I can read your mind."

Lebish was rather puzzled by that last remark. He was also becoming a little bit suspicious of what was going to happen next. The evil toad's voice had changed from sounding friendly (or as friendly as Emled's voice ever could sound) and was now beginning to take on a distinctly nasty tone. Lebish anxiously moved from one hindlimb to the other as he looked nervously about the king's chamber. Although he felt that something was not right he could not for the life of him work out why he felt that way.

"You look as if you are expecting someone," said Emled mockingly.

"Well... er... I am not sure really," answered Lebish hesitatingly. "Just you and... and... and m-me, I think," the podgy senior stammered badly. The truth was he really didn't know what to think.

"You know, my pot-bellied friend, I very much hoped that you would present me with a useful set of proposals but what you have just given me is quite beyond my wildest expectations. It really is quite splendid that you see yourself playing such a prominent role in the future management of our community. You have also provided me with an excellent description of your senior colleagues' shortcomings and failings. Yes, I must admit, your observations and suggestions have been illuminating and a fascinating insight into Seaxe life.

"In fact, my devious and crafty senior, I anticipated a fine response from you and, in so doing, I thought that it would be a great shame if we did not share your words of wisdom. I am sure you will therefore be pleased to know that I have asked a few mutual friends to come and join us. I am so keen for them to also benefit from your marvellous proposals and especially if they can hear them directly from you."

Lebish was totally confused by what Emled was saying. Surely this was meant to be a private meeting involving only the two of them? Emled had asked him to carry out this exercise alone and to report to nobody but himself on the subject. This job was meant to have been top secret. What therefore did he mean by sharing his words of wisdom? And just who were these mutual friends the king said he had invited?

"It's okay, you can come and join us now." Lebish was suddenly rocked back on his hindlimbs and badly shaken as Emled called over his head in the general direction of the entrance to the palace.

Then, as he turned round to see to whom the king had beckoned, he was filled with horror as into the chamber trooped firstly Brylil, Geelan, Chrich and Kejon; the seniors were then closely followed by their respective marsh frog 'Advisers' (including Lebish's); and lastly, hard on their heels, came the villainous pairing of Gawk and Kaara.

Emled waved to the visitors and indicated that they should form a semicircle in front of him and Lebish. He had by this time sidled alongside the petrified senior and put his forelimb around the shoulder of the fat frog as if showing the others how fond he was of the devious creature.

It was just as well that Emled did have hold of Lebish as all the blood had drained from the chubby frog's face and his head had become so dizzy that he would have fallen flat upon the ground had he not been propped up by the toad. In fact, it felt to Lebish as if the whole chamber was spinning round and the sneering, leering faces of those in front of him kept surging backwards and forwards as he passed in and out of consciousness.

"Welcome to you all! I'm so glad you have been able to come." Emled greeted his recent arrivals most heartily as if he hadn't seen them for ages. "I shall not delay in getting down to the purpose of this little gathering. I see no point in keeping you all in suspense." Emled then turned his head and looked at Lebish. "After all it is not me that I want you to listen to, for it is our dear friend Lebish who is today's celebrity."

Lebish was astonished by the king's words. He couldn't grasp what was happening although it was dawning on him that he was being set up in some way. His brain was in turmoil and he hadn't got a clear thought in his head. The faces of his colleagues, and the grotesque expressions of Emled's cronies, and particularly those of Gawk and Kaara, kept swirling around before his eyes as if he was in the middle of a dreadful nightmare.

"Now, when Lebish... dear Lebish, our loyal and much trusted friend, is ready, I will ask him to tell you what he has just told me. He has some very fine ideas about how we should manage our community which I would like you all to hear. A particularly interesting feature of Lebish's proposals is that each and every one of you here is included in his future management structure. Well, that is to say, to a greater or lesser extent depending on quite what view he has taken of your individual abilities."

Lebish was trying desperately hard to make it known that he didn't really have anything worthwhile to say, but, when he opened his mouth, nothing would come out. His throat had gone quite dry and a blackness had filled his eyes. He then heard Emled's voice echoing in his ears.

"Lebish, the floor is yours!"

The only thing that the podgy senior wanted from the floor at this moment in time was for it to open up like a chasm and swallow him whole. He felt sick to the pit of his stomach. How he now regretted his underhand and foolish attempt to seek higher status than his senior colleagues and especially to have betrayed them in the process. He should have seen that he was hopping into some sort of a trap. Lebish knew deep down that it was always going to be an unrealistic attempt to lord it over his fellow seniors but his inner weakness for misplaced power had overridden any sensible or logical thought that he may have had. Why oh why, he now despairingly thought, did he so willingly accept Emled's request to prepare the proposed structure?

If he now reiterated to the assembled audience what he had only minutes before so willingly and enthusiastically expounded to Emled, what would be their reaction? Oh why had he spoken so badly of the frogs he had worked both with and alongside these past few years? They didn't deserve the bad-mouthing he had given them. Surely they wouldn't have tried to do him down in this way had they been in his position.

And then there was Kaara and Gawk, thought Lebish. They would certainly see through his plan for revenge. They would not take kindly to effectively being demoted to a position where they would be subservient and answerable to him. They would undoubtedly realise that he was looking to be able to order them about as he wished. Lebish knew that he had been a fool and that now there was no turning back from this sticky situation nor was there an easy route by means of which he could grovel his way out of the mess in which he now found himself.

In his confused state a terrible thought suddenly occurred to him. Had Emled informed Gawk and Kaara that he had said that he thought the evil duo were planning to overthrow the king?

"Come on Lebish, don't be shy!" shouted Gawk. "Let's hear what you have in store for us!"

"Yes, come on, Lebish," urged Brylil encouragingly. "We would also like to know what advice you have given to the king." Brylil was being very careful not to let on that he and the other seniors previously knew of Lebish's task. In his innocence he of course fully expected Lebish to put forward the many ideas that they had been pouring into his ears during the past two days. Had he known that Lebish had not used a single suggestion that had been given to him then he would certainly not have acted so charitably.

The fat frog was dumbstruck. He was quite unable to utter a word and, unfortunately for him, the desperately wanted chasm in the ground was not going to come to his rescue. He realised that he was doomed!

Then the chanting began.

"*Lebish! Lebish! Lebish!*" First it was the 'Advisers' who called out his name. Then Gawk and Kaara joined in and these two were soon followed by Brylil, Geelan, Kejon and Chrich. The sound of his name being shouted echoed loudly in the king's chamber. Lebish felt as if he was being crushed to the ground by the deafening noise. Finally Emled held up his forelimbs to silence the chanting as at last Lebish began to speak.

At first Lebish spoke slowly and quietly. In fact his words were barely audible so faintly did he whisper. He had resigned himself to having to repeat his proposals knowing that the consequences would be dire. As his voice became clearer and his proposals took shape the four seniors gradually realised that their podgy colleague had stabbed them in the back and that he was not using a single idea they had proposed.

"Traitor!" squealed Geelan who had surprisingly been the first to recognise Lebish's betrayal.

"*Traitor! Traitor! Traitor!*" screamed Brylil, Chrich and Kejon.

"What do we do with traitors?" shouted Gawk, who could see that the four seniors were angry beyond their imaginations.

"*We kill them! We kill them! We kill them! We kill them!*" replied the four seniors who were quite overcome with rage.

"Then take this despicable creep away from here and deal with him in a manner befitting such a scoundrel!" ordered Emled, pointing dramatically at Lebish.

Kaara glanced at the 'Advisers' and nodded towards Lebish, who was now cowering in fright as the hate in the chamber overwhelmed him. The 'Advisers' took the hint from their leader and proceeded to roughly bundle Lebish out of the palace.

The four seniors stood quite still as if in shock. They all knew instinctively that this was the last time they were ever going to see their colleague alive. Dear old Lebish. A frog who had once been their friend... surely he had at one time been their friend... hadn't he?

Emled broke the silence.

"I think that about concludes today's meeting. I must say that once again you have all done very well. I really am most impressed by your speedy decision-making. You took absolutely no time at all in deciding the fate of that good for nothing Lebish... or traitor, as I think you so very aptly described him. Yes, you took no time at all in determining his demise. Well done! You gave me no other option of course but to act immediately on your verdict. Not necessarily the outcome I would have chosen but I am here to support you and honour your wishes."

The seniors were too stunned by the recent events to reply. Emled looked at them and thought how much he despised them, both for their inherent weakness and the blind faith they had invested in the untrustworthy Lebish. The devious toad had of course known all along about the senior's earlier conversation with Lebish in the Boathouse, for Gawk had reported back with a detailed account of the entire discussion that had taken place therein.

Emled then waived his forelimb dismissively at the seniors motioning them to leave the chamber. As they turned to make their way towards the entrance they heard him call after them:

"Oh, and don't you fine frogs forget... *Who cares? Emled cares! I care!*"

*

The four seniors filed out of the palace and made their way to the island's edge from where they swam slowly across to the main river bank. Although not one of them spoke a single word on this short journey they all nevertheless felt deeply in need of each other's company. When they reached the other side instead of going straight back to the main centre of the community they shuffled mournfully along to a quiet area on the bend of the river up towards Kingfisher's Bridge.

There they sat huddled together on some rather uncomfortable lily pads that were surrounded by a particularly thick clump of bulrushes. It was a long while before any of them spoke and when they did it was Chrich who broke the silence.

"What has become of us? Are we now afflicted by the same brand of evil that is the hallmark of Emled and his foul mercenaries? We have just murdered one of our brethren!" Chrich then lowered his head and sobbed heavily.

"Were we like this before Emled arrived?" asked Kejon aloud, but to no frog in particular. "I cannot ever remember even wishing another frog dead."

"The worst fate I ever wished upon another was that he fell off his lily pad on a chilly winter's day." This inane comment came of course from Geelan who proceeded to laugh nervously and noisily but then suddenly realised with great embarrassment how stupid his contribution had been in the circumstances.

"Where is Moha?" cried Brylil. "When Moha was our king we were a happy community. I wish that he were here now. I want to tell him how wonderful he is and how much I love him. How I hate myself for the terrible things that I have said about him. I didn't mean to say such things but I feel that Emled somehow forced me to speak in that way. I want to apologise to Moha and tell him I am ashamed of what I have done. How I want him back."

All four frogs reflected sadly and bitterly as they considered their gross disloyalty towards their great mentor. Everything that they had ever done that was good was as a result of Moha's teaching and guidance. Yet, in the nine long months of Emled's reign, the majority of that good had become undone. Even worse, it had now been replaced by an evil and wicked streak that had been implanted by the malignance that is Emled.

Sad, ashamed and dispirited, the four seniors sat in their seclusion for the rest of that afternoon. None of them felt hungry. They all in fact felt sick at heart. They had let Moha down and they had let their community down. They had also been unfaithful to the ways they had been taught and which they knew morally to be right. They knew, and now realised too late, that when they had been tempted by promises of material gain and better conditions than their fellow everyday local frogs, then they had willingly chosen to follow Emled's evil code in order to satisfy their greed and achieve self-gratification.

Yes, Lebish had been a fool, but he had surely never deserved to die for such a failing. Yet it was they who had killed him as certainly as if they had murdered him with their own forelimbs!

Chapter Twenty-Three

The Teaching of Mars

The teaching of Mars by the wise old blackbird was a process that had to be very carefully planned. It had taken Krakow many years to acquire his level of wisdom and knowledge and it was now essential that everything he knew should be transferred to the young frog. It was vital that the educating of Mars should be conducted thoroughly and successfully as the future of so many creatures rested upon the broad shoulders of the handsome young frog.

Krakow was well aware that the whole learning process should normally be spread over several months. This allows the recipient of the 'Great Learning' to be nurtured with care by his tutor and personally guided in the practical use of the 'Supreme Qualities of Wisdom and Knowledge'. In truth the process should be accomplished with teacher and pupil working side by side during this extensive and intense period, thus ensuring perfect application of the acquired skills.

Unfortunately for Krakow and Mars normal circumstances did not prevail and the entire learning process needed to be completed within a very tight timescale. If, as he expected, Emled was about to step up his bid to search out both he and Mars then there was absolutely no time to lose. In fact Krakow reckoned he would only have about seven days and nights in which to transfer all that he knew to Mars. Krakow's sixth sense told him that the evil toad would already be planning his campaign to catch both Mars and himself. He calculated that at best an attack of some kind would only be a week or so away.

The wise old blackbird needed a place for the teaching where he and Mars would not be disturbed. It had to be a secluded yet safe spot where they could talk and rest in private without any interruption whatsoever. It was crucial to the successful outcome of the learning process that the profound train of thought and deep concentration that must be established during their time together should not be broken.

They also needed an area that allowed sufficient room for them to be able to move about unhindered and unrestricted as a substantial part of the process required great physical as well as mental effort.

Interestingly food was not a problem as fasting is an integral feature of the learning process. Hunger is actually considered to be a sensation that sharpens the body's senses, whereas a belly that is full and satisfied causes tiredness and thereby dulls the natural instincts and reactions of both the pupil and teacher.

Denray had selected an ideal haven for Krakow and Mars. It was some little way upstream from the main centre of Cowall but not too far to be difficult to reach in case of emergency. The actual spot he had chosen was in an area where a small pond had formed about fifty hops or so from where the river curved before making its way down a fairly steep incline. The current, therefore, ran quite quickly at this point and as a result the pond benefited from having a regular supply of cool and refreshing water that flowed in by way of a narrow tributary which linked it to the river.

Masses of bulrushes and reeds grew around the edge of the pond and large sturdy lily pads could be found hidden amongst the foliage. This of course afforded excellent cover for Krakow and Mars and meant they could go about the learning process totally unseen from the banks of the pond. Several large weeping willow trees added to the seclusion which, by overhanging the pond, offered both shade from the sun when it was at its highest as well as providing cover from any danger that might happen to fly overhead.

As the two friends made their way to the place of teaching, accompanied by Denray who had come along to show them the way, they were pleased to feel the warmth of the pale yellow early morning sunshine on their backs. Autumn was now well underway and it would not be long before the chill winds arrived to announce the approach of winter.

*

Mars proved to be the perfect scholar. He was receptive to all that Krakow had to say and whenever he was unsure as to the precise meaning of certain statements, signs or actions, then he would ask the wise old blackbird for clarification.

Trying to absorb the words of wisdom, and taking on board the many years of knowledge that Krakow had accumulated, was an immense task for Mars. After all it had been quite some time since he had been an adolescent sitting with his young friends amongst the reeds and rushes of Seaxe learning from their elders about the ways of the river banks. Now that he was a good deal older recapturing the discipline of sitting quietly, whilst listening and taking in what was being said, required a considerable amount of concentration.

However, there was a great motivation which drove Mars on that would ensure he successfully completed the 'Great Learning'. This was the knowledge that not only was the future of the local frog population of Seaxe reliant upon him but that, in addition, all the other creatures of the rivers and forests would also look to him to save them from the forces of evil. The dreadful and dark forces that were led by the most wicked creature of them all, namely the vile toad Emled!

Master and pupil worked in consummate harmony. As knowledge was passed from the old blackbird so wisdom was being honed in the mind of the young frog. Through the explaining by Krakow of philosophies and science; theories and experience; and tradition and culture, came the development by Mars of new concepts and ideas; new applications and practices; and new probabilities and possibilities.

A vibrant and brilliant comprehension was forming in the young frog's brain and with it he could feel both his mental and physical strength growing by the day.

Sleep had become quite unnecessary for the duo, so intense was the learning process and so high their levels of concentration. Two powerful minds were working together by day and by night. One was seasoned and sure of its ability whilst the other was young, nimble, receptive and in which confidence was blossoming.

In Mars the freshly acquired knowledge was forming a new and broader base which allowed for greater areas of expansion even beyond that achieved by the old blackbird and all the previous holders of the 'Supreme Qualities of Wisdom and Knowledge' before him. Such was the way in which the 'Supreme Qualities' were passed on, for each new recipient needed to improve the 'Great Learning' and be capable of developing the powers of goodness in order to combat the unceasing rise in the powers of evil.

A vibrant and brilliant comprehension was forming in the young frog's brain…

And so it was that as one holder of these 'Supreme Qualities' passed them on so the new recipient began to build upon a wider and higher platform. There was a constant need for the powers of good to be expanded and improved in this way for, in the areas and regions where it had already become established, the seed bed of evil prospered on fertile soil and its abundance of forbidden fruit provided temptation to those creatures who were weak and easily influenced.

*

Towards the end of the sixth day Krakow was sure that Mars had learned all that he had been able to teach the young frog. He could see that in front of him there now stood a creature who had grown substantially in both mind and body during the six days and nights that had just passed. Throughout the process Krakow had emphasised the need for strenuous exercise as well as mental preparation. He preached that one complemented the other and he insisted that it was essential to be physically fit in order to think clearly and logically. He advised that to be able to apply the acquired wisdom and knowledge the mind and body should always be in peak condition.

On the seventh day Krakow suggested that Mars should rest and try to restore the natural energy level in his body by eating and sleeping. Whilst the young frog ate, Krakow recapped on all that they had covered during the previous six days. This was a process and technique that Krakow termed 'prioritising' and its intention was to enable Mars to focus clearly on which of the many vital issues he had learned were the most important and those which were of somewhat lesser importance. It also enabled Mars to identify upon which areas of his personal development he needed to concentrate. This was because although the learning process was extremely wide-ranging, thorough and intense, it had to be accepted that in all creatures, even those of Krakow's and Mars' high standing, it was necessary to constantly look at one's ability and performance in order to identify any weaknesses that needed to be attended to or perhaps eliminated.

Krakow explained carefully to Mars that it was not only one's strengths on which one had to concentrate but it was also just as important that the weaknesses be given appropriate attention.

At the end of the seventh day, as the moon's white beams glistened on the gently undulating water of the pond, Mars fell into a deep and peaceful sleep. The learning process was complete and there was nothing more for Krakow to pass on to his young pupil. He gazed upon his handsome student and he felt a surge of passion sweep over him as he saw how magnificently Mars had grown in stature during the time they had spent together. The old blackbird was proud of Mars and confident that the 'Supreme Qualities of Wisdom and Knowledge' he had personally held for so many years were now in the safest of hands.

Krakow felt strangely weakened by the experience. He was certainly physically tired, but the intensity of teaching Mars in such a short period had caused his head to pound. He knew that the future path for Mars was a dangerous one and upon which sat an obstacle of immense evil and wickedness. Krakow also knew that he personally would not survive a challenge from Emled and this was one of the major reasons why the transfer of the 'Great Learning of the Supreme Qualities of Wisdom and Knowledge' to a younger and potentially much stronger creature had been so important.

Could Mars himself now withstand the onslaught of malevolence that was sure to be cast upon him by Emled? Could Mars overcome such evil powers and deliver the creatures of the river bank and forests into a future that would be full of peace and goodness?

Krakow was troubled that he did not know the answers to these questions. How could he? He had taken his teaching of Mars as far as it was possible for him to go. Now it was up to Mars to pick up the baton of wisdom and knowledge and pursue a way out of adversity and into a better world for all.

Krakow was however certain of one fact which was that Emled, being the master of all things evil, would provide the supreme test for Mars in the courageous young frog's bid to win the battle of good over bad.

*

As Krakow continued to gaze upon the sleeping Mars he knew with much sadness that there was one final personal act left for him to perform. Now that the young frog was full of the 'Great Learning' it was Mars who held the key to even greater wisdom and knowledge. He would find, as did Krakow when he was invested with these high qualities, that it was he alone who must lead and that there could not simultaneously be two holders of such supreme intelligence. The time had therefore come for Krakow to bow out quietly with grace and dignity and leave Mars forever. It would not be possible for them to meet again in this life.

Krakow was saddened that he would no longer be with Mars whom he had grown to love as a true friend. He would never again share laughter with the young frog nor would he be able to physically stand by his side so that they might together stare into the face of evil. He leant forward, and, being careful not to awaken him, he gently caressed the head of the handsome frog with the tips of his wings.

"Goodbye, my friend," he whispered. "Be confident of your knowledge; have faith in your wisdom; and be certain of your decisions. Use your powers of intellect wisely and have the courage of your convictions. Your own future and those of all the other good creatures of the river banks and forests are dependent upon you. Although such a prospect may appear daunting it is not beyond your capabilities to carry this burden. You will succeed in your endeavours, although there will undoubtedly be moments when you face situations that may cause you to feel that success is quite beyond your reach.

"You must never despair, however, and you must remain strong. Remember at all times that goodness must and will triumph over evil. You are that goodness… the evil is Emled!

"Goodbye, my dear Mars."

On these final words Krakow lifted his wings from Mars' head and he hopped off the lily pad on which the young frog slept and flew the short distance across to the bank of the pond. From here he turned and looked towards the place where Mars lay sleeping peacefully and in the faintest of whispers wished him luck and good fortune. He then rose high up into the air and flew off in the direction of the Far North, never once looking back towards Cowall.

Krakow would return to the place where he had lived in exile for so many winters and summers that he had quite lost count of the years. He wanted to live out the remainder of his days in quiet solitude. He was so very sad to be leaving Mars and he was tired and exhausted by his role in the teaching of his friend. He was, however, also very happy that he had been able to pass his wisdom and knowledge on to one so capable. Mars, he felt, would be a credit to the 'Great Learning' and be a fine leader of the creatures of the river banks and forests.

Chapter Twenty-Four

The Power of Evil is on the Move

From across the swamps of Waga came a surging mass of enormous brown marsh frogs. Even though the day had dawned brightly the frogs nevertheless moved under a cloak of semi-darkness. A darkness that had been created by the wings of thousand upon thousand of black carrion crows who flew above the heads of their murderous cohort blotting out the rays of the sun.

Several days earlier Emled had sent Gawk and Kaara back to the Far North community of Tamsid to organise this movement of his most feared army of barbarous creatures. He wanted them in Seaxe ready and willing to move out in his bid to capture Mars and Krakow. The exiled senior frog and the legendary old blackbird had those things for which he craved. Mars had the beauty that Emled truly believed the young frog had stolen from him; and Krakow was the holder of the greatest assets that any creature could possibly possess, namely the treasured 'Great Learning of the Supreme Qualities of Wisdom and Knowledge'.

The evil toad would now stop at nothing to get what he wanted and he had mobilised his notorious army of murderers and madcaps to hunt down his quarry. By his reckoning, he imagined that as soon as he ripped the beauty of Mars from the face of the young frog and squeezed every last drop of Krakow's great qualities from the body of the wise old blackbird, then from that moment on he would be able to achieve total and absolute domination over all creatures. And he was determined to achieve his targets whatever the ultimate cost either to his own army or to those whom he conquered on the way!

*

Josmi had been awoken early on the morning that Gawk and Kaara had returned by a noisy commotion close by his residence. In fact such a racket was being made that he had hopped outside to see what was happening. It must be said that the normally placid newly appointed king of Tamsid was not best pleased to see Emled's two leading lieutenants issuing orders to the local frogs. When all was said and done, he considered that it was his job to give orders in Tamsid, if indeed any orders needed to be given. He was the king, and Gawk and Kaara had absolutely no right bellowing out instructions in his community.

What's more, he didn't like the sound of what was going on either and he even thought he heard several of the marsh frogs asking who it was they were going to slaughter. He therefore decided he would have to intervene and put an immediate end to Gawk and Kaara's meddling.

"*Stop! Stop! Stop!*" shouted Josmi just as Gawk screamed the order for his crows to head due south to Seaxe.

On hearing Josmi's cries of defiance the crow leader turned and saw the impotent king hopping up and down excitedly, the colour of his neck and throat going various shades of purple in the process.

"And just who do you think you are?" Gawk's voice was mean and his body language aggressive and threatening. He clearly held not one iota of respect for Josmi's position.

"I am the king of this community, as you well know," retorted Josmi who was trying very hard to act as he thought a king should do in such circumstances. "It is I who give the orders in Tamsid."

"Don't make me laugh... You the king!" sneered Gawk. "Emled is our king! You are nothing but a useless lump of cold flesh with a mind so full of rubbish that you don't know your hindlimb from your forelimb. You're worthless! A waste of space! Oh, and here's a message from the real king."

With that Gawk swung his beak violently at Josmi and he caught the unsuspecting frog a fatal blow across the top of the head. Josmi fell instantly and he was dead before his face hit the ground.

Gawk turned away as if nothing untoward had happened and he screeched at the mass of assembled crows to move out. Fired up by what they had just seen Gawk do to Josmi, and their appetites now well and truly whetted for whatever evil lay ahead, the manic birds rose in a thunderous clamour of flapping wings and shrieking cries and swept south as ordered.

On the ground Kaara had little difficulty in similarly encouraging his marsh frogs to likewise head off in the direction of Seaxe.

Emled's army was on the move and they were on their way to an inglorious reunion with their evil leader. Death and destruction; chaos and catastrophe; murder and mayhem, were in the air - and that was just the way they liked it!

*

As the marsh frogs and crows swarmed over the swamps of Waga and poured into the Near North, the creatures of the river banks and forests were filled with terror. Some hid in their burrows; some dived for cover in the dense undergrowth; and some simply fled in fear of their lives. Others were so scared by what they saw that in their fear they froze and were slaughtered where they stood by the marauding savages.

Word rapidly reached Seaxe that Gawk and Kaara were returning with an army of thousands and that they were slaying all that stood in their way. Panic was rife in the community and hundreds of the locals gathered around the four remaining seniors demanding to know what was happening.

The everyday frogs of Seaxe wanted to know if they too were going to be attacked and if so what should they do to defend themselves. After all none of them had ever fought a battle before because in all the years that Moha had reigned he had brought peace to both his community and to all those thereabouts.

The locals were very frightened and insisted that the seniors confront Emled in order to find out what was going on. In the crowd's anxiety Brylil, Geelan, Kejon and Chrich were carried along towards the river bank from where Emled's palace on the island could be clearly seen. The poor frogs of Seaxe were near to hysteria and quite beyond any attempt at pacification by the four seniors.

As the mass of frogs approached the river bank a hundred or more huge brown marsh frogs rose up from their concealed positions in the reeds and foliage where they had been keeping guard on behalf of the wicked toad. These particular frogs were Emled's finest warriors and their job, as you know, was to protect the king at all costs.

The first of the frenzied crowd to reach the river bank were immediately cut down by the guards who, when faced with potential danger, had been instructed not to waste time by asking questions. All they knew, or cared for that matter, was that a large crowd of frogs was bearing down upon the palace and that, in their view, signalled danger for the king.

Fifty or sixty of the local frogs met their death in this way at the hands of the marsh frogs as the momentum of the surging crowd pushed those at the vanguard right into the clutches of the fearsome guards. It was not in fact until Kejon had clawed his way to the fore to explain that they only wanted to speak with Emled that the unsolicited killing ceased.

The crowd gradually stopped pressing forward as word was sent back that some of the locals had been struck down and that Kejon had bravely gone to the front to defend them. The noisy shouts of the local frogs had begun to subside as they strained to hear what Kejon was saying.

Meanwhile Kejon was being buffeted by a group of the guards who were a little uncertain as to what they should make of this tough-looking character. The other local frogs had been a push-over but this one, they thought, looked as if he might give them a problem or two.

How Kejon wanted to give them a dose of their own medicine. He could do to, and would, given half a chance! However he knew that before he had been able to dispose of more than two or three of the guards he would himself be overpowered by the others and probably butchered for all his valiant efforts. He therefore reluctantly chose to use his discretion for the moment and called out to the guards that the local frogs of Seaxe had come in peace.

"We are not here to cause trouble! We merely want to speak with the king!" Kejon's voice was calm but he nevertheless spoke firmly and with conviction.

"The king is far too busy to be bothered by the likes of you," replied one of the guards who appeared to be the most senior amongst them. "Clear off or you will be flattened like a lily pad!" he continued as he advanced menacingly towards Kejon.

The guard wasn't to know of course but Kejon had a very short temper at the best of times and he really didn't take kindly to being spoken to in this way. Momentarily forgetting about his discretion the angry senior lashed out at the marsh frog with his hindlimb catching him a hefty blow on his nose. Kejon struck with such force that the guard was knocked out and he lay motionless on the ground at the feet of the gritty senior. Kejon then shaped up to tackle another of the guards as several of them hurried towards him. "This is it," thought Kejon, "but at least I will take a couple of them with me."

At that moment Emled's voice boomed out from over on the island.

"*At ease, you guards! Back off and let him speak!*"

Kejon never actually thought he would be pleased to see or hear Emled but on this occasion he was and very relieved to. He quickly gathered his wits about him and turned to face the king. However, he still kept a watchful eye on the nearest of the marsh frog guards just in case one of them sought revenge for their unconscious colleague.

"Emled! We want to know, and we want to know immediately, why an army of marsh frogs and crows from your old community in the Far North are now marching upon Seaxe? We also understand that these savages are murdering and destroying every creature and every thing that lies in their path."

"You need not be afraid," replied Emled. "They are not going to harm this community. Surely no frog would think that I would allow such a terrible thing to happen or that I could possibly sanction such an act? I am your king and you all know how much I care for my frogs. After all is said and done... *Who cares? Emled cares! I care!*"

"That didn't prevent those assassins from Tamsid carrying out the massacre of the kingfisher family up by Kingfisher's Bridge, did it?" Kejon's tone was angry as he questioned the toad. "We heard that it was your murderous lot who were responsible for that terrible and brutal attack."

Emled's patience had gone. This was the first time any frog in Seaxe had dared to accuse him of having anything to do with that foul deed.

"Shut up, Kejon!" shouted Emled, his whole presence emanating evil and malice. "I've heard enough from you. If you really want to know why my marsh frogs and crows are coming this way then I shall tell you, for it is I, the great Emled, who has ordered them here."

There was a gasp from those local frogs who heard this admission from the king. As the word was passed back and through the assembled masses so the same question came to the lips of each of the anxious creatures.

"Why does he want them here?" was what they wanted to know. There was a great deal of nudging and pushing and those nearest to Kejon willed him to put the question to Emled.

"For what purpose are they required here in Seaxe?" asked Kejon as politely as he felt able in the circumstances, "We are a peaceful community. We neither seek confrontation nor do we expect others to do likewise with us."

Emled was almost bursting with anger and frustration. He was not used to this form of interrogation and he especially didn't like being challenged in front of his guards. After all, they might spot a weakness in his seemingly impregnable power base and that, in the opinion of the odious toad, would certainly never do.

"All you need to know is that I require creatures of their capability to undertake a mission for me," replied the toad. "It is for something that is way beyond the limited skills of you and your weak-kneed compatriots. Now clear off before I do something that you will regret!"

The ordinary frogs of Seaxe suddenly realised that Emled really held them in very low esteem. For some it was actually confirmation of a feeling they had privately held for quite some time, although they wouldn't have dared to let it be known that they felt that way for fear of being reported to Emled via the 'Croak Blower's Charter'. However for others, and these were kindly and good souls who should not be chastised for their naiveté, this announcement came as a shocking revelation and was much too much for them to bear.

Kejon could hear the groans of dismay and disillusionment welling up behind him. He wasn't really sure what to do next for the best. However, with a feeling that was greater than he had ever experienced before, he passionately wanted to do something for his community. He looked around for some moral support from his fellow seniors but the only one he could actually see was Chrich, and Kejon immediately sensed that he would be receiving no help whatsoever from this quarter. At this most critical moment he could see that Chrich was slumped against some thick fern stems holding his head in his forelimbs and clearly in great distress. The old senior looked tired and spent for when it came to the crunch poor Chrich really had no heart or spirit for a fight.

What, you may ask, had become of Brylil and Geelan? Well, it must sadly be reported that in the face of adversity these two seniors deserted their friends and colleagues in a way that no frog in Seaxe would have ever dreamt possible.

Brylil had simply fallen apart at the very first sign of trouble, he knew that it was wrong to run away but the lily-livered senior was just too afraid to stand up to the threat of violence. As soon as the rough stuff began between Kejon and the guards Brylil was physically sick with fright and he had dashed off to some deep undergrowth where he had collapsed and fainted.

With regard to Geelan his desertion can only be described as of the most cowardly kind. As far as he was concerned the whole situation had looked grim from the moment the local frogs determined to march upon Emled's island palace. He had decided that there was no way he was going to get either involved in, or be associated with, anything that might reflect badly upon him, or as a result of which he might collect some bumps and bruises. Therefore the moment the surging crowd had reached the edge of the river bank, and the guards had emerged from their hiding places, Geelan had begun to back his way out through the crowd. Whilst he retreated he made many comments to the frightened locals as to how shocking it all was and that really Emled and his cronies should not be allowed to get away with this outrage. All the time of course he was purposefully edging his way nearer and nearer to the rear of the crowd. When he had finally made his way to the back Geelan slipped unnoticed into some long grass from where he bolted as far and as fast as his hindlimbs would carry him. All he knew, as he made great haste through the forest, was that Seaxe was finished as a community and there was no way he was going to risk his neck on behalf of those local no-hopers.

Incidentally that was the last any frog in Seaxe ever saw of the cowardly senior and the locals just presumed he had been lost in all the terrible events that followed. It is, therefore, only you the reader and me the author who knows the truth about Geelan's desertion. Except of course the stout little frog himself. I wonder if he was ever able to live with his dastardly act? Maybe he died in remorse as a lonely and sad frog? Somehow I can't imagine the cowardly senior being that bothered – can you?

"We will not move until you explain to us just what is happening!" shouted Kejon in his defiance of Emled. He was growing stronger by the second and now felt no fear from either the wicked king or his guards.

"That is for me to know," leered Emled. "Your friends will find out in time... However I don't think that you will be so lucky."

The king then turned towards the guards.

"Guards, take this troublesome creature away and teach him a lesson in manners," he ordered. And then as an afterthought the evil toad added, "A lesson the Tamsid way of course!"

The guards bundled Kejon to the ground. In the tussle he had been severely stunned by a blow to the back of his head but not before he had accounted for the death of two of his aggressors. Unconscious from the injury to his head, Kejon was then dragged to the edge of the river and thrown far out into the fast running water. The marsh frogs who had beaten him had assumed the limp body they had tossed into the river to be lifeless. They watched just long enough to see the strong current sweep the stubborn frog swiftly away downstream, bumping him first into the bank and then pulling him deep below the surface. When Kejon's body bobbed back up again it was face down and spreadeagled. The guards patted each other on the shoulders as they made their way back to the palace. They regarded this as a job well done. Their king would be very pleased with them and that meant an extra special supply of tasty grasshoppers!

Whilst Kejon was being dragged away Emled had ordered the other guards to round up all the local Seaxe frogs. They were to be treated as his prisoners and none were to escape. Emled made it known that any that did try to get away would pay the ultimate penalty.

Following the orders that they had been given the guards turned on the large gathering of Seaxe locals and pushed them back towards the centre of the community. Any frogs who for one reason or another hadn't taken part in the march to the king's palace were pulled violently from their homes and forced to join their friends and colleagues.

Having seen the way in which Kejon was disposed none of the local frogs felt inclined to suffer the same fate and so they meekly did as they were ordered.

The entire community were thus kept under a close guard by Emled's vicious henchfrogs. None of the locals hardly dared to move or croak. It was indeed a sorry and pitiful sight. They were leaderless and had no heart for a fight and most certainly not a fight with such a murderous bunch as they now unfortunately had for their captors.

*

Later on that day, when the sun started to fall below the horizon, the imprisoned local Seaxe frogs looked the very picture of sadness and dejection as they stood shivering from both the cold and fear that coursed through their veins. Suddenly they became aware of a distant rumbling. "Was it thunder?" they thought. "Was it a storm brewing?" They couldn't be sure. Whatever it was, however, it was heading their way and approaching rapidly at that.

The noise became louder and louder as it got nearer and nearer. It was then that the locals realised that what they had been listening to was the drumming of thousand upon thousand of frogs' feet upon the ground. Needless to say it was not the feet of ordinary frogs but instead the feet of the massive army of Emled's marsh frogs pounding on the ground as they relentlessly made their way towards Seaxe.

As the marsh frogs marched belligerently into Seaxe their drumming was accompanied by deafening shrieks from a vast black cloud of crows who flew very low overhead. So low in fact that the frightened local frogs cowered upon the ground for fear of being struck by their large flapping wings.

The din made by the ever swelling hordes of marsh frogs and crows rose to such a pitch that the poor Seaxe prisoners were sure that their eardrums were going to burst. Then, just as it seemed it was about to reach its peak, so the cacophony suddenly died down and an eerie silence fell upon the whole community.

After a while, first very softly and then building up to a tumultuous crescendo, came a spooky and repetitive chanting by the marsh frogs and the crows.

"*Emled... Emled... EmLED!... EmLED!... EMLED!... EMLED!*"

They soon reached a point when they were all shouting as loudly as they could and at that moment they were rewarded by the appearance of their hideous king. As the evil toad emerged from his palace they hailed their leader and he in turn waved a forelimb regally in their direction.

The imprisoned Seaxe frogs saw the figure of Emled rise up over the heads of their captors and they were filled with a great fear. He was not their king. He never had been. All that rubbish about 'Emled cares'. All along he had been deceiving them. Why had they been so gullible? Why had the seniors not been aware of what was happening? And where was Moha? If only he were here now.

"Friends! Friends! My loyal and trusted comrades! Welcome to the charming and peaceful community of Seaxe!" Emled was of course addressing the marsh frogs and crows. He now made no attempt to hide his sarcasm or the contempt in which he held the local frogs of Seaxe. The savage looking marsh frogs and the spiteful crows whooped with delight at Emled's cynical words.

"I trust you have all journeyed well and not met too many obstacles on your way?" continued the wicked king.

At this point the marsh frogs began acting out mock fight sequences graphically illustrating how they had battered and beaten the poor defenceless creatures who had been unfortunate enough to have strayed in the path of the marauding army. The black crows were also getting very excited and were flapping their wings and spiralling up and down in their madcap way in their demonstration to Emled of how they too had carried out many cases of death and destruction to the birds of the forest during the course of the violent journey from Tamsid.

"Good! Good!" applauded the toad. "I can see that you are all nicely in the mood for what I have in store for you."

The hordes of marsh frogs roughly pushed and shoved each other in order to get as close to the edge of the river bank as they could without actually falling in. The whole area of the bank was now covered in their large brown bodies. As for the crows they seemed to occupy every spare branch on each of the surrounding trees. In fact the true colours of the riverside oaks and horse chestnuts were now totally obscured as they wore their masks of black crows.

"Tell us!... Tell us!" demanded the eager marsh frogs and crows.

Emled kept his frenzied mob waiting before he delivered the words he knew they would be pleased to hear. Instead he watched them for a while, keen to pump up their excitement and prepare them for what he wanted them to do. Then, just at the point at which their raving was about to boil over, Emled decided to make his big announcement. He first of all held up his forelimbs as a signal for the boisterous and turbulent army to simmer down. The evil king wasn't going to speak until total order and quiet had been restored. Then, as an expectant calm settled over the horde of marsh frogs and crows, he roared his short but terrifying speech.

"*We are going to war and our enemy is every creature and everything that lies in our way!*"

Great whoops and croaks came from the marsh frogs and ear-splitting shrieks of delight emanated from the crows as all of Emled's huge army rejoiced at his message. This was just what they had wanted to hear. It couldn't be better. The big push for taking other communities was starting at long last with as much murder and mayhem thrown in as they wished!

Emled allowed the cheering and celebrating to continue for several minutes before he again raised his arms to calm his followers and let them know that he had more to say.

"There is, however, one order that I shall give that must on no account be ignored or disobeyed. It is that I want that troublesome frog Mars and that mangy blackbird Krakow captured alive and presented to me in good health. There is a special reward for those of you who bring these creatures to me."

Emled again watched as the villainous army heaved and shoved and pushed each other as if each of the mercenaries was letting those closest to them know that it would of course be them who would be collecting this prize.

Emled however hadn't finished speaking. He wanted to make sure that his army had clearly got his special message.

"I know that Mars headed west and, from what I hear, he was accompanied by a young kingfisher, who I presume had luckily avoided death in that unfortunate incident at Kingfisher's Bridge." Emled allowed a cynical smile to creep across the corner of his mouth as if he had just said something amusing. But then, in an instant, his expression changed to one of great menace.

"If what I have heard regarding the kingfisher is indeed true then I must warn those responsible that such an error was extremely careless and I will not tolerate any similar mistakes in the future." The evil toad spoke these words so coldly and with such a threatening intent that they sent shivers up and down the spine of even the meanest of the marsh frogs.

"I am also fairly certain that wherever Mars goes then the old blackbird will follow," continued Emled. "Just you remember that I want these two creatures delivered to me alive and unharmed and I certainly don't want to see so much as a scratch upon the face of the frog." This was clearly of great importance to Emled as he believed that the face of Mars actually belonged to him.

"If there are any further mistakes made by any of you this time then they will be your last as I shall personally crush the life out of the miscreant." Emled's sinister warning was received by a now rather more subdued audience and the toad was pleased to see that they had all seemingly listened well to what he had to say. He knew, however, that it wouldn't be good for their morale if he were to leave the army on a low ebb so he finished with a rallying call.

"Now, rest well tonight, my friends, for I want you all at you marauding best tomorrow! And remember... *Who cares? Emled cares! I care!*"

With that Emled turned and disappeared back into his palace with the sound of his wildly cheering mob once again ringing in his ears. His thoughts, however, were now firmly concentrated on the night ahead for it was to be filled with a mammoth gorging of his most succulent grasshoppers in the company of his favourite female frogs. Organising death and destruction always gave him such a great appetite!

Chapter Twenty-Five

Bad News Travels Fast

Kejon suddenly regained consciousness with a bump. He was not at all sure how far he had floated down the river but what he did know was that his head, and not for the first time that day, had come into direct contact with something very hard.

For a few seconds he wondered where he was and just what was happening. Gradually, however, the cool water began to bring him back to his senses. Across his mind kept flashing images of the final moments of his confrontation with Emled just before he received what he assumed must have been a blow on the back of the head from one of the evil king's marsh frog guards. After that he remembered nothing until now.

The river's currents had been running swiftly this day and Kejon had been carried along a considerable distance downstream in a south-westerly direction. What had helped him back to consciousness was the fact that he had been firmly swept, and in no uncertain manner, into a tangled mass of tree roots that occupied the recess of a sharp bend in the river. Little by little the roots had become exposed over time by the constant battering of running water as it raced into the bank before being diverted back along its natural course.

The tough and gritty frog hauled himself out of the river and onto the shiny ebony black root system. He didn't know which part of his body hurt most or for that matter which to rub first. In fact everything ached, although he finally decided that his head was rather more tender than any of the other bruises and abrasions he now displayed.

The belligerent frog's toughness and resilience had been what had saved him. Even though he had been given a hefty whack on the head by one of Emled's guards, and blow after blow had rained in on him from several others as he fell to the ground before being dragged unceremoniously away to be thrown into the rapid river, he quickly realised that he must now act fast as the community of Seaxe and all the other creatures of the river banks and forests were in imminent mortal danger from Emled and his cronies.

But what should he do for the best? Should he go back to Seaxe and again attempt to stand up against Emled and his army of thugs? If he did try such a stunt surely the ignoble king would show him no mercy and, given another opportunity, would have him killed as soon as look at him. Although Kejon was mad with anger, and he desperately wanted to go and help his friends and colleagues, he could see that to return alone would be pointless. He couldn't take on the full might of Emled and his army on his own.

Kejon sat and thought some more. He did of course have one great advantage which was that Emled would have assumed him to be dead. After all the wicked toad had seen Kejon felled by the marsh frog guards and they would for sure have reported back to their king that his lifeless body had been cast to the bottom of the river.

The pugnacious frog therefore decided that the best thing he could do for the moment would be to keep secret from Emled and his thugs that he was actually still alive and use this situation to his advantage in whatever way possible. At the very least he would be able to give an early warning to his fellow frogs and other creature communities that Emled was on the warpath and that they must make every effort to protect themselves.

Kejon thought long and hard before determining his next step. It was one thing to tell everyone that they were in imminent danger of attack from Emled and his army, but, if he couldn't say where the evil king was to strike first, then all he would succeed in doing would be to create panic and mass hysteria within the hearts of the very frogs and creature communities he was attempting to protect. If he were to cause such a condition amongst his fellow creatures, then in such a state of disarray, Emled would have absolutely no trouble at all in smashing his way through the good communities virtually at will.

Kejon decided, therefore, that he must try and find out what were Emled's intentions and in particular in which direction he was going to order his army to march. He also knew that he must find Mars, and maybe Moha too, in order to tell them what was happening. He was sure that they would know what to do.

Not for the first time Kejon scolded himself for being such a fool. Why, oh why, had he allowed himself to be swayed by the malignant influence of Emled? What on earth, and indeed on water, did he ever think he was going to gain from turning his back on Moha and Mars and giving his allegiance to the evil Emled? Having spent a great many seasons enjoying a peaceful and caring existence under the loving Moha what was it that happened to cause him to reject all of that kindness in favour of what can only be described as utter and total evil?

Images of Emled again flashed across Kejon's mind. He could vividly see the menacing face of the king as he addressed huge gatherings of frogs in Seaxe, offering promises of care and support to all creatures. Kejon fancied that he could almost hear the sinister voice of Emled saying that he would give the community all of the things that they had so shamefully been denied under Moha's oppressive regime.

The constant barrage of bad-mouthing of Moha that was practised to such a relentless extent by each of Emled, the crows and the marsh frogs, had served its obviously intended purpose of putting negative thoughts about the friendly old king in the corporate mind of the community. It now seemed to Kejon very clear that although what had been said about Moha was completely untrue, the more such lies were expounded by Emled and his cronies the greater was the possibility that the everyday frogs of Seaxe would eventually believe in the stories.

The cunning of the ignominious toad knew no boundaries, and, as he told his lies about Moha in order to put the old king in a bad light, he would say to any frog who happened to be listening how much he wanted to share the pain that had been inflicted upon them as he personally wished he could ease their burden in some way. And of course he would always end his speeches and pronouncements with his favourite phrase of '*Who cares? Emled cares! I care!*"

In the early days of Emled's reign the sound of the new king making such statements encouraged the community of Seaxe to believe that improvements were really going to be made. The odd thing was that no frog was at all sure what Emled actually meant by the supposedly 'bad times' they had experienced under Moha, for they had always enjoyed what they considered to be very good times under the old king. However, if Emled was going to commit himself to making improvements then they would certainly not reject such action.

It was, therefore, in this very strange and confused environment that the ordinary frogs of Seaxe went about their daily business. They were clearly happy that the new king appeared to have their future well-being at the top of his agenda, but, if they had been asked to explain what had been so bad before, then they would have been hard pressed to answer such a question. Of course the way in which Emled described the future sounded good but it really was quite impossible for the local Seaxe frogs to relate what he said about the past to any form of reality.

Gradually, however, and little by little, the continuous bombardment by Emled on the minds of the Seaxe community slowly began to achieve its purpose. It was perhaps inevitable that when faced by such concentrated pressure the good but naive frogs of Seaxe should prove susceptible to Emled's influence. The loving thoughts they previously treasured in respect of Moha were slowly being eroded and replaced by a desire for betterment. This desire then began to take the form of greed and caused one frog to look at another and wonder why he or she should have less than one's neighbour. Such thoughts had previously been alien to the good frogs of Seaxe and they found these new emotions difficult to contain. As a direct consequence of this changing atmosphere unwelcome feelings of envy, jealousy and craving soon became commonplace. And whereas in the past one frog would have regarded his neighbour as a friend, quite irrespective of the latter's status or possessions, such an attitude was now being replaced by feelings of deep suspicion and resentment particularly in respect of another creature's material gain and what could only be described as their personal wealth.

Kejon felt a huge surge of regret spread throughout his body. How could he and his friends and colleagues have allowed themselves to be fooled by all those empty words and hollow promises spouted by Emled? He knew now that he should have listened to Mars. He realised, albeit now much too late, that the young frog must have seen through the evil king from the very beginning. That Kejon had chosen to ignore Mars was of course a mistake but it was a mistake that the stubborn frog shared with all of his senior colleagues as well as the vast majority of the honest and trusting everyday frogs of Seaxe.

In truth the seniors had willingly submitted to the influence of Emled and pandered to his demands as they felt they would personally benefit by so doing. The common frogs in the community, on the other hand, were merely carried along by Emled's psychological attack and targeted assault on their memory of what life was really like under the reign of Moha. At heart they were good and kind frogs but Emled had preyed upon their gullibility and poisoned their minds with his unique brand of morality.

As Kejon again chastised himself for his foolishness the wave of remorse was slowly being replaced by a renewed vigour and fortitude. He was determined that from now on he would make amends for his failings and do all he could to save his fellow creatures from the imminent onslaught by Emled and his flying and marching army of dreadful mercenaries.

Revitalised by this commitment he leapt from the smooth and shiny tree roots and landed on the bank from where he hurried along back towards Seaxe. He had decided that he was going to find out what the evil Emled was planning irrespective of the dangers he was personally likely to face. His deep rooted passion had been stirred. Come on, Kejon! The qualities he possessed, and for which he had been promoted by Moha, of determination; strength of mind and body; and an unshakeable commitment and belief in himself, were now most definitely aroused. He was set on redeeming his past failings in order to make up for his recent sad lapses of character.

*

The river had actually taken Kejon a good deal further than he had at first thought and it was several hours before he entered an area that he recognised as being on the outskirts of his home community. The dusk was drawing in as he arrived and his natural instincts warned him to take great care in his final approach.

As Kejon crept stealthily through the long grasses and the ferns that lined the banks of the river, the raucous laughter of a group of marsh frogs broke the stillness of the cool night air. He immediately crouched down low and crept as near to them as he dared.

"...and I'll bet you a hundred fat and juicy grasshoppers that I will kill more of those Surey frogs than you do," boasted a particularly

Revitalised by this commitment he leapt from the smooth and shiny tree roots and landed on the bank from where he hurried along back towards Seaxe.

mean sounding individual. "And what's more, I'll double my winnings when we move on to Cowall."

"Make that two hundred grasshoppers and you've got a deal," replied a fellow thug. "I'll enjoy murdering those no-hopers even more knowing that I shall have a fine feast to follow, and especially as it will be at your expense."

As their colleagues roared their approval of this grisly wager, Kejon shuddered at the prospect. He wanted to jump out right there and then into the middle of the group of thugs and fight them all. However he realised that this would be stupid as he would almost certainly be overpowered and bludgeoned to death by these vicious creatures. If that happened he would immediately lose the benefit of what he had just heard, for he was now in possession of the extremely valuable information that Emled's line of attack was first into Surey and then on to Cowall.

Something again told him that he must find Mars. He wasn't quite sure what this feeling meant, or why it was so strong, he only knew that he must urgently search for his former colleague.

A tinge of sadness prickled Kejon's leathery skin as he remembered Mars as a friend as well as a colleague. More so than any of the other seniors would have cared to admit Kejon had admired Mars, but he did so without the painful pangs of jealousy that so riddled the minds and bodies of his peers.

He must now find Mars, and fast. So, with this singular thought in his mind, he silently stole away into the night. He would not be stopping to sleep or eat as there was no time to consider his own personal comforts. All he knew was that it was vitally important that he should locate Mars and that the unsuspecting inhabitants of Surey and Cowall be given as much time as possible to vacate their communities and thus escape the plundering of Emled's savage and cruel army.

Chapter Twenty-Six

Mars Awakes

Mars awoke to find that he was quite alone. He somehow knew that Krakow would not be there and that he would never again see the wise old blackbird. He could, however, still hear in his mind Krakow's words of encouragement and he sensed the bird's love and friendship permeating throughout his body. Mars was sad that Krakow had gone but he knew that it must be so. The young frog welcomed the feelings that the wise old bird had left within his heart and soul and he felt uplifted in the knowledge that, although Krakow would not physically be by his side in his fight against the forces of evil, he would nevertheless be with him in spirit.

As Mars stood and looked about him he felt refreshed by his sleep. He also felt an inner strength quite unlike anything he had ever experienced. His body and mind felt more powerful and he was filled with a great belief both in himself and in the future.

Mars sensed that all of his faculties were engaged and focused, and, although he knew that what lay ahead was an extreme threat to the continued existence of the forest and river bank creature's way of life, he felt confident that he was both physically and mentally well-equipped to meet such a challenge. Whether or not he would be successful would of course depend on how well he applied his newly acquired 'Great Learning of the Supreme Qualities of Wisdom and Knowledge'. We shall have to wait and see how he fared.

*

Mars made his way back to the main area of the Cowall community. Maccus had been waiting for him and he greeted him warmly. He could see that there had been a change in Mars for there was a visible aura of authority about him and he hopped along in an altogether more positive and confident manner. The two friends exchanged no words, as words, in such emotionally charged circumstances, were not necessary between creatures who well understand each other's feelings. The respect, loyalty and great friendship that existed between Maccus and Mars was deeply set and they knew that they would each willingly lay down their life for the other.

Maccus skipped alongside Mars as they entered into Cowall's main community centre. It was then that the full force of his new position struck Mars for he was welcomed by a tumultuous cheering and great cries of support from the local frogs.

As increasingly hundreds and hundreds of Cowall's frogs clamoured excitedly around him Mars was somewhat surprised that he did not feel overwhelmed by either their number or their enthusiasm. Instead he felt most able to receive their affection and support and in return he gave them clear signs both of his appreciation and of his undoubted ability to lead his fellow frogs.

Maccus looked on the scene with a huge amount of admiration for his friend. As he did so Denray emerged from amidst the crowd and went and stood by Mars' side. Standing shoulder to shoulder, the two frogs appeared to the community to be a most powerful and handsome combination indeed.

Cheers of approval and shouts of "*Long live Mars! Long live Denray!*" filled the air. These cries were soon followed by a resounding call of "*Three croaks for Mars and Denray. Three croaks for our leaders!*"

This was a great moment for all those assembled to celebrate. It was indeed an occasion that was to have substantial and lasting implications for the many thousands of creatures who lived along the river banks and in the forests.

*

As the cheering continued, and both Mars and Denray were lifted on to the shoulders of the frogs of Cowall, far away in the ravaged community of Seaxe a sudden spasm ran through the grotesque body of Emled. Perspiration oozed from the dry warty skin of the evil toad as he was momentarily overcome by a strange feeling of anxiety. He felt hot all over and extremely uncomfortable. Then, in an instant, he felt very cold yet the perspiration continued to break out all over his unsightly body. Such a condition was, of course, quite extraneous to him as he was not used to experiencing emotions such as fear or anxiety. However, had he appreciated the meaning of fear then he would have realised that it was indeed this very sensation that was currently tripping through his system.

Although he personally did not understand such emotions the greater powers of evil certainly did and Emled's inner senses were suddenly aware that a serious challenger to the forces of evil had emerged. These dark forces intuitively knew that this challenge would come from a creature who sided with all that was good and who would most definitely pose a real threat to their quest for total domination which they sought through the medium of the hideous body of the toad.

Even though he was feeling distinctly uneasy Emled had no reason to believe that it was anything more than an over-indulgence in particularly rich grasshoppers the night before that was the cause of his discomfort. He had no idea what might lie between himself and his personal bid for absolute power and, if he was asked, he would probably say he didn't actually much care about such minor difficulties. It was therefore quite without a concern for the strength or otherwise of the opposition that the wicked toad was driven inexorably on by the evil powers that were embedded deep within him. In truth he was completely blind to anything other than his quest for total domination of all creatures and he was certain that nothing could stop him and no creature could possibly stand in his way! We shall of course in time see if he was right!

Chapter Twenty-Seven

Kejon's Surprise Visit

It was an exhausted and dusty Kejon who stumbled into the community of Surey just as the dawn was breaking. Motivated by the gravity of his mission and the urgent need to give warning to one and all of Emled's imminent attack, he had travelled all through the night hardly stopping to take a rest.

There were only a few local frogs up and about at this early hour but as soon as they caught sight of the weary and grimy visitor they immediately came to his assistance.

Two of the Surey frogs asked him if he needed a shoulder to lean on as they thought he appeared to be a little unsteady on his hindlimbs. Kejon assured them that he personally was really all right, but what he did require was a meeting with their king.

"I have news of such great significance that I must see your king without delay," explained Kejon.

The local frogs sensed from Kejon's all too apparent distress that a matter of the utmost importance had indeed arisen so they straight away bade Kejon to follow them to the king's residence.

The news of the outsider's sudden arrival spread rapidly throughout the community, and, as Kejon was ushered along by several of the locals who had been amongst the first to spot him, a great many others also began to emerge from their sleeping places, all of whom were very keen to see what was going on.

In no time at all a huge crowd had joined Kejon and his escorts hopping about excitedly and asking all manner of questions. All Kejon would say was that he must first of all speak with their king for he would know what to do for the best. This of course only served to add to the intrigue of the occasion and the locals' curiosity was almost at bursting point.

It was an exhausted and dusty Kejon who stumbled into the community of Surey just as the dawn was breaking.

As soon as the thronging crowd arrived at the king of Surey's residence Kejon was taken inside. Although the muffled sounds of the excited crowd could still be heard, he was struck by the feeling of peace and calmness that permeated the atmosphere of the royal chamber. As Kejon looked around at his surroundings he felt safe for the first time in what seemed like ages.

"I understand you have some very important news that you wish to give me." A fine, deep and mellow voice came from behind Kejon.

The Seaxe senior turned to see who had spoken these words and as he did so he found himself face to face with a large and extremely powerfully built bullfrog.

"Please allow me to introduce myself," continued the distinguished and ruggedly handsome bullfrog. "My name is Fara. I am the king of this community."

Kejon's initial thought was how closely this bullfrog resembled Moha. In size, shape and the way he proudly held his head up high as he spoke, it could almost have been the old king of Seaxe himself. The tone of his voice was similar too and it reminded Kejon of the great many times that the kind and caring Moha had put his forelimb upon his shoulder and given him advice on all manner of things.

Kejon introduced himself and as he did so he felt secure in the company of this giant of a bullfrog. Although he had never had the honour and privilege to have met Fara before he had heard many stories told about the noble king of Surey. Fara had an exemplary reputation and he was widely known for his ability to rapidly assess even the most difficult of situations and to then be able to make speedy and appropriately telling decisions. He was as forthright as he was positive and frogs of his acquaintance would always say, "you know exactly where you stand with Fara". He was thus greatly loved by his community and widely admired throughout the river banks and forests.

What Fara subsequently heard from Kejon sounded so outrageous of course that many would have considered the messenger to be deranged. Fara instead, however, listened intently and very carefully to all that Kejon had to say and he allowed the resilient senior to give all of his news. Every now and then the king of Surey would gently raise his hand indicating that he wanted Kejon to pause whilst he asked a question or two in order to enable him to clarify or establish the full meaning of what he was being told.

Fara could sense that what he was hearing was true. He felt that Kejon spoke honestly and from his heart and that the fear that was evident to him in the courageous frog's voice was quite genuine.

"...and coming this way, you say?" asked Fara.

"That's right," replied Kejon. "And they are many in number too. These marsh frogs are the largest and meanest frogs you will ever have seen; and the crows, that appear to have some form of evil alliance with Emled, are as black as pitch and as cunning as can be."

"Are you quite certain that Emled's plan is to attack other frog communities and that he intends to start his campaign of terror by firstly striking at Surey?" Fara didn't doubt Kejon, he merely wanted to confirm that he had correctly understood what he had just been told.

"Judging from what I overheard when I listened in on the conversation of that murderous bunch of marsh frogs my assumption is that Emled's army will be moving out of Seaxe before noon today and that they will be heading straight for Surey. My guess is that they will probably have spent this morning resting after the excitement of yesterday's invasion of Seaxe. I would also expect they will make every effort to ensure that the local frogs of Seaxe whom they have captured are securely imprisoned in order that they will have no chance of escape. They will of course need to leave a contingent of marsh frogs behind in my home community to guard such frogs but I would not think that many of these vicious creatures will be necessary to keep such peaceful beings under control. I am quite certain that my friends and colleagues will by this time be totally confused and bewildered by what has happened there in the past day or so. They are also entirely without any form of leadership and they are certainly very, very frightened.

"Therefore, allowing for an eight hour march, I would estimate that Emled will aim to reach the outskirts of this community by dusk today. I am sure he will not wish to launch his attack at night as he will want to avoid giving you or your frogs even the slightest chance of escaping under the cover of darkness. He will also not want to incur any unnecessary losses in the ranks of his damned marsh frogs and carrion crows this early in his campaign. I would therefore suggest that you can probably expect him to invade Surey at dawn tomorrow."

Fara bowed his head and closed his eyes as he mulled over all that Kejon had said. The Seaxe senior could sense that Fara was deep in meditation as he considered what action he should take. He was therefore very careful not to move or make a sound that might disturb the king of Surey's train of thought.

After a while Fara opened his eyes, straightened his back and raised his head. What Kejon then saw and heard was a very positive king who spoke with the confidence of a frog who knew his mind and how to assess even the most sticky of predicaments.

"Thank you, Kejon, for giving such a detailed account of Emled's activities. You have been extremely brave in your efforts to obtain this information and you have interpreted clearly and rationally Emled's probable intentions. Put to such an acute test you have demonstrated well the sort of qualities that would have made your old king very proud. You are indeed a product of the good King Moha's teaching." Fara was pleased with Kejon and he spoke with warmth to the gritty Seaxe senior. However, he sensed that deep within Kejon there existed a determination that was not just founded on ability and responsibility. Fara felt that in this regard there was an overwhelming motivation which Kejon needed to satisfy and which was driving him on to do good for his fellow creatures.

"We shall move out of here within the hour and march to Cowall in order to join up with Denray and his community." Fara continued to speak, making his statements assertively and with authority. "From what you have told me about the strength of this evil King Emled, and the size and wicked nature of his army of marsh frogs and crows, there is absolutely no benefit to be gained in waiting for them to arrive in Surey only to be massacred in a vain attempt to defend our territory. What is the point in dying for material things such as our homes; the reeds and the bulrushes that adorn the banks of the river that runs through our community; and the supplies of grasshoppers that fill our stores? Such things are of little consequence when they are compared to the well-being and safety of our frogs. The lives of the creatures of our community are very precious and it is they who must be protected from these evil forces whilst a more appropriate strategy is developed to combat the advance of Emled and his army.

"Let's hope and pray that there will come a time in the future when we can concentrate on rebuilding our material losses. After all is said and done it is possible to reconstruct such things as our habitat but we would not be able to bring back to life a dead friend, relative or colleague who had been pointlessly sacrificed to the mercy of this loathsome fiend."

Kejon both knew and felt that he was in the presence of a very kind and charismatic king. However, although he realised that what Fara had proposed was the most sensible strategy in the circumstances, he would personally have preferred a more direct course of action. Kejon was a headstrong creature and his method of dealing with this situation, after having informed all those who needed to be aware of the threat of Emled, would have been to stand against the evil toad's mighty army and fight back with blood and thunder. Unfortunately Kejon's strategy, although typically brave of the senior frog, would of course have been doomed to failure.

Kejon desperately wanted to defeat the evil king at the earliest opportunity and then to have him hung upside down from the tallest reeds that grew along the river bank. He wanted to see Emled ridiculed and taunted by all those whom he had harmed or who had suffered as a consequence of his wickedness. Although Kejon hadn't laid the plans as to how he would actually defeat Emled, this spirited and bold Seaxe senior was nevertheless willing to charge in and leave the outcome in the hands of fate.

"But...!" began Kejon.

Before he could continue, Fara had raised his forelimb in a friendly fashion and motioned for him to stop talking. The king of Surey recognised Kejon for the tough character that he was and he instinctively knew that the Seaxe senior would rather fight fire with fire. He also understood the reasons why Kejon should adopt such an attitude and he sympathised with the tenacious senior's aggressive stance. However the current situation demanded a more conservative policy at this stage, which required safety first tactics, and Kejon would need to accept that as a fact. Fara respected Kejon and admired his honesty and bravery but now was not the appropriate moment for debating what needed to be done. He had made his decision and there was no time to delay further action.

"Kejon, my friend," began Fara. "I'm afraid now is not the moment to discuss our respective tactics. I do understand your feelings but we must move out of Surey immediately." On seeing Kejon's obvious disappointment he paused for a moment or two before continuing.

"Come now, my brave friend, you have been most courageous in your endeavours so far and there is no way that I shall waste the vital news that you have brought to us. It is quite clear to me that if we are to have any chance of standing our ground against Emled we must join forces with our friends in other communities." Fara then paused again before finally saying, "You will have your chance to bloody the nose of Emled... I shall personally see to that! In the meantime, however, you will have to trust in my judgement and understand that I am not running away from this creeping evil. I have a responsibility for the frogs of Surey and I view that role very seriously. As a king of a community I also have a responsibility for my fellow kings and in turn the everyday frogs of their respective communities. Taking all these things into consideration, it is my opinion that a joint campaign against the powers of evil will have a much greater chance of success than if we confronted Emled with merely the resources available to our own community. I am certain that we would be entirely wiped out by Emled's much more powerful army even if we were prepared for his onslaught."

Kejon knew in his heart that what Fara said was right and he acknowledged, albeit a little reluctantly, the wise counsel he was receiving. Kejon was basically a good frog with, as many of his colleagues would say, "his heart in the right place". However, his powers of intellect and analysis were somewhat lacking and were certainly far outweighed by his talent for being a tough, stubborn and single-minded operator when he wanted to be. Although he was never going to have the essential qualities that are required if a frog is ever to progress to becoming a king, he would, nevertheless, always be a valuable comrade to have on your side when your backs are up against the banks of the river.

"Now, my friend, let me see you raise that strong chin of yours and come and join me in passing on this news to my community. I must advise them of the action that we shall be taking. If we are to defeat the evil king it is essential that we act swiftly and decisively at all times. I also want you to be properly introduced to them for I know they will be inspired by your brave exploits."

Fara put his forelimb on the top of Kejon's head and spoke to him in much the same way as Moha had done many times before. What he said reached deep into the tough senior's heart. "I sense that there is more in your mission to help in our battle against Emled than readily meets the eye and that you may feel you have something to prove. If you do have some additional motivation I don't really need to know what it is, for I am confident that you are a good frog and that your intentions are entirely honourable. My only advice is that you consider carefully how you utilise such feelings as none of us will have a second chance against the scale of evil that is threatening our very existence.

Despite his toughness Kejon's throat reddened slightly on hearing these words. It wasn't because he felt any embarrassment that Fara had clearly seen into the inner workings of his mind, it was more that he felt in awe of this king and he marvelled at his powers of insight. Kejon's thoughts then again momentarily wandered to the way he had so easily succumbed to the evil influence of Emled and how he had willingly allowed himself to be encouraged to think and speak so badly of Moha. He pondered on the fact that at the time he did not have any feelings of guilt in respect of what he was doing or saying. He also suddenly felt ashamed and sick at heart for showing no remorse when the wicked king expelled Mars from the community which his one time friend had loved and served so well. In fact Kejon, in keeping with his fellow seniors, had played his full part in encouraging Emled to banish Mars from Seaxe.

Yes, Kejon did have something to prove, and it was as much to himself as to others. He had badly let down frogs whom he once loved and now he was determined to make amends.

*

"...Wc arc therefore going to reassemble here within the hour in order to prepare for our march to Cowall!" Fara's voice rang out to the frogs of Surey. His community had been numbed by the news that a fearsome and depraved army being led by a most vile and abominable king, and which consisted of marsh frogs and carrion crows, was about to descend upon their community.

"Ahead of us I will send a messenger to Cowall, accompanied by our new friend Kejon, to advise Denray that we are coming and to explain the reason behind our mass exodus from Surey. I am also going to ask one of our most experienced seniors to lead a small team, consisting of frogs who have proved themselves to be adept in the skills of orienteering and survival, to travel to the far distant communities of Nolk and Solk to seek assistance from their fine kings Tanal and Cabal."

At this point Fara looked round at his group of seven seniors and he could see that each of them wanted to be the one chosen to head off east towards Nolk and Solk. Fara knew that any one of them would be capable of undertaking the mission although he was aware that there was a high risk of losing valued personnel in such dangerous circumstances.

Fara looked at each of his seniors in turn and decided that Rogar was the one to take on this hazardous task. Rogar was a muscular young frog who had a wise head on very youthful and broad shoulders. He was also quite fearless, but not reckless, and his king was confident that he would be best suited to this difficult mission.

Having made his selection, Fara turned to the gathered crowd and again spoke to them all. His voice was grave and the local frogs of Surey paid very close attention to what he had to say.

"To travel east at this time along river banks and through forests, all of which will probably be occupied by Emled and his army, is certainly going to be a most difficult and dangerous task. I am therefore sure that you will all join me in wishing Rogar, and those brave frogs whom he will select to accompany him, the very best of fortunes in their attempt to reach our friends in the eastern communities of Nolk and Solk. All of our thoughts will be with them every hop of the way. The successful outcome, or otherwise, of their task will I am certain have a great bearing on all of our futures.

"I must now ask you all to gather together your families and prepare to move out within the hour. My intention is that we will aim to arrive in Cowall by dusk tomorrow. It will unfortunately not be possible for you to take stores of food on our travels so I therefore suggest that you all consume as much nourishment as you can before we leave. The journey will be particularly tough for the young; the elderly; and those frogs who happen to be more unfortunate than others. In this respect can I please ask that you give such frogs as much assistance as they may require.

"There are of course no guarantees in this life and so we must make our own luck. I have taken decisions that I feel will at least secure our position until the way ahead becomes a little more clear. This may give us some breathing space whilst we debate what to do with this evil monster Emled.

"Thanks to you all and good luck. I hope and pray that we are delivered safely into a happy and peaceful existence at the end of all this trauma.

"I shall waste no further time in talking. Please now disperse and reassemble here and be ready to go before the sun reaches the top of the oak tree on the far side of the river bank.

"Once again good luck and may the forces of goodness be with you always."

On that note Fara bade his community to go and prepare themselves for the long march which lay ahead.

Chapter Twenty-Eight

Mars Contemplates His Strategy

What was all too clear to Mars was the fact that the resources available in the community of Cowall would certainly not be able to withstand the expected and massive onslaught from Emled and his vast evil army. Despite the enthusiastic show of support and affection by the local frogs of Cowall, plus their unswerving willingness to follow both their own king and Mars into battle, the new leader of frogs was well aware that to confront Emled with just the numbers currently at his command would, without doubt, result in total slaughter for this happy and friendly community. Mars was certainly not about to waste the lives of such trusting and good frogs on such a hopeless cause.

*

Mars, Denray and Maccus sat in silence for a long while. They were in Denray's home and this was Mars' first council of war. The small group were sitting so close that their heads were almost touching. Denray was the first to speak.

"The frogs of my community are willing to die if it means ridding the earth and rivers of something as evil as Emled. If necessary they will stand shoulder to shoulder and put up a determined resistance."

Denray was a proud king and thought a great deal of the frogs in his community. He spoke his words with great honesty and commitment.

"Denray, my friend. To know that you and your frogs would do such a thing fills me with sincere gratification. That we have such resolute and big-hearted frogs on our side does indeed bode well for the future in our fight against evil. However, to take Emled on head to head would be playing right into his hands. He has a murderous army of marsh frogs on the ground and a vicious army of crows in the air each of whom are capable on their own of beating our frogs. It would therefore be foolhardy and totally irresponsible of me to utilise our most valuable resources in such a way. To lay the lives of our frogs at the mercy of Emled would be to send them to their certain deaths."

Denray could feel the urgency with which Mars was approaching the situation but at the same time be could sense the inner calmness with which the newly appointed leader of all frogs was marshalling his thoughts and contemplating his strategy. Mars thought hard for a short while longer and then he spoke again.

"We must think more widely and consider what additional support we may be able to harness from outside of Cowall. We must also try and anticipate when Emled is likely to mount an attack. My immediate estimation is that this will probably happen within the next two to three days.

"As far as the likelihood of additional resources is concerned," continued Mars, "the possibility of adding to our numbers by recruiting frogs from neighbouring communities is now probably severely limited. We must accept the possibility that Surey may already have fallen to Emled as he will undoubtedly march through that community on his way here. We must also accept that it is impossible for word to be sent from Cowall to both Nolk and Solk in time for their armies to arrive here before Emled attacks. If we sent there for help now it would take at least three to four days for the message to get through and for Tanal and Cabal to march their respective frogs back across to Cowall.

"Realistically we may only have Somset who could provide assistance in time, although, by my calculation, we will still be far outnumbered by Emled's army. It is essential, nevertheless, that we send word to Somset immediately. I am sure they will already know of the existence of Emled for dear Moha, who now of course lives there, will have recounted some of the stories of the wicked king's dastardly deeds. I'm therefore certain that full support will come from that quarter once they know that Emled is on the move, as they will fully understand the futility of pitting single communities against such powerful forces of evil."

Mars then looked towards Maccus. The young bird had grown noticeably in both mind and body over the past couple of weeks, although he was as yet not quite confident enough to personally put forward suggestions for such a vital battle strategy.

"Maccus, we shall require support from the air if we are to reduce the impact of Emled's crows. Their unchallenged aerial dominance means that we will have no chance once any of our frogs breaks cover. Please think hard as to where we may obtain such assistance."

Maccus was pleased to be given this responsibility. He had already been wondering along these lines but now that Mars had given him his head on the matter he would be able to focus all his effort on finding an appropriate solution.

"Denray, whilst Maccus thinks on, can you please arrange for a message to be sent across to Somset requesting support to be sent without delay." Denray nodded and both he and Maccus prepared to leave in order to pursue their respective tasks.

"Now," began Mars, "I need some time alone in which I can gather my thoughts and concentrate on what needs to be done. Can you both please attend to your duties and meet with me again back here in one hour for an update on what we have been able to achieve."

*

Left entirely on his own, Mars thought hard about the prospect of tackling the impending invasion by Emled. In his heart he knew that even with all of Somset's frogs, together with those of Cowall, they would still be no match for Emled. There would neither be sufficient depth in numbers nor strength of bodies to successfully fight a war with the battle-hardened marsh frogs, especially with the latter's airborne support from the crows.

As it currently stood, the very best that Mars could arrange with the resources available to him was a strategy based exclusively on defence. Standing nose to nose, not to mention nose to beak, with their adversaries would be most unwise and it would certainly result in failure. The option of a defensive strategy was clearly more sensible although Mars knew that with the wide disparity in the known level of resources it was merely only delaying the inevitability of a crushing defeat for his good frogs.

The young leader of frogs also knew that what he and Denray most needed was more time to build up their numbers to a sufficient level in order to combat Emled's vast army. Time, however, was at a premium and Emled was not about to allow much of it to pass before he launched his attack on Cowall.

It was against such a parlous background that Mars prepared his battle strategy. He was certain that he would only have one chance to defeat Emled and if he was beaten then it would herald the dawn of a new era dominated by the forces of evil. He therefore had to be sure about his battle plans and they had to be successful.

Mars sat quietly and calmly with his eyes closed. Although the odds were at this time massively stacked against him he nevertheless felt undaunted by the prospect. The wisdom that he now possessed gave him a clarity of thought that eliminated the negative and focused entirely on the positive. At the same time the knowledge he had acquired gave him a broad spectrum of experience on which he could draw.

In this mode Mars painted pictures in his mind as he considered first one scenario and then another. He would then occasionally merge two or three of the scenarios in order to test various options and fall back positions. In this way he sought to clarify in his mind the tactics he should employ within his strategy. The young leader of frogs was concentrating hard and focusing exclusively on his battle plans.

*

Meanwhile, whilst Mars contemplated his strategy, an angry and malevolent toad sat back on his hindlimbs gazing over the deserted community of Surey.

Emled was, to say the very least, absolutely fuming, furious and filled with rage. It appeared that he had been thwarted on this the first leg of his planned trail of carnage. The defeat and destruction of Surey was intended to be the initial step on his way to the ultimate take-over of all the neighbouring creature communities. However something had seemingly gone horribly wrong.

Everything, in fact, had been going well up until this moment. Emled had ordered his marsh frogs and crows to approach the main centre of the community from the outskirts of Surey as quietly as possible so as not to alert the local frogs of their impending doom. Then, at the command of the toad's blood-curdling croak to attack, the evil army had been primed to swarm all over the unsuspecting community showing absolutely no mercy and ready to strike dead any creature who stood in their way.

To Emled's chagrin the attack rendered nothing other than the sight of thousands of highly confused marsh frogs and crows falling over themselves in their eagerness to slaughter the inhabitants of Surey. The only problem was that they could not find any such creatures to kill.

As soon as it dawned upon the murderous army that there was actually no opposition they turned upon Emled for an explanation.

"I-I-I really don't know what has happened," stammered the equally confused toad. And then, as his evil mind rapidly began to return to its senses, he blurted out accusations at those who clamoured before him.

"It must be that we have a traitor in our midst!" he shouted. "Come on, who was it that sent a warning which enabled this miserable community to make their escape? Some frog or crow must have advised them of my plans! Who is the traitor? Someone must know who it is! I'll kill him with my own hands when I find out! A thousand grasshoppers to whomsoever can give me the name of the culprit."

The marsh frogs and crows were already filled with an uncontrollable craving for blood and the sound of their leader's ranting and the offer of such a substantial reward only served to increase their murderous aspirations. At Emled's cries of traitor they began looking accusingly at each other and their pushing and shoving quickly turned into punching and clawing.

"It was you!" shouted one marsh frog to another.

"It wasn't me," the accused frog replied. "It must have been him!" he continued, pointing a sinewy forelimb at a frog standing close by him.

"Why me?" replied the surprised creature. "My bet is that it was one of those mangy crows, I always said that you couldn't trust them."

Gawk was nearby and he clearly heard this taunt. Quite without warning he flew at the marsh frog and with his beak he scythed a deep cut across the beleaguered creature's throat. As the frog fell and lay dead upon the ground Gawk turned around threateningly upon a group of marsh frogs who were preparing to attack him.

"Come on then, you shabby bunch of duck fodder... If you want a fight, have a real fight with me and my crows!"

The scene in front of Emled instantly became one of chaos and carnage as frog fought crow; crow fought frog; frog fought frog; and crow fought crow. Feathers were flying and the blood of both sets of creatures was liberally being spattered on the ground.

Within a matter of a few seconds, scores of the evil creatures lay dead or dying. Not even Emled's screams ordering them to stop had any impact as he could not make his voice heard above the frenzy.

There was nothing else for it; he would have to wade in amongst the warring factions himself and put an end to this violence. And so he did, crushing bodies here and squashing others there. As he lashed out at all and sundry he too took many strikes to his body particularly from the beaks of the crows. However, his thick warty skin was able to withstand such blows as if they were mere pin pricks, and he carried on regardless in his attempt to regain control.

As Emled's frantic charging amongst his unruly army caused broken bodies to be scattered to the four winds the mob gradually stopped their fighting. The marsh frogs and carrion crows then began to back away from each other muttering many curses and promises of reprisal.

Emled stood quite still amongst a mass of mutilated bodies. He was panting deeply from his exertions and, as the dust began to settle, he could feel dozens of bruises throbbing on his body. Although the beaks and forelimbs of the crows and marsh frogs had not penetrated his thick dry skin he had received so many direct hits that he now felt rather tender in more than just a few places.

The angry toad ordered Gawk and Kaara to separate their respective fraternities and to ensure that there wasn't a repeat performance of what they had all just witnessed. Emled was by now feeling extremely uneasy. Already his initial plans had gone awry. What's more, he had just lost several hundred of his army in a stupid and unnecessary fight and they hadn't as yet even met up with their intended opposition. He wasn't used to failure and he couldn't understand why things should be going so horribly wrong at this crucial stage.

For the first time Emled was beginning to develop serious doubts about the mentality of his murderous army. He was also concerned as to his own ability to control them when the going got tough. He was becoming increasingly aware that when things were going well they were indeed a mighty force but when things were not so good they became unruly and quite unmanageable. He secretly feared that the next step might be a mutinous move and that possibly Gawk or Kaara, or even both of them together, might attempt to organise a take-over and seek control.

It was, therefore, an anxious and worried toad who stood before his army with the blood of many of his dead colleagues dripping from his forelimbs. Order had been restored but it was a fragile peace that now existed between the marsh frogs and the crows.

*

A sudden burst of noisy activity from just outside the front of Denray's residence interrupted Mars' thoughts. Moments later an excited Maccus hopped into the King of Cowall's chamber closely followed by two very dusty and exhausted frogs. One of the latter two frogs was a rather tough looking character but on this occasion he displayed what appeared to be a great deal of shyness (or was it embarrassment?).

"Kejon! Can it really be you?" Mars was quite shocked to see his ex-senior colleague standing before him and looking so bedraggled. Kejon was clearly lost for words and his head hung so low that his nose almost touched his toes. It was a while before the weary frog answered.

"Yes, Great Leader, it is I, Kejon, your one time friend and colleague. A shallow and unworthy creature who has betrayed all the good things in his past through his lust for power and promises of material gain."

Kejon's head remained bowed and Mars could hardly hear what he said.

"Come, Kejon, raise that proud head of yours and tell me why you have travelled so far and what it is that brings you to Cowall?"

As Kejon slowly lifted his head he began to speak but it was in such a subdued and humble tone that Mars had to listen very hard to make out what his one time senior colleague was trying to say.

"How could I have let you down so badly?" whispered Kejon. "What made me say such terrible things about you and our good King Moha? I am not fit to look you in the eyes."

'Kejon! Can it really be you?' Mars was quite shocked to see his ex-senior colleague standing before him and looking so bedraggled.

Mars could both see and feel the very real remorse by which Kejon was gripped and he knew it was hard for a frog as tough and as proud as his old friend to admit to having been in the wrong. Mars welcomed Kejon's sentiments for he knew they were given with honesty and heartfelt regret.

"Come, Kejon... my friend. Lift your head and let me see your face. It is indeed a long time since we have been together. I have missed you and it is good to see you again." Mars spoke in such an irresistible and friendly manner that Kejon felt able to do as he was bid. Mars then looked deeply into the tough frog's eyes with such warmth and intensity that the gritty senior felt almost as if his heart would melt.

"Now, my old friend, tell me how and why you have come to be here?" asked Mars. "Sadly I sense that you are the bearer of bad news from Seaxe."

Kejon sucked air deep into his lungs as he steadied himself and prepared to explain his reasons for being in Cowall. He wasn't used to feeling nervous but at this very moment he had to confess that he was quite overwhelmed by the importance of the occasion. In addition to feeling highly embarrassed by the admission of his weaknesses he was also greatly taken aback by Mars' magnificence and the visible growth in both his stature and presence.

"The community of Seaxe has been overrun by Emled's army and it is now occupied by many mean marsh frogs and carrion crows. Scores of our local frogs have been killed or maimed and those that are still alive have been captured and are now imprisoned in the central area of the community. The everyday frogs have no leader and they are powerless to do anything about the situation. I'm not certain what has happened to the remaining seniors although I can tell you that Lebish has been killed."

"Lebish!" exclaimed Mars in great surprise. "But why? He appeared to be so close to Emled!"

"No creature can truly regard itself as being close to Emled," replied Kejon. "Lebish tried too hard to please the malignant king and in so doing he made many enemies amongst those who were previously his friends. He shouldn't really be blamed, for he was weak and he fell, as have many others, for Emled's smarmy lies and deceitful ways. Just when he thought he had gained the king's confidence he was slaughtered and we, the seniors, were as guilty of his demise as the wicked king himself.

"I am not sure," continued Kejon, "but I think that Josmi may also have been murdered in Tamsid. It hasn't been confirmed but I did overhear a group of those hateful carrion crows boasting about killing their king, or 'so called king', as they described him, before they left to fly down to Seaxe."

Mars felt an enormous sadness for his old community. There were many questions he wanted to ask of Kejon about the well-being of his close friends and colleagues who he had been so cruelly forced to leave behind in Seaxe. He knew, however, that there wasn't time for such talk at the moment. Instead he had to be mentally strong and practicable, focusing on his battle strategy and concentrating his mind on how best to prepare for the onslaught from Emled.

"Do you know of Emled's plans?" enquired Mars. "Were you able to find out what he intends to do and where he is likely to strike next?"

"Yes I did and that is why I have come, in order to warn you of what is happening," replied Kejon who was now beginning to take on a rather more confident air as he realised that Mars greatly valued his presence and the importance of his information. "His intention is to first of all annihilate the community of Surey and then march upon Cowall and do the same here."

Kejon then let his eyes drop and he looked at a point just in front of his toes as he explained why he thought Emled was coming to Cowall.

"As much as he wants total domination I believe that he sees you as his major prize. His jealousy and hatred of you is intense and he would time and again fly off into a rage at the mere mention of your name. He has never been able to accept the esteem in which you are held by the frogs of Seaxe and he was constantly frustrated that he could not drive the memory of you from their minds. To control the thoughts of our senior colleagues was one thing, and ridiculously easy for a manipulative purveyor of evil such as Emled, but to control the collective mind of the whole community was quite a different proposition. I must say that there are many thousands of Seaxe frogs who would dearly love to be here now and to stand at your side."

Mars felt the responsibility he had now assumed as leader of all frogs rise up inside him but he was again undaunted by the challenge that lay ahead. And, as the new leader stood handsomely and charismatically before him, Kejon wondered if he momentarily saw a glow around Mars' body as if an aura had suddenly surrounded his whole being so enhancing the young frog's magnificent presence and stature.

"What do you know of Surey's fate?" asked Mars.

"I was actually able to reach this community in time to give them sufficient warning of Emled's intention to attack," replied Kejon. "Their good king, Fara, took swift action and immediately evacuated his community. He and his faithful frogs are marching towards Cowall as we speak and if all goes well they should in fact reach here by dusk today. Fara said that he felt it would be foolish for any community to confront Emled alone and that it was much better to combine all available resources with neighbouring communities."

"That is very good news," said Mars. "We will certainly require all the help we can muster. My major concern, however, is that we have so little time to enlist the assistance of our more remote neighbours."

"I have some encouraging news on that front too," said a very excited Kejon. "At the same time as he sent us to Cowall, Fara also dispatched a small group of highly trained frogs to set out for Nolk and Solk in order to ask their kings, Tanal and Cabal, to send support. How successful this team will be in travelling east it is hard to say. The forests and river banks will be teeming with marsh frogs and the air will be thick with the wings of the black crows. We must accept, therefore, that their mission is extremely perilous and the chances of success are quite small."

Mars was uplifted by these words. He was greatly pleased by the news that Surey had been spared a murderous attack and he was heartened in the knowledge that the community of Cowall was not only about to be joined by Somset but that Fara was bringing his Surey frogs here to. Mars' thoughts about the likelihood of the messengers from Surey getting through to Nolk and Solk were similar to those of Kejon and he sadly did not therefore place too much hope in receiving assistance from this source.

Mars quickly assessed the potential number of his growing army and, by his reckoning, with the combined communities of Cowall, Somset and Surey, he considered that they could now at least maintain a temporary holding position against the evil hordes of Emled for quite a while. However, he knew that in all honesty he was still substantially short of the necessary strength to inflict defeat upon the wicked toad. He then listened as Kejon described in more detail the events of the past couple of days and how he had come to leave Seaxe.

"You have done very well, Kejon," said a smiling Mars. "It took great courage to confront Emled and to stand up for your fellow Seaxe frogs in the way that you did. To have then gone back amongst his army after having been beaten and left for dead is the hallmark of a valiant and brave creature. If that wasn't enough you next made your way to Surey and effectively single-handedly saved their whole community. I must say that no frog, myself included, would have chastised you or thought any less of you had you sought a safe refuge far away from these dangerous forests and river banks following your initial recovery from the brutal treatment you received from the marsh frogs. You will forevermore be regarded most highly by your fellow creatures and you will always be remembered for your heroic deeds.

"Come now, my good and trusty friend, there is much more to be done before we can even dare to imagine a future that will have room for quiet, peaceful and loving reflection."

Kejon was immensely heartened by Mars' words and he began to feel that he was a useful and worthwhile frog after all. He was now more than ever determined to stop at nothing to rid the land of the evil that was Emled and, as a mark of his loyalty and commitment, he pledged his undying support for his young friend.

"Now," said Mars, "I have to meet again with my council of war to consider our battle strategy. You, my friend, will be in need of rest and nourishment in order to recover from your ordeal and to prepare yourself for whatever lies ahead."

Kejon made as if to say that he didn't need a break but Mars kindly ushered him out of Denray's residence and arranged for him to be escorted by two of Cowall's senior frogs to a secluded place where he could enjoy a well-earned meal and some much needed relaxation.

*

Mars was rejoined by Denray and Maccus and they were gladdened and uplifted when they heard of Kejon's news. It would indeed have been an understatement to say that their spirits received a massive boost when Mars informed them that Fara was on his way with the frogs of Surey and that there was an outside chance that further support might yet come from the far distant communities of Nolk and Solk.

Denray spoke next and he advised that he had sent his fastest messenger to Somset. By his reckoning, if all went well, it should enable support to arrive back later that very day and certainly before the sun set in the west.

Mars could sense that Maccus was bursting to tell his news and when Denray had concluded he turned to his young companion.

"And Maccus, how have you fared with the aerial support?"

Maccus was indeed greatly excited by the information he had for Mars and Denray and he could hardly wait for the opportunity to speak. He was bubbling over with enthusiasm as he began to tell his news.

"When I was very young and learning to dive for fish up by Kingfisher's Bridge," commenced Maccus, "I came across a tiny and very weak baby chick who appeared to have fallen from its nest. I found it struggling amongst the mud and reeds on the edge of the river bank. The chick was clearly in great distress and seemed to be close to death. I momentarily forgot about the danger of any predators who may have been watching the situation and I flew across to see if I could help the bird out of its sticky situation and onto dry land to a place of safety. After a while I managed to find a safe refuge for the poor creature and I waited by its side hoping that its mother or father might come along and help it back home.

"As I sat with the frightened bird my mother suddenly arrived and in great alarm warned me to leave the chick and immediately fly back to our family nest with her. I had no idea why she was so agitated but there was clearly some danger about and so I followed her straight away. Although I was very reluctant to leave the baby chick behind I knew that it would be wrong to disobey my mother so I did what I was told.

"When we got to our home I looked anxiously back across to the place where the chick was sheltering. It was then that I saw quite the most magnificent and awesome sight, for, as it lifted off the branch on which it had been perched high up in the tall trees of Horse Chestnut Wood, I caught a glimpse of quite the most beautiful and majestic female bird I have ever been fortunate enough to see. However, at the same moment I noticed a sinister black crow who was flapping low over the place where the injured chick was cowering, looking every bit as though it was getting ready to move in to kill the poor defenceless bird.

"My mother saw my concern but as I made to leave our nest in order to ward off the crow and try and save the chick she raised her wing to prevent me from going. At first I began to protest but then she merely motioned for me to look back up into the high trees to where the beautiful bird was gracefully circling.

"Without any warning whatsoever the bird dramatically dropped out of the sky and swooped down towards the chick at a most frightening rate. As she dived she suddenly changed direction and flashed past our nesting hole so close that I almost fell over backwards as her wing tips brushed across my beak. I can still clearly see her glorious colouring. The dark reddish-brown and white of her underparts and her magnificent long dark grey and brown striped tail are as vivid to me now as they were on that day.

"In an instant she veered across towards the place where the chick lay and where the crow was just about to land. The crow was not aware of the presence of the female bird, who I then realised must have been the mother of the young chick. In the split second it took for her to pass our nest and reach her young chick she had hit the crow with such speed and ferocity that the impact rendered the insidious creature dead long before its body hit the ground. A bolt of lightning would surely not have been more effective.

"The next scene was in stark contrast to the quite lethal destruction of the crow for amongst the mass of black feathers that were swirling around in the air I could see the mother bird administering to the chick with much love and tenderness.

"My own mother then drew me back into our burrow and told me that what I had just seen in action was the sparrowhawk, the most feared bird of the forests and farmlands. She said that this bird of prey was able to take out in mid air even the largest of birds and that she was at her most deadly when protecting her young or hunting for food. She warned me that I was not to venture outside for a while in case the mother thought that, like the crow, I also intended to harm her chick. I considered myself lucky to have been spared by the female sparrowhawk but I so much wanted to see both her and the young chick again.

"The next morning I very cautiously went to the spot where I had left the chick. I was relieved to see that it had gone so I assumed that its mother must have helped it fly back to their nest. Whilst I was looking around for the small bird, and quite against all the wise teaching of my mother and father, I stupidly wasn't paying attention to my own safety. Then, just as I was about to turn to go back home, what seemed like an arrow suddenly came out of the sky and pinned me firmly to the ground.

"I immediately recognised my captor as being the mother sparrowhawk whom I had seen the day before. From what I knew of this bird's exploits I fully expected to be carried away and fed to the very same chick I had so recently saved.

"However, just as I waited for my end to come, she spoke very softly to me and said how thankful she was that I had saved her young chick's life and that forevermore sparrowhawks would consider the kingfishers as their friends. She also said that if ever I needed a favour of her or her family then I only had to ask.

"Unfortunately, not long after that incident, we heard that the family of sparrowhawks had left their nest near to Kingfisher's Bridge and as far as we knew they settled somewhere in the west."

Mars and Denray were fascinated by the story that Maccus had told but they were concerned as to its relevance to the matter in hand.

"That is a fine tale, my friend," said Mars, "but I am not quite sure where it is leading. We really do need to focus our attention on Emled and concentrate on how we are to tackle the toad."

Mars could sense again Maccus's growing excitement as the young kingfisher indicated that he was about to get to the most important part of his story.

"When I left our council of war meeting a little while ago I wondered if it might be worth asking around to see if anyone here in Cowall knew of the sparrowhawk family. If they really did move west then I thought they may possibly live somewhere near here. Well, I am sure you will both be very pleased to know, the first frog I asked said that there are indeed some sparrowhawks living approximately halfway between here and Somset and it appears that they arrived at about the same time that our family of sparrowhawks left Seaxe.

"As there was clearly a chance that he could have been referring to the family from Seaxe I thought that I should follow up this lead. I therefore took directions from the frog I had been talking to and made my way towards Somset.

"It didn't take me long to get to the spot that the helpful frog had described. When I first arrived everywhere was very quiet and my initial thoughts were that maybe the frog had been mistaken or possibly the sparrowhawk family had moved on again. Then, just as I was thinking about turning round and heading back to Cowall, something flew past me with such a tremendous rush of wind that my feathers felt as if they were about to be pulled out of my skin.

"As I struggled to regain my balance I looked up into the sky and then immediately realised the cause of my great surprise. Circling high above me, with the unmistakable grace and elegance that is a feature of her breed, was the mother sparrowhawk whom I had first met in Seaxe. She was soon joined by another sparrowhawk, a male bird, whom I also had no difficulty in recognising. It was in fact her now fully grown son... the chick I had once helped to save.

"When the two beautiful birds flew down to where I was perched they said that they had seen me coming from some way off and although pleased to see me they did wonder why I had strayed so far from my home. The young sparrowhawk did not of course recognise me but his mother had often told him of the time he had nearly been taken by the crow and the part that I had played in helping to protect him.

"When I told them of the dire straits in which we now find ourselves, and of the imminent attack that the community of Cowall faces from Emled and his army of marsh frogs and crows, the mother sparrowhawk straight away offered us all the support she had available. There is apparently a flourishing community of sparrowhawks deep in the forest between here and Somset and she said that both she and her son will contact all their friends and relations without delay. She assured me that all of the sparrowhawk community will be only too happy to have an excuse to pulverise the crows. She said that the crow I had seen her kill in Seaxe was the very bird who had scared her chick from their nest and from that moment on her kind had vowed a terrible revenge upon all crows.

"What I then learnt was that the mother sparrowhawk's name is Sona, that is to say Queen Sona, the most wondrous and regal leader of all the sparrowhawk communities. The chick whom I had helped to save back in Seaxe is called Anlaw and he is of course a prince among his species. Unbeknown at the time to both me and my mother I had in fact helped to save the future king of the sparrowhawks, and, as a result of my attempt to protect the young prince, the sparrowhawks now regard kingfishers as lucky omens and we feature prominently in their folklore as good luck friends of their race.

"We now therefore have support from the air to help in our fight against Emled and it is going to come from the most fearsome of birds. They will undoubtedly give Gawk's crows a gigantic fright and knock the leering grin off the monstrous and repulsive face of the evil toad."

Mars and Denray had been engrossed in Maccus's news. Even though it had taken the young kingfisher quite some time to tell his story they nevertheless wanted to hear it in its entirety.

"Maccus, you are to be congratulated on seeking out and finding our sparrowhawk friends. They will certainly prove to be powerful and valuable allies." Mars put his forelimb upon the young bird's wing and then turned to Denray.

"Denray my friend, between the three of us here, plus the most fortuitous sequence of events brought about by Kejon, we are now in a position to put together a force that will begin to rival Emled's army. I know that we will still be far outnumbered but we can surely destroy a great many of his evil followers." Mars then added thoughtfully, "and maybe even Emled himself!"

*

Mars knew that he would have to raise the morale of the frogs of Cowall and the news of his growing army would certainly help in this respect. It was essential for good to triumph over evil although Mars was well aware that realistically, and certainly in terms of sheer weight of numbers, the balance still lay heavily in favour of Emled. Notwithstanding this obvious disadvantage, Mars was nevertheless confident that the evil toad was at least going to get more than that for which he had bargained.

Chapter Twenty-Nine

Battle Plans Are Prepared

By dusk the frogs of Surey had arrived and soon after them the frogs of Somset hopped into the community of Cowall to join Mars' expanding army.

Mars and the three kings of the south-western communities met together for the very first time and they rubbed shoulders and noses in a friendly and unified gesture. This show of harmony was greatly welcomed by the assembled masses and all the frogs of their respective communities cheered excitedly and without inhibition.

The kind and good-hearted creatures of Cowall, Somset and Surey knew that on their own each of their communities was vulnerable against the overwhelming and evil army of Emled. Their togetherness, however, provided them all with a strength that was much more powerful than just the sum of the three communities. With Mars and each of their own great kings at the helm they felt their combined might to have grown ten times at least.

Mars turned towards the multitude of gathered frogs and spread his forelimbs wide in a gesture of greeting and thanks. No words were required at that moment and the enormous congregation croaked loudly, clearly demonstrating their support for the young frog leader. Then, as the thronging masses surged backward and forward and frogs from the neighbouring communities made each others acquaintance, Mars led their respective kings back to Denray's residence. He had already asked Kejon and Maccus to wait for him there along with Sona, Queen of the sparrowhawks.

Mars introduced Kejon to Truda for the king of Somset had not yet met this tough and reformed senior frog from Seaxe. Mars glowingly described Kejon's recent daring exploits and how his old friend had obtained valuable information regarding Emled's intended campaign of death and destruction. Although rather embarrassed at hearing himself being praised in this way, and especially in front of such an esteemed gathering, Kejon nevertheless felt proud to be so admiringly welcomed by these illustrious and good creatures.

What really did need some explanation, however, was the presence of the two magnificent and beautiful birds. In particular the frog kings of Surey and Somset were more than just a little anxious to hear explained how it was that they had come to be standing so close to the regal sparrowhawk. After all she was a bird of prey and the frog kings felt distinctly uncomfortable with her standing so close to them.

Mars firstly introduced Maccus and he spoke of the close relationship that had always existed between the kingfishers and the frog kings of the Seaxe community. He then recounted very briefly his early association with the bird's father, Peeyu, and the horrific events at Kingfisher's Bridge whereat fate had brought him and Maccus together and from whence their friendship had flourished. He also told of his travels to the Far North and of his first meeting with the legendary Krakow and how this led on to the teaching process he had gone through with the wise old blackbird which enabled him to take on the 'Great Learning of the Supreme Qualities of Wisdom and Knowledge'.

Mars then turned towards Sona and introduced her to the three kings. He explained Maccus's association with the sparrowhawks (somewhat more briefly, it must be said, than the young kingfisher had done to Mars and Denray a little earlier) and how these fine birds were not to be feared by frogs ever again as they were in fact now confirmed allies who were ready and willing to fight against the evil forces of Emled's wicked army.

Recognising both the beauty and great value of having the sparrowhawk race on their side, the somewhat relieved frog kings welcomed Sona and apologised for their initial coolness and concern. They said that they hoped she would understand that it had taken them a little while to get used to standing so near to a species of bird that had rightly acquired such an awesome and fearsome reputation.

Sona said that she had no problems with their first reaction and that if she in turn appeared at all anxious to them then it was probably because she was not accustomed to being in an enclosed space as she was far more at ease flying high in the sky or perched in the topmost bows of the trees. She then pointed out that normally the only time she stayed on the ground for more than a few moments was to eat her prey if it was too heavy to take back to her nest.

As Sona spoke these last few words she noticed a nervous shuffling of feet around her so she quickly added, "Present company excepted of course." This immediately brought a smile to the faces of each of the three kings and thus the ice was well and truly broken between the frogs and the sparrowhawks.

*

It was now time for the council of war to discuss their battle strategy and set out their plans for defence, attack and counter attack against the loathsome toad and his army of barbarous marsh frogs and sly black carrion crows. This demanded very clear thinking and firm leadership by Mars with the ability to listen to the suggestions of the others and from this, coupled with his own ideas, to determine the most appropriate way forward. It was vital that he should put together an overall strategy that took on board the proposals of each member of the council of war and that fully explored all possible options.

It was a fact of course that neither Mars nor any of the three frog kings had ever before been confronted by a situation the like of which they now faced. Wars, battles and fighting between communities were matters now confined to history and today such happenings are only mentioned in tales of dark days that occurred a long, long time ago. Even when these stories are told the storyteller purposely does not glorify the past warlike ways of notorious frog fighters such as Vinjo, Norhun, Nobsti or Pesto. Instead the antics of these aggressors are considered to be examples of totally unacceptable behaviour and as such are not to be encouraged and most definitely not revered or celebrated.

Therefore, although the three frog kings who now sat with Mars were fine and very capable leaders of their communities and certainly able to discuss the business of war, they quite understandably looked to Mars for guidance in this most crucial of issues. Mars recognised and acknowledged his responsibilities and he was determined not to disappoint them.

It must also be said that at first Mars had wondered how on earth he was going to organise his resources against the forces of Emled. However, as he considered the number of frogs now available to him, plus of course the valuable addition to the cause of Queen Sona and her sparrowhawks, the newly declared leader of frogs began to feel the recently acquired 'Supreme Qualities of Wisdom and Knowledge' pumping confidently through his veins encouraging him to consider all manner of options that would previously not have occurred to him.

There was for instance the terrain to be considered on which the battle would be fought. Mars had accordingly given a great deal of thought to this critical matter and he could see with clarity how the natural landscape around the community of Cowall could be utilised not only to his advantage but also, and as importantly, to the distinct disadvantage of Emled. Added to the natural features of the battlefield there was also to be considered the method by which he deployed his army. Should he attack at certain points or would he be better advised to defend such positions?

Mars could feel the eyes of all the members of his council of war upon him. He looked lovingly at each of them and he felt proud to be their leader. They in turn were developing a growing admiration for the young frog and their expectation of him, although not unrealistic, was very great indeed.

"Our numbers are far less than those of our enemy," began Mars. "Our kind are also not filled with the bloodlust for murder and mayhem that is a trademark of the damnable crows and marsh frogs that the toad has at his disposal. That doesn't of course make us any the less able to resist their challenge providing of course that we can develop a strategy that focuses on our strengths and at the same time on their weaknesses."

Mars paused for a few moments before continuing. His council of war colleagues sat listening very attentively to what he had to say. In their own minds they were also giving thought to the contributions they each had to offer which they in turn hoped would complement their leader's thinking.

"My assumption," continued Mars, "is that the toad will expect an easy victory. It is therefore likely that he will throw his full might at us in an effort to defeat our frogs in one massive attack.

"He won't, of course, know how many we are although he may assume that Surey has joined forces with Cowall. He will have no idea that Truda has brought the entire community of Somset here and he will most definitely not have the faintest inkling that Sona and her sparrowhawks have pledged their support to our cause."

At this point Mars looked towards the queen of the sparrowhawks. He could sense in the magnificent bird a creature who possessed supreme confidence. Whilst he knew that Sona would act in tandem with the frog communities and do all she could to assist in the battle against Emled he was also aware that she had a personal score to settle with regard to Gawk and his crows. Mars shivered very slightly at the prospect of Sona's involvement and he felt glad that she was on his side.

The council of war then sat and discussed the forthcoming invasion by Emled. Many scenarios were put forward and all ideas were positively considered. Each of the three kings offered valuable advice to the younger Mars and he appreciated their experience and sound views. Sona's aerial perspective gave the frogs great heart and they felt sure her participation would reduce the threat from the air that Gawk and his villainous crows presented.

In this way they discussed their approach in earnest for about an hour. From what was debated Mars was able to identify suitable options so much so that he finally felt able to conclude the conversation and set out for his colleagues the preferred strategy.

"Even if Emled has a more sophisticated campaign planned," said Mars, "I am sure that what I have been able to put together as a result of our deliberations will give us a fairly even chance of beating the toad and his evil horde. I do believe, however, that we will realistically only have one chance of success. To fail of course will spell disaster for the creatures of the river banks and forests as it is only our combined army of frogs from the south and west, together with Sona's sparrowhawks, that lie between our current way of life and a future founded on malevolence and much evildoing."

Those assembled in Denray's residence shuddered at the prospect and huddled closer together both for comfort and to hear what Mars had in store for the rank toad.

With his forelimb Mars began to draw in the soft earth a diagram of the battlefield in order to graphically illustrate his plans. *[See map of the Battle of Boda Moor at the end of this chapter.]*

"Emled will naturally attack through Fir Tree Wood. It is the only clear and safe route into Cowall so his army must come that way. He will have to travel overland as he couldn't risk approaching from the river as the banks are far too high and much too steep for him to mount his invasion. He will surely have assessed that we would have no difficulty in dealing with his marsh frogs if they attempted to scramble up the sheer banks of the river for we would be able to pick them off one by one as they tried to get on to dry land.

"Once his forces have emerged from out of Fir Tree Wood he then has to cross the wide and open area of scrubland that leads on to Boda Moor. It is here that for the first time we will have a good view of his numbers.

"It is also at this stage that the terrain will begin to work to our advantage for I am confident that Emled will know very little about the nature of the landscape around Cowall. I expect that as far as he will be concerned he will assume that the land between Fir Tree Wood and the High Ground is firm, flat and safe to cross. Therefore, what he will certainly not be prepared to tackle are the hazards of Boda Moor.

"My information is that even for experienced local frogs who know Boda Moor well it can be a dangerous place to cross with it being full of deep waters and swamps that are capable of sucking in the strongest of frogs." On hearing these words there were a great deal of knowing nods from Denray and Sona who both knew the treacherous moor very well indeed. "My plan, therefore, is to draw Emled's leading frogs as far as possible into this perilous area before we prepare to launch our counter-attack upon them."

The expressions on the faces of each of the other members of the council of war brightened considerably as they immediately realised what Mars was planning. The young frog then continued to explain his strategy.

"When we do attack it will be from both flanks simultaneously. We will therefore adopt a 'V' formation with the respective armies of Surey and Somset covering a flank each. The frogs of Surey will take the left flank leading out of Cowall which runs all the way alongside Boda Moor and the Open Scrubland. The frogs of Somset will correspondingly be positioned along the right flank covering a broadly similar area."

As he spoke and marked his strategy in the soil so Mars moved effortlessly and confidently about the diagram. All the while he added new elements to the map of the battlefield, gradually building up the complete strategy for his war council.

"We will position the greater part of the Surey and Somset frogs at the Open Scrubland end of the flanks as I suggest that once Emled's army has been drawn into the sticky wastes of Boda Moor we should then be able to close in behind them. My intention for so doing is that this will both cut off their ability to retreat as well as enabling us to mount a surprise attack from the sides whilst they are confused and rather preoccupied by the difficult conditions they will be experiencing underfoot.

"The bait we will employ to actually draw Emled into Boda Moor will be the vision of me on the High Ground at the far end of the swampy lands. Alongside me will be Denray and behind us, and out of view to the marauding mob, will be the good frogs of Cowall. My plan is that Emled will find the very sight of me, at the vanguard of what will appear to him as a seemingly small opposition, a quite irresistible opportunity to order his army to charge across the Open Scrubland and effect our mass slaughter."

Mars paused for a moment and asked if there were any questions. Denray had one point that be wished to raise.

"What about our friend Sona?" he asked. "Where will the sparrowhawks be positioned and what role will they play?"

"I sincerely hope that it will be something to do with the demise of the crows," said Sona, with an icy edge to her voice. "We know of Gawk from way back. He and a bunch of his thugs once attacked one of our sparrowhawk families and smashed several eggs that were about to hatch. For both that, and a host of other reasons, my hawks and I would welcome the chance to gain our revenge on those despicable creatures. Gawk will find out that there is nothing so terrifying and lasting as the pent up vengeance of the sparrowhawks."

For a few seconds, although it seemed like much longer, there was complete silence. Sona had spoken her words with such conviction that the others on the council of war were quite stunned by her coldness. It was nevertheless just the example that they needed if they were to adopt the right attitude to combat Emled. Now was not the time for faint hearts. Nothing less than full commitment to defeating the vile toad was acceptable.

Mars welcomed Sona's fighting talk and advised her that it was indeed the crows that the sparrowhawks would be required to tackle. Once again the young frog leader said that his intention was to catch Emled's army unawares and attack them when they least expected to be hit. Mars explained that in the circumstances, with the joint army of the south and west being substantially outnumbered, the element of surprise was to be one of their greatest assets.

"Sona," began Mars. "Your position will be in The Weeping Willows on the far side of the River Som. Gawk's army are carrion crows and as such they will follow after the marsh frogs hoping to deal with the dead or dying. They are callous and cowardly creatures by nature and do not relish a fight on equal terms. As soon as they have followed the marsh frogs out of Fir Tree Wood I suggest that you circle high out of The Weeping Willows and then swoop in over Fir Tree Wood from the north-west and attack Gawk and his obnoxious band from the rear."

Sona nodded appreciatively. She said that she would enjoy her role in the battle and she knew her sparrowhawks would be extremely pleased to exact their revenge on the hated Gawk and his insidious crows.

"If there are no further questions I suggest that you all return to your respective armies and advise them of our plans. Tonight we will all need a good rest and plenty of nourishment in order to prepare for the battle that lies ahead. I want all our frogs and sparrowhawk friends to be in position before the dawn breaks tomorrow. My feeling is that the toad will be looking to attack some time during the early morning. We must therefore be ready and waiting when he comes!"

Mars looked around at the faces of his council of war colleagues. All had strong, determined and resolute expressions and the young frog leader could see that they were ready to go into battle and fight for all that was good. With their help he had prepared a strategy which was now complete. Even so, although he was confident that he had made the most of his resources, Mars could not be certain that it was enough to halt Emled's evil advance, let alone inflict defeat upon the malignant toad.

Mars held out his hands to his friends and each of those who looked upon him gained great strength from his presence. Through every vein of their bodies coursed the blood of the courageous and in every sinew and muscle a power they had never felt before began to emerge. They were all prepared to stand against the forces of evil and fight to the very last breath if necessary.

"All that remains for me to say tonight is to wish you good luck for tomorrow and may the powers of goodness be with us all and enable us to ultimately triumph over the dark forces of evil."

*

The three frog kings and Queen Sona left Denray's residence and returned to their fellow creatures. Kejon also departed as tiredness was beginning to overwhelm this tough and determined frog. After all of his recent and courageous exploits it was not surprising that their effect was at last taking its toll. Nevertheless, as sure as tadpoles are tadpoles, Kejon could be relied upon to be up way before first light refreshed after a couple of hours deep sleep and raring to do battle against Emled.

Only Maccus stayed behind with Mars. He instinctively knew that the young frog leader needed a friend close by him at this most difficult of moments. As they sat together, in silence for a while, they exchanged a few smiles of mutual support which meant more than a thousand words ever could in such circumstances. Mars was thankful to have such a friend as Maccus.

The young kingfisher was the first to break the stillness for he had noticed that in the last few minutes several deep furrows had appeared across Mars' proud brow.

"Denray and the others see you as the saviour of all the frogs and creatures of the river banks and the forests. They support you totally and have placed all their faith in your ability to lead them in the defence of our communities. Your wise words have given them strength, the kind of which they have never before known. It is a strength that is full of dedication and firm resolve to fight alongside you in order to hold back the evil that Emled is so intent on spreading throughout the land. You now command an army of creatures that is relatively small in number but huge in spirit."

Maccus paused for a few seconds. Mars was grateful for his friend's keen observation of their fellow war councillors.

"And yet," continued the beautiful bird, "I detect that you are greatly troubled. Would it help to talk and maybe share some of the worries that you have?"

"Maccus, my dear friend. You, more than anyone since Moha and your father, know my feelings only too well. I am indeed deeply troubled." Mars sat back on his haunches and raised his eyes staring far beyond the tree roots and black soil that formed the ceiling of Denray's home. "I have developed a strategy that I feel is about as good as it can be, given the resources that are available to us and the terrain on which the battle is to be fought. I have accordingly set out a plan that if all goes well and good fortune is in our favour then we will have a fair chance of matching Emled's evil army. However, even with the best laid plans it is of course impossible to predict the outcome against such a malevolent being as the foul toad, for an imagination does not exist that could dream of the malice of which the dark forces of evil are capable of conjuring up. What really concerns me most of all is that the only thing of which I can be certain is that I will be sending many good frogs to their death tomorrow and that means many families will be left to grieve the loss of their loved ones as a direct result of my commands."

Maccus touched Mars very lightly on the shoulder with the tip of his wing. He needed to give his friend reassurance that in the face of great adversity such monumentally difficult decisions have to be taken and it is only the most capable of creatures who can possibly be entrusted with this unenviable responsibility. He spoke softly yet positively to the young frog leader.

"You know you have the ability to think clearly even in situations where many a good and strong creature would crumble under the sheer weight of their duty. You have also been blessed with the 'Supreme Qualities of Wisdom and Knowledge' that have been passed through many generations of the most venerable creatures of our communities. Your competence to correctly judge situations and make the right decision will not be questioned as you are now the pre-eminent leader of leaders – a king of kings. What you are doing has to be done. There is no other way."

"You are right in what you say," replied Mars. "It is indeed my responsibility to lead in these circumstances and I must trust in the qualities that have been bestowed upon me. Krakow warned that being the holder of the 'Great Learning of the Supreme Qualities of Wisdom and Knowledge', I will face formidable dilemmas, although he also assured me that I will be equipped to deal with such situations. My fellow creatures will be looking to me for guidance and I must therefore be strong, positive and confident in all that I do. I must not let them down. Maccus, my friend, I will not let them down!"

The unbreakable bond of friendship and love that Mars and Maccus shared for each other grew stronger as they sat closely together on this night; the eve, as it would prove to be, of the most important day in the lives of all the creatures of the forests and river banks.

"Such is the dilemma that faces me now," concluded Mars. "I have to make plans that I know will cause much fine blood to be spilt and good lives to be lost in order to combat the evil that marches upon this land. I willingly accept my role as leader but I know that whether glorious in our victory or brave and courageous in defeat the blood of my fellows will forever be a stain upon my breast. This night will be the longest and darkest of my life. Stay with me, Maccus, and keep me company. This is not a time that I wish to be alone. Knowing you are here by my side will give me warmth and the strength for what lies ahead."

THE BATTLE OF BODA MOOR

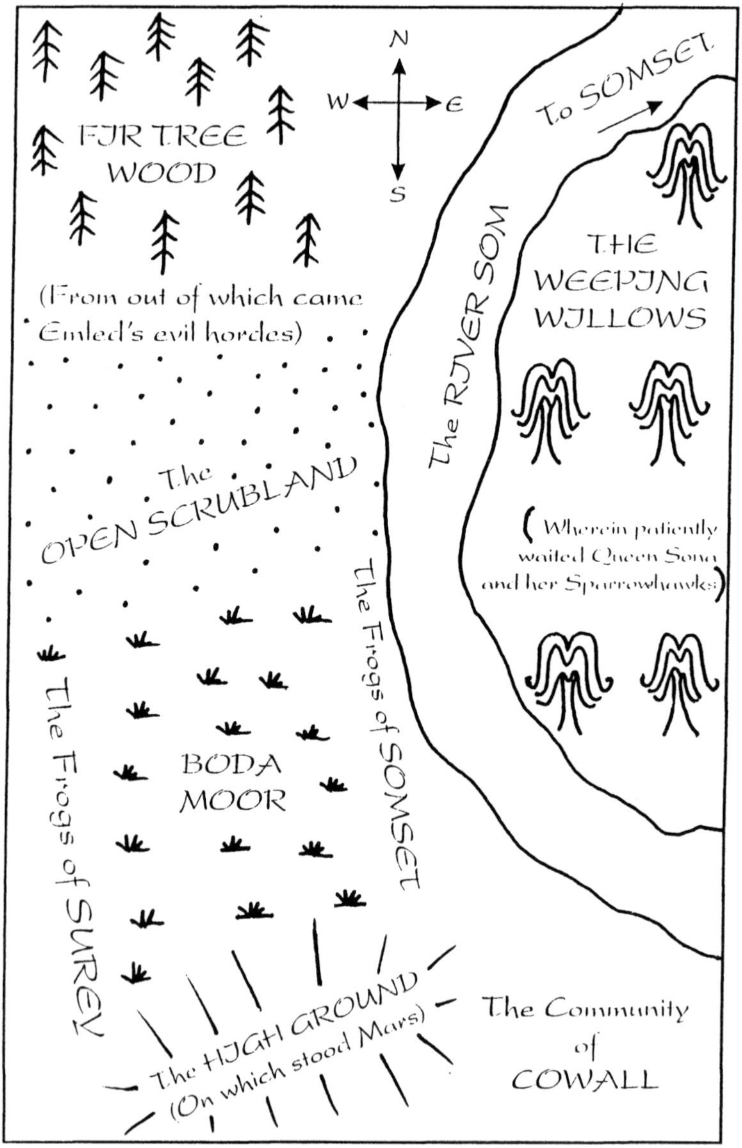

Chapter Thirty

The Battle of Boda Moor

The Calm Before the Storm

On the far distant horizon to the east a barely traceable hint of the new dawn was forming. Stars were still shining brightly in the night sky as intermittent beams of light from the moon filtered down through broken clouds interrupting the cloak of darkness which covered the battleground and casting eerie shadows that floated like wraiths across the Open Scrubland and the swamps of Boda Moor.

Mars stood on the High Ground and surveyed the area that lay between himself and Fir Tree Wood. Not a sound could be heard. No bird sang to greet the dawn on this day and what little breeze there was seemed hardly dare to disturb the leaves on the trees. Mars wondered momentarily if he would ever again be able to stand in this position to see the birth of another new day. Would the events that were to follow later this morning result in him standing victoriously overlooking the battleground, or would defeat confine the good creatures of Cowall and all the surrounding lands to a future as desolate and bleak as that which had befallen the Far North following the emergence of Emled?

Mars shook his head to rid himself of such negative thoughts. Of course he would live to see another new day dawn. He must, otherwise evil would have triumphed and all that was good would have been crushed under its wicked power.

The handsome young frog refocused his thoughts and concentrated on his battle strategy. He knew that he must remain courageous and be confident in his ability to out-think the toad. The young frog leader clenched his hands and told himself to be bold and to think positively.

Mars had already been down to the front line and he had spoken personally to many of the frogs of Surey, Somset and Cowall. Somewhat earlier and under the cover of darkness the frogs of these three communities, led by Fara, Truda and Denray, had quietly assembled along both flanks of the battlefield and in the area behind the High Ground.

As he had hopped along the front line, Mars had been impressed with his army. He had not seen any fear on the faces of his valiant frogs although he knew that deep within their hearts there must linger an understandable feeling of anxiety as to what fate had in store for them.

These were frogs who cared about their families and their friends and who were not accustomed to fighting, let alone killing. In stark contrast to Emled's army the frogs from south of Waga enjoyed the simple pleasures of life and looked forward to a long and happy existence. They would normally no more consider hurting one of their number than passing up the opportunity of a good feast of juicy grasshoppers whilst swapping tales of great deeds as they sat upon their favourite lily pad on a sunny summer's afternoon.

Now, however, everything was so very different as the frogs of Mars' army waited patiently in the shadows of the rising dawn. Today was to bring for them an experience of happenings and events the nature of which would stay in their memories for ever.

What Mars had also witnessed as he visited his front line were indomitable frogs with resolute expressions and stout hearts. Frogs that were determined to repel the evil that was Emled. Frogs that were ready and willing to stand up against the malevolent toad and his unprincipled army and if need be to fight to their last drop of blood or final puff of breath.

Yes, Mars was impressed. He was also very proud. Proud of the courage he had already seen displayed and proud of the creatures who followed him and supported him in the essential battle to protect all that was good.

In the quietness a faint rustling sound came from across the river as an errant early morning breeze stirred the long draping tentacles of the weeping willow trees. On hearing this sound Mars became aware that the first light of dawn was now clearly evident and the far eastern horizon was now alight with a yellow and blue glow as the clear morning sky suddenly reflected the golden rays of the waking sun.

As he had hopped along the front line, Mars had been impressed with his army.

Mars thought how ironic it was that such a beautiful morning could herald the awful scenes that were surely to follow during this day.

The young frog leader peered through the half-light of the battleground away to his right towards The Weeping Willows. There was no visible sign of Sona and her sparrowhawks although Mars knew instinctively that they were there, concealed deep within the foliage of the trees. Mars was as certain as night follows day that Sona would be perched, calmly yet passionately, among the gently swaying and pendulous branches awaiting the chance to punish Gawk and his villainous crows for their past wrongdoings against her race. A massive store of pent up fury and hatred for Gawk and his followers was soon to burst upon the despicable carrion comrades of Emled.

Mars shivered a little at the prospect of Sona and her sparrowhawks swooping fast and true upon the crows. Gawk and his mercenaries would be shown no compassion. Then why should they? They had themselves never shown any pity or mercy towards any living creature, choosing rather to cause pain, suffering and death to those unfortunate enough to cross their path. Mars knew that now was neither the moment for displaying charity towards such wicked creatures as the crows, nor was this the right time to be thinking about reforming those creatures who were inextricably woven into the wicked web of evil. Such malignance needed eradicating not re-educating. The evil that was Emled, Gawk and Kaara must be destroyed along with their followers who had all grown up knowing nothing other than the teaching and example of their diabolic leaders.

Mars hoped that there would soon come a time when he could once again think compassionately and be able to offer compromise in an environment where peace, and not war, flourished. Unfortunately he knew that now was not the appropriate moment for such sentiments or action. It was the business of battle that lay before him and this was a matter which required extreme effort as well as a cold heart and a clear head if it was to be won. Indeed winning the battle was the only real alternative open to the good creatures of Mars' army, for to lose would almost certainly mean the end of their civilised and harmonious way of life causing it to be replaced by… well… something too horrid to imagine!

*

The flanks to the left and right of Mars' command point on the High Ground were lined ten deep with the good frogs of Surey and Somset. Unseen from the entrance of Fir Tree Wood these brave frogs lay hidden with their respective kings, namely Fara and Truda, awaiting the signal from Mars to charge. In fact the only visible sign of life that Emled would see when he emerged from out of Fir Tree Wood was the sight of Mars and Denray standing on the High Ground with a hundred or so of the front line of Cowall's frogs just behind them. It was Mars' intention that this should provide sufficient bait to tempt Emled into ordering his army to make a direct assault from the front and in so doing getting themselves caught up in the sticky expanse of Boda Moor. Mars also wanted the toad's attention to be firmly focused on the High Ground in order that the frogs of Surey and Somset could mount their counter-attack from the flanks with the added advantage of the element of surprise.

During the past hour or so an eerie calmness, some may even say 'spooky calmness', had descended on the battlefield and surrounding areas. As the sun had risen steadily in a clear blue sky so the breeze, what little of it there was, had dropped completely.

Not a sound could be heard, and yet, all around the battlefield, both on the flanks and to the rear of the High Ground, many thousands of good frogs crouched low quietly praying for victory.

Mars peered across to the entrance of Fir Tree Wood for what seemed like the hundredth time since dawn. Whilst he did so a rush of air swept across him as Maccus landed gracefully by his side.

"I have just spoken with Sona," whispered the resplendent bird. "She wants you to know that she is in position and ready to do her duty."

Mars gave his friend a warm and knowing smile. "Thanks, Maccus. That is really good news. I'm sure she is ready."

Both Mars and Maccus allowed their thoughts to momentarily drift across to The Weeping Willows where, in their mind's eye, they could see Queen Sona and her sparrowhawks hiding in the foliage eagerly anticipating what was to come. These magnificent birds, much more so than any of Mars' gallant army of frogs, were supremely prepared for battle. They were built for speed and they could strike an enemy in mid air with devastating results for the luckless recipient. A crow would be no match for a sparrowhawk. It was indeed only the vast number of Gawk's flying army that could pose a threat to Sona as the crows outnumbered the sparrowhawks by fifty to one at least.

The two friends stood side by side and they were soon joined by Denray and Kejon. Four pairs of eyes now concentrated on the darkness that was the mouth of Fir Tree Wood from whence Emled must surely soon emerge.

"The Forces of Evil Are Upon Us!"

A chilly breeze suddenly sprang up from out of the north that ruffled the gloriously colourful plumage of Maccus and caused each of the other three frogs to shiver. Then, barely perceptible at first, but gradually becoming louder and louder, there came a steady pounding noise from deep within the heart of Fir Tree Wood. As the pounding grew louder so it appeared to draw closer and closer to the edge of the wood although no visible sign could be seen as to its source.

Accompanying the noise came a gusty breeze that became stronger as the pounding became louder causing the tops of the fir trees to bend under its force and the long fringes of the weeping willows to whip up and down excitedly.

Then, all at once, dark clouds from out of the Far North began to scud across the sky and heavy drops of freezing cold rain swept over the Open Scrubland and Boda Moor. As the black clouds careered overhead so eclipsing the brightness of the day Mars noticed that one particularly massive cloud, as black as pitch, dropped down from the rest and swirled this way and that before settling on top of the firs of Fir Tree Wood.

This was, however, no ordinary cloud and very soon the shrieks of hundred upon hundred of crows filled the air their manic screeching rising and falling on the gusts of the stormy winds. It was in fact the arrival of Gawk and his insidious flying army!

Mars watched as the squawking black mass poured into the upper branches of the fir trees. Although it was impossible to see from where he stood on the High Ground had Mars been a little closer he would have witnessed much clawing and pecking as individual birds fought amongst themselves for the best vantage points. The spiteful and malicious nature of a crow was not just reserved for other creatures. Their selfishness and vile minds knew no bounds and they would be as likely to plunge their long beaks into the neck of a fellow crow as into the body of another creature if there was something to be personally gained from so doing.

The demonic shrieks from the crows now filled the air, seemingly mocking the frogs of Cowall who they could see grouped behind the High Ground on which Mars, Denray, Maccus and Kejon now stood. It was a mocking that suggested they soon expected some easy pickings.

Along the flanks and beyond the High Ground the hearts of many frogs fluttered at the blood-curdling sound of the crows - yet their resolve did not weaken. In The Weeping Willows the mood of the sparrowhawks hardened on hearing the arrival of the fulsome birds, and many powerful wings were being flexed - they knew the day of retribution had come at last.

On the High Ground Mars could now be certain that today was indeed the day for the great battle. Gawk and his murderous crows would not be here by sheer coincidence. Their presence must therefore signal the imminent arrival of Emled!

Just then a tremendous crash of thunder caused the very earth to shake and the trees to shudder. Almost instantaneously a bright flash of forked lightning lit up the gathering gloom and the deafening noise of it ripping deep into the middle of Fir Tree Wood caused all the creatures of Mars' army to cower down a little lower in their hiding places. Even the jet black cloud of crows rose up from the trees in a cacophony of screeching before settling back down again like a funereal drape over the upper boughs.

Mars however stayed tall; not once did he flinch from the sudden violence of the storm nor did he allow his eyes to be averted from the entrance to Fir Tree Wood. Those who saw him standing there marvelled at his courage and were heartened by his example. Word of his fearlessness spread along the ranks of his army almost as quickly as the fork of lightning zipped across and into the forest floor. A renewed and enthusiastic air of hope and optimism filled the hearts and souls of the frogs of Surey, Somset and Cowall. They were indeed ready and willing to follow their supreme leader into the battle to end all battles!

One after another a tremendous barrage of enormous claps of thunder then burst above Cowall. Whilst this clamour in the heavens continued, seemingly unabated, a series of jagged lines of lightning dived angrily into the surrounding trees.

It was during this violent atmospheric interlude that a vast silhouette appeared at the mouth of Fir Tree Wood. At first it was difficult to make out just what the shape was, so large and unworldly it appeared to those on the High Ground. But then, as countless flashes of brilliant white streaks of lightning seemed to fuse the whole wood, it was possible to see clearly the outline of a toad. This was no ordinary toad however. It was a huge gargantuan creature, the like of which had never been seen before in Cowall. Yet, and despite the disbelief on the faces of those who gazed upon this spectre, it was a toad. It was Emled!

A powerful odour had begun to fill the air around the battlefield. It slowly became more and more pungent and it pinched the noses of the frogs of Mars' army. Never in any of their lives had the creatures defending Cowall smelt anything quite so disgusting. Mars and Kejon, however, recognised the foul stench as being the unmistakable and putrid trademark of Emled.

"Emled!" whispered Mars instinctively. "The King of Evil has come! The forces of evil are upon us!"

Within seconds of the appearance of the toad came an earth-shattering roar of thunder accompanied by a simultaneous and vicious rapier of lightning which ripped into and exploded a massive fir tree some hundred metres or so behind where Emled now stood. The blazing red embers rose high into the sky and then fell to the ground like a fantastic scarlet fountain. Then, as quickly as the crescendo of thunder and lightning had arrived, so it disappeared and an eerie silence once again descended upon the whole battlefield area.

The pounding noise that had filled the ears of Mars' army in the moments leading up to the start of the sudden storm had ceased. Not a sound could be heard. Not a trace of wind disturbed the trees. Every leaf, twig and blade of grass was still. Not even a crow dared to move, let alone squawk. Every frog in the vicinity held its breath. Hearts beat faster and blood ran quicker through the veins and arteries of all the assembled creatures whether they sided with good or evil. Mouths became dry and to swallow was uncomfortable. Tummies churned, guts twisted and heads thumped.

Such was the intensity of all those who were preparing for battle. Such was the excitement; the expectation; and the very real emotion that filled the hearts, souls and minds of all the gathered masses.

Emled Makes His Demands

With the passing of the tempestuous storm the brightness of the morning clearly revealed the amphitheatre of the battlefield. In the daylight it was also becoming possible to see into the outer fringes of Fir Tree Wood. To the horror of those on the High Ground there was now revealed the source of the heavy pounding that had risen steadily from deep within the wood. It was the terrifying sight of Emled's army. Rank after rank of numerous huge brown marsh frogs clustered behind their leader. So many in fact that even though they were at present motionless it was quite impossible to count their number. In any event the ranks were so many that they actually extended way back into the forest and far beyond the area where sunlight had been able to penetrate.

In years to come stories would be told of an invasion by hundreds of thousands of Emled's evil marsh frogs, but then, as you know, frogs do enjoy being a little extravagant with the facts when telling their tales.

"*Mars!*" The huge booming voice of Emled broke the stillness and its resonance echoed in the distance.

Mars did not answer but instead focused his gaze even more keenly across Boda Moor and the Open Scrubland and fixed his stare unswervingly into the eyes of the obnoxious and ugly toad.

Emled cast his eyes first to the left and then to the right of Mars as he desperately searched for a sign of Krakow. Seeing that the legendary old blackbird was not there, the toad instantly guessed that the 'Supreme Qualities' had already been passed on to the handsome young frog.

"*Mars!...* You have something that belongs to me," continued Emled. "Something that only the true leader of all the frogs and all the creatures of the river banks and forest can rightly possess. You hold the key to the 'Supreme Qualities of Wisdom and Knowledge' and that is something which should be mine and mine alone, for I am the all powerful king of communities and the natural leader of all creatures, *I therefore demand that you pass the 'Great Qualities' to me at once!*"

Mars replied in a steady, clear and authoritative voice, choosing his words with care.

"The 'Qualities' to which you refer are most valuable to the good creatures of the river banks and forests. They are handed down from generation to generation paying great heed to ensure they are entrusted only to those that practise all that is good in our world. For the 'Supreme Qualities of Wisdom and Knowledge' to fall into your hands, the hands of unspeakable evil and wickedness, would surely destroy them forever. You are the epitome of all that is bad and you will never be allowed to possess the sacred 'Qualities' that have been bequeathed by our forefathers."

Emled was fast becoming angrier and angrier. He knew that Mars would certainly not relinquish the 'Qualities' he possessed without a fight and, although of course it suited him and his rotten army to plunder the community of Cowall and cause death and destruction to all those that refused to surrender, he rather liked the idea of Mars being seen to yield to his demands. That, he felt, would make Mars look like a coward who bowed under the pressure of a superior being, so proving that the young frog did not have the stomach to stand up for his principles.

Both Emled and Mars were also aware, as Krakow had informed Mars during his teaching, that it was only possible for one creature at a time to possess and apply the 'Great Learning'. Therefore, whatever Emled might say about Mars passing the 'Qualities' to him, it was certain that the evil toad would also strive to kill the young frog in the process.

Realising that the handsome young frog would never submit to his demands, the ugly toad decided that he would keep Mars talking to see if he could get an idea of the size of the opposing army. He didn't of course fear the opposition. Why should he? After all he was certain that his murderous marsh frogs far outnumbered the frogs at Mars' command – even if they did turn out to include both the communities of Cowall and Surey. However, all he could see at this moment in time was the front line of Cowall's frogs who were standing behind Mars and Denray. Along the flanks, and well out of sight of course, were the gallant frogs of Surey and Somset, crouched low preparing for the battle.

*

Although Emled was open about his wish to possess the 'Supreme Qualities of Wisdom and Knowledge' this was not his main target. He knew of course that by acquiring the precious 'Qualities' it would guarantee his being able to reign supreme, but then again, due to his size and strength and the fear he engendered in all those whom he encountered, he could achieve total dominance without such an acquisition.

What he really wanted most of all, however, was the face and beauty of Mars; and, in obtaining such a prize, that would certainly mean the death of the much adored young frog.

Emled's own hideous face could not hide the hatred he felt for Mars for he blatantly leered at the beauty of his handsome rival and he felt sick with jealousy that he didn't have a physique so well proportioned and lithe as that of the young frog leader.

"Will you be so heartless and irresponsible as to send the poor frogs of this peaceful community to their certain death by ignoring my request?" questioned the toad in a mocking tone. He then addressed the frogs of Cowall directly, hoping to provoke some support for his views. As he looked over the heads of Mars and Denray he shouted out for all to hear... "Surely your own king would prefer that you avoided unnecessary bloodshed? Why don't you tell him to give up this futile act of defiance and hand to me, the true leader of frogs, the 'Qualities' which so rightly should be mine? Don't you realise that he is just playing with your lives in order to satisfy his desire to lord it over you?"

Denray had stayed silent whilst Emled hurled his comments across the Open Scrubland and Boda Moor. Now, however, he felt he could keep quiet no longer. He wanted the malignant toad to know that it was Mars whom he and all the good-hearted and fair-minded creatures of the lands south of Waga supported. He wanted Emled to be certain that they would rather fight to the last frog in their efforts to repel the march of evil than meekly succumb to the toad's insane craving for power.

"You and your murderous hordes represent only malice and malevolence," shouted back Denray. "Our communities support the power of all that is good and will stand by Mars in order to defend such virtues. If necessary we will fight you until our final breath is taken and our last drop of blood falls upon the ground."

The evil toad had not really intended to take much notice of what Denray had to say as his mind was focused on humbling Mars and belittling him in the eyes of his followers. What he did not want to do was give too much credence to any obvious show of support for the young frog leader, an example of which had just come from the King of Cowall. However, as Denray had spoken, Emled's interest was suddenly pricked by the reference to "communities".

"Aha!" Emled thought to himself. "If I heard him correctly this fool talks of "communities". This must mean that there are indeed others hereabouts, in addition to the pathetic frogs of Cowall, who are preparing to do battle with me."

The eyes of the toad suspiciously swept the landscape that lay both to the front and to the sides of the Open Scrubland and Boda Moor. Emled of course had no way of knowing the condition of the land that lay between him and Mars but right at the moment this was the least of his concerns. Unfortunately, from the clue that Denray had just unwittingly given him about the potential level of support for Mars, Emled now sensed that the young frog might actually have been able to recruit the assistance of other communities and that he might well therefore have positioned some of these additional creatures along the flanks of the battleground as a means to trap and encircle any charge that the marsh frogs might be planning.

Denray had spoken with the very best of intentions and he had meant his words to demonstrate the substantial level of support that Mars enjoyed. His use of the word 'communities', however, had given Emled a warning that it was almost certainly not only the frogs of Cowall who stood between himself and his quest for total domination. In so doing Denray had alerted Emled to the possibility that at least one other community had joined forces with the local frogs. Emled accordingly considered that his earlier assumption that the Surey frogs had departed for Cowall was now clearly confirmed.

Turning around to his left, Emled beckoned to Kaara to come forward. As the hateful leader of the marsh frogs came alongside him the foul toad raised his forelimb to his mouth and spoke in a harsh whisper to his most villainous marsh frog lieutenant.

"My guts tell me that these stupid frogs expect us to walk into a trap. If I am not mistaken I believe that they may have positioned some of their number along the flanks with a view to attacking from the sides and possibly from behind. If I have interpreted that fool Denray's comments correctly then it is probably to here where those damn frogs of Surey have fled."

"Then we will just have to outmanoeuvre them, my King," replied the treacherous Kaara. "And give them a real lesson in battle tactics."

"Quite right!" rasped Emled. "Quite right, my dear friend! Although it will be a lesson that none of them will ever live to remember!"

Emled ordered Kaara to take two substantial detachments of marsh frogs from the rear of the massed ranks of his army with a view to each of these battalions of savages doubling back through the forest in two wide arcs so bringing them up behind the frogs of Surey and Somset on their respective flanks. The wicked toad's plan was that an attack from the rear of these frogs, if indeed the flanks were so covered, would come at the same time as he ordered a final frontal advance on the hill upon which stood Mars, Denray and the frogs of Cowall. Without their support from the flanks Emled considered the remainder of Mars' army and the young frog leader's position on the High Ground to be totally vulnerable and definitely there for the taking. He was now sure that the battle was going to be even easier than he had at first imagined.

Kaara melted back into the body of the thronging mass of the army and acted out Emled's instructions. So it was that many thousands of marsh frogs, who had been standing at the rear of Emled's army in the gloom of Fir Tree Wood, slipped away silently and unseen by Mars and Denray and prepared for their attack on the unsuspecting frogs of Surey and Somset who were themselves lined along the flanks.

In order to give the two detachments time to get into position Emled boomed out a further demand to Mars.

"Mars, my misguided little friend, I will give you just a short while longer to reconsider my request. In your hands lies the future of all those frogs who appear to support you. Their own lives, and the lives of their families, now depend upon your seeing some sense and not trying to be a hero in the face of impossible odds. Surely they would prefer that you voluntarily pass on to me the 'Qualities' that you for some reason possess rather than have me fight you for them. After all the only losers will be the poor souls of Cowall." Emled took great care to emphasise the word 'Cowall' in order to give Mars the impression that he was working on the basis that it was only this community against which he may have to do battle. He certainly didn't want to give away the fact that he had guessed there may be rather more than just Denray's frogs preparing to repel him.

"You will have lost nothing by giving me the 'Qualities' as they should be mine as of right," continued the toad. "You must realise that the only possible outcome of a battle between us is that many, if not all, of the good frogs of Cowall will die... and for what purpose? With me as their leader they will enjoy a full and meaningful life. Come now, be sensible, why not give all of your supporters` the opportunity for an enriched future under my kind and loving leadership. Surely every frog knows by now who really cares... for it is Emled who cares... *It is I who cares!*"

With these words the despicable toad threw open his forelimbs and then clasped them so hard to his chest that the slap of his horny hands hitting his vile body could be heard all around the battlefield.

Emled had spoken in the over-friendly drawl that he always used when he was being deceitful or when lying to an audience about what he could do for them. Mars, however, sensed that the ugly toad's persuasive powers were beginning to infiltrate the minds of the frogs around him. Such was Emled's cunning and his ability to influence and delude that even in these tense circumstances, where only moments before the good frogs of Cowall, Surey and Somset were clear that Emled was their enemy, he was nevertheless able to confuse them and sow some seeds of doubt.

Mars knew that he had to quickly counter the harmful influence of the ignominious toad before hearts and minds were lost. Therefore, in a loud voice that carried across the wastes of Boda Moor and the Open Scrubland and far into the darkest recesses of Fir Tree Wood, the young frog leader shouted...

"If I was to explain to the frogs of both sides the atrocities you have carried out against harmless and innocent frogs in the name of your youth policy then I expect that the support you currently have at your command would rapidly evaporate. Do your own frogs know for instance of the thousands of young Tamsid frogs that you have sacrificed to the humans just to satisfy your belly?"

Emled was far from happy to hear that Mars had learned of his exploitation of the young frogs of the Far North and even less so for him to be making such a pronouncement in front of his fearsome army. He now had to think fast on his hindlimbs for if it was to become known that he had colluded with humans then such a fact would instantly finish him as a power in the forest and river bank communities.

Apart from his closest 'personal aides' who regularly accompanied him on his mass deliveries of young frogs there was not another Far North frog, not even the most loathsome of their kind, who would have associated with humans for any purpose whatsoever. Such an act would have been regarded as more despicable and abhorrent than could possibly ever be described. Accordingly if they knew that Emled had liaised with humans, and had actually taken food from their hands in return for the lives of their off-spring, then they would most definitely have mutinied and slaughtered the fiendish creature right there and then.

The foul and malignant toad glanced slyly over his huge shoulder at the faces of his army. He didn't need to look twice to see that many of them were shuffling about uneasily and nudging each other, exchanging gestures that clearly indicated they were interested in what Mars was saying.

"How can you say such things?" retorted Emled, making a great display of being flabbergasted and utterly shocked by what he had just heard. "Please don't degrade yourself by telling such lies. I am sure that every creature here will realise that all you are trying to do is undermine me with cheap and nasty propaganda. Well, it won't work! Every frog knows how much I care about them and that with me it is always 'frogs first'!"

Emled then turned with a theatrical flourish to face his army. Firstly he stretched out his forelimbs towards the massed ranks of his marsh frogs and then he extended them upwards in the direction of the crows who were anxiously squabbling and squawking in the tops of the fir trees. As he did so he boomed out his favourite phrase.

"*Who cares...? Emled cares! ...I care for you all!*"

On hearing this familiar cry the marsh frogs loudly croaked their appreciation as they hopped and tumbled ever each other in delight at their master's rallying call. The crows, although somewhat less excited by Emled's attempt to elicit support, nevertheless danced crazily on their treetop perches and screeched their pleasure at Emled's words.

It was clear to the hideous toad that he was winning back the support of his army. He also knew that he needed to strike quickly before Mars was able to implant any further doubt into the minds of his evil followers. Any more references to atrocities or the like and

Mars might just succeed in penetrating the psyche of his villainous marsh frogs and crows and cause insubordination in the ranks.

Emled slowly turned back around to face Mars and the frogs of Cowall. The menace that was in the toad's eyes at that moment would have frozen the fastest flowing river on a hot sunny summer's afternoon, so icy was his stare. Mars watched as Emled raised his right forelimb high above his head and held it there whilst he venomously and threateningly spat out his next command. It was just the call for which his barbarous army had been waiting.

"The time has come for these mealy-mouthed frogs to be taught a lesson by the Far North!" Emled shouted. "Just remember that Mars is mine and woe betide any creature who takes my quarry!" No one was in any doubt what that meant... it was bound to be something horrible as well as fatal!

"As for the rest of these weak-limbed excuses for a tadpole... they are yours to do with as you will and they must be annihilated!" Emled was screaming now at the very top of his voice, and, as he drew his forelimb down sharply to his side, he issued his blood-curdling order to attack.

"CHAAAAAAARRRRRRRGE! DEATH TO ALL OUR ENEMIES!"

In a Sticky Situation

At his command the brown mass of marsh frogs lurched forward their minds full of savage intent. Rank after rank detached itself from the gathered hordes in Fir Tree Wood hopping wildly and excitedly in the direction of the High Ground. From above the battlefield hardly a patch of earth or a blade of grass could be seen beneath their hindlimbs, so thick was the advancing swarm.

"Death to our enemy! Death to our enemy!" They chanted as row after row and column after column poured out of the darkness of the forest and surged forward into the Open Scrubland and ever closer towards the bogs of Boda Moor.

Mars, meanwhile, held his forelimbs outstretched and at shoulder level waiting for exactly the right moment before signalling his frogs to counter-attack.

The young supreme leader of all the good creatures of the river banks and forests felt confident that he would be able to exercise sound judgement in this battle, even though he had never before experienced anything so terrifying as that with which he was now confronted. He somehow knew in his heart and in his soul that the teaching of Krakow had given him great inner strength as well as the ability to make quick and accurate decisions even in the most critical of circumstances.

Mars carefully surveyed the battlefield area that stretched out in front of him from the High Ground across to the edge of Fir Tree Wood. He was relieved that the stench of the monstrous toad had momentarily drifted away, so he took full advantage and drew in a huge lungful of the cool and crisp morning air into his body. He proudly and defiantly pumped up his chest in readiness for the battle.

By this time the marsh frogs were now flooding across the Open Scrubland and the first ranks had reached the edge of Boda Moor. With their minds totally focused on butchering their enemy the leading marsh frogs gave absolutely no thought to the ground beneath their feet and, in their frenzy, they hopped madly into the bog trying vainly to plough their way through the sticky swamp.

It was quite impossible for those marsh frogs who were some way behind the leaders to see what the terrain was like ahead of them. In addition, save for those hapless invaders immediately behind Emled's front line, none of them even realised or was aware that their colleagues in the vanguard were now not so much hopping across the battlefield as squelching their way through some extremely thick and cloying mud.

As those behind roughly pushed their way forward, their minds overwhelmed by hate and looking forward to the killing and slaughter of the Cowall frogs, they began tumbling over those in front who were becoming stuck fast in the bogs of Boda Moor. Very soon hundreds upon hundreds of the marsh frogs were similarly ensnared and were feverishly trying to extricate themselves from their gluey trap.

Those marsh frogs who had been at the forefront of the charge were soon being trampled deep into the bog by the mad, crazed killers behind then. Those crushed in this way only served to act as a grisly platform for their comrades who charged on regardless of the dangerous terrain. Driven by their lust for blood all that these evil creatures succeeded in doing was to gain a few extra metres across the embedded bodies of their comrades before they too became immersed in the swampy mud and were themselves in turn trampled under the surging mass of yet more maniacal hordes.

Whilst mayhem reigned in the ranks of the marsh frogs Mars watched dispassionately from his vantage point still withholding his command to counter the attack from Emled's floundering army.

High above the battlefield, Gawk was slowly circling and he looked down on the marsh frogs with disdain.

"Fools! Fools?" he cried. Then, swooping low towards Emled, he rudely shrieked at the toad to take corrective action.

"Come on, get them out of there, this is a trap and just like your idiot marsh frogs you have fallen right into it! There is no way through the swamp to the High Ground!"

Emled could now clearly see what was happening. He didn't need Gawk to point out the painfully obvious fact that Mars was out-thinking him by cleverly applying tactics of which he himself would have been proud to have employed. However, the evil toad had other ideas. Now was not the moment to retreat. There was no way he would dream of backing away from an opposition seemingly as weak as that led by Mars.

Feeling confident that despite their sticky predicament his army continued to far outnumber that of the handsome young frog, Emled ignored the pleading of Gawk and instead even more enthusiastically roared on his troops to carry out their assault on the High Ground. He had decided that if the only way for the majority of his army to reach the area occupied by Mars was to lay a carpet of dead marsh frogs in the swamps of Boda Moor then so be it. After all, what were the lives of several thousand of these inconsequential creatures worth when compared with his ultimate goal of taking Mars' beauty?

A demonic grin spread around the mouth and nose of the toad giving his face a hideously disfigured appearance. The expression became transfixed and he displayed no further emotion as he watched the dead and dying marsh frogs form their macabre platform which was slowly extending towards the High Ground.

Mars sensed Emled's plan and was not surprised at the callous and wanton disregard that the toad displayed even for the lives of his own army. For a moment Mars considered the plight of those marsh frogs who were being sent to such a sticky end. Even creatures as despicable as they undoubtedly were must have families who will grieve at their not returning home after this battle has ended.

The young leader of frogs could, however, only allow himself a fleeting thought for the well-being of the marsh frogs as the advancing thick brown mass was moving ever closer. Mars nevertheless remained calm and continued to hold his forelimbs aloft steeling himself for the exact moment to give the signal for the army of Cowall to defend the High Ground, whilst their comrades from Surey and Somset attacked the marsh frogs from both flanks.

Gawk Gets in on the Act

The crows were becoming restless. They were unruly and untrustworthy at the best of times, but, when things were going badly wrong, as they certainly appeared to be at the moment for Emled's army, then what little discipline they had very quickly evaporated.

"Come on, Gawk!" shouted one of the crow leader's sidekicks. "Let's get those gutless frogs of Cowall! If those damned marsh frogs can't do it let's show them how!"

Gawk didn't bother to wait before agreeing to this request. Why should he just remain on his perch and watch the marsh frogs' inept attempt at a charge through a swamp when he could quite simply fly over it and descend right into the heart of the enemy? What's more, he was sure that a little earlier that morning he had seen the flashing colours of a kingfisher's feathers reflecting in the rays of the sun as a small bird flew across from The Weeping Willows and landed by the side of Mars. If he wasn't mistaken that brilliant plumage belonged to a kingfisher from Kingfisher's Bridge.

He had been inwardly consumed with a mixture of horror and rage at the sight of this bird as it confirmed Emled's information that there had indeed been a survivor of the massacre of Peeyu and his family. Gawk's orders from Emled had been to destroy the entire family of kingfishers. He thought he had done so and reported as much to the toad on his return from the massacre at Kingfisher's Bridge. In fact so sure had he been of the total success of his cruel and brutal mission that he had conceitedly boasted to Emled that if ever he wanted a job done well then he could always rely on a crow.

The sight of the kingfisher had therefore caused a cold sensation to run along his spine. He would never be able to live down the embarrassment of such a failure if Emled got to know that one of the family had in fact survived the slaughter. He determined, therefore, to see to it that this mistake was eradicated once and for all. He would personally ensure that this time the kingfisher would be well and truly slain and the evidence of his blunder at Kingfisher's Bridge consigned to the murky depths of the swamps of Boda Moor.

Without further ado Gawk flew up into the air and excitedly shrieked his orders for his crows to swoop upon Mars and the frogs of Cowall. Within seconds every single one of his crows was airborne.

Sona serenely watched the antics of Gawk and his madcap army through clear, cool and impassive eyes. She had remained perfectly still throughout the frantic activity above Fir Tree Wood and not until she was totally satisfied that not one of the crows had been left behind in the trees did she order her birds to leave their post. Then, with a grace and beauty of movement that only served to enhance their fearsome reputation, Sona's sparrowhawks rose high into the morning sky circling around the back of The Weeping Willows in order to approach Boda Moor over the tops of the trees from the rear of Fir Tree Wood.

As Gawk and his crows flew over the Open Scrubland and focused their attention on both the sticky progress of the marsh frogs and their target of Mars and the brave frogs of Cowall on the High Ground they were completely unaware of the danger that was looming overhead. Therefore, as the eyes of Gawk and company were concentrating on events below, some way above the black mass and positioning her imperious brigade in a direct line between the sun and the crows, Queen Sona gave her command to attack.

At breathtaking speed the sparrowhawks plunged deep into the black cloud that was Gawk's flying army. The sight from the ground was awesome. Both Emled and Mars looked upward and stared almost in disbelief at what they saw. The advancing army of marsh frogs were bewildered and had stopped their forward push as they too could only wonder at what was happening to their crow allies. And, from the cover of their hiding places along the flanks, Fara and Truda looked on, for the first time witnessing the full horror and scale of battle. For them, and for all the good frogs of Cowall, Surey and Somset, there was a quite frightening realisation that if the fight was to be won, and not lost, then the conflict had to be about cold-hearted killing and not just offering hearts and souls in support of the cause. They held their breath and steeled their emotions as they watched Sona and her valiant comrades go expertly about their work.

The sparrowhawks were wreaking havoc amongst the crows as Sona and her warriors dived time and time again into the black mass.

Whether from above or below; from the right side or the left side; or from the front or from the back, every strike was made swiftly and with great precision. Each time a sparrowhawk swooped and entered the black cloud so another crow fell heavily from the sky.

Gawk's wicked troops had no answer to this onslaught. Individually they were no match for a sparrowhawk, but even with the advantage of far greater numbers they could not counter the effusion of rage and vengeance that had for so long been stored in the hearts of Sona and her intrepid birds.

Very soon the black cloud was beginning to thin out and disperse, and, as a result of the unerring accuracy of the sparrowhawks, the ground below was becoming littered with the debris of black feathers and the broken bodies of a multitude of dead and dying crows.

Not one crow was allowed to escape, and, as the naturally cowardly instinct of such birds encouraged one after another to fly away rather than fight, so a sparrowhawk would give chase and knock such faint hearts to the ground.

So great and so swift had been the revenge of the sparrowhawks that Emled had not even been able to shout a warning to Gawk or give his battle orders to the crows for them to retreat or fight back. He had merely stood open-mouthed in his astonishment as Sona and her swashbuckling brigade tore through and destroyed Gawk's entire army.

Finally all that was left of the crow contingent was Gawk himself. The sparrowhawks had purposely saved him till last. It was to be Sona's privilege to personally dispose of this most despicable carrion eating creature.

Gawk looked down at the carnage beneath him as he flew around in ever decreasing circles trying to get his bearings. He had been stunned by the suddenness of the attack and was totally disorientated by such a massive defeat. As he peered through air that was thick with the fluttering black feathers of his slain army so he glimpsed the magnificent, but for him terrifying, sight of Sona heading straight at him. It was in fact the last thing that Gawk ever saw as the Queen of the sparrowhawks struck him a fatal blow right between the eyes with her beak. Sona hit him with such great power that the crow leader fell out of the sky like a stone, his neck thoroughly broken. Gawk was dead long before he hit the ground.

Sona had incredibly not lost one of her birds in the attack and yet the sparrowhawks had accounted for every one of Gawk's crows. She regrouped her warriors with great discipline and flew them low past Mars, Denray and Maccus who stood admiringly on the High Ground. They waved their heartfelt thanks and marvelled at the supreme ability of these magnificent birds. The frogs of Cowall cheered at the glorious sight and were hugely buoyed up by what they had seen.

The sparrowhawks then rose high up into the late morning sky before disappearing over The Weeping Willows and away to the peace and tranquillity of their nesting places deep in the forest. For Sona her part in the battle was done and her vengeance on Gawk and his contemptible crows was complete. She at least could rest peacefully in the knowledge and satisfaction of her spectacular victory and glorious revenge.

Mars Closes In

Emled, meanwhile, had to shake himself in order to regain his senses. Directly in front of him was a squirming mass of marsh frogs who were ploughing their way with extreme difficulty across the swamps of Boda Moor; below these creatures were the bodies of many hundreds of their compatriots whom they had trampled into their muddy graves as they obeyed their leader's command to continue their advance on the High Ground; and all over the battlefield and the surrounding areas the ground was strewn with the broken bodies of Gawk and his crows.

Things were clearly not going as planned for Emled yet his manic desire for the 'Qualities' that Mars possessed, and above all for the young frog's beauty, drove the malevolent toad menacingly onwards towards his obsessive goal.

"*CHARGE! CHAAARRRGE!*" screamed the foul toad as the carpet of trapped marsh frogs stretched further and further across Boda Moor's sticky clutches. "*CHAAAARRRRGE*," he cried, his excitement mounting at the prospect of reaching Mars' command point on the High Ground no matter how many lives of his own army were lost in the process.

From Mars' and Denray's vantage point it had seemed as if a never-ending flow of marsh frogs was pouring out of Fir Tree Wood spurred on as they were by their fanatical leader. However, at last it appeared that the final battalions of Emled and Kaara's brown marauders were at the edge of the forest. With the leading marsh frogs now about halfway across Boda Moor it meant that virtually three-quarters of the entire battlefield was now covered with the villainous creatures.

Mars knew that very soon he would have to determine the right moment to order his counter-attack. He was well aware that the terrain on the second half of the moor that led up to the high Ground was a good deal firmer than that part in which the marsh frogs were now labouring. This was due to the fact that the land gradually rose up towards the High Ground and the rainwater, when it fell, ran down the slopes, causing most of it to be collected some way in from the swampy boundary on the High Ground end of the moor.

Emled's army were now coming within range of this safer ground and Mars, therefore, was preparing himself for his call to arms. He was also gauging what would be the best moment for the frogs of Surey and Somset to move in from the flanks. He wanted them to be able to push inwards from the drier edges of the swamp's perimeter as well as close in from behind the marsh frogs by way of the Open Scrubland. This strategy would have the effect of forcing the marsh frogs into the soft centre of the bog where many of Emled's army had already perished as a result of the toad's uncaring command to continue with their advance.

Despite the clear advantage that was developing for Mars on the battlefield he nevertheless felt that something was missing. He was sure that the last of the marsh frogs who had congregated in Fir Tree Wood were now out in the open and yet he was surprised at their numbers. From the various accounts he had received from both Krakow and Kejon he had estimated there to be at least twice as many marsh frogs under the command of Emled than those which now floundered below him on the Open Scrubland and in Boda Moor.

There was however no time to ponder on what may have been incorrect information. He knew that against all the odds he now had an opportunity, even if only an outside chance, to defeat Emled. With the limited and inexperienced army he had been able to put together Mars had to strike quickly and effectively. He certainly didn't have sufficient numbers to make provision for all eventualities and he knew that when the right moment presented itself he had to give his order to attack with the whole of his army participating. Anything less would result in certain defeat for the good and brave frogs of Cowall, Surey and Somset; which in addition, of course, would result in the loss of the 'Supreme Qualities' to the vile toad. Irrespective of the predicament that the marsh frogs were in they still far outnumbered Mars' army and of course individually benefited from much greater size and body strength.

Mars raised himself to his full height and breathed in very deeply. From their concealed positions on the flanks Fara and Truda watched their young leader and waited anxiously for the signal to launch their attack. Then, as soon as the advancing marsh frogs had almost reached the first traces of firm land leading up to the High Ground so Mars dramatically raised both his forelimbs above his head. He looked first to the left and then to the right and received positive acknowledgements from Fara and Truda that they and their communities of Surey and Somset were ready. Mars then glanced one more time at Emled before refocusing on the invading marsh frogs.

The young frog leader felt a wave of passion rising within his firm athletic body and he knew that now was the moment he had to signal his counter-attack. With a flourish, and with great aplomb, Mars dropped both his forelimbs to his sides so giving the pre-arranged signal to Fara and Truda to go over the top and put in motion their offensive from the flanks.

The hapless marsh frogs on the battlefield had no idea that they were going to be outflanked. Not only that but as Fara and Truda led their armies into battle and closed in from the sides so Denray and the valiant frogs of Cowall raced passed Mars and simultaneously mounted their forward offensive from the High Ground. Some marsh frogs turned and tried to beat a hasty retreat but the vision of Emled lashing out at any of them who had decided to run away or desert their post struck almost as much fear into their hearts as did the sight of Mars' combined armies bearing down on them from both the flanks as well as from the front and back.

Many frogs from both sides, good and bad, fell in the opening skirmishes of the Battle of Boda Moor. Gradually, as the fighting raged on, the bigger and more impassioned hearts of Mars' combined army began to gain the upper hand. Despite the greater physical strength and size of the marsh frogs the latter had been severely weakened both by their long trek from Seaxe and by the exertions of their march across the bogs of Boda Moor. Very soon, therefore, they found themselves wilting under the well planned and sustained counter-attack of Mars' enthusiastic army. The much fresher frogs from Cowall, Surey and Somset, fired up enormously by their desire to defeat Emled and rid the earth of his evil and malignance, were now proving to be more than a match for the contingent of marsh frogs on whom they were steadily closing in.

Increasingly, more and more of the marsh frogs were being slaughtered at the forelimbs and hindlimbs of Mars' army. Then, seeing that there was little chance of successfully fighting off their buoyant assailants, many of Emled's followers who could fight no more (or were too scared to do so) offered to surrender in order to save their own lives.

Seeing what was happening Emled screamed at his army to march on. He seemed quite oblivious to their plight and urged them ever forward into what was fast becoming a hopeless cause. As marsh frog after marsh frog fell to the passion of Mars' fearless fighters so the toad bellowed even louder his threats of a much worse fate that would await them if they dared to desert or surrender.

Regardless of the toad's rantings, his army could fight no more. To a marsh frog they were exhausted and thoroughly spent. The armies of Cowall, Surey and Somset encircled their quarry waiting for Mars' instructions as to what should be done to their prisoners. Although victorious, if called upon by Mars to do so, they would even now show compassion to the vanquished marsh frogs who were grouped together in a bedraggled and sorry state before them.

The Tables Are Turned

An eerie hush had fallen on the battlefield as the realisation of what had just taken place began to sink into the minds of the bloodied and bruised of both sides. For the marsh frogs their thoughts were of utter and complete disbelief. How was it that they had been beaten by a much smaller army? Not only that but also by one that was so much weaker and entirely unaccustomed to battle. The marsh frogs hung their heads low in their shame. They had considered themselves to be invincible. Was it not their king, the indestructible and all powerful Emled, who had told them so? Surely he could not be wrong?

As for the good frogs of Cowall, Surey and Somset, their immediate reaction was of great elation coupled with a liberal amount of relief. For those that had survived the battle, and thankfully a great many had done so, they looked in on the marsh frogs and felt very fortunate and proud indeed.

The silence seemed endless even though it had only lasted for less than a minute. The marsh frogs were seemingly too embarrassed to utter a word; and the frogs of Mars' army, triumphant as they were, each held their breath as they were almost too frightened to say a thing for fear of breaking the spell of this magical moment.

The two main protagonists eyed each other from opposite ends of the battlefield. Between them lay the carnage of an embittered battle where the forces of evil had failed in their attempt to reach and take the High Ground. Mars' strategy of tempting Emled to enter the swamps of Boda Moor and then outflanking him had apparently worked and the toad had been defeated. Frogs from both sides now waited for the next moves in this horrific fight. Would Emled surrender graciously? Would Mars order the final and complete elimination of the evil and wicked army of marsh frogs? Or would the young and victorious frog leader show compassion and spare the lives of those that were now the captives of his own army?

Mars, however, still felt that all was not as it should be. He had expected more from Emled and the fact that the toad had remained rooted to his position at the entrance of Fir Tree Wood throughout the titanic struggle made Mars feel very uncomfortable indeed. Why hadn't Emled joined in the fighting? His sheer presence in the heat of battle would have been worth a thousand marsh frogs and would surely have put great fear and uncertainty into the hearts and souls of the brave frogs of Cowall, Surey and Somset.

Mars held Emled's gaze and noticed that an expression, even more menacing than he had ever seen before, was beginning to creep across the evil creature's face.

Suddenly the silence that had blanketed the battlefield was shattered by the rasping sound of Emled laughing out loud. It was a sickening and mortifying cackle that froze the very blood in the veins of the frogs of Mars' army.

Emled leered at Mars and cried out, "Did you really think that I would be so easy to defeat that the likes of you and your minuscule army could beat me into submission?"

Emled again laughed out loud as the mocking tone of his words reverberated in the deathly hush of Boda Moor.

Those who were close enough to the evil toad and who survived what happened next will say that as Emled bellowed at Mars they were certain that from the pores of his warty skin there began to ooze a strange milky fluid. Many were overcome by the dreadful stink of the foul creature's excretion and they fell upon the ground struggling for air, suffocated as they were by his obnoxious odour.

Those not affected in this way watched as the malignant toad rose up threateningly on his hindlimbs to what appeared to be an even greater elevation than his full height. As he did so the hideously ugly creature puffed up his chest and filled his lungs with air contaminated by the putrid smell of rotting flesh that emanated from his own body. Seeming to thrive upon the rancid stench, as if it were a fuel that fed his evil intentions, Emled then gave vent to a massive raucous roar that shook Mars and his faithful army to their very toes and fingertips.

"*DEATH TO OUR ENEMY! DEATH TO ALL THOSE THAT STAND BEFORE US! CHAAAAAARRRRRRGE ON ALL FRONTS!*"

The frogs from Cowall, Surey and Somset could not believe their eyes as from the flanks, where they had themselves only recently advanced, there now appeared thousand upon thousand of huge brown marsh frogs.

Mars had been outwitted by the cunning toad and the anxiety that he had felt at the relative ease by which he and his army had beaten their invaders' initial advance was now unfortunately very clearly being explained. In respect of numbers, the crafty toad had literally halved his army into those whom he would use to attack the High Ground from across the Open Scrubland and Boda Moor and those whom he would utilise to circumvent the flanking strategy that the young frog leader had employed along the perimeter of the battlefield. Mars now realised, alas too late of course, that Emled must have suspected such a manoeuvre and so he had countered it by retreating a large portion of his army out of Fir Tree Wood in order to move them in on the battlefield from way beyond the flanks on which the good frogs of Surey and Somset had taken up their original positions.

Given a choice, at that very moment in time, Mars would rather have ordered his army to surrender than fight on in the face of such immensely unfavourable odds. That way at least he might have been able to save the lives of those valiant creatures who had battled so bravely in defeating Emled's first onslaught. However, the toad's cry of attack came so fast that it gave him no opportunity whatsoever for seeking any form of compromise with the toad. In fact all Mars could really do in the circumstances was to infuse his own army with a passion to fight back this second flood of marsh frogs as best they could.

A slaughter of unspeakable proportions was inevitable as wave upon wave of marsh frogs smashed their way through the ranks of Mars' joint army, crushing the life out of the defenders of all that is good by their superior strength and lust for murder. Then, as the skirmishing progressed, Emled began wading through the seething masses paying absolutely no heed to the carnage and butchery that was taking place all around him.

The forbidding and monstrous toad had his eyes totally focused on Mars. He was out to get that for which he came. Whilst he was certainly determined to obtain the 'Supreme Qualities of Wisdom and Knowledge', which would undoubtedly make him the most powerful creature in all the forests and river banks, there was a prize that was much more valuable to him and for which he craved above all else. He was going to take the greatest prize of all. The prize which this insane 'thing' truly believed should be his of right. Namely, the beauty of Mars'.

As soon as Emled reached the High Ground he hopped aggressively and menacingly up towards Mars. The handsome frog leader, boldly and without nerves, bravely stood his ground. He felt no fear for the toad, and, if he was to lose his life in an attempt to protect the values of all that was good and right, then so be it. In such an event, and in the face of his substantially more powerful adversary, he promised himself that he would go down fighting and make it as difficult as he could for the brutish toad to take from him the 'Supreme Qualities' that he possessed. To Mars, along with the well-being of his loyal army of brave-hearted frogs, this was paramount in his mind; whereas, had he been totally aware of Emled's prime purpose for mounting his attack, the loss of his beauty to the mad craving of the paranoid creature would have been of secondary importance. Conversely, or rather perversely, it was Emled's insane jealousy and lust for Mars' magnificent features that were at the forefront of the demonic toad's mind.

As Mars and Emled came nose to nose the warfare upon the battlefield began to subside as, one by one, frogs of both sides turned their attention towards their leaders. Very soon every frog stood quite still watching with bated breath and waiting for what might happen next. Once again a silence had spread across the entire battlefield save for the occasional groan of a wounded or dying creature. The words spoken by Emled and Mars were therefore clearly audible to all of those who witnessed this monumental event.

"You have no other option than to admit defeat and to finally pass to me, as their rightful owner, the 'Supreme Qualities' that you are fraudulently looking after for me," demanded Emled in his most forceful and booming voice.

"Never!" replied Mars defiantly. "I would never willingly give them to you. You will have to fight me for whatever it is that you want!"

Emled laughed out loud. He knew that even full of passion there was no way that Mars would be a match for his superior strength and craft in the art of fighting.

Then, with a sudden spring that defied his size and bulk, Emled leapt forward at Mars knocking him over on to his back. Mars fell heavily with a thud against the ground. A further hop forward and the toad now sat astride Mars, pinning him firmly to the soft dry earth of the High Ground.

All around the battlefield the silence was broken by a mixture of gasps and cheers from the two armies. The good frogs of Cowall, Surey and Somset were distressed to see their young leader seemingly bowled over so easily, although they were to a frog most impressed with the way he had faced up to the giant figure of Emled. They all realised that it took a special kind of strength to defy this gross monster and what Mars was displaying was a measure of courage the like of which had never been seen before by any living frog. Indeed it was only in tales of far distant times that there were recorded feats of bravery that could at best possibly equal what was now happening on the High Ground. There certainly were none of greater standing than Mars' defiance of the wicked toad of Tamsid.

The way things were going, however, it appeared that the demise of Mars at the forelimbs of Emled was now only moments away. The brown masses of marsh frogs cheered on their leader calling for the death of Mars and the total destruction of the civilised societies of the south and west.

The frenzied toad grasped Mars' face with his forelimbs and held him tightly, the tips of his fingers pressed deep within the young frog's skin. He then leaned forward and spoke very quietly into Mars' ear so that no other living creature could hear his terrifying words.

"You stole my beautiful face and left me ugly and unsightly. When once I was handsome and much admired, now I am left a distorted and hideous freak. I shall rip off your face and take my beauty back for the handsome features you now display are indeed my own!"

Emled's nose was almost touching Mars' face and the toad's fetid breath made the young frog's head swim with dizziness. He nevertheless managed to keep his wits about him and never once let his eyes be diverted from those of his aggressor.

"I am the rightful owner of that beautiful face," continued Emled, still speaking in an evil hiss that only Mars could hear. "I know I am, for I used to be able to see it looking back at me in the reflection of my favourite bathing pool."

Finally, and in preparation for the killing of Mars, Emled could control his anger, frustration and jealousy no more. The monstrous toad threw his head back and shouted out in his great booming voice so loudly that every creature on the battlefield cringed at the power of his thunderous and resounding tone.

"*IT IS I, EMLED, WHO IS THE MOST WONDERFUL AND HANDSOME FROG OF ALL, AND ON YOUR DEATH THE 'GREAT LEARNING OF THE SUPREME QUALITIES OF WISDOM AND KNOWLEDGE' WILL BE MINE FOREVER!*"

Great cheers and whooping croaks of delight came from the clamouring ranks of excited marsh frogs. Their wicked king was about to murder the young frog leader. They sensed more wanton bloodshed and could themselves hardly wait to resume the slaughter of what remained of Mars' brave army.

"*NO, EMLED!*" cried back Mars, his words too reaching the ears of all the assembled and battle weary frogs. "*YOU ARE NOT A FROG... YOU ARE A TOAD... A WICKED AND ODIOUS CREATURE WHO HAS NO PLACE IN OUR WORLD. YOU ARE A MURDEROUS MONSTER WHO HAS CORRUPTED THE FAR NORTH AND...!*"

Emled had heard enough and he certainly didn't want his followers to hear any more. From their immediate reaction he could sense again that Mars had created a spark of interest in the minds of his evil army and many heads had now turned as if they were keen to learn some more. Gasps from the marsh frogs indicated their shock and amazement at what Mars had just revealed and many questioning cries of "A toad...? Did he say a toad...? Emled is really a toad...?" ran like wildfire throughout the confused hordes of Emled's vast battalions.

Emled knew that he now had to deal quickly and finally with Mars. He could delay for not a moment longer the destruction of the handsome young frog who was the new leader of all that was good in the world of the creature communities of the river banks and forests. The evil monster therefore lashed out and struck Mars hard across the side of his head which dazed him as he lay on the ground entrapped by the enormous weight of the massive toad. As Mars tried to regain his senses, the loathsome and repulsive beast then dug his fingers even harder into the skin of Mars' handsome face as he got ready to rip off the young frog's beautiful features.

The cheering and chanting of Emled's army had faded away as the effect and realisation of Mars' words carried over the battleground. The marsh frogs had become increasingly perturbed and perplexed and were not at all certain of what to do or say next. What was all this talk of a toad...? Had they heard Mars correctly? Did he actually say that Emled was really a toad...? Surely not! They hadn't been following a toad for all these years...! Had they? They couldn't possibly have been fooled by such a creature...! Could they?

Emled Can't Believe His Eyes

As Emled made to destroy Mars a faint beat of drumming filtered into the quiet of a pregnant pause that had momentarily developed as the massed ranks of both armies anxiously waited for Emled to deliver his final and fatal blow in the one-sided combat between the two rivals. At first the sound came and went as it drifted lazily on the light morning breeze. Some of the frogs who had been amongst the first to hear it thought that it must have been their imaginations but then the sound came again, a little louder this time, and possibly getting closer. The drumming then became much more audible and was clear for all to hear. Even Emled heard it in spite of all his vile roaring and croaking.

Although he was at the pinnacle of his rage Emled slackened his grip on the young frog leader as he too listened more carefully. He looked questioningly at Mars and then cocked his head on one side as if trying to establish just what it was he could hear. For the moment the only thing of which he could be certain was that it was definitely getting louder and that it was coming towards the community of Cowall.

Emled couldn't be sure, in fact he hoped he was wrong, but was it also the sound of chanting he could make out that was accompanying the drumming noise? Surely, he thought, he must be mistaken and in the heat of the battle it was his ears that were playing tricks on him! He turned again to face Mars who by this time had fully regained his senses.

The young frog leader could certainly hear the sound of chanting. Not only that he could also clearly make out the words. They were words which filled his heart with joy and he felt a supreme surge of strength race through his whole body.

"*Mars is the king…! Long live Mars!*
Death to the toad…! Long live the king!
Mars is the king…! Long live Mars!
Death to the toad…! Long live the king!"

As the new-found strength permeated his every muscle and sinew Mars kicked upwards with all his might at the lower part of Emled's body. The toad, who was still sitting astride Mars, was taken completely by surprise at the young frog's power and he was sent cartwheeling backwards over and over, only finally coming to a stop when the hideous creature landed with a fearful crash as his head banged hard against a sharp rock.

In great pain the evil toad slowly staggered to his hindlimbs clutching the side of his head from which blood was now trickling. Hatred had filled his eyes and with every wart on his body he determined to kill Mars.

The sound of drumming was almost upon them and the chanting was now clear for all to hear. A strange compulsion caused Emled to turn his head and look towards the edge of Fir Tree Wood. It was then, through eyes becoming blurred with a mixture of hate and the blood from the gash on his head, that there appeared to the evil toad a vision of a magnificent old bullfrog. Emled blinked several times as he tried to focus his eyes on what seemed to him to be an apparition, for around the outline of the bullfrog was a wonderful golden aura which glowed brightly as the sun's rays embraced and lit up his body.

As the toad's eyes began to clear he then saw that upon each of the two flanks of Boda Moor a statuesque and identical frog had appeared. He now felt sure that he was seeing things and that his eyes were deceiving him so he rubbed them hard and blinked again. No, surely it couldn't be true, they were both still there, equally splendid in physique; distinguished in features; and majestic in their presence. Not only that but behind these two noble creatures were their massive armies which were huge by any frogs' reckoning and several times greater than the number of marsh frogs remaining under Emled's command.

Although the toad did not know it, these two proud and stately frogs were none other than King Cabal of Solk and King Tanal of Nolk, the most highly esteemed twins who had simultaneously risen to lead the vast frog communities that lay far to the east of Seaxe.

Then, to add to Emled's misery, behind the stupendous figure of the bullfrog there emerged from out of the depths of Fir Tree Wood the many thousands of frogs who represented the community of Seaxe. These frogs were rampant with a fire that burned in their bellies. A fire that was fuelled by a spirit to both avenge the ignominy and humiliation inflicted upon them by Emled and his marsh frogs plus a passion to save Mars and install him as the true king of their community.

Mars immediately recognised many of his friends and he rejoiced in their presence. He also momentarily noticed that he could not see any of his former senior colleagues, but that thought only fleetingly passed through his mind.

Those brave creatures from Cowall, Surey and Somset who had survived the final onslaught from Emled's outflanking manoeuvre regained their hearts and hopped towards the perimeter of the battlefield to join the friendly ranks of the legions of frogs from Solk, Nolk and Seaxe. The beleaguered marsh frogs, however, remained motionless. They were stunned into disbelief by the amazing turnaround in events and were clueless as to whether to fight on; run for their lives; or meekly surrender, faced as they now were by insurmountable odds against them ever winning this battle.

"*You are finished, Emled*!" The old bullfrog's rich mellow voice swept across the Open Scrubland and the bogs of Boda Moor, causing the toad to tremble with a cocktail of fear and anger. It was a familiar voice. A voice that was as clear as it was calm. A voice that Mars knew and loved. A voice that unmistakably belonged to Moha, the greatest and proudest king ever to have reigned over the community of Seaxe. "*Your campaign of terror is at an end*!"

Emled's mind had cleared sufficiently for him to consider what move he should make next, and, both as a bluff and in order to give himself a little more time to think, he continued to stagger, giving the impression that he was still suffering from the bash he had just received to the side of his head.

Emled therefore lurched about clutching his head with his forelimbs and grossly exaggerating the extent of his injury. All the time he was gradually moving closer and closer towards Mars. He had decided that if Moha was right and he was indeed finished then he would take the life of Mars with him as his final vile act.

"What will become of me?" whimpered the toad, making a pretence of being humbled but all the while purposefully shuffling nearer to Mars whilst he assessed his best opportunity for a final strike at the handsome frog leader. "I never meant to harm any frog or any of the other creatures of the river banks and forests. I am so misunderstood. I really do care for you all."

Whilst he spoke these words Emled had crept to within one long hop of Mars, and, although the toad still held his supposedly aching head in his forelimbs, Maccus was the first to spot the veil of humility drop and the flash of hatred return to his eyes as the toad prepared to spring at the young frog leader.

The vigilant kingfisher's call for Mars to watch out for the treacherous toad came just in time. As the evil creature sprang at him so the athletic young frog side-stepped to the left, and, before Emled could recover, Mars then in turn leapt at him with lightning speed and with his hindlimbs caught the toad a powerful blow full across the chest.

The surprise of Mars' deft movement, together with the stunning blow to his body, caused Emled to topple backwards, whereupon he rolled to a point only a metre or so away from the slope which ran steeply down from the High Ground to the swamps of Boda Moor below.

During this tremendous struggle Fara had made his way from the battlefield up to the High Ground and was now standing next to Kejon. The Seaxe senior hadn't been aware of Fara's arrival until he felt the king of Surey place a forelimb upon his back and quietly whisper in his ear.

"Kejon, now is the moment for me to fulfil my promise to you," said Fara as he gently ushered Kejon forward. "I said that you would one day have the opportunity to bloody the nose of the wicked king. Well, that moment has now arrived. Go on, my brave friend, for your king and all your fellow creatures, go boldly before the evil creature and exact your vengeance!"

On hearing Fara's voice, and being inspired by his words, Kejon hopped quickly past Mars to stand between his regal friend and the monstrous figure of Emled. The surprise on the face of the toad at seeing a creature he had considered to be dead was a sight to behold.

"*You!*... What are *you* doing here? *I ordered your death!*"

In one movement, and quite before Emled could recover from the shock of seeing Kejon, the courageous senior leapt at the toad, catching the fulsome beast a solid blow with his hindlimbs right on the centre of his nose. The sheer force of Kejon's kick, which had been fuelled by a fury that had long been building up in the angry senior, caused Emled to topple over the edge of the High Ground and roll over and over down the steep slope to the swamps of Boda Moor below. The toad tumbled and rolled crashing into rocks and uprooting small trees as he gained speed in his inglorious descent.

Emled finally came to a stop, but only after he had hit a prominent rock which had sent him hurtling through mid-air in the last part of his downward journey, plunging him head first into an extremely wet and boggy patch of the moor.

All those who watched this momentous scene held their breath as the bruised and battered body of the toad lay motionless face down in the swamp. Every creature waited, fully expecting Emled to haul himself up and mount a further attack on the handsome frog leader. Mars was also anticipating such a reaction and he braced himself for a further encounter with his arch-enemy.

Instead the impossible appeared to be happening. Emled had made no move to extricate himself from the bog's sticky clutches and he continued to lie perfectly still. Then, very gradually, the swamp began to suck the toad downwards into its hidden depths. Within a matter of seconds, although it seemed more like hours, his whole body had disappeared and the swamp, which had moments earlier lazily opened its jaws wide to consume him, now closed in above its prey. Only a few bubbles rising to the surface provided a sign of its satisfying feast.

Frogs from all communities stood spellbound for a few moments not daring to speak or move. Surely, they were thinking, any second now the toad would erupt from the swamp like the deranged monster that he was, promising vengeance on all and sundry. Every creature waited, therefore, full of expectation and, if the truth were known, a great deal of fear.

Several minutes elapsed before one frog started to look both nervously and anxiously at another as the realisation began to dawn on the vast assemblage that Emled was not coming back and that he was dead! He was, in fact, dead and buried deep within the bogs of Boda Moor! A more fitting end or a more appropriate grave it would have been difficult to imagine, it having been the scene of the greatest triumph of the powers of all that was good and righteous over the forces of all that was most evil.

The deathly hush was broken by the rich, warm and friendly voice of Moha who began to gently and clearly chant his support for Mars.

"*Mars is the king,*
Long live Mars.
The toad is dead.
Long live the king."

Very soon all the frogs of Cowall, Surey, Somset, Solk, Nolk and Seaxe were chanting victoriously. A great battle had been won and a new king had been born who had led them through a period of great adversity. The power of good had triumphed over the forces of evil, during the course of which many heroes had been created and villains vanquished. Tales would certainly be told of great deeds for many years to come, although it was difficult to imagine that even the most creative of frogs, with quite the most fertile of minds and who was prone to the most outrageous extravagance when it came to spinning a yarn or swapping an anecdote or two, could possibly improve upon some of the heroic acts we have witnessed in this story.

Chapter Thirty-One

And Then...?

As soon as the Open Scrubland and Boda Moor had been cleared of the aftermath of battle, there began a great celebration in the community of Cowall. Never before had the good frogs of Cowall, Surey, Somset, Solk, Nolk and Seaxe had the opportunity to all meet together, and what a wonderful event it was that now marked this first famous occasion. In their common happiness they were gleefully united and they rejoiced in the glorious defeat of Emled and the forces of evil.

Every door of every home of every frog in Cowall was thrown open and their visitors were invited in to rest-a-plenty and to eat and drink their fill. Every available lily pad too was brimming over with frogs who were either telling stories or listening intently whilst another did so. There was first this version of some marvellous or infamous act and then there was that version. There was a little spice added here and a little garnish there. There were heroes made into legends and there were villains turned into demons.

For as long as the talking and the storytelling and the joyful celebrations continued so an abundant supply of the most juicy and succulent grasshoppers gave much needed nourishment to the jubilant frogs. There had never before been such a feasting seen anywhere in the forests or along the river banks. Of course to have commemorated the occasion in any lesser fashion would not have been the way of a frog. After all, those frogs of more advanced years would always say to their younger counterparts... "If a feast is worth having then it is worth having well!"

When the last frog finally dropped off to sleep it was just as the new day was dawning. Almost a full day had therefore passed since the evil and wicked toad had emerged from out of the gloom of Fir

Tree Wood to launch his assault on Cowall and do battle with the good frogs of Mars' army. Such a lot had happened in such a short period of time!

*

As the celebrations began Moha had clasped Mars tightly in the warmest of embraces. They were truly great friends who were bonded by love, respect and loyalty. In great spirit they then sat down to feast with the other frog kings; together with Maccus, Kejon, Rogar and, at Mars' special request, Brencro and Marpol, who were two of his most faithful assistants from his time as a Seaxe senior. This historic gathering gave all of these brave and valiant creatures the opportunity to recount their own exploits and to explain to one another their experiences of the past few days leading up to the Battle of Boda Moor.

Everyone, of course, wanted a full description of what had happened and absolutely no detail was to be omitted. A frog of course doesn't need to be asked twice to tell a story, so not only did they pay attention to every aspect of their individual exploits but they also ensured that the occasion was not missed to elaborate on all the best bits.

In order to record such detail as was discussed that night it would probably be necessary to write another book on the subject – maybe two, knowing the ability of a frog to tell a tale! However, and just for the moment, a brief résumé should be sufficient for you the reader in order that you can piece together some of the more important events that took place outside of Cowall in the two or three days prior to the battle.

Rogar's Route East

The supremely well-timed arrival of the eastern kings onto the flanks of the battlefield was of particular interest to Mars. It was Rogar, you will recall, who undertook to travel to Nolk and Solk in order to try and gain the support of their two fine kings, namely Tanal and Cabal. He had been specially selected by his own king, Fara of course, who knew that if ever there was a frog capable of successfully undertaking such a perilous mission then this was a task most suited to a frog of Rogar's natural and adventurous talents.

As he told his story it was clear that Rogar's small team had encountered great difficulty almost immediately after they had left their home community of Surey. Although they checked and double-checked they had found to their frustration that every route through to the east was either guarded or blocked by what they assumed to be the huge brown marsh frogs from the Far North. Although Rogar had never previously come nose to nose with one of these vile creatures he was nevertheless able to recognise them from Kejon's description.

Rogar said that after a great deal of fruitless searching for a safe passage he had reached a point where he was almost on the verge of giving up and leading his team out of this very dangerous zone when, all of a sudden, an old bald-headed blackbird seemingly appeared from nowhere and offered to be their guide. How the ancient bird knew where they were heading or what was the purpose of their mission Rogar could not even begin to hazard a guess. Neither of course could he be sure that the old bird was not going to lead both himself and his team directly into a trap. However, having already explored what he considered to be all the feasible routes himself and finding them impassable, Rogar felt that he had exhausted all of his forward options. He had therefore been faced with the unenviable alternative of either going back to Fara without the much needed support from the eastern communities or accepting the blackbird's offer of assistance.

Rogar said that something inside his body convinced him that the ancient bird was genuinely trying to help and so he decided to place his faith in their rather strange visitor and agreed to him leading them through the area that was quite literally crawling with the marsh frogs. Rogar then recalled how the blackbird constantly and expertly flitted backwards and forwards checking first one route and then another in order to bypass Emled's army. Rogar and his party of Surey frogs had been amazed and enthralled by the dexterity and agility displayed by their bald-headed guide who, he rather shyly admitted, on first appearances looked far too old to fly let alone run the gauntlet of the scurrilous and mean-minded marsh frogs.

However, in no time at all, and by virtue of taking a series of long disused and overgrown paths which the old blackbird said he hadn't travelled upon since he was not much more than a chick, they had passed through the area infested with Emled's army and were on their way to the Far East. By Rogar's estimation this was an incredible feat and he marvelled at the old bird's canny ability. Unfortunately, before he or any other member of his team had been able to express their heartfelt thanks for the help they had received, or even had the opportunity to ask the blackbird his name, the stranger had briskly wished them all good luck and in a flash he had disappeared into the dense undergrowth of the forest.

Mars caught Moha's eye and smiled knowingly. He then looked around at each of the illustrious creatures who were gathered together in a circle of friendship.

"That was none other than Krakow the Wise," explained Mars. "He who is the legendary old blackbird and of course the one from whom I have received the 'Great Learning of the Supreme Qualities of Wisdom and Knowledge'. The part he has played in all of our lives and the influence he has had on our future has indeed been enormous. He is without doubt quite the bravest and wisest creature who has ever lived."

The Liberation of Seaxe

Moha's role in the lead up to the Battle of Boda Moor had been rather different although just as crucial. He too had been in contact with Krakow and the ancient blackbird had told him all that had taken place since Emled had taken over as the new King of Seaxe. Moha therefore knew of the toad's intended march upon Surey and he rightly assumed that the next step on the venomous creature's murderous and potentially all-conquering rampage would be either Somset or Cowall.

Moha was also aware from Krakow that the community of Seaxe had fallen totally to Emled and that it was now under the control of the marsh frogs. Even though he had resigned as their king, and it was a tradition that no interference should ever be made once a king had relinquished his position, Moha nevertheless determined that he should return to his old community and do all that he could in order to try and save them from their terrible fate. Therefore, the day before King Truda left Somset with his entire community to join up with Denray at Cowall, Moha set off for Seaxe.

The old bullfrog had decided to travel alone. He was confident that he would be able to navigate a safe route and in any event it was widely agreed that there was not a creature in all of the river banks and forests who knew the land as well as he did. No frog, therefore, was better equipped to plot a way through an area that was full of hazards and, most dangerously of all, patrolled by Emled's marauding army of marsh frogs and crows.

The ability to move unseen and with consummate deftness was a skill that both Krakow and Moha possessed in abundance. Although large in body the giant bullfrog was never once spotted by either a marsh frog or a crow. In fact he even remained hidden, concealed deep in the undergrowth, whilst the full might of Emled and his mad-crazed army passed all around him as they marched on Surey intent on plundering this peace loving community.

Moha knew that he had to act quickly, and, in the knowledge that Emled and the vast majority of marsh frogs and crows were heading away from Seaxe, the courageous giant of a bullfrog hopped swiftly and positively in the direction of his much loved old community.

When he arrived at the outskirts of Seaxe, Moha was saddened to see that the whole of the community had indeed been taken over by marsh frogs and all of its occupants were now held as the prisoners of these vile brown creatures. However, it wasn't all bad news and Moha was pleased to see that only a small number of Emled's thugs had been left behind on guard duty. In fact he could count only twenty. Just twenty, he thought. How on all the lily pads in the rivers and ponds could the community have allowed itself to have the life knocked out of it to such an extent that it needed only twenty marsh frogs to control the many thousands who lived there?

The old bullfrog kept himself well out of sight in some long grass near to where the Seaxe frogs were being contained. He waited there patiently until he could get word to any of the locals who might venture close enough to hear him call. Fortunately he didn't have too long to wait as fairly soon two female frogs wandered to within a short distance of the prison camp's perimeter quite unaware of his presence. To Moha's relief and great delight it was Marpol and Brencro who were ambling towards him. These fine mature female adult frogs had both been very close and loyal colleagues of Mars when he had been their senior.

When they heard a soft, strong, yet wonderfully familiar voice call out to them they were somewhat taken aback to say the least. However, these were sensible and well-disciplined frogs who were quite capable of controlling their emotions even in the most extraordinary of

…the full might of Emled and his mad-crazed army passed all around him as they marched on Surey…

circumstances. Recognising the voice to be that which belonged to Moha, and immediately understanding the need to keep his presence secret, they sauntered a little closer to where their loveable old ex-king was hidden.

The unsuspecting guards just assumed that the two female frogs were aimlessly passing the time of day with some idle gossip so they didn't pay any particular attention to their activity. "After all," thought the ignorant marsh frogs, "what else would any of these lily-livered frogs be doing? Why, they haven't got a tadpole's worth of fight left between the lot of them!"

In this way, and without difficulty, Marpol and Brencro were able to advise Moha with regard to the exact number of guards on site as well as inform him of just what had been going on and who was now leading the good frogs of Seaxe. The old bullfrog was saddened by what he heard next although in truth he was not totally surprised. The two frogs told Moha that none of the Seaxe seniors had proved worthy of their high status, for when faced with the greater power of Emled and his marsh frogs they had been flattened either psychologically or, quite literally, physically. They said that both Josmi and Lebish were dead and that they feared the same fate had befallen Kejon. And as for Brylil, Geelan and Chrich, well, the everyday frogs of Seaxe had nothing but contempt for these cowardly individuals. Marpol and Brencro explained that once the community at large realised that the seniors had purposely both bad-mouthed Moha and been instrumental in driving Mars out of Seaxe, and that it was clearly for the prime purpose of ingratiating themselves with Emled for their own benefit, then all faith and any residue of respect they might once have held for 'the six' had disappeared into thin air. In fact, they informed Moha, the little creep Geelan was actually thought to have run away when the first signs of difficulty arose from Emled and the marsh frogs. They said it was generally considered by all the local Seaxe frogs that if the cowardly and stubby senior never showed his face in Seaxe again then that would be too soon.

The result of all this, explained Marpol and Brencro, was that the community was now leaderless and rudderless.

This depressing news only served to re-enforce Moha's resolve. He told the two faithful frogs that he was going to lead them, together with all the other good frogs of Seaxe, out of their imprisonment. He emphasised that time was of the essence as the community was needed urgently in the south-west to give assistance to Mars in the fight to prevent Emled's quest for total domination. Moha then advised that they must return to their colleagues and tell them that in exactly two hours' time he would give the signal for a mass breakout. He also suggested that twenty Seaxe frogs should be detailed to each of the marsh frog guards, and, immediately he gave his signal, the guards were all to be simultaneously overpowered. Moha made it clear to Marpol and Brencro that none of the guards was to be allowed to escape, and, if necessary, and if they attempted to do so, then they were to be killed.

Moha could see that the two Seaxe frogs looked slightly shocked at his advocating that one of their kind should be encouraged to kill another creature. He therefore made a point of saying that they were all in the middle of a terrible war which, if it were to be lost, would almost certainly result in the end of civilised living as they knew it. In such circumstances drastic measures needed to be taken and it was essential that the marsh frog guards should not be permitted to evade capture in case they got word back to Emled of Seaxe's liberation from their brutal control.

Marpol and Brencro assured Moha that they understood what was required. They then hopped away, as casually as they could, in the direction of their colleagues between whom they accordingly circulated whilst at the same time discreetly passing on the news of Moha's return and the planned mass escape.

Exactly two hours later Moha emerged from the deep grass in which he had been hiding and gave the call for the frogs of Seaxe to rise up and make their bid for freedom. The overpowering of the guards and the subsequent departure from Seaxe took place with very little difficulty. Marpol and Brencro had done an excellent job in making sure that every frog knew what was going to happen. They had checked the positions of all the guards and allocated to each of them twenty strong young frogs. They also made it clear that when Moha called for action there should be no dithering or half-hearted efforts. Total commitment to the cause was what was required... nothing less would do!

On Moha's powerful cry for action all of the guards, without exception, were taken totally by surprise and bundled to the ground before being trussed up with bind weed. So excited and so pleased were the local frogs to see their old king that they quite forgot the awful recent experiences they had gone through. Their spirits were indeed substantially revived and they felt invigorated by the sight of the reassuring frame of Moha. They were also amazed at their own courage and even though it had only been twenty marsh frogs with whom they had to contend they had proved to themselves that they were capable of aggression when it was required.

As it hadn't been necessary to actually dispose of any of the marsh frogs during the breakout, Moha determined that two hundred Seaxe frogs should be allocated to stay behind in order to guard them. As for the rest of the community they willingly followed Moha in their long march to Cowall.

On the way to the south-west Moha explained to his travelling companions, as far as he knew, what had been happening. Although understandably worried about the advance and spread of Emled's brand of evil the Seaxe frogs were filled with hope and joy when they learned that Mars had been bestowed with the 'Great Learning of the Supreme Qualities of Wisdom and Knowledge'. That their loving and immensely admired friend had been elevated to the position of leader of all frogs added further fuel to their burning passion to defeat Emled.

They were also amazed that Krakow, the legendary blackbird who they thought was long since dead - if ever he existed at all - was actually still alive and playing a major part in the fight against evil. They agreed that it somehow gave the whole matter a quite unreal feeling, almost as if they were living through some sort of a fairy tale!

At this stage you may well be wondering if Moha and the enthusiastic army of Seaxe were joined by the remaining ex-senior colleagues of Mars. Well, the short answer is... *no, they were not*! Both Brylil and Chrich felt that there was so much for them to do back in the community that they just could not spend their valuable time "gallivanting across the countryside", as they described the bold and courageous march to Cowall. So, rather than journey to Cowall to fight alongside Mars and the valiant frogs of his combined army, they chose instead to busy themselves with tidying up their lily pads and reorganising their larders. After all, they had said, these are priority matters and ones that require the attention of frogs with senior standing in the community; and what's more, if they didn't perform such important tasks, then who would?

Unfortunately for Brylil and Chrich, from that day on they were regarded by the frogs of Seaxe as creatures with very little value and their credibility plummeted to zero. It didn't of course have very far to drop anyway, but the two seniors had missed out on a golden opportunity to at least restore a little pride, both in themselves and in the eyes of their colleagues, through showing some degree of resolve and commitment by joining in the fight against the relentless spread of evil.

It was in fact only as a great favour by all concerned, plus the compassionate and forgiving nature of Mars, that these two seniors were ever even tolerated again by the frogs of Seaxe. However, for the rest of their lives they literally lived as hermits close by a small weed covered pond on the northern outskirts of the community. It was indeed a bleak place, well suited for such faint hearts, where juicy grasshoppers were a rarity and lily pads were thin and sank low in the water when sat upon.

As they mooched about in their lonely isolation these two sad seniors would occasionally forget their past indiscretions and begin to gabble excitedly about this and that before remembering why they were where they were. They would then become overwhelmed with remorse and embarrassment and their conversation would die down as their chins once again fell heavily upon their chests. They would remain in this way for many hours pondering on their past lives and inwardly chastising themselves for succumbing to the power and influence of Emled and the terrible craving they had developed for status and material benefits, all of which had been brought on by greed, jealousy and hate.

Oh how they wanted a second chance to be able to go back to the time before Emled arrived! They promised themselves that if they were ever given such an opportunity then they would be hard working seniors, loyal to Moha and faithful to the community… I'm not so sure about their honesty and integrity though… Are you?

A Dark Shadowy Figure

And what of Emled himself?

Well, all those creatures who took part in the Battle of Boda Moor clearly saw him swallowed up by the swamps, never to be seen again! His army of crows had been entirely wiped out by Sona and her sparrowhawks; and the whole of his massive horde of marsh frogs had either been killed or taken prisoner by Mars' combined army.

Indeed those marsh frogs who had been captured were subsequently sent to a far distant place to live out the rest of their lives in contemplation and reflection on what evil and atrocities they had committed. On the whole these creatures gradually became better souls, although they would unfortunately never be fit enough to be integrated back into a normal community. Any young that were born to such remotely located marsh frogs were, however, immediately removed and transferred to a whole variety of communities ranging from Nolk in the extreme north-east of the region to Cowall in the west. Such young frogs were welcomed lovingly into the families of these good communities and, with kindness and careful nurturing, they grew up to be virtuous and well respected creatures… if a little larger and rather darker in colour than the other children of the families into which they were adopted.

There was, however, one very worrying occurrence that happened deep into the night which followed the Battle of Boda Moor. It was that just after the last of the victory celebrations had finally come to a close, and whilst a thick shroud of mist hung heavily over the bogs and swamps of the treacherous landscape, a dark shadowy figure was to be seen skulking through the gloom of the now silent battlefield. Whoever, or whatever, it was seemed confidently to sense that there were no eyes upon it, and, despite the extraordinarily large shadow that it cast whenever it was caught by the moonlight, it moved surprisingly fast and quietly too.

When the unworldly figure reached the far edge of the Open Scrubland by the entrance to Fir Tree Wood it stopped and appeared to look back. It was impossible to be certain, because almost at the same time a single clap of thunder suddenly crashed without warning in the clouds above, but it sounded as though an angry and evil voice roared out threateningly from this wraith-like figure the following words… "*I'LL BE BACK!*"

Then the figure was gone. Hurrying away in a northerly direction in a fashion that suggested it feared none of the night's predators whether they were the regular creatures of the river banks and forests or humans lurking in the half-light of the rising dawn.

*

It must be said that neither the bodies of Emled nor Kaara were ever recovered from the battlefield. However, as we of course know, and there were many thousands of witnesses to the fact, Emled was drowned and sucked deep into the bogs of Boda Moor following his epic duel with Mars. Therefore, if the shadow had actually belonged to any living creature and was not merely a spirit of some poor lost soul restlessly floating over its boggy grave, it could only have been Kaara's. If indeed it was him, he must somehow have avoided capture by hiding in a secret place whilst the area was being cleared of the debris and dead bodies of battle.

Yes of course it must have been Kaara... Or was it?

On the morning after the battle a pungent milky slime was observed lying exactly on top of the place where Emled had been drawn down into the swamp. The popular belief was that the foul smelling scum had appeared because not even the bog could bear to retain such an evil substance and so it had squeezed the revolting fluid from the odious toad and let it rise to the surface for it to evaporate into the air.

It's a nice explanation of course and one that would favourably and quite quaintly complete this momentous chapter in the lives of all the characters in this story. After all, anecdotes such as this are the foundation of all good fairy tales and are just the sort of thing on which myths, legends and folklore are based.

We would, however, all be a lot happier and sleep a little more soundly in our beds if only we truly knew to whom that mysterious shadow belonged which silently and stealthily stole away from the swamps of Boda Moor under a cloak of mist and darkness.

Was it Kaara...? Or was it...? No, surely you can't be serious...! Not... EMLED!